If Birds
Fly Back

If Birds Fly Back

CARLIE SOROSIAK

MACMILLAN

For my parents, who said I could do anything

First published 2017 by Macmillan Children's Books
an imprint of Pan Macmillan
20 New Wharf Road, London N1 9RR
Associated companies throughout the world
www.panmacmillan.com

ISBN 978-1-5098-3586-7

Copyright © Carlie Sorosiak 2017

The right of Carlie Sorosiak to be identified as the
author of this work has been asserted by her in
accordance with the Copyright, Designs and Patents Act 1988.

1 3 5 7 9 8 6 4 2

A CIP catalogue record for this book is available from
the British Library.

Printed and bound by CPI Group (UK) Ltd, Croydon CR0 4YY

Linny

1.

If you watch enough movies, it becomes pretty darn obvious when momentous things are about to happen. Classical music booms ominously like thunder. A character bites her bottom lip and gazes meaningfully into a sunset. Everything unfolds in slow motion. Occasionally, there are swans.

In real life? No swans. Just a somersaulting feeling that blooms in your belly and works its way to your hands until your fingers refuse to function as fingers. Which is exactly what's happening right now.

I blink, keep blinking, but he's still there. Álvaro Herrera. One of the most enigmatic writers in the history of cinema. His book *Midnight in Miami* inspired my all-time favorite cult film. It's even better than *The Rocky Horror Picture Show*, if you can believe it. Even better than that supercool biopic about a guy who carves through mountains with spoons.

But I'm not staring at Álvaro because he's famous. I'm staring because he's supposed to be dead.

The last time anyone saw him, he was at a party in Miami's Art Deco District, and the next day – *poof!* No Álvaro. He stopped showing up for film openings, for lunches with friends. After three years, people assumed the worst.

So naturally I think I'm hallucinating, as all five foot six and potbelly of him sways unsteadily in the Silver Springs parking lot. Present-day Álvaro still looks like book jacket Álvaro: same brown skin, same brilliant smile, same black hair fanning across his forehead like a crow's wing, except his hair's probably dyed now because he's – what? Eight-two? So old, he's even wearing those white orthopedic shoes that my grandpa used to have. Behind him is a black sedan, and he turns and raps twice on the trunk with his knuckles.

This is the perfect shot. I can tell because my shoulders are tingling (call it a sixth sense or whatever). If I panned slightly to the left, I could get everything in frame: the slanted light filtering through the palm trees, the conch-shell pink of the apartment building across the street, the supposed-to-be-dead writer knocking on the mysterious black car. Every single thing is harmonious, intriguing, *significant*. In film, most people think that the big picture is what's most important – the entire effect. But really it's the smallest details: the sparkling glint of the windshield, birds swooping in the distance, that perfect shade of pink. Pair this shot with some fast-paced guitar music, and voilà – I'd have the opening to a kick-ass documentary, something to show UCLA's admissions committee.

I should be whipping my video camera from my backpack, capturing the gravelly sound of Álvaro shifting like a shadow onto the curb. But I've found that shoving a lens into strangers' faces is a good way to scare them away. (Or to have them toss neon-blue slushies in your direction. Either one.)

And I can't afford to lose Álvaro Herrera. Not when he's about to change my life.

Ten feet away, Álvaro is pawing the air as if grasping for an invisible cane. Even from here I can smell his liberal application of aftershave. I tiptoe closer to him – one inch, two inches. The banner above our heads reads OVER THE HILL BUT NOT OUT

OF OUR HEARTS! Underneath in smaller letters: Welcome New Residents and Volunteers. He gestures to it and announces to me, '*Este lugar esta hecho una mierda.*'

'True,' I say, because this place *is* shitty. Silver Springs Retirement Community, a monstrous cement structure sandwiched between fancy condos in Miami Beach, is hardly the Ritz. Here and there are Art Deco leftovers, shards of marble and colorful geometric tiles, but most of the building's beauty has been stripped out or jackhammered away. It's what my sister, Grace, would call 'a soul-sucked place.'

More Spanish flies from Álvaro's mouth, and I hold up my hands to catch it, tell him my foreign-language skills are *así así*. Only so-so. Everyone assumes I'm Cuban or Colombian or Puerto Rican on account of my copper-brown skin and two feet of dark curls that Hula Hoop in the humidity. At least once a week I have to run through my genealogy when strangers chuck Spanish at me in the supermarket. I'll admit, sometimes it's annoying. 'My grandpa was Nigerian' doesn't immediately register in Miami Beach, where even the gas stations sell Cuban sandwiches.

'Ah, *lo siento,*' Álvaro says. He squints into the sun, woolly mammoth eyebrows blocking half of his vision. Then, for some reason, he asks my name.

'Marilyn,' I say, extending a hand like I'm on a job interview. 'Well, Linny.'

My name, chosen by my parents in a fit of nostalgia for past Christmases, when Great-Grandma Marilyn was still alive and kicking, isn't so cool for a sixteen-year-old. Forget the Marilyn Monroe connection. (My parents certainly did; why else would they've named me after a white sex symbol?) Generally speaking, 'Marilyn' is for older women with cat's-eye glasses, for country-club goers and savings-bond buyers. Silver Springs is the first place I've volunteered where 'Marilyn' actually fits.

I prefer Linny.

'Marilyn Wellinny,' he says, as if tasting the words. There's something beautiful about the way his tongue curls around English, like it's another language altogether.

'Just Linny,' I say.

He shakes my hand back, and it's like squeezing tissue paper. 'Tell me. Shouldn't you be in school?'

'Um, it's June . . . the summer.'

He lets the words linger for a moment and then swirls his head around, double-checking the season. '*Sí*,' he says. 'So it is.'

Up close, I notice that a newly healing cut lightning-bolts above his right eye. (What's *that* from?) The rest of his face looks gooey, like it's sliding off his bones, and he has enough underarm skin to flap and fly away. His flamingo-patterned shirt is unbuttoned into an uncomfortably low V, revealing a serious tan and a sprawl of black chest hair. I wonder if he dyes that, too.

And then I wonder why I'm deeply contemplating chest hair. It's just so . . . abundant.

Focus, Linny. Focus! 'You're Álvaro Herrera,' I say.

He laughs. '*Sí.*'

'And you're going to live here?'

'*Desafortunadamente.*'

'Yes, unfortunately, but I was kind of wondering why you came back?'

He cocks his head at me, extracts a cigarillo from his chest pocket, and fumbles around for a match. 'You ask a lot of questions.'

'Oh. Sorry, yeah. Sorry. It's just –' It's just *what*? How do I even begin to explain this?

A driver steps from the mystery car, yanks a suitcase from the trunk, and walks over to us, extending an arm for Álvaro to hold. 'After you, sir,' he says.

Álvaro waves good-bye, but I follow them. *Of course* I do.

Because here's the thing: my eighteen-year-old sister, Grace, climbed out of her bedroom window five months ago, and I haven't seen her since. (There were no swans then, either; she disappeared soundlessly one night, as if slipping into a crack in the sky.) Feeling very much like an unwanted sofa left at the curb, I tried everything I could think of to reel her back: calling a hundred motels in cities where I suspected she was, tracking activity on her credit card, placing ads on missing people websites, checking and rechecking to see if she reactivated her phone plan. For three days the police shuffled in and out of Grace's room; my parents clung to each other; we're not prayer people, but we prayed.

Nothing happened.

So I started a log of people who disappeared and came back. To say I'm obsessed is like saying Martin Scorsese is *sort of* a good director (i.e. a vast understatement). I spend an unfathomable amount of time trolling the internet, collecting stories about mysterious reappearances; other people have hobbies like beach volleyball and croquet – I have movies and my *Journal of Lost and Found*. My thinking is, if I can discover why people return, then I can figure out a way to bring Grace home. But until right now, I'd never actually witnessed a person re-enter the world. More than a miracle, Álvaro feels like *my* miracle, because if he can swoop back into this life, then my sister can, too.

My sister *will*. I've never been more certain of anything.

When we were in elementary school, our friend Cass had a ginormous Map of the World rug on her bedroom floor, and every day after class, the three of us would grab hands, close our eyes, and spin on top of it, promising that no matter where our feet eventually stopped, we would travel there together someday. Turkmenistan, Chad, the middle of the Indian Ocean – it didn't matter. Right before the spin, Grace would grip my hand extra, *extra* hard so she didn't fly away without me.

That's how I know she's coming back.

In the Silver Springs lobby, the driver politely drops the luggage with a 'You're here, *Señor*,' and Álvaro pays him with a fifty-dollar bill.

To a nurse behind the front desk, Álvaro says, *'¡Estoy aquí!'*

A purple badge on the nurse's substantial chest indicates her name is Marla, and she's Happy to Help. Her expression, puckered up like a tortoise, suggests otherwise. A few banana fritters rest half eaten near her keyboard. 'Honey,' she says. 'Ooooh no, honey. *Gracias* and *hola*'s the only Spanish I know. So let's try it in English.'

'I'm here,' he says again.

Marla says, 'All right, honey. Let me just get your welcome packet and fix you up and then we can –'

But Álvaro is already shifting away, leaving his luggage in the lobby like a stood-up prom date. A nurses' aide follows him down the hall, calling, *'Señor Herrera! SEÑOR HERRERA!'*

Marla pushes back her chair, revealing her yoga-ball girth, and peers at me over the desk. Sugary fritter residue glistens on her fingers as she licks them one by one in between. 'Can . . . I . . . help . . . you?'

Oh, right. Me. Probably acting extremely suspicious here. I tug at my white T-shirt. 'Yeah, please. I'm one of the new volunteers. Linny Carson.'

'Ah!' she says, friendlier. 'Got us another high school do-gooder! Lord, I can't believe it's that time of year already!' Grabbing a clipboard, she flips through a numbered list. 'I've got a Marilyn Carson here. That you, honey?'

I nod reluctantly, craning my neck around the corner. Did Álvaro make a left or a right?

'You overachiever beavers put me to shame!' Marla howls. 'When I was y'all's age, growing up in Georgia, we just hung out at the beach.' She tells me to leave my backpack behind her desk and then makes a 'follow me' motion. I trail behind the twitch of her butt cheeks.

Silver Springs is laid out like an octopus: a gigantic midsection with corridors like tentacles. The hallways are cramped, claustrophobic, and confusing. I keep hoping that Álvaro Herrera will pop out somewhere, lost, asking for a map, but I only see four or five residents. As if on cue, Marla says, 'Most of them are baking by the pool like chickens. Days like this, we herd them out there. Get some sunshine in their veins!' She pulls at her chest. 'These scrubs do not breathe! I'm sweating. You sweating?'

I have a near-constant stream trickling between my boobs. The summer's already the kind of hot that makes a nudist colony seem mildly appealing. *It's Florida*, I want to tell her. *Everyone's sweating*.

A gust of scorched air smacks our faces as we step into the courtyard, where at least a hundred residents are sprinkled across the concrete. Ever seen *Birdman of Alcatraz*? Somehow Silver Springs reminds me of a prison movie. There's a pool, but no one's swimming. On the back wall is a faded mural of the ocean, and I can't help but wonder: *When was the last time these people saw the real beach?* It's only two blocks away.

Marla says that for the next three hours I'm to introduce myself around the courtyard and 'make friends.' Handing me a sticky 'I Am a Volunteer' badge, she adds, 'My fritters are getting cold. You all right here?'

Am I? I vaguely nod, although all I can think about are the residents dead asleep in the courtyard. Mummifying in the sun. They are left-behinds, just like me. Their children – maybe their grandchildren, or their partners – have stuck them here and skipped off to better things.

When it comes to movies, I'm drawn to drama like this (complications, grittiness, imperfect relationships), but in real life, these things are far from stellar. I didn't fully understand that until dysfunction found my family, tapping us on the shoulders and dumping a bundle of grief into our laps.

Hey, wait a second.

The Left-Behinds. That's actually a decent title for my screenplay. I started it a few months ago – to process what happened to my family, what happened to Grace, what's still happening to me. Okay, this might sound a little hokey, but ever since my sister disappeared, I've been living in black and white. Full-on classic movie without any of the good bits. It's the sad channel, twenty-four seven.

I'm convinced that when Grace left, she dragged all the color with her.

I'm convinced that Álvaro's going to help me get it back.

THE LEFT-BEHINDS (scene 1)

Open on:

GRACE'S BEDROOM – LATE EVENING

The room is bright and remarkably colorful: vibrant greens, yellows, and blues.

A full moon hangs high in the sky as GRACE, guitar slung over one shoulder, opens the window and climbs halfway out. On the windowsill, she leaves a cup attached to a long line of string. Another cup is in her hand. As she launches into the air, yellow-feathered wings unfold from beneath her sundress.

She is gone in an instant.

The room quickly fades to black and white.

An unspecified amount of time later, LINNY appears and picks up the cup, transfixed. She begins to whisper into it.

LINNY
      Where did you go?
(beat)
      Grace? Where did you go?

A pause before GRACE's voice trickles down the string.

GRACE

>You remember when Mom used to read us *Where the Wild Things Are*?

LINNY

>Yes?

GRACE

>It's nothing like that.

LINNY

>Oh.

GRACE

>Hey, cheer up.

LINNY

>I can't. It's like you disappear a hundred times a day.

GRACE

>What do you mean?

LINNY

>Well, I could be brushing my teeth or doing my laundry or painting my toenails, and a memory of you will explode inside my chest.

GRACE
(remorseful)

>Sounds painful.

LINNY

> It is. Like, remember how you used to empty the kitchen
> cabinets of pots and pans, forming makeshift drum sets, and
> I'd draw crowds with chalk on the driveway – a pink-and-
> green blob for each one of your fans? Or how when I was six
> and you were eight, you developed the habit of wedging your
> leotard between your butt cheeks in ballet class? You'd yank
> the fabric as high as it would go and duck-waddle over to the
> mirror, urging me to do the same. Well, I'll want to joke about
> this with you – and that's when the stumbling feeling will hit,
> over and over again, because you're not stretched out in our
> backyard hammock, a book like *Into the Wild* balanced on your
> knees. And you're not in the band room at school, showboating
> on the piano, a crowd of boys leaning in to catch a whiff of
> your Granny Smith apple body lotion. And you sure aren't
> planning epic trips to the middle of the Indian Ocean with me,
> or knocking on the wall separating our bedrooms, complaining
> that it's two a.m. and you're too wound up to sleep.

(beat)

> Grace?

LINNY drops the cup and sticks her head out the window, her neck
craning to the sky.

LINNY (continued)

(angry)

> Grace?

The scene is rewound, as if going back in time.

Sebastian

2.

'Of course dark matter is invisible, but that doesn't make it any less real.' *A Brief Compendium of Astrophysical Curiosities*, by Dr. Boris P. Mangum, p. 8

For the last seventeen years I've made up stories about my dad. The guy bolted before I was born — and that's all I know about him. That he left.

So I thought: *Maybe he's a physicist.*
Or a tuna fisherman like on the Discovery Channel.
Or an archeologist, stuck in another dimension.
I scribbled the following in the margins of my favorite book:

A THEORY FOR ABSENT FATHERS #1:
Invisibility necessitates imagination.
$x + y = z$, *where* $x = $ *clues,* $y = $ *stories, and* $z = $ *who he is*

Mom neither confirmed nor denied my suppositions, only said things like 'Sebastian, can this wait?'
'Sebastian, not at the table, *mi amor*.'
'Sebastian, we'll talk about this later.'
So I built an image of my dad based on possibilities. I assembled clues. *Hechos*. Like how Mom kept a blank postcard from Italy in her nightstand, which clearly suggested that my father was a Venetian gondolier. Or how there was a baseball in the back of

her closet, which almost proved that my father was a professional sports player.

Clues turned into stories. I figured that even if my dad was invisible to me, that didn't make him any less real. He was as real as my stepdad, Paul, who (incidentally) can't pitch a baseball at ninety miles an hour.

It's 10:30 a.m., and I'm reclining in our living room La-Z-Boy. Chowing down peanut butter toast. Paul rounds the corner in his black suit, his sandy-blond hair perfectly coiffed. He does a double take. 'Change your mind, champ?'

I massage the area above my lip. 'I – uh – it's just a bit of stubble.'

Paul is a helicopter pilot and a big believer in mustaches. I don't think I've ever disappointed him more than last week when I said I didn't want to grow one. *He* has a massive handlebar and looks perpetually prepared for the rodeo.

'Right,' Paul says, deflating. 'Well, when you change your mind, I'll let you borrow my kit.'

The man has a *mustache kit*.

My real father better not have a mustache kit.

I give him a thumbs-up and go back to my toast. It's not that Paul's an awful guy. He just has a specific look that he reserves exclusively for me. His eyes squint in a question: *Where did you come from, and what the heck are we going to do with you?* Unlike me, Paul is buff and into all kinds of martial arts. My best friend, Micah, and I often substitute his name in Chuck Norris jokes.

Balancing my toast in one hand and phone in the other (it's an art form), I text Micah: **When Paul does a push-up, he isn't lifting himself up. He's pushing the earth down.**

My phone dings back a minute later: **Paul is the only man to** ever defeat a brick wall in a game of tennis.

Hah. Good one.

I hear Paul's BMW revving in the driveway – then skidding down the street. I turn the TV to the Science Channel, where Morgan Freeman is talking about wormholes in that voice of his. In the hallway, my five-year-old half brother, Louis, is lining up his toy soldiers. I woke up with seven of them in my bed this morning. Imprinted into various parts of my body. Butt. Elbow. The left side of my neck. *And* I had Play-Doh in my hair. Apparently I am the deepest sleeper in the history of sleep.

Louis lion-roars and then swats his hands through the soldiers. They scatter, thumping against the wall.

Every time I hang out with Micah lately, Mom reminds me that I'm missing valuable bonding time with Louis. 'When you're at college, we'll hardly ever see you.' What she doesn't know is, you can love someone to pieces and hate them at the same time. Going to Cal Tech at the end of the summer is the equivalent of someone offering me space in a lifeboat.

Maybe I'm still angry because I was the last to know. Paul married my mom six years ago, right before she got pregnant with Louis. The wedding date was on the kitchen calendar before Mom bothered to mention it, and she told the checkout lady at Fresco Mart about Louis – *that's* how I found out I was going to have a brother. I overheard it at the grocery store. When Mom and Paul brought him home from the hospital, the three of them looked – I don't know. Complete? I wasn't aware I was missing that kind of bond until I saw it right in front of me. Louis, with both his parents. Louis, with his dad.

It made me want to punch the air.

The phone rings, and Mom yells, '*¡Yo lo contesto!*' And then again, in English: 'I'll get it!' I hate when she catches herself. Before Paul, we only spoke Spanish in the house. Had *ropa vieja* for dinner on Fridays. Pulled up all the living-room rugs so Mom could teach me salsa steps. Paul's parents are Danish immigrants, so you'd think he'd get the 'I want to hang on to my culture' thing. But no. Apparently only *certain* cultures are worth holding on to, while others are chucked aside. Paul preaches assimiliation above all else.

In the kitchen: Mom's voice. She isn't laughing. Usually she laughs on the phone – even with telemarketers. Maybe it's her boss, asking if she wants another shift at the diner. A kitchen cabinet slams.

Louis has decimated his entire regiment of soldiers and has fixed his sights on the TV.

Do NOT cut off Morgan Freeman. Anyone but Morgan Freeman!

Right as Louis starts pushing buttons on the remote, Mom enters the living room, still gripping the phone. Wet faced. Her voice reminds me of a dying dinosaur. 'Louis,' – scratchy throat – 'I need to talk to Sebastian alone, please.' When my little brother doesn't budge, she yells, 'Louis, *ándale, ándale*!' and then cracks a bit more, realizing he doesn't know that language. Eventually – from facial expressions alone – he gets the picture and scrams.

All the while my stomach is in my shoes.

'Uh, what's up?' I say, nervously biting the last piece of peanut butter toast.

Her dark hair fuzzes around her in waves. Disorientated, rubbing her eyes – 'You know that man who wrote about Miami?'

'Be more specific,' I try to say. But the peanut butter's firmly cemented to the roof of my mouth. It comes out like 'Beeee maaaa sppefff,' followed by strange clucking noises where I attempt to extract said peanut butter from said roof of mouth.

Then she drops the bomb. Nagasaki style.

'Álvaro Herrera. He's your father. Oh God. Oh *God.*'

I suck in. Peanut butter lodges in the back of my throat. I don't even know who Álvaro Herrera *is*, but I can't believe she's finally told me! I can't believe I'm choking!

'Sebastian?' Mom says. 'Sebastian!'

I heave forward, out of the La-Z-Boy. Mom thwacks my upper back with the palm of her hand – six times, by my count – until I retch a chunk of toast onto the new carpeting. It's vaguely the shape of Michigan.

'Oh my God,' Mom croaks, dropping to her knees. 'Oh my God, Sebastian.'

My throat is a bit irritated, but this does not dissuade me from speaking. 'Who . . . is . . . he?'

Hands on her face – 'You don't recognize the name?'

I shake my head. The room feels too warm.

'He's a – well, he's a writer. *Midnight in Miami.* You've probably heard of the movie. He wrote that book.'

I startle. '*That* guy? The dead guy?'

'He's alive, Sebastian.'

'Wait. Who was that on the phone?'

'Your aunt Ana. Remember, she works with geriatrics? She heard through the nursing home circuit that he's back, and I –' She gathers her breath. 'Someone spotted him in Miami.'

'A *nursing home*? How old is he anyway? Know what – doesn't matter. *No me importa.* I'm going to Miami.'

'You most certainly are not!'

I scrunch my eyebrows, confused. 'What?'

'I said: You. Most. Certainly. Are not!' She glances into the hallway, where Louis is peeking into the living room. We must be a sight: on our knees. Mom on the verge of sobbing. Me, crouched like a scared monkey.

'Why the hell did you tell me then?' I say.

'Sebastian! Language.'

'Fine. Why the *heck* did you tell me?'

'Because!' She throws up her hands. 'Because if you asked another question about it . . . I panicked, okay?' Gesturing to the TV screen – 'What if he's on the news? What if I walked in tomorrow and you were watching him on the screen, and I'd have to *lie* to you, Sebastian?'

My voice has too much growl in it. 'How's that any different from what you've been doing for my entire life?' Was I the last to know about this, too?

'Hey. Not fair. Everything I've done, I've done to protect you.'

'From what?' I point at the TV, as if Álvaro Herrera is about to pop out of the box. 'From a guy in a nursing home who I've never met? ¿*Seriamente?*'

'*Sí!*' she shouts. '¡*Exactamente!* That is exactly right! He *left* me, Sebastian. Do you understand?'

'No! I don't. How could I when you've never told me anything?'

She clamps her teeth together. 'Fine. We met at a film festival before I moved to California. I was trying to launch my acting career, and Álvaro – he saw my first movie. I had a small role, but he said I was good and we hit it off. Four months later, he proposed. He had a ring, Sebastian – plans for a wedding, the whole thing. And then he left. I was pregnant with you, and he . . . never found out. After he left, I didn't think he had the right to know.'

That's awful. Incredibly awful. But . . .

'I'm sorry,' I say softly, standing up. 'I'm *really* sorry that happened. But just because he left you' – choosing my words carefully – 'doesn't mean I can't know him. Maybe he's changed.'

Mom sounds so tired. 'People don't change.'

Theoretically, everything is explainable. That's why I like physics. If you want to know why a pineapple and a slice of pizza fall at equal speeds when dropped off a building, there's a reasonable answer for that. Plus there are all these outrageously named theories. Like, I kid you not, the Hairy Ball Theorem.

In the last year alone, I've read *A Brief Compendium of Astrophysical Curiosities* by Dr. Boris P. Mangum seven times. I write theories in the margins. About physics, about my own conundrums.

I thought: *If I can solve the mysteries of the universe, then I can sure as hell figure out the mystery surrounding my dad.*

I thought: *Rational explanations and order should exist everywhere in the world.*

Should being the operative word.

A tuna fisherman I understand. Stuck in another dimension I understand. An eighty-two-year-old presumed-dead writer wasn't even on my radar.

A THEORY FOR ABSENT FATHERS #2:
The end of invisibility directly correlates with the beginning of complication.

All morning, I Google 'Álvaro Herrera' in my bedroom. Find a website called findalvaro.com, where someone has posted three hours ago: Silver Springs. Miami, FL. I swear it's him. There

are twenty-five responses, all saying something like No shit!
Take a picture!

'Álvaro Herrera' gets thirty thousand image results.

Álvaro on Hollywood Boulevard.

Álvaro in Havana.

Álvaro on the set of *Midnight in Miami*.

I skim some of the attached articles. They tell me he never
had children. (Inaccurate. Am I the only one?) They tell me that
Álvaro's novels are translated from Spanish, that he came to the
US in 1961 as a political refugee, and that Warner Bros. adapted
his first novel, *Midnight in Miami*, in 1963. It's about a bartender
named Eduardo Padilla who gets wrapped up in a spy ring. There
is side-boob in it but no actual boobs. Álvaro has a cameo.

Looks like the type of people interested in Álvaro also have a
healthy obsession with Bigfoot, Bat Boy, and Elvis. He's famous,
sure. But mostly with conspiracy theorists, die-hard movie buffs,
fans of Cuban literature, and the Latino community. I doubt 95
percent of the population would recognize him. And those who
do would probably want to invite him to dinner. Take a billion
pictures. Steal his underwear or something.

By the fifteenth article, I've made my decision. Hell, I'd made
my decision at the exact moment Mom blurted out his name.

(That's part of my problem. I do everything too fast. I swear
I only have one button: Go. Someone forgot to install the brakes.)

I log on to the Silver Springs home page, which profiles a
white and faded-blue building surrounded by palm trees. A
cheesy talking flamingo juts onto the screen and offers a virtual
tour. (Wish I were kidding. I couldn't make up that crap.) So
I follow this flamingo to the Volunteer section and fill out a
form. *Boom!* Twelve minutes later, I receive an email saying my

application has been approved. I start tomorrow.

Next step: plane tickets.

This is the hardest bit, because I'm flat broke. Can't-even-find-a-dime-in-my-sofa broke. So I do the only thing I can: I sell my Chinese fossil collection on the internet. I kiss every one of them good-bye, box them up, ship them to the highest bidder. Then I spend a thousand bucks on a one-way, last-minute ticket from Los Angeles to Miami. Boarding: seven hours from now.

Ay stomach lurch.

I'll call my aunt Ana when I touch down. I've met her a bunch: every Christmas, some Easters. She's cool. Hopefully cool enough to let me crash on her couch for part of the summer.

Mom keeps knocking on my door. She never comes in unannounced because of . . . because of that one time. So I put on my headphones – I have *A Brief Compendium of Astrophysical Curiosities* on audiobook as well – and enter a staring contest with the poster above my bed. The cast of *X-Men* glares back.

All the while, I'm going over the plan.

Step 1: Fly from LA to Miami.

Step 2: Talk to Álvaro Herrera.

Step 3: Glue all my broken pieces back together.

Dr. Mangum is saying, 'A supernova is so bright that, even if but for a moment, it can outshine a whole galaxy. Scientists do not yet know the detailed mechanism of igniting stars.'

I write in the hard copy:

THE STARS-ARE-LIKE-SECRETS PRINCIPLE:
Both can run out of fuel. Even if they remain dormant for years,
all it takes is a catalyst. One day, they will explode.

Linny

3.

WHO: *Santiago Lopez, host of the popular Argentinian game show* Arriba!

WHEN: *2012, shortly after his nightly broadcast*

WHY: *He disappeared for six days, and when he finally returned to the set, his only explanation was 'The grand prize last week was a Hawaiian vacation. I thought to myself, If they can go, why can't I?'*

NOTES: *Maybe Grace is on an extended vacation? Maybe she'll come back on her own a few days from now — sunburned from the beach?*

I don't spot Álvaro Herrera for the rest of my shift, but I resolve that – the next time I see him – I'm going to get some answers.

In the Silver Springs parking lot, my phone buzzes with a text from Ray: **Hope you didn't party too hard with the old people.** Attached is a selfie of him and Cass lounging at the beach. She resembles a praying mantis in her wide-lensed sunglasses, but her bathing suit is very Cass: aggressively pink, fringed, rhinestone studded. Ray is rocking a pair of orange swim trunks that mimic his fiery hair.

I squint at the picture for a sec before trying to whip out a reply, but then it occurs to me that the un-freaking-believable news is best shared face-to-face. I unchain my bike and fast-pedal down to Cass's favorite beach spot: by the Hilton, next to the constantly shirtless ice cream man with the six-pack abs. I park between two red convertibles, kick off my Chuck Taylors, and hotfoot it through the burning sand.

When Ray sees me, he says, 'Sup, Linny!' and I scoot onto his towel. Although we've only known each other four and a half months, he greets me with the biggest smile, like we've been best friends for our entire lives.

'Just a warning,' he says. 'I might've had three ice-cream cones within the space of an hour. Half of my body is sugar.'

Cass affirms, 'It's true. And now he keeps asking me to go for a run with him. I've explained to him the mechanics of boobs without sports bras, but it's not sinking in.'

'Care to join me in the sugar high?' Ray asks.

I laugh and shake my head. It's funny – sugar is actually the reason we're all friends. Cass and Ray met at Dylan's Candy Bar, the ultrahip sweets boutique where they were coworkers for an ill-fated seventeen days. (Ginormous lollypops. Accidental fire. You get the picture.) Although Ray joined our trio after Grace left, I still find it intensely weird that he only knew of her.

But I do adore him. He's on the track team and is constantly trying to drag me into sprint workouts to, as he claims, 'reduce my anxiety'. I refuse most of the time (running is his thing, very much not mine), but it's nice to be asked. And honestly, it's nice to be understood. Ray came out the week before summer break, and even though almost everyone was cool about it, some people (aka dickwads) weren't. He knows what it's like to walk around under a spotlight.

He and Cass are my only friends who don't give me that look – a mixture of *Aw, poor you, little sisterless girl* and *Your family must be so screwed up for Grace to disappear like that*. It involves heavy eyebrow arching and an upward pout of the lip. What's unbelievable is, sometimes I catch my glance in the mirror, giving *myself* that look. Because it does suck, and no one knows that better than me.

Pulling out my camera, I switch it on so I can film Cass's and Ray's reactions to the Álvaro news. I call out, 'Take one.'

Cass is largely preoccupied with spritzing bronzing oil onto her endless legs to attract all the boys, as if every guy within a fifty-mile radius didn't already have a moth-to-flame reaction. Fresh conquests perpetually snake their arms around her shoulders. She parades them through Miami Beach Senior High's halls like prized kills, raccoons she's just snuffed with her BB gun. Last month I shot a short movie of her getting ready for a date. The lighting was all wrong, but with her chalky eyeliner and mass of blond hair, she still looked luminous, more of a Marilyn Monroe than I'll ever be. (Not that I lack curves. The curves are aplenty. I just prefer to be behind the camera, capturing the things that no one else sees: all the seemingly insignificant details that add up to something wonderful and big. I love that about movies, the way they dive into you as deep as you dive into them.)

When Cass hears 'Take one,' she snaps to attention. So does Ray. He lifts his head from my lap and throws one shoulder forward into an exaggerated pose. 'What's our motivation in this film?' he says.

Cass says, 'How about . . . we're criminals?'

'*Sexy* criminals,' Ray adds.

'Yes! And we are on the run because we are *literally* too sexy for anyone to handle.'

'From now on, I will only answer to the name Fabio. Or the Red Falcon!' He actually flaps his arms. We're attracting curious stares from passersby on the beach; an older man and his much-much-younger wife actually stop in their tracks.

I slap my hand on my thigh. 'Guys. Pay attention. Ask me about Silver Springs.'

'Sorry,' Ray says, withdrawing his wings. 'So, how terrible was it? Like, on a scale from one to I'm About to Be Eaten by Vultures.'

'Actually,' I burst, 'it wasn't bad at all. I –'

'There was Jell-O, then?'

'What?'

'Well, I assumed you must've gotten free Jell-O or something.'

'No, I –'

'Because the last time I visited my nan, I got free Jell-O, and she *smoked* me at canasta –'

I cut him off. This is bigger than desserts. I adjust to close-up. '*Ray*. I saw Álvaro Herrera.'

I expect Cass to drop her bronzing oil or Ray to drop his jaw. I get neither.

'So . . .' Cass says. 'He is . . . who?'

Slowing my speech and enunciating, as if this will do the trick, I say, 'Ál-va-ro Her-rer-a.'

'Nope,' Ray says. 'Still don't know who you're talking about.'

'Oh, come on,' I say, flicking off the camera. 'Really?'

'Wait, wait,' Cass chimes in. 'Didn't you tell me about him? Famous writer guy. What's that website: findalvaro.com? You can submit a video of him and win, like, a thousand bucks.'

'Thank you,' I say, gently punching Ray's shoulder. 'At least *one* of you was paying attention.'

Cass says, 'Well, did you get a video, Camera Girl?'

That's one of her nicknames for me. Half of me likes it, because it comes from a good place; the other half hates how I sound like the subject of an endangered species documentary. *Behold, the elusive Camera Girl in her natural habitat!*

I shake my head and straighten out a curl, press it between my lips.

'Ugh,' Cass moans. 'Why not? Do you know how many Pie in the Sky croissants that would buy?'

'Um, yes,' I admit. 'We could fill the bottom of a swimming pool.'

'Then what's the deal?'

All during high school, I've carried my camcorder everywhere, gathering images like crows collect shiny objects. How can I explain that seeing Álvaro means more to me than every single one of those images combined? That it has everything to do with my sister? Whenever I get into a situation like this, I picture Brad Pitt in *Fight Club*, except he's saying: 'The first rule of Grace's disappearance is you do not talk about Grace's disappearance.'

I settle for a white lie: 'I – um – just couldn't get my camera out fast enough.'

'But he's definitely alive?' Cass says.

'Or definitely a ghost walking among us.'

'Don't be creepy.'

'In that case,' Ray concludes, 'we'll meet you outside the lobby in the morning.'

I cock an eyebrow. 'You can't be serious.'

He smiles with all his teeth. 'We never joke about celebrities.'

Around five o'clock, just before biking home from the beach, I check my texts: eight panicked messages, all from MomandDad.

Where are you?

Please call when you can.

Linny, you have a curfew.

Linny. Call in the next fifteen minutes.

It escalates from there.

I call them 'MomandDad' because, in the weeks following Grace's disappearance, my parents started becoming the same person, as if their unanimity would somehow hold our family together. They're developing similar faces: tight skin, fake smiles, shiny cheekbones. Mom's skin is five shades darker than Dad's, but if you squint, the color differences blur. Even before Grace ditched us, they liked uniformity in everything. Case in point: most houses on our street are painted a tasteful Dolphin Egg Blue, and they *like* that. 'Seriously,' Grace used to say, 'what the hell is a dolphin egg?'

Parking my bike, I check our mail (no letters from my sister, again) and have barely stepped onto the porch when Mom swings open the door with 'Why didn't you return my text messages?' Lysol fumes trail from the kitchen. We have a cleaning lady, but Mom now insists that Ella misses spots, that merely *clean* isn't good enough. I think she's trying to scrub out every stain my sister left behind, to give me a stable environment or whatever.

'I – I didn't hear it ring,' I say.

'Then turn it up louder.'

Inside, I flop belly up on the living-room couch, and she hovers over me, her nose razor-sharp from this angle, all her curls pinned in a knot at the back of her head. 'Really, Marilyn? Ella *just* had those pillow covers dry-cleaned. . . . She was supposed to, at least.' Although the outside temperature is trending toward ninety degrees, Mom shows no evidence of sweating in her gray pantsuit (a perfectly reasonable outfit for cleaning?). If she has one superpower, besides her uncanny ability to stress me out, it's her freakish tolerance for the Miami heat. 'And you're all drippy. And sandy. Those pillows are *pashmina*,' she says, as if the word should resonate.

When I film people, I often focus on their mouths. Most directors say that 'the eyes have it,' but I disagree. Mouths straighten out in anger and purse in frustration and pucker in love. From below, I can see all the way into Mom's mouth: the arc of its roof, the sharpness of her molars, how wide she opens her jaw when she speaks – like an anaconda accommodating its prey. I start mind-filming the scene: on set there would be a great storm cloud behind her. A tornado or a hurricane.

'Well,' she says, 'dinner's in fifteen. You can tell us all about your day at Silver Springs.'

I roll over and firmly press my face into the pillows. Mom wasn't kidding: they do smell clean, like spring. I hear her heels *click-clack* back into the kitchen, then the frustrated snap of rubber gloves, the suctioned pop of the cleaning-solution bottle, opening, spilling again onto white tile.

Mom is laying silverware on the table, and she no longer sets a place for Grace; it makes me nauseated.

It's a Monday – and we used to grill *suya* on Mondays (from Grandpa's spice mix recipe). We are now a take-out family: Chinese noodles, Mediterranean deli grape leaves in plastic boxes, pizza and more pizza and did I mention pizza? Tonight it's hot dogs with ceviche (trust me, the combo works) from one of my favorite restaurants in town. Mom looks like she wants to disinfect everything before we eat it, but I dive right in. I'm tempted to shout at her: *And I've only washed my hands seven times today! ONLY SEVEN TIMES!*

What makes you stay silent when every inch of your body wants to scream?

Dad is still in his white doctor's coat, his blondish hair slicked to precision. 'Excellent flavor profile,' he says, biting into his hot dog. We discuss food a lot to avoid discussing other things. I'm not sure that any of us has said Grace's name out loud in months.

And I can't exactly talk to them about their work – because I have been forbidden to say 'vagina' at the dinner table (although I hardly think it's a dirty word). MomandDad are gynecologists. Every adult on my dad's side is a doctor. Like swallows, this family has a predetermined life cycle: Miami to Princeton to Miami again. A recent article in the *Miami Home Journal* called Dad's work 'majestic,' a peculiar adjective that should be reserved for deep-sea photographers, ballerinas, and unicorn trainers – not people who spend most of their waking hours examining vaginas. Mom graduated second in her class at Princeton Med (just above Dad). Although born in Florida, she's always talking about how different this country is from Nigeria: 'There were so few women practicing medicine in Lagos. So few! I wanted the best for myself – the best for you girls.'

You girls – meaning Grace and me. MomandDad think we should be doctors, too, and that's 80 percent of the problem. I haven't told them about *The Left-Behinds* yet. My goal is to finish it by the end of August so I have time to tweak it before applying to study film at UCLA. MomandDad won't take it well – film school, my screenplay, none of it.

'So,' Mom says, eating her hot dog with a knife and fork. 'Meet anyone nice at Silver Springs?'

Against my better judgment, I tell her about Álvaro Herrera.

'That pervert writer?' she asks. 'Didn't he write that really trashy book?'

Leave it to Mom to bypass THE FACT THAT HE'S SUPPOSED TO BE DEAD and jump straight to sex. I roll my eyes and wish I could delete my words from the scene. 'He's not *actually* a pervert.'

'Anyone who writes about intercourse like that is a pervert.'

'*Mom*. Isn't sex, like, your business?'

She purses her lips. 'There's a difference.'

According to MomandDad, discussing sex in a medical capacity is acceptable. They take issue with the practical application, especially when it comes to their daughters. Not that I'm having sex. My experience with guys extends to two quick groping sessions under the school bleachers and one liquor-propelled tongue tangling last winter, which ended in Todd Banbury vomiting all over my new jean jacket. I'm still very much the Virgin Marilyn.

Dad says, 'You really need to meet residents more suited to your life goals. Why not find some retired doctors to network with?'

Right, because that's what volunteering at Silver Springs is about: beefing up my Princeton pre-med application and networking with other do-gooders who'll grow up to pursue do-gooder careers (and make lots of money, have Dolphin Egg Blue houses, yada yada yada). At least, that's what this summer *was* about. Now I'm focused on figuring out where Álvaro went and why he came back, along with finishing *The Left-Behinds*.

Mom's palms are pressed together, a prayer. 'Please, you need to make an effort. The biggest barrier between you and Princeton is your attitude. Attitude, attitude, attitude! What am I always telling you about networking? Every encounter is an opportunity.'

'Got it.'

'You're so close.'

'Yep.'

'*So* close.'

'Oh wow,' I say, 'this hot dog *is* supertasty,' and they both agree. I wish I could fight with them but I can't. Not yet. For one, Grace always flung herself into the front lines – saving me from the impact – and I never learned the art of combat. But the main reason is, my sister didn't leave a note for MomandDad. She only left one for me:

> *I just have to get away for a while, okay? Feed Hector 4-5x a week, pls.*

Hector is Grace's pet box turtle who she found injured near a pond a few miles away and was nursing back to health. My sister dictated care instructions for a flipping *turtle*, but didn't say goodbye to our parents.

So I had to tell them.

I had to show them the message in her handwriting. I had to watch as their souls tried to escape from their mouths. I had to memorize the take-out menus; answer questions for missing-person reports; look at my mother on the couch, her hair zigzagged around her like lightning bolts, as if she'd spent the last few hours trying to pull it out. I remember she didn't smell like Mom – not like rosemary and latex gloves. She smelled like sadness. (That's when I learned that sadness has a smell.)

Now we jump every time the phone rings. We clench our hands at news reports about missing girls. We leave the porch lights on all night, just in case she comes home.

My family is a newly formed tripod. Any little thing could topple us.

THE LEFT-BEHINDS (scene 2)

CARSON FAMILY GARAGE

Full color.

LINNY (ten years old) and GRACE (twelve) are crawling through a labyrinth of cherry planks – a massive bird's nest.

LINNY (Voice-over)
> Remember the summer Grandpa died, and we got all his woodworking equipment?

GRACE (Voice-over)
> God, that got so ridiculous. Dad was always complaining about how much money he'd get for the wood on eBay.

LINNY (Voice-over)
> Yep. The garage was such a mess.

In the center of the nest is a clear space with a little movie set – two feet by two feet of plywood dolled up with wallpaper scraps and flowers. Balls of clay are rolled into miniature people. LINNY and GRACE arrive in the center. LINNY provides stage directions while GRACE maneuvers the clay people around the set.

CLOSE-UP –

GRACE's back: in places, smooth skin gives way to puckering, as if something is growing beneath.

LINNY (Voice-over)

>   That world made me so weirdly happy. You know, being the
>   director and the scriptwriter. Not just Camera Girl.

GRACE (Voice-over)

>   But you remember what happened next, right?

LINNY (Voice-over)

>   Of course I remember.

CUT TO –

CARSON FAMILY DRIVEWAY

DAD cracks the movie set in two, maybe thinking it is junk. MOM
leaves the pieces by the mailbox for the garbageman. It is a clay
people massacre.

GRACE (Voice-over)

>   Want to know a secret?

LINNY (Voice-over)

>   Yeah?

GRACE (Voice-over)
(whispering)

>   I'm still not over it.

Sebastian

4.

'This is all hypothetical, of course. Which means that one day, it could be proven true.' *A Brief Compendium of Astrophysical Curiosities*, p. 340

'Death by peanut butter toast?' Micah says, after I've sneaked out of my house and into his.

'How tragic is that?' I say.

'That's like "I decided to take a piss in the middle of a field and accidently peed on an electric fence and died" type of level.'

My flight to Miami leaves in two hours and forty-five minutes. In the meantime, I'm recounting this morning's events to Micah as he fights off enemy troops in *Dark Ops Resolution*, our favorite video game. The *boom-boom-boom* of semiautomatic weapons fills his basement.

I've just told him about spending the summer in Florida. He looked confused. Then pissed. And now he's pretending he's over it and is mainly focused on securing the high ground behind the bridge.

I left out the small, insignificant little fact that Álvaro Herrera is my dad, except he doesn't know he's my dad, and now I'm traveling to Miami to tell him. I don't say anything because 1) It's a heaping gulp of words, 2) Micah would lose his shit, and 3) We cannot simultaneously lose our shit. I'm still working out answers myself.

I mean, where has Álvaro *been*?

A THEORY-IN-PROGRESS FOR NEWLY DISCOVERED
FATHERS:
All hypotheses are fair game.

He could have mysteriously disappeared like those astronauts in 'And When the Sky Was Opened' – the best episode of *The Twilight Zone*.

Or maybe he's a time traveler – actually gone a few seconds, but everyone *thinks* he's been gone three years.

'Incoming! Incoming!' Micah yells. The whoosh of a grenade launcher and then 'God! Shitting! Damn it! Where's your head, dude? You're killing us.'

'We still have half our troops.' The sound of a bomb blast. 'We still have a third of our troops.'

Micah's thumbs dart all over the controls. He's a finger ninja. 'And you're volunteering at an old-people's home? Jump left! I said left! I bet you'll meet an eighty-year-old babe with a healthy appetite for younger men.'

'Jesus, Micah –'

'God damn it, Sebastian! Left! With an *L*! She's going to fall so head over heels in lust for you that she's going to write you into her will. "To my teenage lover, I bequeath you my cardigan sweaters and set of wooden golf clubs."'

'You're going to make me barf.'

'I'm just saying, you're undermaximizing your dating potential by missing out on the over-eighty demographic. Something to think about. LEFT!'

'*Bueno*, got it, got it.'

'I've stuffed your suitcase full of condoms.'

'*What?*'

'And your wallet. There are three in your wallet. DO YOU SERIOUSLY NOT KNOW THAT *LEFT* IS DIFFERENT FROM *RIGHT*?'

We curve around the abandoned amusement park, staying low. It's hard to focus.

Partly because I keep thinking about my eighth-grade field trip. My class went to the California Science Center to see bodies without their skin – nothing but muscles and veins and bones. That's how it feels: like I've been stripped down. Like my insides are no longer *insides*, but I don't want everyone to see the mess.

And also because I'm going to be thousands of miles away from Micah this summer, and we're going to different colleges this fall (me: Cal Tech for astrophysics, him: Berkeley for God knows what). Say what you will, but bromances are real. We've been friends since fifth grade, when his Christian missionary parents adopted him from a Korean border town. One of his favorite anecdotes is about the origin of his name: 'It *was* Chung-Hee, but in their infinite wisdom, my parents thought that wasn't American enough, so they named me after a rock instead. Personally, I would've liked "Bald Eagle." Might as well go full-out.'

To his credit, Micah goes full-out on everything. Like last year when he decided that not being a rocker couldn't stop him from looking like one. The result: hair buzzed short in the back but long enough in the front to braid.

I kind of envy him.

Blood splatters all over the screen. Micah throws down the controls and sighs. 'Dude. You suck.'

'You were always better at this game.'

'Don't say *were*.'

'What?'

'Don't say *were*. Like you're dying or something.'

I push his shoulder. 'You ol' softy.'

He shrugs me off and looks at the clock. Two and a half hours until takeoff.

I load my suitcase, which is twenty-eight condoms heavier than at last check, into the back of his rusted-out Ford Fiesta. We drive with the windows down.

'One last alphabet game for the road?' he asks, tapping the wheel.

'Sure.'

'*J*,' he says.

'Jennifer Lawrence,' I say. We came up with this game in middle school: listing all the girls who'll never sleep with either of us.

'Julie,' he counters, 'the redhead from the video store.'

'Jessica O'Conner.'

'Cheerleader Jessica?'

'Yep,' I say.

'I don't know, man. She might sleep with *you*.'

Micah is always quick to point out that I dated a cheerleader. Savannah. One and a half disastrous months that I'll never get back. During that time, Micah came up with no less than a hundred euphemisms for Savannah's 'pom-poms.'

'That was a fluke,' I say. 'I was a project or something.'

'Don't minimize that victory. She was capital *H* hot. Just *slightly* less hot than your mom.'

'Find. Another. Comparative.'

'All I'm saying is, if I had your mom, I wouldn't be leaving her at home for the summer.'

'And all *I'm* saying is, if you don't stop talking about my mom, I will have to suffocate you in your sleep.'

Micah chuckles. 'So, she really doesn't know you're leaving?'

'Nope.'

'Why not?'

'It was a spur-of-the-moment decision.'

'Uh, and she's going to be . . . fine with that?'

'Nope.'

'Well, that's a shit storm waiting to happen.'

At the airport, I hug Micah good-bye. You know, a man hug. Double pat on the back. And two hours later I'm in the sky.

AN ALTERNATE FORMULA FOR DISCOVERING ABSENT FATHERS:

$x\,(y) = z$, *where* x = *concrete information,*

y = *travel to the subject, and* z = *the assembly of broken pieces*

Linny

5.

WHO: James Willis, singer for the band Middlehouse
WHEN: 2013, after he skipped out on the MTV Video Music Awards
WHY: From what I can tell, no one knows why he disappeared, but he came back eight days later to open for Maroon 5.
NOTES: Grace actually went to this concert in Orlando. . . . Connection? (She said it was the greatest Middlehouse performance ever – and she knows best.)

The morning before Grace disappeared, she slipped her headphones over my ears while I was sleeping. I woke up to see her standing over me, every one of her curls tightly coiled – a ready-to-burst appearance. Two fake butterfly tattoos were dancing on her collarbone, highlighted by her scooped tank top that she absolutely *swore* Joan Jett once owned (the guy at the vintage shop told her so).

'Thank God you're awake,' Grace said. 'I've been waiting for*ever*.' I miss that about her – how she stressed the second syllable of important words, how she had the husky voice of a thirty-five-year-old lounge singer, and I was always shocked when it came out of five-foot-three her.

I didn't have time to ask, 'Jeez Louise, what's with the headphones,' because she shushed me with her index finger and declared, 'This song will change your life.' An electric guitar solo began to rattle – fast and alive – through the headphones, and I started bobbing to the beat, because she was right. As the family music virtuoso, Grace is always right about life-altering songs. She can play eleven instruments (if you count the kazoo, which I totally do) and is the proud owner of no less than two hundred records, mostly of women who wore their hair all big in the eighties.

'Not bad,' I told her, and she pounced on me – sat on my stomach like she was squeezing closed a suitcase – until I admitted, 'Okay, okay, it's *great*.'

I remember this, and then I remember that she's gone.

The missing her practically blows me off my feet.

It's eight in the morning, I'm (shakily) standing outside Silver Springs waiting for Cass and Ray – and there's a man in a red baseball cap photographing the building from between two palm trees. He calls out to me: 'Do you mind moving about three feet to the right? I'm trying to get a good shot!'

'Oh,' I mumble. 'Um, sure.'

News of Álvaro Herrera's appearance is spreading slowly – but it *is* spreading. According to findalvaro.com, only the die-hard followers believe that he's alive and at Silver Springs. I wonder how long it'll take before other people discover that the rumors are true.

Fashionably late, Ray and Cass rock up in Ray's clunker of a truck, which is old enough to be a resident of Silver Springs. In places it's graying – stripped down to the metal frame, green paint hanging on in fragments. On the sidewalk, they describe their plan, which includes claiming they're visiting their grandma Ethel (who would be a very lovely woman, if she existed), obtaining visitor badges under aforementioned pretenses, and gawking at Álvaro Herrera from afar.

'So you're going to lie,' I say, slightly regretting my decision to tell them.

'It's only a white lie,' Ray says, pointing to the building. 'I'm sure *somewhere* in there's an Ethel.'

'True,' I admit. 'But I still classify "falsely entering a nursing home" under "morally dubious activities."'

'Chill out, my little Lin-zer Torte,' Cass says, and my stomach drops a notch. Grace came up with that nickname. 'We are superstealthy when it comes to celeb spotting.'

Turns out that Marla's not at the front desk, so I sign myself in while Cass and Ray scurry through the lobby. We check the courtyard – no Álvaro. And the halls – no Álvaro. So we spend a nice morning in the game room, playing Ping-Pong with two women in canary muumuus, one of whom is named Ethel. (Ray gets such a kick out of that, Cass has to pinch him to stop the giggles.)

And then, in the cafeteria at lunchtime, there's Álvaro Herrera, sitting alone at one of the long plastic tables with an ashtray in front of him, studying the smoke mushrooming from his lips.

'*That's* him?' Ray says.

I nod. 'Try not to stare.'

A small crowd has formed, and a ripple of voices drifts across the room. 'Is that really . . . ?' 'I thought he was . . . ?' 'I saw him yesterday, but . . .' Three nurses hold up the wall behind him, but none of them moves to snatch his cigarillo.

And there's something else. *Someone* else.

I notice a guy my age – or maybe a bit older – leaning against the vending machine and staring at Álvaro. Like, *staring*. He has a slightly offbeat look, like a puzzle improperly put together, and if I'm reading it correctly, his bright-green T-shirt says I Believe in Science. He has dark, wild hair. (Side note: *Wild* is not a word I use lightly. His hair is like Ringo Starr's in the mid-sixties, if Ringo got caught in a windstorm.)

Even so, something about him makes me acutely aware of my outfit: tattered jean shorts and a baggy white blouse that matches the chipped polish on my nails. I fiddle self-consciously with a few renegade curls. Most of my hair is woven into a fishtail braid after a lost battle with my straightener.

Ray and I grab trays and silverware while Cass plops down at one of the tables. With her sparkly silver crop top and sheet of blond hair, Cass usually draws attention, but no one notices her, or us lesser mortals, or anyone but Álvaro.

A cafeteria worker serves something that resembles meat loaf (or turkey?), and Ray and I take seats next to Cass, who's been smacking the same piece of cinnamon gum for the last half hour. I offer her some of my meat substance, but she points to her mouth and says, 'Nah, I'm good.'

'Go talk to him,' Ray urges me.

'I will,' I say. 'I'm just waiting for the right moment.'

The air conditioner must be broken, because the room feels like a jungle. Heavy-duty fans are positioned in the corners, creating a wind tunnel effect and eating up most of the whispers. So it's impossible that Álvaro hears Cass when she leans over our table and says between smacks of gum, 'He's . . . *so* different . . . from what I thought he'd be,' but that's when Álvaro begins banging his hands against the table. A frantic look shoots into his eyes. They widen. His jaw clenches. *BANG, BANG, BANG.* Palms flat, slapping the plastic in a repetitive motion like a wind-up toy. Focusing on his mouth, I expect him to say something – scream, shout, whatever – but his lips remain synched together.

BANG, BANG, BANG

Ten seconds pass.

BANG

Ray's neck has gone a dark pink, and he keeps side-eyeing me like: *We should do something, right?* But I have no idea what to do. Most of us don't. Except the nurses, who rush to his side, and the puzzle boy, who darts from the room. I wonder where he goes.

BANG, BANG, BANG

It takes all three nurses plus Marla, who has run from the office, to calm him. 'You're all right, honey,' she says. 'You're all right.'

Clearly that's not the case. Clearly something's wrong.

THE LEFT-BEHINDS (scene 3)

CARSON FAMILY BACKYARD

LINNY (eleven) and CASS (eleven and a half) are collecting fireflies. Each girl has a Mason jar with ten or so, their little butts lighting up the darkness.

GRACE (thirteen) rushes out the back door and into the yard, barefoot and screaming. Clearly something is wrong. The skin on her back is no longer puckering, but giving way to lines of soft spikes.

GRACE

   I told you not to do that!

CASS
(confused)
>   What are you talking about?

LINNY
(guilty)
>   We aren't going to keep them. You know, just look at them for
>   a while.

GRACE
>   They're wild things, Linny. Let. Them. Go.

So LINNY and CASS unscrew the lids and watch the blinking lights
fade away. GRACE reaches out to them with her fingertips, trying to
lift off the ground.

Sebastian

6.

'Scientists have deeply speculated about the possibility of multiple universes, existing side by side.' *A Brief Compendium of Astrophysical Curiosities*, p. 177

Something is very wrong.

I'm ten feet away from Álvaro. His breath is raspy. Like a helicopter struggling to get off the ground. And then he starts completely losing his shit. *BANG, BANG, BANG.*

I have only three thoughts:

What's happening?

Why's that blond girl on her phone at a time like this?

Why is nothing – literally nothing – going as planned?

I was *just* about to speak with him, and now . . .

It happens fast. Like teleportation. One minute: in the cafeteria. The next: in the hallway, trying to catch my breath.

Damn it.

Theoretically, everything is explainable. But right now, I can't explain why this moment doesn't match the fantasy I've been harboring for – oh, I don't know – the last six thousand days of my life.

If I could hibernate for the rest of the summer, I swear to God I would. But since evolution has yet to extend me the ability to slow my heart rate substantially and drop my body temperature, I settle for the next best thing: I skulk back to Ana's condo. Wedge myself between couch cushions. Hide in *A Brief Compendium of Astrophysical Curiosities*.

Reading. Thinking.

Thinking about another Sebastian in a parallel universe. Wondering if Other Sebastian feels as broken as I do.

AN ADDENDUM ON THE MULTIVERSE:
A shitty situation in universe 1 may have little to no effect on universe 2.

Meanwhile, my cell phone keeps flashing *MOM*. I ignore it. She'd want me to explain myself, and I have no explanation other than: I needed to do it.

Around four o'clock, I open a bag of salt-and-vinegar potato chips and flick on the TV. Maybe Aunt Ana has the Discovery Channel?

But it's already programmed to News 6 Miami. On-screen is a shiny-looking newscaster in a purple pantsuit. 'This afternoon,' she says, 'more shocking news coming out of the most unlikely place . . .'

The TV shows shifty footage of a pool and a cement courtyard.

I think: *Hey, that looks familiar.*

I think: *Holy shit, it's Silver Springs.*

I think: *GRAN DIOS, IT'S ÁLVARO.*

The cameraman inches closer to Álvaro, who is thwacking the keys of his typewriter at one of the pool tables. In the distance, someone shouts, 'Oh naw! Turn that thing off!'

Footage then switches to a YouTube video. And, oh shit – I'm in it.

The angle looks like . . . *Espera un segundo* . . .

That blond girl! She filmed the whole thing with her phone! Who *does* that?

The newscaster provides a dramatic voice-over: 'This footage clearly shows that Álvaro Herrera, known for his book *Midnight in Miami*, is alive. The video is currently gathering steam on social networks, garnering even more speculation about this mysterious man. This evening, the questions on everyone's mind are: Where'd he go? Why's he here? Is this episode symptomatic of psychological issues or – ?'

Click.

I sort of punch the remote with my fist. The living room seems devoid of any oxygen.

Five minutes later, enter Ana, home from her shift at University of Miami Hospital. She drops her pocketbook and unties her massive ponytail. Wavy hair flops every which way. Groaning like a harpooned sea lion, she begins picking at two red specks (ketchup? blood?) on her sleeve.

'Is that . . . ?' I say.

She winks. 'Better not to talk about it.'

Because it's Florida, my aunt Ana (aka Nurse Ana) gets a lot of dementia patients – eighty- or ninety-year-old women who blow through traffic lights and cause four-car pileups. Although she *says* it's best not to discuss it, I've learned over the last seventeen years that Ana is a talker. She lets out a three-minute diatribe about the risks of operating a vehicle without functional use of your legs.

'*Ouch*,' I conclude.

'Major *ouch*.'

She really is cool, my aunt. She's seven years younger than

my mom. Single. And obsessed with healing crystals. There are crystals everywhere. Purple crystals. Pink crystals. A two-foot-tall rock crystal near the kitchen sink.

Ana picks off the last bit of ketchup and says, 'Why are you so quiet?'

Quiet. It's the first time in my life I've been called quiet. When I was little, Mom would chase me around the house with superglue and pretend she was going to seal my lips together ('Sebastian, you talk too much for your own good!'). It never scared me. Her point was: I babble to anyone about anything. Two-hour debate about alien spacecraft and the possibility of life on Mars? Lecture on quarks, hadrons, and high-energy collision? No problem. Then I saw that news report, and a strange vocal paralysis set in.

Maybe I'll take up nonverbal communication. Smoke signals. Morse code.

I shrug. 'I'm just listening.'

Ana *hmmm*s at me and hits me with this whammy: 'Please tell me you called your mom.'

A pause. 'Not in the classical sense.'

'Sebastian.'

'I just need some time to figure out everything without her. *Por mi cuenta.*'

Sighing – 'Well, I spoke with her twice on my shift. She's really worried about you, but . . . I understand where you're coming from. Just call her soon, okay?'

'Okay.'

'So, was Silver Springs good?'

What a loaded question. PLEASE let something drag her away into the kitchen. I would give anything for the phone to ring. For a small asteroid to strike the condo roof . . .

I say, 'Not so hot.'

'You don't have to tell him, sweetie. Just . . .' She grasps for the words. Literally grasps for them. Fingers twitching in the air. 'Get to know him, but don't get your hopes up too much.' Then she leans across the couch to ruffle my hair. Never in my seventeen years have I enjoyed a hair ruffle, despite good intentions. I can already sense this summer is going to be one long hug-a-thon. (I read that oxytocin, the 'bonding hormone,' is only released when people hug for over twenty seconds. A twenty-second hug? Kill me now.)

Ana uses her nurse voice. Sweet yet detached. 'Did you see the news?'

'Yep.'

'I'm so sorry . . .' She winces. 'Is the couch working for you at least?'

'Oh yeah,' I say. 'It's great.' I sound convincing, although the couch is a blob masquerading as furniture. Last night before bed, I prayed that the blob wouldn't swallow me in the night. I picture myself waking up like Jonah in the belly of the whale. Granted, that would *still* be an improvement over home.

Clapping her hands together – 'Know what would help?'

'Time travel.'

She opens her mouth to say one thing but reconsiders. 'I'm just going to skip over that and say COOKING!'

'Cooking?'

'COOKING!' Grabbing my hand, she drags me into the kitchen – which is decorated with, you guessed it, crystals. 'Your mom says you don't know how to cook *bistec empanizado*.'

'I'm not even sure *she* knows how to cook *bistec empanizado* anymore.'

'You're kidding.'

'Nope.'

'You're *kidding*.'

'Um . . . no?'

She slaps three cloves of garlic into my palm. 'Then peel.'

Every few minutes she shouts another direction: 'Chop the onions!' 'Beat the eggs!' 'Give it more salt!' Until I almost forget about the news. Almost.

'This calls for music,' she says. I hear her switch on the kitchen radio. The static buzz, systems humming awake. But three seconds later I catch the words: '. . . there are still speculations about the former whereabouts of Álvaro Herrera.' Then *clang-clash-clang* – pots falling as Ana scrambles across the kitchen to turn off the news.

Now in the house there is an eerie stillness. I think the steaks are burning.

* *AN ADDENDUM TO AFOREMENTIONED ADDENDUM:*
Or, in every universe, shit is still shit.

Linny

7.

WHO: Richard Thorpe of Thorpe Brothers Truffles
WHEN: 1865
WHY: He was responsible for the greatest disaster in the history of chocolate making — two thousand gallons of liquid chocolate flooded the streets of the Bronx after a system malfunction. To avoid further embarrassment, Thorpe fled the city for the Catskills but returned two months later when the company's board threatened to remove him as chief executive.
NOTES: Lure Grace back by threatening to give away her records? Something else important to her? (Also, just an observation, but a chocolate flood doesn't seem like the worst thing in the world.)

In John Hughes films, I always pay particular attention to people's rooms – how absolutely everything speaks to their characters. The pink messiness and overstuffed throw pillows in *Sixteen Candles*. The mishmashed patterns of Ferris Bueller's rug and quilt. The sad thing is, if my life were a movie, my room would say more about MomandDad than me.

Early last March, Mom painted every wall in our house white – to sterilize it, I guess. To give me a fresh start, even though I didn't want one. I want black sheets over mirrors that no longer reflect Grace – a complete state of mourning – because isn't that what this is? In some ways, doesn't it feel like she's died?

Through my viewfinder, I pan around my room. Even the

bedding and the carpet are like snow, which totally sucks. If Grace were here, she'd suggest a cure for all this white: an emergency tie-dye dance. In Cass's garage is a relic from her parents' hippie days – a massive tie-dyed flag strung up in the rafters. As a result, when the lights flicker on, the whole room illuminates in psychedelic colors. Grace always cranked up her music ultraloud, so we just *had* to dance, hips shimmying and hands high in the air. She was always doing this – pulling me out of my comfort zone, giving me experiences, pushing me to be a better filmmaker. 'Linny,' she'd say. 'No one ever made a good movie by sitting on her ass. Live. You have to *live*.'

Am I living now, Grace? Huh? All this researching reappearances, eating silent dinners with MomandDad, volunteering at an old-people's home, spending evenings hand-feeding a box turtle. (Side note: I know that none of this is Hector's fault, and I do not resent him. After Grace left, I moved his terrarium onto my dresser and take him on walks whenever I can. He is especially fond of kale.)

The back of my closet is the only place MomandDad left unsterilized – the only place where I can watch footage of Grace without them freaking out. Before breakfast, I grab my laptop and tunnel into its cocoon of throw pillows – no pashmina here, just tribal-printed fabrics that Grandpa brought back from his final trip to Nigeria. Snatching a fistful of M&M'S from the pocket of my winter jacket (a natural hiding place since the coat rarely leaves the closet), I log on to my computer, click on the file marked 'The Left-Behinds Inspiration,' and start sifting through shots. Grace fills the screen – gap-toothed smile, rock star hair, her voice low and rambling through the speakers. I love her this way: happy, bouncing, *here*.

It's becoming increasingly obvious that I lived a bold, colorful life because Grace did. I was brave because she was brave. Now, at home, I'm trending toward turtle: head firmly in shell. (No offense, Hector.) Cass once said, 'It must be *so* hard that your sister is always in the spotlight,' but that couldn't be further from the truth. When Grace took center stage, she towed me along with her.

From underneath one of the pillows, I pull out my *Journal of Lost and Found* and open it to the first page. Taped to the creamy white paper is the note Grace left on my desk the day she disappeared. She hasn't written me since. Would it kill her to send a note that says: *Hey Linny, how's it going*? Or, *By the way I'm in Utah and here's my phone number*? Would it have killed her to tell me that she was planning on leaving in the first place?

At first I'd hoped that Grace was running toward something instead of just plain running away. Music festivals were my first inclination, so I stapled a map of America to the back of my journal, marked red dots in places I thought she would go: a dot over Indio, California, for Coachella, for example, another one for the Savannah Music Festival in Georgia. Then I posted pictures of her online, asking festival-goers: Have you seen this girl? A lot of people said they had (one claimed she was onstage banging a tambourine with Middlehouse), but no one could prove it.

Are you still running, Grace? Because I'm still chasing you, and my legs are about to give out.

I don't realize until it's too late that I'm crushing the M&M'S in my hand.

Another chocolate disaster.

*

For breakfast, MomandDad make pancakes from a box, because serious discussions demand heavy carbohydrates and maple syrup. Dad slides a copy of the *Miami Daily* across the table and taps the front page. Just below the June 8 date stamp is a black-and-white image of 1950s Álvaro – sharp suit, sharp smile – beneath a still shot of a video. The newer image shows Álvaro iron eyed, his hands suspended in midair, right before the *BANG*.

Mom sets a pancake stack and some blueberries on the table. 'You washed your hands, right? I saw you petting that turtle. Did you know reptiles frequently carry salmonella?'

'Mm, fascinating,' I say, grabbing the paper and squinting at the caption: A YouTube video uploaded last night by Cassandra49213 shows Álvaro Herrera alive.

Holy bananas. Cass? *Cass* filmed this? I text her under the table: Explain????????

A few seconds later, she responds: You're so uptight lately

Me: I'm not being uptight. Just, take it down, okay?

Her: No, you're not the only one who gets to be Camera Girl ☺

A whirlpool of frustration begins twisting my intestines into a Gordian knot. Now that everyone knows Álvaro's at Silver Springs, will I even get the chance to speak with him? Plus, what happened yesterday seemed so . . . personal. A few days after Grace left, I sort of did the same thing – threw stuff at the walls, gripped my hands into fists – and I wouldn't want images of *that* splashed across the internet.

The funny thing is, when I glance at the newspaper picture again, the first person I notice isn't Álvaro. I notice the boy with the puzzle face. He's slightly out of focus, but it's like he's looking right at me. As I start tracing his blurred outline with my finger, I remember what MomandDad told me a few summers ago when I began showing a tangible interest in boys: 'They're a distraction, Linny. You can't list "hanging out with boys" on your college application under "extracurricular activities."'

Dad's chewing methodically, dissecting the situation. 'Maybe you can incorporate some of these experiences at Silver Springs into your admissions essay.'

I shove half a pancake into my mouth. The incapacity to speak is helpful, given this is sure to be another lightning round of Let's Prod Linny About Princeton.

Patting her lips with a napkin, Mom says, 'Have you finished your rough draft yet, sweetheart? You can't expect to write these things overnight.' Dad nods in solidarity. Or perhaps their identicalness is such that Mom's thoughts automatically control Dad's movements.

I point to my mouth to indicate I'm still chewing.

Mom gives me her X-ray eyes, like she's not looking at me but administering a pelvic scan.

I say through a mouthful of pancake, 'We'll taa-lk about this laa-ter,' although I have no intention of discussing it at all. I snatch a few berries for Hector, then the newspaper from Mom as she begins wiping away a syrupy smudge from the front page.

At Silver Springs, there are three reporters in the parking lot, and I practically have to wedge my way through them to enter the lobby. One shouts in my ear, 'Just one question, one question: Has Álvaro gone crazy?' which prompts my first ever 'talk to the hand' gesture.

That's it. I *have* to get some answers from Álvaro, just in case these people force him to skedaddle. Dashing upstairs like my curls are on fire, I start with the first hallway and work my way in a circular pattern. Every door boasts a construction paper sign with the resident's name written in swirly ink. Halfway down the third hallway, I see: MR. HERRERA.

Here goes nothing.

I knock, and his gargled voice answers, 'Come in, come in.'

Inside is like the aftermath of *The Perfect Storm*. Stacks of books and piles of paper are everywhere. His twin bed and armchair are submerged beneath the chaos. I can barely see his typewriter, which sits on a tiny desk. Although his bathroom has one of those fancy walk-in tubs they advertise on TV, it would be a Herculean feat to access it. How'd he manage to clog up the room so quickly?

In the dead center of the space, immersed in his cave of paper, is Álvaro. He's in silk pajamas, reclining in a chair, his legs propped on the collected works of Philip Roth. The room is filling with smoke and the sound of a Spanish guitar thrumming on the radio. It's the kind of song Grace would love.

He fumbles deep in his shirt pocket and fishes out a matchbox with an 'Aha!' As he lights another cigarillo, smoke claws up his face. 'Would you care for one?'

I wade toward him, careful not to disturb any piles. 'No thanks, I don't smoke. . . . Should you really be doing that in here?' I have a vision of him improperly extinguishing the cigarillo, the room going up in a sudden blaze.

He considers the question by massaging the cut on his forehead. 'You know the "an apple a day keeps the doctor away" saying, yes? Well, these are my apples.' He's so nonchalant that I wonder if he's aware that news of his reappearance is spreading like a virus, that *I'm* partly responsible. He says, 'Remind me of your name, *niña*.'

'Linny.' I gently stack the papers on the armchair and sort of wiggle in. 'Can I ask you something?'

The left corner of Álvaro's mouth twitches upward, revealing teeth shaped like Chiclets. 'It seems you will anyway, no?'

'No. Well, yes. I mean . . . I need to know why you came back.'

'*¿Necesitas?* This is a need? You will die without it?'

What, is he making fun of me? 'Not *die*, exactly. But it's really important.'

He leans forward, lowering his voice. 'Came back? Why do you say "came back"? Where do you think I went?'

Well, this is fun. 'I was hoping that you'd tell me.'

Álvaro puffs once more on his cigarillo. 'Do you like movies, *mi amor*?'

Maybe getting answers won't be as easy as I'd thought. 'Yeah, I do, but what does that have to do with –'

'Everything!' he shouts. 'Love! Romance! Memories! They are never better than in the movies. It has everything to do with everything. You know this, yes?'

'Um, yes,' I say, for lack of anything better. 'So, where *did* you go?'

He reclines thoughtfully and places both hands behind his head, the dangerously low V-neck popping farther and farther open, until I can see his belly button. It's hairy, too. The *ewwww* in my mind extends fifteen syllables.

'How do you like this place?' he finally says.

'What place?'

He motions his arm around. '*This* place.'

'Oh, Silver Springs? Um, it's okay.'

With both distaste and genuine surprise, he says, 'There are so many *old* people here.'

I'm about to get us back on track when the smoke alarm begins to beep. And when I say beep, I actually mean: simulate a Godzilla death cry. At first Álvaro's eyes widen, and I think I'm in for a repeat of the cafeteria scene. But then he shouts 'Bah!' up at the ceiling and lifts himself from the chair. 'I thought I took care of that, but I guess not! Now, escort me to *la cantina.*'

Is that it? Our conversation's done?

I help him up and start clearing a pathway through the papers.

That's when I open the door and see the puzzle boy clearly for the first time. It's hard not to, considering he's hovering statue-still roughly two feet from my face. Under the fluorescent lights, his hair is flopping everywhere. He looks Hispanic – or maybe multiracial like me – and his eyes are so gray, they're almost metallic. His arm is extended in midair, ready to knock on the just-opened door. He sucks in a breath.

I can't understand why, but just for an instant, he looks at me like we have the same secret.

THE LEFT-BEHINDS (scene 4)

<u>BOOKS & BOOKS – EARLY AFTERNOON</u>

LINNY (twelve) wanders through the bookstore, checking around each corner.

LINNY
(peppy)
> Marco!

GRACE
(from afar)
> Polo!

LINNY
> Marco?

GRACE
(closer)
> Polo!

In the next nook, there is GRACE (fourteen), back resting uncomfortably against a bookcase. Fuzzy yellow feathers are poking out from the sleeves of her dress. She is reading an oversize book called *Alaska, Atlantis, and Beyond.*

GRACE
> What took you so long? I've been waiting forever.

LINNY plops down beside her. We see a page of the book: a brightly colored illustration of an early plane, flying over glaciers.

LINNY
> Where's that?

GRACE
> Somewhere we're going.

GRACE smiles, then:

GRACE (continued)
Just don't tell Mom and Dad.

LINNY rests her head on GRACE's shoulder.

LINNY
It'll be our secret.

Sebastian

8.

'Readers, please forgive the pun – but the mechanism behind the sun's magnetism is hotly debated.' *A Brief Compendium of Astrophysical Curiosities*, p. 203

I don't even get to knock. The door swings open, and there's Álvaro and the girl from the cafeteria. The girl whose friend filmed everything. All my words get stuck. Hell, even my arm gets stuck. I watch it linger in midair and try to recall it silently, like, *WTF, arm, get back here this instant! ¡Rápido!* It reminds me of a journal article I read about split-brain syndrome, where people sometimes lose control of half of their limbs.

The girl stares at me. Her lips are O shaped, like she's sucking on something. My eyes pinball from her to Álvaro.

Mostly to her.

One of her hands is on Álvaro's shoulder. The other grips the bottom of her C'est la Vie tank top. I try not to focus on two things in particular: 1) the slight see-through-ness of her shirt, and 2) the shirt's annoyingly accurate translation.

Why is she here? Why is she here *now*?

AN OBSERVATION ON MAGNETISM:
People are either attracted to or repelled by each other
at random.

I take in everything about this girl. Freckles. Brown skin. Mass of braided hair. How she smells of sweat and honeysuckle and strawberries all at once.

She's derailed me. Killed my words.

If only I could summon superpowers: telepathy like Professor X in *X-Men*. Then I could infiltrate this girl's brain space. Tell her she can't be here. Not for this.

But I can't summon shit, because telepathy doesn't *really* exist (yet) . . . and because this girl is mind-blowingly hot.

Two thoughts:

What's with the alarm?

Why, of all days, did I wear this goddamn periodic table T-shirt?

Álvaro's looking at me like I'm an alien, and I think I might vomit or cry or laugh about the stupid, stupid luck of it all. None of the steps in my plan included a girl crashing into my orbit like intergalactic space junk, opening a door that Álvaro Herrera was supposed to open. She is directly in the spot where I should be standing.

My fight-or-flight response kicks in. I turn and speed-walk away, barely making it to the stairs before Álvaro's voice echoes down the hallway. 'Weird kid. Do you know him?'

Weird kid. Awesome first impression.

That night, Ana paces around the living room, on the phone with my mom. '*Lo sé, lo sé*. Just give him some time, Luna. He'll come around.' Pause. 'I know, but he doesn't want to come home right now – he wants to be in Miami, with his father. . . . It's hard, *sí*. I know it's hard, but he's going off to college in the fall. You won't be able to control him then, either.'

Hurting my mom is the last thing I want. But I need to do this without her.

To distract myself, I cook *arroz con pollo* using Ana's recipe. I burn the chicken. And the rice. (Apparently you're supposed to cook them *together*.)

Ana insists I'm getting better. 'It always tastes good when you make it yourself,' she says after hanging up the phone, sitting down at the table.

I take a bite then immediately spit it into a napkin. 'Let's agree to disagree.'

'Well, I like it.' She spoons some rice into her mouth and smiles. Then coughs. Spits it out, too. 'Okay, I have mac and cheese in the freezer.'

I can't do anything right.

Over Dinner Plan B, I ask, 'How's my mom?'

'She's' – struggling with her words – 'coming to terms with the fact that you're making your own decision.'

'Oh.'

'You both will be just fine.' Ana pats my hand with hers. 'Speaking of . . . how's it going at Silver Springs? Have you talked to Álvaro yet, by any chance?'

'Nope.'

'I'm just . . . I'm just worried that you're getting your hopes up too much, you know? Real-life reunions aren't like Disney movies, and you look so upset and –'

'There's this *girl*,' I explode.

'Oh,' Ana says, and then: 'Oh, oh! *Ooo!* A girl! Tell me, tell me.' She's even shimmying her shoulders.

'Not like that. Definitely not like that. Whenever I try to talk to Álvaro, she's *there*, like a curse hanging over me or something.'

'¡Ay, dios mio!, Sebastian, and you don't think that's a sign?'

'Yes. I do. A sign that my life is going to shit. That random things happen for no reason at all.'

She swats her hand at me, waving away the air. 'Don't be so dramatic. What does she look like?'

'She's . . .' Hot. Damn it, she is so hot. And also cute. A formidable combination. 'It doesn't matter what she looks like.'

Ana raises her eyebrows in my direction. 'Sure it doesn't.'

The next morning, I realize Californians don't know heat. Here, it's brain-turned-to-sludge weather. To make matters worse, there are fifty thousand people in the Silver Springs parking lot.

Fine. I'm exaggerating. There are eleven. But six of them *are* from major TV networks. Univision, Fusion, Fox News Latino printed on the sides of their cameras. As I step off the bus and shove my way through the lot, questions rocket through the air:

'Young man! Any news about where Álvaro Herrera's been?'

'Are the rumors true?'

'Is he dating anyone?'

The last question whips my head around. The man disappeared for three years and this asshat wants to know if he's *dating anyone*?

Screw him. Screw them all.

Inside the lobby I let out a breath I didn't realize I was holding. Marla shuts the door behind me and shouts through the glass, 'YOU PEOPLE NEED TO MIND YOUR OWN BUSINESS!' Turning back around, she pulls a card from her pocket. Hands it to me with the words: 'Here, honey. Phone's been ringing off the hook, and you betcha life, it's going to get worse. I'm giving all the volunteers swipe cards. If your card doesn't work' – leaning in, whispering – 'the code's zero-zero-zero-zero.'

Before I can tell her that 0-0-0-0 is hardly high security, she says, 'Got one for you, too, Miss Marilyn.'

Oh. There's someone else in the lobby. The girl from yesterday.

'It's Linny,' the girl says.

I hate her. God, how I hate her.

My face reads like an obscene hand gesture. At least I hope it does. There's a fine line between looking angry and looking constipated.

Marla motions between us. 'Y'all two met before?'

Si. And no. I dig my hands into my pockets, ballooning them out like puffer fish.

The girl doesn't move. I can tell she's replaying yesterday's speed-walk down the hallway. Her narrowing eyes give it away.

Marla says, 'Linny, Sebastian. Sebastian, Linny.'

Neither of us says hello. Linny blows a curl from her eyes. She's wearing jean shorts and Chuck Taylors like yesterday, but her blue T-shirt isn't so see-through this time. On it is a picture of a yawning kitten. The fabric slips off one of her shoulders.

Smacking her hands together, Marla says, 'Right. So here's what y'all need to know. Last night one of the reporters broke in through Ethel Markovitz's bathroom window again. We found him wandering the second floor. I'm hiring a security guard, but in the meantime, I need y'all to make sure Álvaro's not wandering anywhere he shouldn't be wandering. Make sure no one's wandering into him, if you see what I mean.'

Linny asks, 'Why do we get to do it?' and Marla says, 'Look around, honey. We aren't exactly swimming in volunteers.'

'So basically,' I croak, 'we're stuck together.'

Marla crosses her arms. 'Maybe you'll even like him. Ever think of that?'

But I didn't mean stuck with Álvaro.

On the way upstairs, I remind myself that avoiding confrontation is simple, if I stick to a proven plan.

Step 1: Feign interest in the floor.

Step 2: Count the tiles to keep your mind occupied.

Step 3: Whatever you do, don't speak first.

Except I speak first. Halfway up the steps it dawns on me that it could be a long-ass summer if I don't get a few things off my chest. I take one of those I'm-the-wolf-about-to-blow-your-house-down breaths. Turn around and say, 'Look.' The tone of my voice is very Mr. Benson, my chemistry teacher, when he's scolding us about lab safety.

Linny recoils.

Three steps ahead, I tower over her. 'I know it was your friend – that girl – who, you know, filmed the whole Álvaro thing, and I just wanted you to know that I think it was really shitty, filming him when he was . . . you know. Stressed. Really, really shitty.'

Linny studies the two stairs between us like a demon's about to jack-in-the-box out of them. But do I stop? Heck no.

'Who *does* that?' I shout. 'What kind of person has *friends* like that?'

Linny tugs at the long braid behind her back. Then she looks up. *Bam!* Her eyes are really brown and super big.

I remind myself that I hate her. That she keeps getting in the way.

She says, 'Sorry, I didn't . . . Cass . . . I didn't know she was filming it, okay?'

'No! It's not okay!'

'It's not okay that I didn't know?'

I shake my head. 'That's not what I meant.'

Linny huffs. 'I said I'm sorry. And I *am* sorry.' She reaches out and grips my arm. Hard. All fingertips. 'I swear,' she says. 'I swear I didn't know. I even tried to get her to take it down, but, well –' Just as abruptly, she pulls back.

The complicated truth of it is, I would give my left eyeball for her to touch me again. Suddenly my body feels weighed down. Like I've swapped all the oxygen for heavy elements.

A SECOND OBSERVATION ON MAGNETISM:
Repellency and attraction can occur in quick succession with
supermassive force.

We stand silently for several days.

Then she says, 'Why do you care so much anyway?'

I cross my arms. 'What makes you think I care?'

'You just yelled at me in a stairwell.'

'Right.' Pause. 'I'm –' Pause. 'Well, I'm –' Pause. 'I'm the president of Álvaro's fan club.'

Linny scrunches her nose. Like she doesn't believe me. 'You are?'

'Yes. Absolutely. That is I. *El presidente.*'

'Oh, um, cool . . . So, are we going to . . . ?' She points to the door at the top of the stairs.

'Yes. Yes. Climbing. Upward. Motion.' Why the hell am I speaking like a robot?

I tell myself to refocus. I tell myself that I don't exactly hate her but I don't exactly like her, either.

DO NOT FOCUS ON THE HOT GIRL.

It almost works. The rest of our twenty-eight-step walk

consists of me recalculating what my first word should be to
Álvaro. Hello? ¿*Hola?* Something snappier? Maybe I should come
right out with it. All in one breath: 'I-know-you-don't-know-
me-and-have-other-things-on-your-mind-but-by-the-way-my-
mom-had-your-baby.' Oh! How about the reverse Darth Vader
approach? '*Álvaro, I am your son.*'

I rap on the door with my knuckles. (Finally! A complete
knock!)

Sounds inside: papers shuffling, footsteps swiping the ground.

Álvaro wrenches open the door. He is so old it stops my heart.
It's one thing to know old age abstractly and another to smell it.
Like stale vinegar and bad cologne.

Physiologically speaking, he looks decent for eighty-two.
(Everyone assumed he was worm food, so I guess not having holes
in his face is a win.) Still, I can't stop staring at his droopy flesh.
He looks blurrier than on TV – all form with no edges. An amoeba
beneath the microscope. Although I saw him yesterday and the
day before, it feels like I'm *seeing* him for the first time.

Hyperventilation happens. Quick *he-hoo-he-hoo* breaths. So
my first word is not technically a word but a combination of *hello*
and *Álvaro*. 'Halvaro,' I say. Which undoubtedly helps with the
weird-kid perception. (Sebastian, zero. Paralysis, a hundred.)

Linny says, 'Can we come in?'

Álvaro: a blank expression.

Us: standing there awkwardly.

Álvaro tilts his head, like viewing us from another angle might
help. 'Sure, sure,' he grumbles. 'You will have to excuse me.'

But he doesn't say for what.

Shuffling back to his desk, he sits. Massages his knees. Returns
to his typewriter. Linny and I take a few exploratory steps inside.

Entering is like landing on the moon: unknown territory. Papers scattered on the floor. Everything is white.

'Bah!' Álvaro shouts. He rips a sheet from the typewriter and tosses it over his head. '*¡Ay qué relajo!*' Translation: What a mess.

Estoy de acuerdo. I agree in every way.

Linny cranes her neck and rises to her tiptoes. 'So, what are you writing?'

Not to us, but to the typewriter, Álvaro mumbles, 'A new novel.'

She rocks to flat feet, leans back. Like that information is blowing her away. 'Oh, wow . . . after all this time?'

In response, Álvaro swivels around in his chair. It is the world's slowest swivel. 'What can I do for you?'

Linny says, 'We want to – you know – hang out with you for a bit.'

Álvaro: blank face again. Then, 'We should play dominoes.'

I nod enthusiastically, like dominoes is exactly what I want to do. Not like I'm desperate to talk about literally anything but dominoes.

I'd rather he played Fill in the Blanks.

I left your mother because _____.

The last few years, I have been hiding in _____.

If I found out I was your father, I would _____.

Five minutes later we settle into a corner of the game room. Next to us is a group of women in hats playing cards. One of them is saying, 'My grandson just got a neck tattoo. *A neck tattoo.* Nothing says "employ me" like a neck tattoo.'

Álvaro carefully sets his personal set of dominoes on our table. They have Cuban flags on them and smell of perfume. I swish them around.

'Every Saturday, I play dominoes,' Álvaro says. 'Every Saturday. Me and Joe. Do you know Joe?'

It's Thursday. And I don't know Joe.

Linny's eyes carve a hole into the side of my face.

I sidestep Álvaro's question. 'So, how do you start?'

'You don't know? I will teach you. Any fool can play, but I'll teach you to win. The first thing you must learn is how to fight.' He winks at Linny and me. 'In dominoes, people scream, sing, make jokes! Shout at the top of their lungs!' There's a cigarillo between his lips. He strikes a match. 'Let me hear you shout.'

Linny and I exchange glances.

'*Ándale*,' Álvaro urges. 'Shout!'

So we do. Give weak *aaaaaaah*s. The card-playing women turn in their chairs to glare at us.

'We'll work on that later,' Álvaro says, waving a hand to tell us: *Okay, shut up now.* Then to me, eyes narrowing: 'You remind me of someone. Have we met?'

My muscles constrict. Does he know? Is it an innate thing – a father recognizing his son?

I completely choke. 'No . . . but . . . I, you know –'

'Sebastian's the president of your fan club,' Linny offers.

Álvaro takes a first puff, pauses for a cripplingly long moment, and repeats my name with a flourish. 'Sebas-TI-AN! Sebas-TI-AN! Saint Sebastian. Patron saint of archers and dying people, no?'

I guess? Never knew that.

'So you two are' – gesturing between me and Linny – 'you two are together, yes?'

'*Nooo*,' Linny says.

'I'm from California,' I say, as if this explains everything.

Jesus. I've *practiced* this. My first real conversation with my father, I was going to reel him in with my favorite scientific facts.

Butterflies taste with their feet.

The known universe has fifty billion galaxies.

Statistically, a meteorite will strike a human once every hundred years.

But Álvaro's giving me a strange look. Like he and Paul have conferred – and they've both decided I'm a weird kid. *Mierda*.

Linny's phone keeps buzzing in her back pocket, distracting me. I don't mention it. That's admitting I'm *looking* there. Which I'm not. Just like I'm not looking at her kick-ass clavicle (the most underrated body part).

'Officially speaking,' Linny says to Álvaro, 'if the fan club wanted to interview you about your – um – *history*, would that be okay?'

Álvaro shrugs. 'I do not mind.'

Linny straightens up. Shoulder blades almost touching. 'Great, I'll have Sebastian set it up.'

Excuse me?

I just nod. Nodding seems like the thing to do.

Suddenly, the game room door flings open. It's Marla. 'MR. HERRERA! I KNOW YOU'RE NOT SMOKING INDOORS AGAIN!'

Álvaro's face says: *Who, me? I would never!* (Although the cigarillo's still between his fingers.)

Then the smoke detector, *BEEP BEEP BEEP*.

Maintenance comes with a key and kills the alarm.

My nerves = completely shot.

Somehow, I make it through the next few hours. We have lunch. Watch an episode of *Wheel of Fortune* and three-quarters of a baseball game. Teach Álvaro – very, very unsuccessfully – how to play Ping-Pong.

Then it's just Linny and me, gathering our stuff. She practically pins me against the fig tree in the lobby.

'I know you're not president of his fan club.'

I falter. 'No, you don't.'

'Yes, I do. The president runs findalvaro.com and is a fifty-year-old man named Jorge Rodriguez.'

'I could be fifty. You don't know that.' What. Am. I. Saying.

Raising a hand – 'I don't really care, okay? You have your reasons, and I have mine.' She shoulders her backpack and looks me square in the face. 'I think we should work together.'

'Uh –'

'It's really obvious that you want to know him. I need to find out things, too, and as it is, you're kind of getting in the way of my investigation. It makes sense if we pair up.'

I'm getting in the way? But I've heard worse ideas. 'Fine.'

'Fine,' she says.

'What exactly did I just agree to?'

'We're going to read his books. Re-watch his movie. Do some sleuthing. Basically, find out where he went and why he came back. Which reminds me . . .' She does a goldfishy thing with her mouth – opening and closing. 'Who do you think Joe is?'

The same question has been rolling through my mind. The best answer I have is very nonspecific. 'A friend?'

Her lips twist to the side. It's kind of adorable. 'Don't you think it's weird that he said he played dominoes *every* Saturday? Because that means someone was with him the last three years.'

My mind races as I play devil's advocate. 'Maybe he meant before he disappeared.'

'No,' she says. 'I think it's probably more than that.'

I think it is, too. But before we can compare hypotheses, two sets of footsteps pound down the hallway. A man with an SLR camera strapped around his neck makes a hairpin turn around the corner. He's moving at sonic speed, Hawaiian shirt rippling with motion, *National Enquirer* baseball cap threatening to fly off his head.

Marla is close behind. 'I hope you got a really nice picture,' she shouts at his back, 'because you betcha behind, you're never getting in here again!'

The man loses his footing, skidding on the lobby tiles and into Linny. To avoid another clash, I quickly swipe my key card. The sliding door whooshes open. He disappears into the parking lot.

Linny follows him. Walking backward. Pointing in my direction like she's picking me out of a crowd. 'We start tomorrow.'

Linny

9.

WHO: British film director Timothy Cross
WHEN: 2001
WHY: Cross was supposed to shoot a contemporary version of Tarzan and His Mate, *but he couldn't handle the pressure of filming. In the greatest overreaction ever, he vanished into the jungle. Crew members later found him living with an indigenous tribe. Several times, Cross had returned to the set in the guise of a costume assistant to watch the rest of the film get completed by the new director.*
NOTES: Maybe it's wishful thinking, but does Grace spy on us sometimes? Should I set up cameras around the house? (I could totally see her in the jungle, tree-climber that she is — Mom used to call her 'a wild thing.')

Cass tries to call me three times after my shift, and then comes a flurry of texts:

It's really not a big deal

ANYONE could have filmed that, it would've happened sooner or later

Linnnnnny, come on! I'll split the thousand bucks with you

Are you mad at me?

… Linny?

I check and see that her YouTube video has ten thousand hits. She almost messed up absolutely everything, my one shot at finding out how to bring Grace home. So I delete all her messages.

There's another thing, too – something I can't quite voice. The truth is, even though Cass doesn't give me the 'you poor sisterless girl' look, she has a habit of prying at doors I want closed, and maybe the smallest part of me is searching for a reason to lock them all, to keep her out.

After dropping a few leaves of lettuce into Hector's terrarium, I crawl into my closet, turn on my flashlight, and pull out my *Journal of Lost and Found*, writing under the Álvaro Herrera Notes section:

'Me and Joe. Do you know Joe?' Who the heck is he? Álvaro's long-lost sibling? His neighbor? Maybe he's the one who brought Álvaro back into the world. But if Joe's so important, then why isn't _he_ the one playing dominoes with Álvaro?

Next I Google 'Álvaro Herrera and Joe' but find nothing except an old picture of Álvaro at an independent bookstore. The caption reads: *Midnight in Miami* Author Visits Joe, North Carolina! Signed Copies! Complimentary Cookies!

It's not exactly what I'm looking for, so I generalize my search. 'How to disappear.'

There's tons of material – even a step-by-step guide featuring information about selecting hoodies for maximum facial coverage (to reduce recognition). The guide suggests moving to the West Coast, taking up migrant farming, hunting for mushrooms. On the bottom of the page, the final piece of advice is: 'Tell no one. You are on your own.' I guess the only way to leave is to disappear completely.

But still – jeez.

Sometimes I wonder if Grace contacts anyone, if she's holed up in some seedy motel in Nebraska, writing letters to her old guitar teacher – *Dear Justin, I'm finding my sound on the road.* Or maybe she's prank-calling her most notable ex-boyfriend – that bass guitarist with the swoopy blond hair who ripped her heart at the seams. (Cass and I nursed her through it. Lots of peppermint ice cream and inspirational Debbie Harry quotes.)

It's a selfish thought, but I let myself think it anyway: *If she isn't contacting me, then I hope she's contacting no one.*

God. How is it possible to love someone more than the moon – to miss them and worry about them *this* much – and be so angry with them at the same time? I cringe. Did Álvaro follow the rule of *tell no one*?

What if he had someone with him, and Grace could have brought me along but didn't?

Focus, focus, focus.

But when I bat away images of my sister, Sebastian rattles into my head. (What's his deal anyway?) Tomorrow I'm planning on dragging him to Books & Books, my favorite indie store, to buy all Álvaro's novels. I know I'm being overly idealistic, but part of me thinks these texts might hold some insight – that all those years ago, Álvaro was already planning his marvelous return. I jot down a list:

Midnight in Miami
Ten Years in Havana
In the Hour of the Spring
The Emperor's House
Memories from No-Man's Land

Divvying up the titles, I assign *Ten Years in Havana* and *The*

Emperor's House to Sebastian and give myself the others.

Outside the closet is a muffled sound – a soft tap of knuckles on my door – followed by Mom's voice: 'Linny, lights-out.'

It's just after 9:00 p.m.

After suppressing a groan, and leaning back and knocking my head three times against the wall, I open the closet door and switch off the overhead lights.

'Thank you! Good night,' Dad says, because of course they have *both* been *waiting directly outside my door*. Their footsteps swish on the white carpeting, all the way down the hall. I listen for the zipping of blinds in the master bedroom, the rustle of the comforter as they pull back the sheets – good, they're in bed now. Movie time.

I found Grace's headphones in one of her desk drawers when I practically ransacked her room. They're blue, with yellow lightning bolts, and mold perfectly to my ears. Popping in *Breakfast at Tiffany's* – my favorite nighttime movie – I climb into bed with my computer and pull up the covers to my chin, thinking about dominoes on Saturdays and the way Sebastian's shoulders pitch forward when he's talking and how darn much I miss my sister.

Outside, a paper moon hangs flat against the black sky. I make a wish on it – because wishes shouldn't be exclusive to stars – and fall asleep to Holly Golightly's voice trailing into the dark.

'It's the mistake you always made,' she says, 'trying to love a wild thing.'

THE LEFT-BEHINDS (scene 5)

CARSON FAMILY BACKYARD

LINNY (thirteen) and GRACE (fifteen) are lying on beach towels under two orange trees, LINNY on her back and GRACE on her stomach. There's a large mound under GRACE's T-shirt, as if she's stuffed her wings beneath it.

LINNY

What does it feel like?

GRACE

It's hard to explain.

LINNY

But will I know when I feel it? Like Holly and Paul in *Breakfast at Tiffany's*?

GRACE

Of course.

LINNY

How?

GRACE

You just know.

LINNY

But –

GRACE rolls her eyes.

GRACE

> Love isn't like chicken pox, Linzer Torte. You don't get spots
> or anything. It's just like . . . like . . .

LINNY

> Like finding the perfect shot in film?

GRACE

> Okay, let's go with that.

LINNY

> My shoulders tingle.

GRACE laughs, then:

GRACE

> Okay. The first time a boy tingles your shoulders, you have to
> tell me before anyone else. Promise?

LINNY

> Who else would I tell?

GRACE

> Just promise me, Linny.

LINNY

> Promise.

'You mean this is *all* for him?' says Sebastian, hunching over a pile of fan mail beginning to resemble Everest. He puffs out his cheeks and runs a heavy hand through his hair, which this morning looks like the 'before' picture for a Supercuts ad. One of his parents must be half lion.

'Every last one, honey.' Marla dumps another bag on top of the sprawling mountain, over a hundred letters that we're supposed to sort into three piles: Keep, Toss, and Report to the Police (because people send suspicious things through the mail). Álvaro is at a doctor's appointment, so we're trapped in his room for the next three hours, reading.

Crouching down, I cross my legs and nestle into the letters. We're almost knee-to-knee, Sebastian and I – close enough to know he smells of vanilla and pine and something distinctly *boy*. (Oh boy.)

Marla trudges back into the hall and shuts the door.

'I have something for you,' I say, handing Sebastian the Álvaro list. 'You read some, I read some.'

He grabs the paper and nods, but doesn't say a word.

'Maybe there could be clues in the mail,' I say. 'Like, what if the person who hid him wrote a letter?'

Silence.

Switching tactics, I hold up an envelope postmarked Beijing. 'Kind of amazing, huh? And this one, too! Who knew he had fans in China?' I show them both to Sebastian, who side-eyes me and groans.

I mess with my fishtail braid and wonder if I've said something stupid. Time slows. I can literally feel it passing, the earth rotating, the stars shifting. The two mutes in *The Heart Is a Lonely Hunter* manage better conversations. (Good movie. Sad ending.)

'You're *really* quiet,' I say.

'Why does everyone keep saying that?'

'Because it's true?'

Sebastian drums his fingers against a package from Argentina. 'Everyone knows Álvaro so well.' His voice sounds rusty, like he's left it out in the rain.

I'm not an idiot; I can tell he's trying to shove down an emotion – and hard – but my mouth can't seem to quit. 'We just have to keep digging, that's all.'

At that, Sebastian chucks a letter onto the pile, closes his eyes, and leans back into a stack of travel books. A sliver of skin appears just above his waistline.

What sort of feeling washes over me, I'm not sure, but I zoom in on him like a camera lens. Can't help it.

Sebastian's definitely a different species of attractive: too willowy to be a jock, too imperfect to be astoundingly popular. Nothing about him *should* work, yet it *does*. Even the T-shirt he's wearing – a green, screen-printed number that looks like the sun ate it and spat it out in neon – somehow complements his brown skin. It's like someone's edited him and ratcheted up the color.

Was I ever like that? Maybe when Grace was around, but now? I feel color drained.

I shake the thought from my head and try to shake out Sebastian as well. No, I can't have him in there, because inevitably he's going to leave – just like Grace. Figuring out this mystery should be the only thing I'm worried about.

'We're going to a bookstore after our shift,' I say, quickly adding, 'you know, for investigative purposes.'

Without opening his eyes, he slowly breathes out and says, 'Yeah, okay . . . mind if I turn on the radio or something?'

Oh. 'Sure.'

To our left is a small white transistor radio that he flips to the first station. For the next three minutes, The Beatles' 'Hey Jude' plugs the gaps in our failing conversation. It's ridiculously awkward.

Wordlessly, I slice open an envelope with my index finger. *Dear Señor Herrera,* it reads. *You have no idea how long I've been wanting to say hello.*

Then Sebastian's voice: 'Hey, Linny?' It comes out like the song. 'I was thinking about it and I think you're right I mean I'm not *sure* you're right but you're probably right about the Joe thing because statistically speaking someone must've seen him in the last three years or helped him out because he's really old and stuff and I doubt he could live by himself.' His hyperventilated soliloquy reminds me of the Scripps National Spelling Bee champions on TV, how they always talk extra-speedily, like they have so much material batting around their brains, they have to expel it or burst. It wouldn't surprise me one bit if Sebastian was a genius. Yesterday, he told Álvaro he'd gotten into one of the best universities in the world: Cal Tech. For astrophysics! (I made a mental note that 90 percent of Miami Beach Senior High's guys probably couldn't *spell astrophysics*, and the other 10 percent . . . Well, let's just say that the Science Olympiad members generally sport aggressive unibrows.)

He's waiting for an answer, palming his knee offbeat. *Hey.* Whack. *Jude.* Whack.

So I tell him about looking up Joe.

Sebastian leans in. 'Well, did you find anything?'

Our knees touch, but neither of us moves. (Okay, he's officially back into my head!) Words burble out like unset Jell-O. 'Just a photo of him at some bookstore. But no Joe.'

Sebastian considers this by chewing his bottom lip. He says nothing else.

My mouth proceeds before my brain can tell it not to. 'Why are you *here*?'

'Is that . . . do you mean, like, on this earth?'

I roll my eyes. 'No, at Silver Springs. Why are you here if you're not even from Miami?'

He clears his throat – awkwardly, for an extended period of time. 'Can't I just, you know, love old people?'

'And there aren't any old people in California?'

That cracks him up, splintering his puzzle face for a moment. 'Nah. Just gym rats and fake-tanned people.'

I lightly shove his shoulder, something I saw Grace do all the time with boys. 'I'm serious.'

'So am I.'

'I don't believe you even the tiniest bit.'

He crosses his arms. 'Why are *you* here, then?'

'Because my parents are obsessed with me going to Princeton and becoming a doctor, and tending to old people looks good on an application.'

'*Tending* to them?'

'Yes, tending.'

'That makes you sound like a gardener. Like they're your shrubbery.'

Just for a second, I laugh – another thing I can't help. The boy might be strange, but he also knows that *shrubbery* is an abnormally funny word. He adds, 'I don't believe you, either, by the way.'

'Um, what I said is true.'

'Maybe. But you're not obsessed with Álvaro's disappearance because your parents want you to go to Princeton.' The way he says it is inarguable, like he has me all figured out.

I shoot back an immeasurably mature 'Whatever' and then pretend I'm immediately reabsorbed in my pile of letters.

At least the silence is less awkward now – and although none of the letters so far have contained any clues, they *are* interesting. Some are rather to the point and grammatically dubious: *Hey hombre, glad to see your alive.* Others are from incredibly creepy people – people who've snipped Álvaro's face from vintage magazines and drawn devil horns on his forehead; people who say if he ever writes a book like that again, there'll be 'hell to pay.' (That's a direct quote from Mrs. Roberta Tully in Tuscaloosa, Alabama, who I imagine as a middle-aged woman who owns several Snuggies.)

The majority of letters, however, splinter the solid bits inside of me. Divulging your personal life to a stranger is something I'll never understand, but here it is, over and over again:

Hi Álvaro,

To my dearest,

Only you will understand,

I haven't told this to anyone,

We've never met, but I feel like we have.

Out of nowhere, Sebastian mumbles, 'It's kind of like the Mars Voyager 1 Golden Record.'

Um, sure? Is he kidding? I squint at him, trying to figure out if he actually expects me to identify with this statement.

'Oh, sorry,' he says, picking up on my confusion. 'I do that sometimes.' Messing with his hair – as if it could get messier – he resumes his Speedy Gonzalez speech. 'It's just this collection of images that NASA sent up with the Voyager spacecraft so that anyone who found it could know about life on Earth and it's kind of like this wish to not be alone and to connect with people or nonpeople and that kind of reminded me of the letters.' Pause for breath. 'Aaaaannnnd now you think I'm the biggest nerd ever.'

The corners of my mouth turn up. 'Yeah, pretty much.'

Sebastian throws his head back – probably with the intention of laughing – but in the process he whacks it on the edge of the wooden bookshelf, which makes him *really* start laughing. His whole face participates; it's an event.

I say, 'You all right there?'

'Just perfect,' he says, hand massaging the back of his skull.

Since I'm preoccupied with Sebastian's minor head trauma – and Sebastian's general Sebastian-ness – I don't hear the doorknob twist open, but the smell of aftershave hits me like a camel's kick. In the doorway stands Álvaro, clutching a cane with flame decals shooting up the side. A part of me wonders if he actually needs the mobility support or if it's a weapon for the next time Marla tries to confiscate his cigarillos. On the positive side of things, his high-collared shirt doesn't reveal masses of chest hair, but it *is* conspicuously inside out – and horizontally striped, matched with vertically striped pants. He looks like a candy cane that's been chopped up and wrongly reassembled.

Squinting, he mumbles a stream of incomprehensible Spanish (someone turn on the subtitles, please) and then points to his desk.

'Get my hat. I need to go.'

In my mind, I hear the theme music to *The Great Escape*.

Sebastian

10.

'It is simply astounding how the spark of an idea can replace the last two hundred years of belief. Take Einstein's theory of relativity, for example, which radically supplanted the Newtonian model. That is all it takes – one moment of breakthrough to change the world.' *A Brief Compendium of Astrophysical Curiosities*, p. 23

Linny grabs her backpack, and we follow Álvaro. He wears a fedora with a spiky red feather.

The man can *move*. You wouldn't think it, with the cane and the shuffling. But when he's motivated? *Voom*. He leads us into the empty kitchen, past the industrial freezer.

Linny whispers to me, 'He's not doing what I think he's doing?' Her breath smells like bubblegum.

My response stutters out: 'I think he's – er – doing exactly what you think he's doing.'

Under the exit sign, Álvaro fishes into his pant's pocket and pulls out a scrap of white paper. Next to the door is a keypad. With a shaky finger he presses 0-0-0-0.

How the heck does he know the code? Maybe he saw someone typing it in?

Now I understand the purpose of outdoor and indoor security: to stop people from breaking in *and* out.

Wedging the door open with his cane – 'You are coming, yes?'

Massaging the back of my still-throbbing head – 'Such a bad idea.'

Correction: This is a *horrendous* idea. All the things that can – and probably will – go wrong tick through my mind.

He could fall and break a hip.

Or give an interview to a crackpot reporter.

Or wander back to where he came from and never be seen again.

Or be eaten by alligators.

Okay. The last one is ridiculous, even in Florida. But the previous three are distinct possibilities.

Trying to coax him back upstairs, I say, 'We're going to miss *Jeopardy!*' Linny's eyes narrow at my pitiful effort, like *That's the best you've got?*

Apparently so.

'I know it's awful,' Linny offers. Sweetly. Reasonably. 'But we're *really* not supposed to leave.'

Álvaro sucks on his teeth and rubs his free hand against the door frame. 'I have no choice, you see.'

Linny again: 'I mean, you haven't broken out yet. We can just go back upstairs –'

Álvaro's chest expands so much that he runs the risk of combustion. 'No. No.' His face clouds over. 'What I mean is, I have no *choice*. This place is always: You eat now. You sleep now. Do this. Do that. Know what I want? To do something by myself.'

Right now would be the obvious time to mention he is, in fact, not alone (we're accomplices), but what kind of asshat would I be if I said that?

Álvaro adds: 'One hour. One hour, and I promise we'll come back.' Opening the door a tad wider – 'It's a beautiful day.'

I peer over at Linny, who's already looking at me, and we exchange an uneasy shrug.

We don't cave because it's sunny and blue outside, which it is. And it's not because we're excitement starved after an hour of reading letters, which we are. The real reason is: Álvaro's little speech was one of the saddest things I've ever heard, and judging by the way her shoulders sank, I think Linny feels the same way.

In the back alley, Álvaro picks up the pace and tips the fedora over his eyes. A few days ago I found it implausible that a man his age could escape public notice for years. This experience makes me a believer. I'm kind of proud of him.

Are we having our first father-son moment?

Behind me, Linny looks like she's experiencing a hernia. 'Am I correct in thinking that we probably shouldn't be doing this? God, if Marla finds out . . .'

In front of us, Álvaro adds an extra spring to his step. So I say to her, 'Sometimes the right thing isn't so black and white.'

We end up two blocks away, at the beach.

Álvaro steps out of his loafers and wiggles his wrinkly toes in the sand. Down to the surf he goes. I follow. Linny kicks the crap out of a few seashells and refuses to leave her backpack unattended.

Álvaro and I wade up to our knees and line up like celestial bodies. Side by side. The water is warm and feels good on my skin.

This is it. *Ahora.*

There won't be an opportunity more perfect than this. I should tell him about my mom, about me.

THE BREAKTHROUGH CONJECTURE:
Opportunities for breakthrough come in sets of finite moments and therefore must be instantaneously capitalized on to ensure world change.

The lump in my throat is the size of Jupiter. 'I – can we talk about something?'

Álvaro mumbles over the sound of the waves, 'You mean *una entrevista*? We should do an interview now, yes?'

'That's not what I –'

'What is that saying? No time like now?'

'The present,' I answer, heart plummeting.

'Hmm?'

'No time like the present.'

Wisps of his hair flail in the breeze. 'You are right, *mijo*! Seize the day!'

Mijo. A combination of *mi* and *hijo*. My son.

It's an expression. Just an expression. He doesn't mean anything by it. . . .

Does he?

Behind us, Linny's sitting knees to chin on the sand, filming the waves as they roll in and out. Álvaro sees her. '*Niña*, with the camera. It would be good to get this down. . . . *¡Oye!*' he shouts to Linny. '*¡Trae tu cámara!*'

She tilts her head at him, confused. Maybe she's not fluent in Spanish? I point to her backpack and press cupped hands to my left eye, like I'm filming.

She gets it. Whips her head back and forth between the sand and us. Oh, she probably doesn't want to get the equipment wet. After a moment, she seems to make a decision, bouncing up and into the surf, camera in hand.

'Take one,' she says, and then is silent for a century. When she speaks again, it's sudden. 'I'm just . . . establishing the shot! Getting my bearings.'

'Oh,' I say. 'Right.'

I don't add anything else. I'm busy looking at the dark curls that frame her face.

BREAKTHROUGH CONJECTURE #2:
The world change one originally hypothesizes may not be the world change that occurs in the course of human events. (See also: catastrophism; radical redirection theory*)*

Then I'm looking at the freckles on her arms.

At her jean shorts. Which are too short for me *not* to notice. But I hate myself for it anyway. I shouldn't have any attention to spare. I should be focused entirely on Álvaro.

Although *Álvaro* isn't the one wearing short shorts . . .

Oh, *Jesus*. The imagery.

'Álvaro,' Linny says, 'why don't you fill us in on your disappearance?'

I cock my head and mouth to her: *Subtle*.

Unfazed by the question, Álvaro answers, 'Growing up in Havana, *mi padre* took me to see a magician, Rolando the Great, who pulled me on to the stage. I went behind a curtain, and – gone!' When he stops, I assume he's just taking a breath. That the story will continue. But it doesn't. He grins at the camera like he's just won *Jeopardy!*

'Oh, okay,' Linny says. 'Cool. What about the past couple of years, though? What have you been up to?'

'Many things.'

'Like what, exactly?'

'My book – I write all the time. When I was younger, I wrote for many hours by the sea, near the Malecón in Havana.'

'But you haven't been in Cuba since the 1960s, right?'

Álvaro jerks his shoulders slightly up, slightly down. 'These places. No matter how long you are away, it doesn't feel like you're gone. These places, they stay with you.'

'Hmmm.' Linny swishes her feet in the water. 'What about Little Havana?'

'Little Havana?'

'Yeah, I mean, I used to go there as a kid. Look at all the mosaic-tile murals and stuff. You hung out there when you were younger, right?'

'*Sí.*' He winks. 'For the cigars.'

'Have you been there lately?'

'As I said, these places – time does not matter.'

It proceeds like that. Linny: asking questions about his disappearance and return. Him: evading the questions like a greased dolphin. He tells us about a pet rabbit he had when he was five. About the inspiration for *In the Hour of the Spring* (his grandfather was a gardener). About his first love, a girl named Mirabelle. He was seventeen, like me. They would sneak off in the dead of night to kiss by the railroad tracks. (Top things I don't want to talk about with my father: Kissing. Women other than my mom.)

I tap my imaginary wristwatch. 'Time to go soon.'

'*Uno momento,*' Álvaro says. 'You must ask me about movies.'

'Yes!' Linny says. 'Absolutely. What about movies?'

He kind of leans back in the air. 'It's strange, no? Life on a small screen has no texture. Smooth as paper. All these little bumps, that is life. Given enough time, *todo se cura*.' Everything heals? I hope so. 'And if you do not like your script,' he says, 'you must write a new one. You *must*. You must.'

He repeats it three or four more times. Like a mantra. 'You must, you must.' It guts me, for some reason. It feels like he's admitting something. It feels like we're getting somewhere.

But Marla interrupts his chant. 'MR. HERRERA!' she calls from the shore where she's rolling up the pant legs of her scrubs. Two male nurses are by her side, glaring at us. 'MR. HERRERA, GET OUT OF THE WATER!'

Every time we get closer, something pulls us further apart.

Linny

11.

WHO: *Olympic swimmer Claudia Jones*
WHEN: *Two months after she won the bronze in the 800-meter butterfly at the Sydney Olympics*
WHY: *She disappeared during a charity event in Puget Sound. When a rescue crew found her eighteen hours later, she was floating on her back more than fifteen miles from the finish line. Apparently she said: 'I never would have come back closer to shore, but the cramp in my left leg was something fierce. I would've just kept swimming. God, it felt so good to be free.'*
NOTES: *Is this how Grace feels, like Álvaro at the beach? Free? (How on Earth do I induce a leg cramp in another person? How weird do I sound right now?)*

Álvaro is beaming, illuminating the shot, the corners of his eyes crinkling against the sun. In *Midnight in Miami*, he makes a cameo halfway through – and completely steals the show. He only has two lines ('Where have you been? I didn't expect to see you again.'), but it's obvious that the camera adores him. Most actors – even superfamous ones – don't have that gift, the ability to light up from the inside out.

Behind him, the waves roll softly along the horizon, and a flock of seagulls dip and dance in circles off to the left. The blues are *spectacular*: the iridescent turquoise of the waves, the robin's egg of Álvaro's button-up, the cloudless Miami sky. I pick up a symphony of noises: my own breath, toddlers giggling as they kick down a sand castle, the flapping of beach tents in the gentle breeze.

And then there's Sebastian.

Sebastian.

Standing two feet from Álvaro, he's ramming his hands into his pockets, head tilted down toward the surf, so I can see the length of his eyelashes – longer than a boy's have a right to be. I zoom in, then zoom in further. It strikes me how much they look alike: the brown of their skins, similar smiles, gray eyes. Up close, Sebastian's wild hair isn't so wild. It has sort of a pattern, actually – twisting clockwise from the top of his head, fanning out like palm tree fronds. It's cute.

No, it isn't, I tell myself. It isn't cute. Once I start thinking he's cute, it's over.

Focus.

'I'm just . . . establishing the shot!' I blurt out. 'Getting my bearings.'

But for the rest of the interview, I keep one eye on Sebastian, until Marla starts screaming from the shore ('MR. HERRERA, GET OUT OF THE WATER!'), and we are sucked out of a moment where I feel so suddenly happy and alive.

Between Marla's face and her hands on her hips, it is immediately obvious that we're – What's that horrible phrase Ray says? Oh yeah. Up shit creek without a paddle.

Explaining that yes, Alvaro's safe and no, we did not kidnap him takes fifteen minutes. Back at Silver Springs, Marla orders Sebastian and me to sit in the lobby as she towers over us. You'd think we were gone five days the way she steamrolls on, like we're the villains in a Bond film. The only things missing are a polygraph machine and a hundred-watt bulb to shine into our pupils.

In my mind, she grows steadily – first her hands, then feet; finally, her legs stretch like a hundred-year time-lapse of forest trees. The fraying hem of my jean shorts is still soaking, and I spend the first third of the interrogation praying that I'm not water-staining the pleather couch.

'Do y'all have any idea what could have happened?' she screams.

Sebastian says, 'But we thought –'

'No, you didn't think. That's your problem.' She stabs the air. 'So let me enlighten you – this man is eighty-two years old, and under my care. *My* care, not yours. If he had wandered off into the ocean and drowned, that would've been on me. We don't wanna see anybody get hurt.'

Eyes firmly on my shoes, I say, 'We weren't trying to hurt him.'

'Things happen, Miss Marilyn. Things out of our control.'

'But he looked *happy*.'

Marla sighs, and in my mind she shrinks a little. 'What matters is his safety. That's just the way it is. The way it's got to be. I'm sorry . . . but one more stunt like this and y'all are gone.' Her general appearance resembles pulled taffy: all drawn out. 'Just' – she wipes the air with her hand – 'just go home for the day.'

As she rounds the corner, I whisper to Sebastian, 'Well, that was horrible.'

Rubbing his face with his hands, he says, 'That's such bullshit.'

'You don't think it was horrible?'

'No – it was. It's just, what's the point of him being safe if he isn't happy?'

I'm not sure if he expects an answer, or if there *is* a good answer, but I start thinking about what Álvaro said about having no choice, how sometimes I'm bitter about the same thing. Although Grace never confessed it, I think I know why she left, because sometimes I feel that way, too – like MomandDad are stuffing me into a container and sealing the lid, and I'd give anything for the space to uncrunch myself. Being trapped in a nursing home isn't entirely different from being trapped at my house. A cage is a cage. 'Some people think they know what's best,' I offer, 'even if they've never asked the person what she wants.'

'She?' Sebastian peeks through his fingers.

Biting my tongue to avoid another slip, I stay silent as Sebastian's eyes flicker across my face. Usually when someone's staring this hard in my direction, one of two things is happening: I'm with Cass or Grace, or there's a camera in my hands. Without the technological barrier, I'm exposed. The look Sebastian's giving me – truly giving *me* – makes me feel like it's pep rally time in the school gym, and I'm standing at the half-court line in my underwear.

'Go on,' he deadpans, straightening his back to attention. 'Give me an example.'

The whole butterfly population of the Amazon battles for space in my rib cage as I tug the neckline of my T-shirt. 'Can we just forget I said that?'

'If you want.'

Although he says it sincerely, in the ensuing silence, I still blurt out: 'If you really want to know, my shoes.'

'Your shoes?'

Idiotically, I stick out my Chuck Taylors for examination. 'Well, one of my friends, she draws all these cool designs on her shoes. Like flowers and skulls and tic-tac-toe. One time my mom saw them and said how horrible they looked. How I should *never* do that with my shoes. . . . Maybe I'm not making sense.'

Rambling. I'm rambling.

I might as well have blurted out my whole life story. *By the way, Sebastian, not only do I have footwear issues, but I also despise shiitake mushrooms and sometimes still sleep with my stuffed-animal giraffe.* Maybe the soliloquy thing is catching.

'I get it,' he says, standing up.

My immediate thought is that I've just driven him away with my excessive verbiage, but then he walks over and grabs a black Sharpie from the front desk. Stooping down at my feet, he flicks the pen between his knuckles.

'May I?'

The whole scenario is so monumentally strange, but when he lifts my left shoe and sketches three little shooting stars on the white rubber, my first thought is, *Even Cinderella didn't have it this good.*

'There,' he says, and almost immediately adds, 'if you hate it, you could probably white it out with some – um – Wite-Out or something. Oh . . .' My foot is still in his hand, and he drops it abruptly with a *clunk*. 'Sorry, you probably want that back.'

'Thanks,' I say, nose throbbing pink, pinker, pinkest. I'm sure my freckles are glowing like a million headlights in the dark.

In the scope of things, maybe this is an insignificant moment – a simple exchange, the type of scene that gets edited out of movies. But for me? It's like: *kapow*. If I could, I'd press Pause and Rewind over and over again. If I could, I'd run home and tell Grace.

THE LEFT-BEHINDS (scene 6)

CARSON FAMILY HOUSE

GRACE (seventeen) is on the roof of the two-story house, sundress blooming in the breeze.

LINNY (fifteen) yells at her from the ground.

LINNY

How'd you even get up there?

GRACE
(nervous)

I need to tell you something.

LINNY

Just get down, okay?

GRACE

That's just it.

LINNY

Grace, you're kind of scaring me.

GRACE

Don't – don't freak out.

LINNY

What are you talking about?

GRACE takes three steps to the edge of the roof – and jumps.

LINNY
(shrieking)
>   Grace!

Over LINNY's scream is a thwwwt sound: GRACE's beautiful yellow wings unfolding. They're as wide as she is tall. With two flaps, she floats gently to the ground and looks at her sister.

GRACE
(half in awe, half petrified)
>   They work.

Sebastian

12.

'The topology of space remains a marvel. In the standard cosmological model ($k = +1$), space is spherical, and it is possible to argue – as did Wheeler – that the universe has no singular boundary.' *A Brief Compendium of Astrophysical Curiosities*, p. 78

Shoe. I *drew* on her *shoe*?

We're at Books & Books on Lincoln Road. Linny's perched on a stepladder, on her tiptoes. I get a good look at the stars.

A TOPOLOGICAL THEORY FOR INTERACTIONS WITH GIRLS:
If a girl lets you draw on her shoe, then the outer limits of the aforementioned relationship are yet to be reached.

Grabbing a book on the top shelf, she passes it down to me with a 'Here, hold this.' It's *Ten Years in Havana*. The front cover is a bold green. 'Looks like we're in luck,' she says. 'They're having an Alvaro-has-miraculously-returned-from-the-dead special. Buy one get one free.'

Her phone rings in her back pocket. Like it's been doing for the last twenty minutes. Her ring tone is the theme from *The Breakfast Club*, which is an excellent song the first three times you hear it in an hour. Not so much after that.

'You going to answer your phone?'

She huffs. 'I should.'

I take a shot in the dark. 'Is it your . . . boyfriend?'

Stepping down the ladder – 'Why would you say that?'

I shrug. 'Hot girls usually have boyfriends.'

Oh *no*. Oh no. No. I did not just say that. No. I close my eyes and wait for the shit to hit the fan.

'I am not hot,' she says. Something in her voice tells me she's even more desperate to get away from this conversation than I am.

Furiously backpedaling – 'I just meant, I – Hey, I think we've left out a title.' Yes! Switching topics! I flip through the books in my hands. 'We need *Midnight in Miami*.'

Biting her bottom lip – 'I know I have an old copy somewhere, but it wouldn't hurt to buy another. There's a display by the front door, I think.' She waves me around the corner, takes a few steps, and then jolts like she's been electrocuted.

'Err – are you all right?'

Brushing a curl from her eyes, she says, 'Yeah – I just thought I saw . . . My sister shops here.'

'Oh.'

'Yeah.'

Why do I have the feeling she wants to say so much more?

She seems sad. But I don't press her on it because she mildly terrifies me. What's even more terrifying is, I *like* that she terrifies me. The resting human heart rate is sixty to one hundred beats per minute. Right now, I feel more hummingbird than human. But I'm feeling . . . something.

I used to think I was defective. That I wasn't capable of normal feelings. (I'm *supposed* to like Paul. But I won't grow a mustache for him. I'm *supposed* to love Louis. But I can't stand watching his shitty soccer games. I'm *supposed* to still feel things for Savannah, my first and only girlfriend. But she thought that Cuba was a state, and there's no getting past that ignorance.)

I thought: *What if there's something's missing inside me, because my dad's gone? Because my mom and I can't speak Spanish in the house? Because it's impossible for me to wake up without Play-Doh in my hair?*

I thought: *Maybe I'm more broken than I realize.*

But no more.

Palms: sweating.

Jugular: pulsing.

I'm alive. I'm okay.

I'm staring directly at *Our Bodies, Ourselves* on the third shelf of the Women's Health section.

Linny says, 'Do you, um, want to buy that or something?'

'Oh,' I say. 'Nah.'

'You sure? Because you were eyeing it for a good thirty seconds.'

'Let's just check out, okay?'

I buy the first three books. She buys the last two. And outside, just before I get on the bus and she hops on her bike, I ask, 'Hey, on Monday can you show me the footage from the beach?'

The sunlight is too harsh, I think, because she squints and backs away. 'Um, maybe. But . . . probably not, the shots weren't that great. Just read the books over the weekend, all right?' On her bike she gives a small wave and pedals away quickly, frantically, until she's just a speck at the end of the road.

'Savannah asked about you,' Micah says on the phone that night.

I'm stretched out in the low grass across the street from Ana's condo. Braving the itchiness because I want to see the stars.

'Since when are you hanging out with my ex-girlfriend?' I say. Not in an accusing way. I'm just shocked.

'Dunno. Since you left.'

'Er – okay. What did she say?'

'Nothing much. Just asked what you were up to. I told her you'd ditched us for a bunch of old people.' A pause. 'Hey . . . are you still . . . I don't know, into her?'

A better question is: Was I ever? Once I got past the awesome fact that she wanted to stick her tongue down my throat, there wasn't much to be *into*. Whenever we kissed, my eyes were always open. One or two times she caught me. ('*God*, Sebastian. Weird much?') And it *was* weird. Like my brain was beeping: Does Not Compute, Does Not Compute!

Today with Linny things computed.

I say, 'Nah, man. You know we broke up weeks ago.'

'Oh, good. Because I am.'

'Am what?'

'Into her.'

'Seriously?'

'I know it's probably weird for you, but . . . she's so . . . well, she's smokin'.'

I probably should feel strange about my best friend dating my ex-girlfriend (and genuinely using the word *smokin'*). But when I say 'Then go for it, man,' I know it's the truth, and it doesn't make me feel at all defective.

'Good,' Micah says. 'I'm gonna ask her to prom.'

I almost laugh. 'Dude. Two problems. First, prom isn't for another eleven months. Second, you've already graduated high school.' A third problem that I refrain from mentioning: at our senior prom (where Savannah was my date), Micah spent the majority of the evening splayed out in the boy's locker room after a freak allergic reaction to shaving cream. (Long story. Don't ask.) You'd think he'd forever have a Pavlovian response to all dance-based activities.

'Hah!' he exclaims. 'Here's where you're wrong. Savannah's almost a senior, so *she'll* have a prom.'

'Okay, good luck with that.'

'You sure you're all right with this?'

'Positive.'

'Because all you have to do is give the word, and –'

To prove to him I'm not about to fling myself off the nearest cliff, I tell him about Linny. The limited amount there is to tell.

Immediately, he says, 'What's her last name?'

Dangerous territory. I *do* know it from her Silver Springs ID badge. But if I give him that, he'll be analyzing her Facebook photos within five seconds.

'You embarrassed or something?' he says. When this fails to get a rise out of me, he switches tactics. 'Oh, come on. It's the least you can do after abandoning me this summer.'

Fine.

Sure enough, a few seconds later – 'Dude, she's *hot*. Like, hotter than your mother.'

'I really wish you'd find another comparative.'

'And *I* really wish my parents would buy me a Porsche for my eighteenth birthday. But' – he starts singing – 'you can't always get what you waaa-aaant.'

'SHUT UP.'

'Okay, no more Mom jokes. But seriously, even this girl's *friends* are hot. How much is a plane ticket from LA to Miami?'

'An entire Chinese fossil collection.'

'Cool. You must introduce me to this blond-haired vixen called' – a pause as he's probably squinting at the page – 'Cassandra.'

Cass, Linny had said. *I didn't know she was . . .*

Cass. The girl who filmed everything.

My voice is a bungee cord ready to snap. 'Why don't you focus on one girl at a time? Savannah. Prom. Remember?'

'*Touché, mi amigo.* Unless your mom accepts my Facebook friend request. Then I'll have to reconsider.'

Another reason for not telling Micah about my predicament: that would lead to a discussion about how lucky Álvaro is for sleeping with my mother. I'd rather dip my head in gasoline and then light myself on fire.

'Hanging up now,' I say.

'Sayonara.'

Linny

13.

WHO: *French ballroom sensation Brigitte Beaulieu*
WHEN: *Four days in 1959*
WHY: *There were rumors that she and her dance partner were fighting. She reappeared at a dance competition in London where she and her partner were scheduled to perform. 'I refuse to go out there without him,' she reportedly told the judges. 'I cannot go on without my best friend.'*
NOTES: *How can Grace go on without me? How can any of us go on without her?*

On my honor, Sebastian will *never* see that beach footage. Too many close-ups of him, too much given away. The bright side is, he thinks I'm 'hot,' although his perception is skewed: he's never seen Grace. Everything I am, she is times a thousand – the type of reckless beauty that should be heralded with trumpets. She's a teensy bit darker than me (just enough for people to notice, and for ruder people to comment on), and I've always been jealous of her skin tone. When we were little, I imagined Grace as every beautiful girl in the Nigerian folktales that Mom would read us.

Compared to her, I'm . . . Well, there really is no comparison.

At home, I check the mail (hopes up, then nothing) and sink into the weatherworn hammock in our backyard, which is mostly palm trees and vines. We have a pool, but MomandDad filled it in with gravel and dirt a few years ago – why would Grace and

I want to swim when we could be studying? Now it's a massive planting bed for their miniature orange grove.

Tonight's muggier than it's been all June (and the boob sweat's already lining up in formation), but somehow I can't stomach the thought of reading *Midnight in Miami* inside the house.

No. Outside feels freer.

So I grab Hector, carry him into the backyard, and let him do turtle things as I research. Resting the book in my lap, I flip it to the back, where Alvaro's smiling wide, dressed in a white pantsuit and ruffled top like the Cuban Austin Powers. And the chest hair. So much chest chair.

I only get past the first few sentences –

We sit by the pool, as we do on blistering days, and sip pineapple slush through short straws. We are good with our mouths but terrible with words.

    'Eduardo?'

    'Sí?'

    'The towels.'

– before someone bangs on the back gate, the one MomandDad erected along with the massive fence to avoid witnessing Mrs. Landry's naked sunbathing. Getting up, I peek through the keyhole to see Cass in my driveway, the straps of her lime-green bra popping from beneath her tank top – the same bra she urged me to buy at the mall two winters ago. 'It'll push your boobies up,' she said, and I countered, 'So *you* buy it.' There was no way I could toss it in the laundry without a speech from MomandDad about the over-sexualization of minors.

'*Linny*, come on,' Cass whines, twirling a piece of straw-colored hair around her index finger. 'I can see your eyeball.'

We haven't talked since she uploaded that video. Even during eighth grade, when her mom forced her into wilderness camp in the Poconos, we never lasted more than twelve hours without contact. But now, every time my phone flashes *CASS*, I contemplate chucking it into the nearest body of water, because filming Álvaro during a breakdown was distinctly uncool – and I still feel like it almost mucked up everything.

Taking a deep breath, I open the latch. 'Hi.' I don't *mean* for the word to sound aggressive, but it almost has teeth.

Cass has a smudged appearance, like she hasn't washed off her eye makeup for days. 'Hey,' she trills in a breezy way that makes me bristle. 'I rang the doorbell but no one answered, so I figured I'd check back here.'

Here's the part when I'd normally invite her into the backyard, ask if she wants lemonade or a Diet Coke, but instead the air ices between us, even in the blistering heat.

Cass inspects an electric-blue fingernail. 'So I'm guessing you got my texts? I sent like a gazillion.'

I deleted like a gazillion.

'And my Facebook messages? And my calls? Jeez, Linny, I thought you were dead or . . . something.' What she doesn't say, probably wants to say: *Or gone like Grace.*

'Well,' I say, 'I'm not. Obviously.'

I get the distinct feeling this is not unfolding as she expected. With her high-heeled sandal, she kicks at a chunk of dirt next to the fence.

'Anyhoo,' she says, forcing a smile. 'Are you like . . . friends with him now?'

I shake my head. 'What?'

'With Álvaro. I saw you at the beach. I was waving and calling your name and stuff, but you guys were already heading back to the boardwalk.'

Arguing with Cass is like entering a duel: you know there's a fifty-fifty chance you'll get fatally shot. This has always dissuaded me. Not today. Today, a primordial sound escapes me – so forceful that I almost swivel around to see if a more powerful being looms behind me. '*Ugggghhh*,' I say, 'are you stalking him now or something?'

I'm acting irrational. I know I am.

I peer down and see Hector munching a lettuce leaf by my foot. Even *he* looks judgmental.

Cass's eyebrows scrunch together as she jerks her head back. 'Oh my God, are you kidding me? I was just *there*. And now I'm just trying to have a conversation with you. You know, stay involved in your life?'

There was a time when that was all I wanted. In elementary school, she collected friends like Girl Scout badges, and I felt privileged just to make a cameo in her harem. She was Grace's friend first – because *everyone* wanted to be friends with Grace – but soon none of our scripts read right without each other. (We even had the same phases, like our Pocahontas phase, when we were convinced that we could speak with trees.) Maybe it sounds stupid, but Grace and Cass elevated me somehow, like their whirlwind personalities were bold enough to make up any lack I had.

You can probably guess what happened. Things changed. As much as I want to think the YouTube video was the trigger, Cass and I were fracturing long before then. Like, five months before. I texted her the picture of Grace's good-bye note, and she biked right over. I can still hear her pounding on our front door. How when I opened it she gasped, like I was about to tell her Grace disappeared all over again. We hugged in the doorway, and when I released her, neither of us knew what to say. It was horrible. Grace was the glue between us, and now we were unsticking. I felt like everyone could see the cracks.

So we no longer sneak into clubs with fake IDs; we no longer have sleepovers on Grace's bedroom floor; we no longer call emergency tie-dye dances in Cass's hippie-colored garage.

We are no longer us.

Why didn't Grace realize that would happen? And why isn't she here to see what's happening now? It's like she set fire to our lives then walked away.

'*Say* something,' Cass shouts abruptly.

I shout back, 'What do you want me to say? That I think what you did was really intrusive and crappy?'

'Yes! Fine! Just as long as we're *talking*, because we don't talk anymore, Linny. Do you realize that? And I don't mean just for the past three days.'

I square my shoulders to her, facing off like we're in a Western film. Instead of guns for weapons, we have guilt. 'We talk all the time.'

'Sure. I tell you about the new boy I'm dating. You tell me how many hallways you mopped at Silver Springs. We talk about nail polish and the weather and bike tires and – God, we never talk about *her*.'

Grace.

It's not one of those if-we-don't-talk-about-it-then-it-won't-be-real type of things. I literally don't have the vocabulary. No one has invented words for the things I need to say.

Echoing my thoughts, Cass yells, 'Why *is* that?' The only noise is the wind swiping a few blades of grass across the driveway. 'I've been reading a few books on loss and stuff, and you're really supposed to talk about it.'

'Cass. Those books are about people who've died.'

She pauses. 'Doesn't it feel like she has?'

Just for an instant, I want to tell her: *I've thought this, too. But it's worse. Barring suicide, death isn't a choice. Leaving is.* But then I think: *Who are you, Linny? What type of person has thoughts like that?*

There's another long silence between us. Finally, Cass says, 'God, say *something*.'

'I'm *angry*, okay?'

'And you think I'm not? You think I like that she's gone and all that's left is –'

I step backward. 'Me?'

Cass takes a remarkably deep breath, like she's inhaling a hurricane. 'You *know* that's not what I was going to say.'

'No. No. It's fine. I feel that way, too. It seems like the world's most unfair swap. Out of the three of us, *she's* not who I'd choose to go away.'

She bites her lip, hard, her whole face going red. 'Thanks for that, Linny. Thanks for that.' Her voice is rough, like she's speaking through steel wool. 'I took down the video, you know. Last night.'

And then she closes the gate herself, leaving me incredibly alone. I want to shout after her: *You probably should have opened with that!* Instead, I count the blades of grass around my feet as thoughts needle the back of my mind.

I'm unsure of who I am without Grace.

And I don't like who I'm becoming.

THE LEFT-BEHINDS (scene 7)

SHOUT NIGHTCLUB, MIAMI BEACH – BATHROOM

The lighting is low except for neon signs above the sinks. Pulsing techno music vibrates the stalls as LINNY (fifteen and a half) knocks on the bathroom door.

LINNY
    Are you okay? Grace? Let me in.

GRACE
(barely audible)
    Go away.

LINNY
    Come on, open the door.

We hear the latch flick aside. LINNY gently pushes open the door to see GRACE on the floor, hands clutching her knees. Mascara drips down her cheeks like nail marks on a chalkboard. Her yellow wings are on full display, hugging her, but are dirty and drooping.

LINNY crouches to the ground, obviously worried. She places two fingers under GRACE's chin and lifts up her face. GRACE's eyes carry a blank expression.

LINNY
    Talk to me.

GRACE

Do you think I'm different now?

LINNY

I mean, a little, but –

GRACE

(sighing)

I just – I just don't know who I am with them.

LINNY

What do you mean?

GRACE

(after a long pause)

The wings. I don't know what I'm supposed to do with the wings.

Fast-forward to six-thirty, when Dad drifts onto the back porch in his white coat and calls across the yard that Mom's staying late at the practice. Since it's Friday night, should he order pizza?

I say, 'If there's extra pineapple,' and an hour later we're huddled around the steaming pie in the dining room. He offers me a knife and fork, but I pick it up with my hands, like a heathen.

When we were kids, Grace and I'd hang out with Dad all the time: Saturday mornings at the Original Pancake House, beach days during the hot, slow summer. For my thirteenth birthday, Dad gave me a Sony Trinicon wrapped in silver ribbon. It's funny to think about that now – how he was the one to give me my first video camera – considering the whole Clay People Smashing fiasco. What's even weirder is, he refuses to be on film, ducking from the lens like he's dodging a wasp, or like I'm trying to steal his soul. (Mom says he's afraid of seeing himself age on film, but I'm not buying it.)

On Sunday nights the three of us would watch movies together, kid films like *Mulan* and *E.T.* and *Finding Nemo*. Eventually, Grace and I graduated to the harder stuff. *Mr. Smith Goes to Washington*, a few documentaries, and some Nollywood films (from the Nigerian Hollywood). I started asking questions about maybe pretty please going to New York City for film camp. Two things happened in quick succession: firstly, Mom acted like I'd just declared my intention to become a stripper, and secondly, she signed Grace and me up for a summer biomedical program. Five weeks of dissecting fetal pigs while choking back vomit. Even without Álvaro Herrera, Silver Springs beats that by a landslide of biblical proportions.

Last year I entered Miami Beach Senior High's seventh annual documentary competition. My film, *Grace in the Wild,* profiled her first live musical performance, outside of choir or band. She played the guitar onstage, sang her own songs, and looked unbelievably radiant. I cut those images with home videos of her growing up, learning to play all the instruments now gathering dust in her room. In my film, there's only one clip of the two of us together; she's showing off her flute skills to the camera, fingers moving up and down the keys like Pan reincarnated, but the only thing I'm interested in is looking at her.

The movie took me *ages*. I worked on it every day before and after school, and for three nights in a row left flyers on MomandDad's bed with my name circled in red ink.

I won first prize at the competition. Neither of them was there. When Grace and I got home from the screening, she went ballistic in my room – gripping her curls and screaming into the throw pillows. I hated seeing her like that, so I told her it was okay. It wasn't worth it. Just drop it. She crawled into my closet after me, bringing my head to her chest so I could listen to her angry breath. We fell asleep like that, curled together, and the next morning we pretended like there was no film at all.

Three months later, she was gone.

I'm almost finished with my second pizza slice when out of nowhere Dad announces, 'I found your book in the hammock.'

Oh boy.

A lie forms on the tip of my tongue: *It's for AP English next year*, I'll say, even though the school district banned *Midnight in Miami* in the 1960s.

Dad takes a sip of milk and carefully rests the glass on the table. 'You know, I really loved that book when I was your age.'

Say what? Truth be told, I always thought of Dad as a guy who never read anything besides medical textbooks and the occasional presidential biography. He's too . . . stiff. Even on the weekends, he irons his shirts – *and* his jeans, a perpetual joke between Grace and me.

Dad says, 'Have you gotten to the part where Eduardo has to say good-bye to Agustina?'

I shake my head. Pizza grease dribbles down my chin, but I'm too stunned to wipe it away.

'Great scene. Very sad.' Dad clears his throat and pushes back his chair. 'Anyway, I have some paperwork to do before your mom gets home.' Standing up, he begins to take his plate to the kitchen but then stops, squints, peers down at my feet. 'And Linny?'

'Yeah?'

'I think you have something on your shoe.'

Sebastian

14.

'I find the extreme properties of physics particularly fascinating – materials that weigh billions of tons per teaspoon, for example. Sometimes the smallest objects yield the most interesting research.' *A Brief Compendium of Astrophysical Curiosities*, p. 17

A GENERAL RULE FOR SMALL-SCALE OBJECTS IN RELATION TO FATHER-BASED MYSTERIES
Never ignore any element, no matter how seemingly insignificant.

Turns out *The Emperor's House* isn't about an emperor at all. It's a metaphor for places that feel like home. All Sunday, I race through its chapters. Getting to know my dad.

Okay. Full disclosure: every page I read, I'm one step closer to discussing it with Linny.

When I get to Silver Springs at eight on Monday morning, she's already set up in the game room. At a corner table, like the mafia.

There is a half-naked man sitting next to her. He smiles and waves at me as I pull up a chair. He's largely toothless. His robe's completely open in the front. I really hope he's wearing underwear. Or at least a washcloth. A fig leaf, even.

Sitting down, I say to him, 'Hello there.' He continues grinning. Bobs his head. Says nothing.

'Right,' Linny begins, putting down the folder she's holding, 'we should get started.'

'Um . . . are you . . . ?' I turn from her to the man and back again. 'Is he going to . . . ?'

Linny shrugs. 'He was here when I got here. It was the only open table.'

'Oh.'

'So I've assembled a list of people to talk to as well, based on *Midnight in Miami*. It mentions Joe's Stone Crabs a lot – that restaurant on Washington Avenue? Maybe that's Joe! Do you think that's Joe? We could talk to some of the waiters there, see if anyone knows anything. Also, I did some digging, and I think the hotel he talks about is the National Hotel in the Art Deco District. The one with the infinity pool? Oh, and there's also his real estate agent, Juan Ramirez. He sold Álvaro's house in South Beach right before he disappeared.'

I process this. As does the half-naked man, who nods vigorously. Like he's intimately involved in the conversation.

'What about *The Emperor's House*?' Linny asks.

'I loved it. There's this car chase on the causeway that – it's just – it's really sweet.'

'That's great . . . but did you find any, like, clues?'

'Oh no. Don't think so.'

She draws in a deep breath. On the exhale – 'Okay, we'll just work from what I have, then.' Gathering up her papers, she adds, 'We should go say good morning to Álvaro.'

'Wait . . . What if . . .' Where am I going with this? Put on the brakes! 'What if the explanation is different than we think?'

Perking up, she says, 'I'm listening.'

I lick my lips. Chest pounding. 'Have you ever heard of *A Brief Compendium of Astrophysical Curiosities*? Or *The Twilight Zone*?'

'Please tell me you are not one of those people.'

'What people?'

She giggles. 'The type of person who believes in aliens and stuff.'

'For your information, evidence of life may have been found on Mars. And . . . I just think the real reason for his disappearance could be a lot more complicated, that's all.' I cross my arms, lean back. Defeated.

After a moment, Linny pokes me with her voice. 'Hey.' And when I don't respond: 'Hey, Sebastian. I don't think you're a nerd or anything.'

'You don't?'

'Well, maybe a little bit. Maybe a lot. But it's . . . it's cool. You know what you're into and you don't apologize for it.' Standing, scooping up the rest of her papers – 'You coming?'

For a moment I just look at her. Game room lamps washing her in light. Freckles on her nose. Shirt slipping off her shoulder again.

If I didn't already suspect I was into her, this is a big fat clue.

God damn it. What happens now?

What happens is, after four hours at Silver Springs, we sit too close to each other at the Miami Beach Regional Library. The reference desk librarian drops a pile of something she calls 'microfiches' by an ancient reading device. I incorrectly pronounce them 'microfishes.' Like minute sea creatures.

'What are these, exactly?' I ask Linny when we're alone.

Yes, alone — but does it count if you're in a governmental reading institution?

'Old newspaper clippings,' she says, sliding one of the microfiche strips under what appears to be a microscope. 'Anything that references "Álvaro Herrera." Like' — pressing her eye to the scope, removing it quickly — 'look at this one.'

I read the opening sentences aloud: '"Friends of Álvaro Herrera now wonder if foul play is involved in his disappearance. Richard Gonzalez, Mr. Herrera's long-time dentist, spoke yesterday with the *Herald*. 'Álvaro's such a fixture here in Miami. I can't imagine why he'd want to leave. No, it doesn't make any sense. Something must've happened to him.'"' Lifting my head, glancing at Linny — 'You actually think someone, I don't know, kidnapped him?'

She makes a face. 'And left him visibly unharmed for three years, only to drop him off *safely* at an old-people's home? Seems unlikely to me.'

'What about this Richard Gonzalez guy?'

Whipping out her phone, she does a quick internet search. 'No luck. He passed away last year.'

I grab another newspaper clipping, peer through the scope: 'Hey, get this. "Álvaro Herrera was spotted with *12 Bandits* film producer, Robin Carlisle, over dinner at Joe's Stone Crabs on the eighteenth of February. The two reportedly shared seventeen martinis and — "'

Shoving me (almost gently) out of the way, Linny says, 'Let me see. . . . Yes, okay.' She snatches her backpack from the ground and pops up. 'That can't be a coincidence. To Joe's!'

'But we just got here.'

'I don't want the trail to run cold.'

'Linny. It's a *three-year-old* mystery.'

She rolls her eyes and slides on a pair of black sunglasses. 'Then it's high time we solved it.'

I follow her for two miles before she bolts directly into the restaurant. As we're waiting in line at the hostess stand, Linny squares her shoulders to mine. 'Just act cool, okay? I'll do the talking.'

But maybe someone should have warned *her* to act cool, because when we get to the hostess, Linny attacks her with enthusiasm: 'Hi! Hi. We're looking for Joe!'

The hostess, a girl in her midtwenties, grins toothily. 'And has he already been seated with the rest of your party?'

Linny: 'No, I mean *Joe*, of Joe's Stone Crabs!'

Hostess: 'Ha. Good one.'

Linny: 'No, really.'

Hostess: 'Uh.' She waves us along, smile a bit more menacing. 'Next in line, please!'

Linny: 'But –'

Hostess: 'NEXT IN LINE, PLEASE.'

Googling it outside, we discover that Joe Weiss of Stone Crabs fame opened his lunch counter in 1913.

'So,' I say, 'he's either *Guinness Book of World Records* old or very dead. I'm thinking dead.'

Linny groans.

Our additional investigations crash and burn in similar ways. We get kicked out of the National Hotel because we're not guests and can't afford infinity pool passes. We call Juan Ramirez, who tries to sell us a condo in South Beach for 'a cracking good deal' before realizing we're not even eighteen. He hangs up shortly after that.

No closer to solving the mystery. But I *am* getting closer to

Linny. Whether or not that's a positive thing is undetermined. In this situation, doesn't it make me a shitty person for thinking so much about a girl? I mean, 72 percent of the time, questions on my mind include: What sort of shampoo Linny uses. If she's ever had a boyfriend. What *exactly* did she think when I said she was hot?

Yeah, definitely a shitty person.

Nine days into my time at Silver Springs, I still haven't spilled the I'm-Álvaro's-son beans. Not to Micah. Not to Linny. *Especially* not to Álvaro, even though I urge myself every day to tell him. The longer I wait, the more I wonder: *What if he doesn't like me? What if I say, 'Guess what? I'm your son!' and he jumps out the window? What if he has no interest in being a dad?*

Linny and I track his movements. He does the same thing every day.

Mornings: orange juice, eggs with hot sauce.

Midday: dominoes, cigarillos, and more cigarillos.

Lunch: Jell-O and a rant about the lack of high-quality cable channels.

Afternoon: *Jeopardy!* and crossword puzzles.

Evening: Marla tells us that, at night, he spends hours at his typewriter. Clacking away. Probably working on his new novel.

Most days, he holds court in the game room or by the pool, entertaining anyone who'll listen with stories that make his hands fly up in exaggerated motions, and Linny captures it on film (Álvaro insists she should).

'Eight kilometers of sea,' he says. 'The Malecón in Havana, near my old neighborhood. You know it; yes? You must; everyone does. Lovers! Poets! Philosophers! Everyone meets there at sunset and – You've never seen it? I will tell you. It is beautiful but falling down now, from the ocean. Sometimes the waves become so big' – expanding his arms to full wingspan – 'they thunder over the wall. *Boom! Boom! Boom!* Sweeping into the street. On those days, the road has no cars, and you can walk barefoot and wet through the empty lanes. I tell you, it is freedom.'

'That's beautiful,' Linny says, probably zooming in.

He shrugs like it's no big deal. 'Everyone in Cuba is a poet.'

Linny: 'Did you ever want to write poetry?'

'Of course! To many women, when I was very young.' Stretching his arms again, grandly – '"*My heart is a winged bird that only flies for you. . . .*" I am much better at writing other things.' Then he bursts into laughter.

When Álvaro's in a silent mood, he picks out works of Cuban novelists to shove into our backpacks – Alejo Carpentier, Cirilo Villaverde, and Guillermo Cabrera Infante – and we watch movies on Linny's laptop. Better than the crap on TV in the game room (kind of agree with Álvaro on this one).

Anyway.

Today we're watching *Roman Holiday* in his bedroom. It's the Anya-gets-her-haircut scene. Absentmindedly, I pick up one of Álvaro's typewritten pages from the floor behind me. Get through three words – *hold the avocados* – before he frantically snatches it away.

His eyes bug out. 'It is not ready! It is not ready!'

'Your new novel?' Linny says, half watching the movie.

He just repeats: 'Not ready,' louder this time. Loud enough that I'm afraid the nurses will come rushing.

Everything is cryptic with him. Like the small scraps of paper he keeps in his chest pocket. At random moments he scribbles down words with his fountain pen and crams the note in with the others, right next to his heart. He looks like he's growing a boob.

On the way to lunch today, one of the scraps falls from his pocket. Linny scoops up the note and flashes it at me. *SeasHore,* it says. No additional context.

(*See A GENERAL RULE FOR SMALL-SCALE OBJECTS IN RELATION TO FATHER-BASED MYSTERIES*)

Once Álvaro disappears around the corner, I say, 'What do you think this means?'

'It says "Seashore,"' Linny says.

'*Obviously*. But why did he write it on a scrap of paper and keep it in his pocket?'

She presses one of her curls between her lips. Thinks. 'He seems a bit off sometimes, doesn't he?'

'No. He's just . . . eccentric. Most writers are eccentric,' I say, like I've known a single writer other than Álvaro.

'Mm, you're probably right.' But she folds the note in the palm of her hand and tucks it in her pocket.

Wouldn't it be awesome if words came out as bubbles like in comic books? Then we could prick them and watch them disappear. But since real words are unprickable, I'm halfway through a bona fide sermon about space ice cream.

'I can't *believe* you've never tried it, Linny. It's freeze-dried and vaporized, and it's kind of like a brick that crumbles, and the spoon! It comes with this mini plastic spoon. . . .'

Jesus. Just shut up. *Cállate, cállate, cállate.*

How did I even get onto this topic?

Linny sits cross-legged in front of me. Her hair falls in spirals across her shoulders.

She's listening. Álvaro's not. He hovers by his bathroom door in a silk robe. Because *I* obviously can't cork my mouth, he does it for me.

Shuffling across the room to his desk – 'There are a few things I'd like you to find.'

It's almost eerie, the way he says it. Like he's delivering a prophecy. Briefly I wonder if I could be the Chosen One.

Unlikely.

He jots down something on a piece of paper, then crinkles his eyes, stretches his neck, and writes down more. Flipping over the sheet, adding another item, he stabs the pen to dot the page. 'There!' He hands it to me. I read the list to myself as Linny peers over my shoulder.

212 SeasHore Drive
Manuscript – chapter Two
Montblanc Pen
Pictura
Humidor

'What's this?' Linny says.

A few years ago, I read about an Italian biologist who attached transmitters to goats to see if they could predict volcanic eruptions. The answer is, yes. Six hours after they fled Mount Etna, lava spewed. Now, my senses aren't *that* developed, but somehow I just know that Álvaro's answer will, in one way or another, erupt my life.

Again.

Álvaro scratches his chin and responds slowly. 'I've been working on this book for years . . . too many years, but I must finish. It would be very nice for you to pick them up, these things I need. I left very quickly, you see. It's . . . *la mesita de noche*. They're on the nightstand.'

Linny cups the paper with both hands. Like she's cradling a baby bird.

212 SeasHore Drive

A REVISED PRINCIPLE FOR SMALL-SCALE OBJECTS:
The unraveling of a great mystery can be attributed to one said object.

Linny

15.

WHO: Formula One driver Louis Lind
WHEN: Three weeks in 1967
WHY: Basically, he completed the last lap of a Grand Prix in record time, and he never achieved first place again. He disappeared one night in Monte Carlo so he could see his face in the papers one more time. Eventually he got sick of hiding, reappeared, and traded in his race car for a truck.
NOTES: Will Grace get sick of it, too? Sometimes I wonder if I care less – if I stop my search – the novelty will wear off for her. Is that too optimistic?

'I need to borrow your truck tonight,' I say when Ray answers his phone.

'Well, hello to you, too.'

'Hey – sorry.'

'Why are you panting?'

In an attempt to pump ideas into my brain, I've been circling my neighborhood for the past forty-seven minutes. My legs no longer feel like legs, but on the bright side, I *have* come to the following conclusion: asking MomandDad to borrow the family Volvo is too risky. That would reveal that I'm planning on driving halfway across Miami in the dark, with a strange boy, to knock on a stranger's door.

Plus, they haven't let me drive since Grace disappeared. I think they're afraid that behind the wheel I'd follow the same instinct – drive off into the sunset or something.

'I'm not – panting,' I lie, propping my bike against the garage. The front tire resembles a limp balloon.

'Yes, you are. If you took me up on some of those 400-meter sprints every once and a while, you'd—'

'*Ray*. The truck. Please?'

He takes a moment to consider it before saying, 'Are you and Cass still at each other's throats?'

In order of topics I want to discuss, my fight with Cass ranks somewhere alongside ingrown toenails and my parents having sex. Through a groan I manage: 'Did she tell you about it?'

'More or less. I hope you don't expect me to pick sides, because Cass scares the shit out of me when she's angry. It's her *eyes*. Like a wolverine or something. A lady wolverine. A wolverina, if you will.'

'Pretty sure that female wolverines are still called wolverines. Is she really, really angry?'

'Does the pope have a balcony?'

I guess that's a yes.

I sink down to the bottom step of the porch and kick out my legs. Three stars blaze back at me from my left Chuck. Every night I hide my shoes in my desk drawer so Mom doesn't sneak in and scrub off the marker.

Ray continues to yammer about how Cass and I need to 'move past our issues,' because he just doesn't understand. How could he, without knowing Grace? While I don't resent him, I was still in my heavy-mourning period when Ray crash-landed into our trio; it's almost impossible to forget the one-to-one exchange – how he's here and she's not. And although his hip-to-hipness with Cass is generally adorable, it's also a reminder that things are different now. That *we're* different now.

Eventually, he gets to 'So what do you need my truck for?'

'Um.' The last time I involved anyone except for Sebastian in an Álvaro-based activity, things got *so* complicated. 'To run an errand.'

'Could you be any more cryptic?'

'Yes. I have an errand . . . in the state of Florida.'

'Hardy har. You can't take your bike?'

'Flat tire.'

'Or the bus?'

'Wrong route.'

'Oh my God, Linny, just spill it.'

Something about this conversation leaves me yearning for Zen. Cradling the phone with my neck, I pry the address from my jean pocket and start folding it into an origami crane. Swiftly my fingers create points and edges – two wings, a narrow beak.

Ray hums the *Jeopardy!* theme song, like, *Hurry the duck up*.

'I have one condition,' I finally say, holding my crane up to the fading sun. 'Under no circumstances can you get weird about it.'

The line goes silent for a moment as he considers this. 'Deal. But that means I get a condition, too. It's only fair.' His giddiness practically seeps through the phone. 'I get to come.'

'You don't even know where we're going.'

'No. But if you don't want me to get weird about it, it must be good.'

I tell him the details, pushing away a twinge of guilt for not telling Cass. If his muttering is anything to go by, he's slightly disappointed we're not A-list celeb scouting or something cooler like that, but he says anyway, 'I'm coming over right now.'

'I need to take Hector for a walk first.'

'You lead a sad, sad life.'

Half an hour later I scribble a note for MomandDad – *At the library, be home in a few hours* – as Ray honks his horn by my mailbox. Across the street, the Saresons are sipping white wine spritzers on their front porch and glaring at Ray's painfully old truck. Over the *chung-chung-chung* of the engine, I almost miss Ray shouting across the lawn: 'C'MON, WE'VE GOT SOME ROAD-TRIPPING TO DO!' Unsure if I heard, he sticks his shock of orange hair out the window and yells it again.

Sorry, Mr. and Mrs. Sareson.

I heave open the truck door, slide across the hot leather interior, and pull out the map I just printed from Google. 'I'd hardly call twelve miles a road trip.'

The map has two stops: one at Sebastian's house (he said he had to go home and talk to his aunt before we left) and the other at 212 SeasHore Drive. The more I look at the paper, the more the strange capitalization is kind of throwing me. Did Álvaro mean Sea*horse* instead of Sea*shore*? It's only now occurring to me that I should have asked.

'How do you even know it's in Miami?'

'What?' I say.

'The address. How do you know it's not in, like, Texas or something?'

Oh boy. Why hadn't I thought of that?

The only response I come up with is 'He wouldn't ask us to get chapter two of his manuscript if it *wasn't* in Miami, right?' I don't even manage to convince myself. That somersaulting sensation crawls into my belly. It doesn't help that Ray's swerving all over the road like we're in Mario Kart and he's trying to collect points. To calm myself down, I stick my hand out the window and feel the resistance, let my fingers rise and fall in waves.

'So,' Ray says at a stop sign. 'I may or may not be dating someone.'

'Really?'

'Really.'

'Ray! That's awesome.' I can't control the grin spreading across my face. This is a huge deal. 'Who is it?'

'Lawrence Scully.'

'No. Way.'

'I know, right?'

Last year, Lawrence was the captain of the track team and the junior class president. Due to his (I'll just go ahead and say it) impressively muscular physique, at least a third of the girls in school have tried to date him. I say, 'I didn't know he . . .'

'Neither did I! Until a few days ago, when we bumped into each other running on the beach. We listen to the same music and like the same track events, and he wants to be a veterinarian. A veterinarian, Linny. The guy wants to cure sick kittens. What's not to love?'

I nudge him very gently. 'Love?'

Blush creeps up his neck. 'Not really, not yet, but . . . It's . . . Everything is so new, and it feels like anything is possible. You know what I mean?'

Um, no. Definitely not. Not at all.

Now it's my turn to blush.

'Tell me,' Ray says, noticing my sudden change in demeanor. 'Who's this guy we're picking up?'

'Just a friend.'

'And you wouldn't happen to be – just taking a shot in the dark here – attracted to this friend, would you?'

'No,' I say too quickly, like a girl who's covering her tracks. Am I attracted to him? He's just . . . Sebastian. Weird, weirdly good-looking Sebastian.

Ray's left eyebrow arches halfway to the moon. 'So on a scale from the Elephant Man to Leonardo DiCaprio, where would you rank him?'

'Can we drop it?' I say as the truck pulls up to a blue condo. The address Sebastian texted me matches the Sandstar Estates sign by the mailboxes. 'This is it, I think.'

'I'm going to need your ranking, then.'

On the bottom floor, one of the condo doors swings open, and Sebastian jingles his keys, locks up.

As soon as I hiss to Ray, 'We are *not* having this conversation,' he proceeds to sing in a stage whisper, 'You two are gonna have SEX AND BABIES AND SEX AND BABIES AND –'

I clamp his mouth with my hand. 'Not. Another. Word.' He licks my palm until I surrender.

'Am I interrupting something?' Sebastian says, all neon shirt and long limbs of him hovering outside the truck window. His hair's whirl-winded around his head like a crown.

And he is not hot. *Not* hot . . .

Oh, who am I kidding?

Stomach pirouetting, I practically shout no in his face.

Ray grins, lips stretched so thin it's a wonder he can say, 'Don't just sit there, Linny. Slide over and make some room.' Almost as an afterthought, he adds, 'Oh, I'm Ray. It's really nice to meet you,' and then he *winks* at me. Not a covert wink, either – a big, theatrical scrunch of his eye. (Note to self: Ray is about as subtle as a hippopotamus. Never invite him to participate in activities with weirdly attractive boys.)

I end up sardined in the middle seat. Before, I reasoned that if Ray continued on the Sex and Babies brigade, I could stunt-roll from the vehicle like they do in movies. Now I'm stuck.

Ray plugs in his iPod and turns up the volume, swearing

that this dubstep album will 'change our lives.' A collection of syncopated drumbeats ping through the cab as Ray bursts, 'This is the perfect song! Is this not the *perfect* song?' I bite my bottom lip to keep from screaming, because it's exactly what Grace would say.

Beside me, Sebastian squirms like a netted squid. Maybe it's because we're smashed together from ankle to shoulder, the overwhelming scent of air freshener pine invading our breathing space. Okay, the smell is bad. But the closeness? Let's just say I can feel every inch of my skin. Ray's voice, the engine's chugging, the music – they all evaporate as I step inside a silent movie in which Sebastian and I are the only actors.

How cheesy does that sound? God, I'm in so much trouble.

Focus, focus. Remember why you're doing this. Remember it's about Grace.

Grace.

A nighttime road trip to run a mysterious errand at a mysterious location? She would love this.

Ray drags me back to reality, yelling, 'Aaaaaaahhhh, missed the exit again!' He has the navigational abilities of an artichoke. Twelve miles turn into twenty. By the time we jerk to a halt in front of 212 Seashore Drive, all the streetlamps are blazing.

Ray virtually trampolines in his seat. 'So what are we going to say?'

'I think it would be a *really* good idea if you stayed in the truck,' I tell him, and Sebastian adds, 'It'll only take a minute.' Ray pulls a face like we just kidnapped his puppy, but we leave him in the truck to trudge up the long driveway of a ranch-style house in the middle of the suburbs. The porch light hurls spiky shadows over several Nerf guns that sprinkle the lawn. On the window ledges hang baskets of petunias.

This doesn't seem like somewhere Álvaro would hide. I envisioned a secluded penthouse apartment or a castle with an iron gate. This is so average.

'*Do* we have a plan?' Sebastian whispers.

I freeze in the driveway. 'Um – no.'

'No? You *always* have a plan.'

I whisper at him, 'I've been a little distracted with all the other plans. Joe's Stone Crabs? That was all me. This was just sprung on us.'

'So what should we do?'

'Okay. Okay, think. We can just . . . make it quick. Tell them we're here for Álvaro's things and leave it at that.'

'That's not exactly a plan. That's just ringing a doorbell.'

'Well, it's the best I've got.'

Little pink lights illuminate the path. Palms sweating, I rap twice on the front door. A man wearing a Miami Dolphins T-shirt opens it a few moments later, his bloodhound jowls quivering as he says, 'Yeah?' Everything about him is massive: massive frame, massive voice, massive glass of beer in his left hand.

'Good evening,' Sebastian says, like we're in Victorian England. Beneath his steady voice I can sense an undercurrent of nerves. 'Álvaro Herrera sent us to pick up a few things. Chapter two of the manuscript, the humidor? He said they were on his nightstand?'

The massive man adjusts his crotch region in response. 'Very funny, kids.'

Sebastian says, 'I know it's kind of late, so sorry we're bothering you, but if you can just give us the things, I promise we'll –'

'What are you playing at?' the man says. 'Joke's over.'

It occurs to me that, in all likelihood, Álvaro never lived here, that this man thinks we're just a couple of mischievous kids substituting Álvaro Herrera jokes for ding-dong-ditch. But this doesn't occur to Sebastian. Obviously he hasn't seen enough horror movies. Even as I'm grabbing his wrist, he presses on. 'Please, if we can –'

'You've got until the count of ten to get off my property,' the man grunts.

Fear replaces all the blood in my body. We were *way* off the mark.

'Ten. Nine. Eight. Seven . . .'

This sure went well.

We fly at a thousand frames per second, stumbling on the Nerf guns as we cut across the yard. Sebastian must've twisted his ankle on one of them, because he lets go of a string of obscenities and then says, 'Linny! Help!'

'Oh-my-gosh-this-is-a-disaster.'

'Gee, Linny! *Is it?* I'm aware! *Shit.*'

I grab his left hand and place it on my shoulder, creating a crutch of sorts, and he fast-limps back to the truck like he's fleeing a war zone.

Ray's reading *People* magazine against the steering wheel.

'Go, go, go!' I shout once we're safely inside the truck.

'Did you get the stuff?' Ray says. 'Why are you guys so out of breath?'

'RAY!' Sebastian and I say in unison. 'GO!'

He catches wind that we *really* mean it, so he floors the gas pedal, which moans on account of never going from zero to sixty before. Pressed against each other, Sebastian and I take deep breaths as one: inhale, exhale, inhale.

In my mind, Grace is laughing next to me – 'Now *that* was fun,' she says – and I'm sucker-punched by a desire to reach out and touch her hand.

THE LEFT-BEHINDS (scene 8)

GRACE'S BEDROOM – LATE EVENING

Once again, we watch GRACE launch out of her window and up in the air, yellow wings carrying her away.

Fade to black and white.

CUT TO –

THE CARSON FAMILY'S STREET – SUNSET

There are long shadows from cardboard palm trees as the sun curves off to the left. Cardboard cutouts of Dolphin Egg Blue houses line the street in orderly rows. LINNY stands alone among them, hands cupped over her mouth.

LINNY
(yelling)
> OLLY-OLLY-OXEN-FREE!

(louder, more forceful)
> OLLY-OLLY-OXEN-FREE!

All of a sudden, the cardboard houses and cardboard trees fall flat – a world collapsing. Everything is colorless except for a single yellow feather, dancing across the empty street.

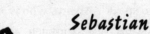

Sebastian

16.

'All scientists should attempt to defy physics. How else can we determine the bounds of what is possible?' *A Brief Compendium of Astrophysical Curiosities*, p. 2

'Was it Seahorse?' Linny says. The cafeteria lights dance in her curls.

I rip my Cuban sandwich in half with unnecessary aggression.

'Seahorse?' Álvaro repeats.

'The address you gave us yesterday,' Linny continues, 'to go pick up your things? We tried to get them but – um – I think you gave us the wrong address. I was wondering if you meant Sea*horse* instead of Sea*shore*.'

Shaking his head twice – 'I am . . . mmm . . .' He bites into his sandwich, yellow mustard and Swiss cheese oozing out the sides of the bread. Chewing carefully, he appears to be thinking about the address, but when he swallows he says, 'If this sandwich was a women, I would make love to her.'

Barf.

A jolt through the table as Álvaro slaps it. 'Oh! Seahorse. Yes, Seahorse.' He laughs. '*Lo siento.*'

Linny jots it on the back of her hand with a blue pen. '212 Seahorse Drive. Got it. . . . So, this is where you lived when you disappeared, right?'

Álvaro smooths back his hair. 'That is all in the past, *mi amor.*'

'Yes, but . . .' She raps the pen twice on the table, like she's deciding whether or not to speak. 'Álvaro, who is Joe?'

Álvaro casually picks up the sandwich again. 'We play dominoes together.'

'On Saturdays,' Linny says. 'I know, but you haven't exactly –'

'Mmmm,' he says, pointing at the napkin container next to my elbow. 'Can you pass me *una servilleta*?'

I slide a napkin across the table and say, 'I need to get some air or something.' My ankle's swollen, so I limp into the hall. Like I'm a zombie in a video game. A nurse's aide by the vending machine throws me a concerned look. *The* last *thing I want is a hug*, I tell her in my mind.

Hands, on knees. I bend over and breathe. This is just so *screwed up*. Was Álvaro messing with us yesterday? Did he give us the wrong address on purpose?

And what's up with Ray? Are he and Linny *together*?

Behind me is the squeak of rubber against tile. All of a sudden Linny's at my side, fingers pressed against her lips so her speech comes out muffled. 'Are you okay?'

I wheeze out an answer. 'Oh. I'm fine.'

'You don't *look* fine. Is it your ankle? I heard a *pop*.'

Shaking my head until I feel something spring loose – 'This is stupid,' I burst. 'What's finding where he went going to prove? I'm all about mysteries, but –'

'More's at stake now,' she says. 'It's like we have this chance to help gift his new novel to the world. So what if we waste a few days knocking on people's doors?'

'Well . . .' I begin.

She's becoming more animated. The most enthusiastic I've

ever seen her. 'And I know you're curious, maybe even more curious than I am. Can't we just see where this goes? How we can be a part of it?'

Ha. I'm already 50 percent his DNA. How much more a part of it can I be?

Still bent over, I have a good view of her shoes. The stars – she hasn't washed them away. Maybe that's why I tell her – because from what I know, she's got a messed-up family, too.

And if I don't talk to someone about this – someone who knows Álvaro, knows this mystery – then I'm going to flip.

Wiping the corners of my mouth, I straighten up and meet her eyes. One gulp. Two gulps. Then out with it: 'He's my dad.' That combination of words – said out loud – feels just as wonderful and as horrible as I'd imagined.

Linny blinks. 'Who's your dad?'

'Álvaro. Álvaro's my dad.'

Her eyes pop. I can almost hear the *click* of pieces as she slots them together. 'You're serious?'

I frown at her. 'Why would I lie about something like that?'

'I don't know! It's just' – throwing her hands up in the air – 'why didn't you say anything? This is baffling. I mean, he's so *old*.'

There are too many people in the hall. Three residents slow-walk past and give us a uniform once over. *Whoosh* – the flush of a toilet as I realize we're standing right outside a bathroom. Anyone can hear us. I gently grab her arm and pull her into one of the adjacent hallways. Her skin is so damn soft I almost forget about everything else. 'Can we maybe talk about this someplace private?'

'Sure,' she says, looking at my fingers on her arm. I snap back my hand and quickly pocket it. 'Where were you thinking?'

'Just somewhere . . . outside. I don't know.'

She nervously tugs at her earlobe. 'Um, sure.' Turning on her heels back to the cafeteria – 'Let me just let Álvaro know we're leaving.'

Outside, my lungs work again. My feet act independently of my mind. I don't know where I'm leading her until we arrive at a playground two blocks south of Silver Springs. It's relatively quiet, other than a mom shoving her kid down the slide and a dachshund taking a leak on the bushes. I open the gate. Breathing = easier. Even my limp has improved. Maybe I just needed to be someplace where everyone isn't dying.

It wears on you, Silver Springs. Sometimes I catch whiffs of urine in the halls. People chew with or without their teeth. Almost everyone is sick. Or getting over being sick. Or about to be sick.

It's hard to stomach that my dad's elderly like them. Harder to stomach that one day I will be, too. I'm not opposed to growing up, but I have come to realize that I'm opposed to growing *old*. It's like looking down a long, dark tunnel, and I can see the black hole at the end.

'You're doing that quiet thing again,' Linny says.

'Sorry, just thinking.'

'About what?'

Adult diapers. Dentures. Mortality. 'Swings. You want to go on the swings?'

'Yeah, okay.'

We pick sides – her on the left, me on the right. It's a tight squeeze considering neither one of us is eight years old. Up, up, up we go. My legs are too long, so I hook them at the bottom to keep them from dragging against the ground.

We're on opposite pendulums. I fly up; Linny comes down.

She speaks between leg-pumps. 'So are you going to' – pump – 'talk to me' – pump – 'about what's going on?' – pump – 'Because I have to tell you' – pump – 'this is' – pump – 'so weird.'

An (admittedly childish) idea comes. 'Yeah' – pump – 'but not before we' – pump – 'see who can' – pump – 'jump the farthest.'

In elementary school, there were rumors that a kid flew so high on the swings that he spun all the way around. According to Newton's second law of motion, that's impossible. But as I climb higher and higher, I wonder if *I* could be that kid. If for just one moment, I can defy physics.

THE PLAYGROUND PRINCIPLE:
Testing the bounds of possibility directly correlates to the amount of effort put forth by the tester.

'Ready?' Linny shouts. 'Jump on three!'

'One!' I say.

'Two!' she says.

'Three!' we say.

We are weightless.

We are free.

We are so goddamn stupid for not factoring in the possibility of injury.

As I land, my already-weak ankle twists in a pocket of sand. Linny smashes into me on the ground, elbow jabbing into my ribs. *Uggggg* – I grunt like a Cro-Magnon. The mom stops pushing her kid down the slide. Picks him up. Carries him away from the two delinquent teens.

'Oh my God!' Linny says, hovering over me. So close.

Count-her-freckles close. 'Did I hurt you?'

Everything feels cartoonish. I should have stars or little birdies circling my head. The impact of the fall has rattled my words loose. 'You're the first person I've told,' I blurt out, struggling to sit up.

She presses her eyebrows together. 'Me? Why?'

'I just knew you'd . . . get it?'

Massaging her temples – 'Do you think we could just rewind for a second? I'm still trying to wrap my head around how he's your father.'

I go for the condensed version, the story I've been replaying since Mom told me. About the film festival in Miami. About Álvaro buying a ring. About him leaving. I conclude with 'My mom made it seem like the only thing he was ever really good at was disappearing.'

'But does he know that you're his –'

'Son? No. He left before my mom could tell him she was pregnant. And then afterward, she didn't feel like he had the right to know. She didn't even tell *me* until my aunt called and told her Álvaro was alive and in Miami.'

'How could your mom keep something like that from you?'

'I think she was afraid he'd be just as horrible to me as he was to her.'

'Still.'

'Yeah. Maybe she was embarrassed? I mean, she was in her thirties, and Álvaro was sixty-five. *Sixty-five*. It's actually kind of a miracle that he was still, I don't know, not shooting blanks.'

We both shudder. I suppress a Viagra joke.

'So are you going to let him know?' Linny says.

'Eventually. It's not exactly easy to bring up.'

She nods, peering down and tracing a circle by her knee. 'Thank you, by the way.'

'For what?'

'For telling me.' She pauses, closes her eyes. I think the conversation's over, but then she leans back and lies flat. Spreads her fingertips through the grains of sand. She's covered in pops of light, curls haloing her head. 'I'm starting to think there are two types of people in this world. People who leave and people who stay.'

I clear my throat. 'And which type are you?'

Her shoulders go up and down, indenting the sand. 'I haven't figured that out yet.' Pause. 'Sebastian?'

'Linny?'

'I *do* get it. I know what it's like to be the one left behind.' A deep breath. 'My sister completely bailed after last Christmas, and I have no idea where she is, and I got it into my head that maybe if I – I don't know – figured out why all these missing people come back – why *Álvaro* came back – that I'd catch on to some way to bring her home. Because I miss her. I miss her all the time. It's like –'

'Like you're a balloon floating around without a tether?'

'Exactly.'

'It sucks.'

'*Completely* sucks,' she says in a choking voice. A few tears pool in the corners of her eyes. She bats them away as they slip down.

The obsession with Álvaro's mystery makes sense now. Well, partial sense. It's still kind of out there.

I want to say 'I'm sorry,' but that feels inadequate somehow. So I say, 'What's her name?'

'I – um – *God*, I haven't said it out loud in so long.'

'Who is she, Lord Voldemort or something?'

Linny lets out a solitary laugh and slaps my knee. 'Sebastian!'

'Sorry. That was insensitive. So . . . you weren't always this neurotic?'

Another slap. Another laugh. 'No, I guess not.' She swallows. 'Grace. Her name is Grace.'

Neither of us says anything else. No words needed.

We stay like that. Her: lying in the sand. Me: kind of curved around her.

AN ADDITION TO THE PLAYGROUND PRINCIPLE:
For a tenth of a second, it is possible to defy memory. It is possible to forget that anything is wrong in the world.

Linny

17.

WHO: *Jessie Love, daughter of guitarist Richard Love*
WHEN: *One week in April 2008*
WHY: *Okay, she didn't <u>really</u> disappear. Every night after the police left, Jessie would switch places with her twin sister, Jolene. The twins wanted to see if anyone could truly tell them apart; Jessie returned for good after Jolene's boyfriend discovered that she didn't kiss the same.*
NOTES: *There's so much a kiss can do. . . .*

As soon as I say 'Grace,' I feel the name floating above me, like I can reach out and poke it with my finger. I silently roll it around on my tongue — a muscle memory. *Grace, Grace, Grace.* And it's gutting, but not as much as I thought it would be. Having Sebastian here makes it easier, because he's a left-behind, too. The way I see it, Álvaro and Grace were cut from the same flighty cloth.

Just look at us — marooned on our little island of grief and sand, like we've survived the same shipwreck. I gaze up at him, hovering to my left, gray eyes half closed and kind of sad, and my first thought is *Good God, Linny, you cannot be serious. Kissing someone at a playground?* I argue with myself for a few seconds, and I'm not sure if I win or lose — but suddenly I'm sitting up and thinking, *Maybe people fall together when they're falling apart.*

'What?' Sebastian says.

'Nothing.'

And then I kiss him, my hand mussing through his messed-up hair, his mouth warm and parting in surprise. He reaches quickly for the side of my face and kind of clips my ear in a semipainful way, but to be honest, I couldn't care less – for approximately six seconds, the black and white at the edges of my vision blurs. As strange as it sounds, it feels like he's pouring color back into me.

Then I break away, slightly panicked, snapping to my senses. 'Oh jeez, I didn't mean to do that.'

His hand is still on the side of my face. 'Er – me neither, I guess.'

'I'm sorry.'

Confused, dropping his hand, he says, 'You don't need to be sorry.'

That's when a toddler ten feet behind us says, 'Mommy, what they doing?' A playgroup has invaded the jungle gym, and I didn't even notice. Three mothers are throwing us nasty looks.

Hurriedly swiping sand off my arms, I say, 'We should probably go soon or Marla's going to have a cow.'

'Yeah,' Sebastian says, face a mask of disappointment, 'sure.'

I can still feel the sensation of Sebastian's lips on mine as we head back. And he's clearly ignoring me. *Of course* he is – I just kissed him and then *apologized*. He must think I'm totally cuckoo bananas, and I'm not entirely convinced he's wrong. He just looked so . . . sad, like me, and for a moment I thought we could put each other back together, or something overly metaphorical like that.

Truth is, sometimes I roll my eyes at movie romances, at girls who bat their eyelashes and boys who lift them off their feet, but now that I have the possibility of – well, of whatever this is – the idea doesn't seem half bad.

Wait a minute – what am I saying? *He's going to leave, Linny.* I might as well add him to a list of people who flee, because he's definitely going to Cal Tech in the fall, and I'm definitely unready for this brand of happiness. Does falling for someone – possibly falling out of black and white – mean accepting that Grace is gone? I haven't even thrown away her empty shampoo bottles in our shower; this is ten thousand steps beyond that.

We pause at the back entrance of Silver Springs, the kiss looming over us.

Should we just be friends? *Can* we be friends after this?

I blurt out: 'Do you think we should play dominoes this afternoon?' My mind's ping-ponging, trying to settle on anything but that kiss.

He appears hurt. 'If you want.'

'I know we should probably talk about what just happened but –'

'It's cool. Don't worry about it,' Sebastian says, in a tone that suggests I probably should.

What have I done?

We find Álvaro in the game room with five other residents, all watching television. One of the women – a redheaded lady with fantastically long nails – is in the middle of shouting at the TV, 'Wheel! Of! Fortune! *Wheel of Fortune!*' And Álvaro's in the middle of telling her to can it and switch coverage to the Miami Marlins game.

It's hard to look at Álvaro the same. Instead of a cult writer, instead of a person who disappeared and returned, all I see is a father. All I see is how complicated things really are, how I've just made them a million times worse with that stinking kiss.

On the way out of Silver Springs, Sebastian and I stop in the parking lot. Only the hard-core reporters remain (like the *National Enquirer* guy who broke into the lobby), plus the evidence of the others: a few McDonald's bags, some cigarette butts, a Pepsi can that Sebastian kicks with the side of his sneaker. Framing him is a fading orange sky, so he's half human, half silhouette. As he swings his foot, I realize this is the perfect series of images: sky, swing, summer; and it seems like a great way to break the tension. Plus, my shoulders are tingling, so I say, 'Pause right there.'

His foot hovers two inches above the ground. 'Is there a bee or something?'

'No, I'm going to shoot you.'

He startles, dropping his foot. 'You're going to *what*?'

'With my camera.'

'Oh, right.'

Maybe this makes me a Camera Girl freak – telling a boy I've just awkwardly kissed to *pause right there* as I pan around him, capturing how the streaking sunset reflects in his hair. But I don't care – a good shot is a good shot. And both of us are visibly more at ease.

I switch off the camera. 'Perfect, thanks.'

'Are you making a movie or something?'

'I just like filming beautiful things.' And when I realize what I've said – that I've just called *him* a beautiful thing – I backtrack. 'You know, the sunset and stuff.'

The conversation stalls, but Sebastian gets it moving again. 'It's Friday night,' he reminds me. In the summer it's easy to forget. 'Any big weekend plans?'

Reading *Midnight in Miami* again probably doesn't rank high on the Cool-o-meter, so I tell a half fib. 'Ray invited me to a party.' I *was* invited; I just wasn't planning on attending. Somehow at parties I always end up being the one camping out on the lawn, filming the party instead of, you know, *partying*. Or I'm holding back some girl's hair (Cass's, namely). And ever since Grace vamoosed, a neon sign has been hanging over my head, flashing SISTERLESS GIRL in bright-yellow light. Grace became the legend, and I became the *other* sister who everyone pities at parties.

'That's cool,' Sebastian says. Then he puffs out his cheeks Godfather-like, as if he's about to *make me an offer I can't refuse*. 'I thought that – er – maybe if you're free tomorrow during the day, we could visit that second address? Because you're right – it's worth a shot, and I looked it up on my phone and there's a bus that stops nearby. I mean, it's okay if you don't want to –'

'I want to,' I say, a bit too eagerly.

The relief on Sebastian's face makes my heart sing. So much singing! Choir auditions, over here. (*Stop, Linny. You can't like him, remember?*)

'In that case,' he says, 'as friends, maybe we could also – um – watch a movie afterward? Eat something?'

My voice does a decent job pretending this isn't one of the greatest things I've heard all summer. 'Yeah,' I say, perfectly smooth.

'Yeah to which bit?'

'All of it.'

Sebastian grins, and it's contagious. By the time I get home, my smile muscles are sore. I throw cold water all over my face.

*

That night, while Ray's getting ready for the party, he eyes my white T-shirt up and down. 'Please tell me that tomorrow you'll wear something less . . . tentlike. It's big enough to shoplift a turkey from Publix. With peas. And carrots. Everyone would just think you're preggo. Why don't you borrow something of –' He bites his lip, because he's said too much.

Borrow something of Grace's, he means. The sister with the style. Even though he doesn't *know* Grace, he glimpsed her fashion in the halls.

It's not like I haven't thought about them – all those Goth-fairy-punk dresses hanging unworn in her closet, along with one yellow sundress that rarely sees the sun. She wore that sundress to school once, and I think half of the twelfth grade fell in love with her that day.

Spaghetti straps are generally a no-go for me. That's the mentality you develop when your mother pretends she doesn't have female body parts. The most exposed I've ever seen her was in a tastefully ruffled swimsuit, which she kept strap-snapping to ensure its durability and full coverage. As if one nipple slip would ruin her life.

Cass looks like she has something to add; she keeps opening her mouth and then shutting it closed. I didn't know she was going to be here. When I entered Ray's room, Cass was flipping through a Victoria's Secret catalog on his bed, and he kicked the door shut with, 'We settle this one of two ways. You can race it out, or you can talk it out, but none of us is leaving until you two stop looking like you want to kill each other.' Before becoming friends with Ray, I sort of knew him from the road races that circled around my neighborhood. He always had the most intense faces. I've never really seen that outside of running, until now.

'You should wear the yellow dress,' Cass suddenly says, and then clamps a hand over her mouth.

'Good!' Ray exclaims, clapping. 'Bravo! Communication! Nice! Keep going!'

I'm slumped in a beanbag chair, eyes flicking between the two of them. They're dressed for the party – Ray in a crisp blue shirt, Cass in a very-Miami hip-hugging dress, boobage fully elevated with that lime-green bra.

She says to him, 'Can you just give us some privacy?'

'No,' he says. 'I need to *see* you two smooth things out.'

Cass grabs him by the collar of his shirt, like a mother cat with a kitten. Opening the door and chucking him into the hall, she says, 'We'll send you a picture.' She shuts the door, grumbling, and turns back to me. 'I need to say something before you go all ape shit on me.'

'I never went ape –'

'*Please*. Just let me get this out.'

Dragging my fingers across my lips, I pretend to zip them.

'I'm sorry,' she says. 'I'm sorry I didn't say sorry that day at your house. And I'm sorry that I tried to convince myself that it was okay. I'm just really, totally, completely sorry.'

I raise my eyebrows. Wow. Apologies are not Cass's style. Softening, I try to say 'Sorry' back, but she cuts me off with 'Wait, I'm not done. You'll be happy to hear that the Humane Society of Greater Miami, North is now a thousand bucks richer with findalvaro.com money. . . . Okay. Nine hundred and ninety-five bucks richer. I may've bought some lip gloss before I came to my senses, but you have to know that I didn't want everything to end up like this, especially when things have been so shitty the past year. And I *wasn't* going to say that I wish you'd left instead of her. I was going to say that she left all this' — fluttering her hands around like birds — '*carnage*, you know?'

In a small voice, I say, 'Yeah, I know.'

She plays with the ends of her hair. 'I'm going to start volunteering at Silver Springs, one day a week, to make up for everything.'

My heart skips three beats. 'Seriously? They let you do that?'

'I guess not everyone knows I'm the one who filmed Álvaro. Anyhoo . . . are you okay with it?'

Let's see. *I* am, because it's obvious: Cass is trying to reapply the glue to our friendship. But Sebastian? He'll probably throw her looks like he's about to huff and puff and bite her face off. 'One condition,' I say.

'Anything.'

'No cell phones or cameras allowed.'

She bobs her head back and forth as if deliberating. 'Deal.'

On the other side of the door, Ray's voice: 'Is that reconciliation I hear?'

Almost. Not completely. But Cass and I both murmur, 'Yes,' and Ray bursts in, beaming.

I film them getting ready for the party as we pretend that everything is 100 percent normal. Cass takes two shots of rum from Ray's secret stash, and afterward I zoom in on the fog their noses make when pressed to the mirror. The whole make-up thing is something I should try sometime, Ray notes as I film his fingers, slick with hair gel. 'You're *so* pretty, Linny. We just have to get you out of the nunnery.'

He's partly right about the nun thing. Maybe tomorrow I'll let Grace's sundress live up to its name. I wonder if it will still smell like her.

Cass finishes applying a fifth coat of gloss and smacks her lips. The *pop* sounds great on film. 'So how long have you and – what's his name? Sebastian? How long have you been you two?'

'We're not actually together.' (Minus the fact that I said *Think fast!* with my mouth.)

'So you haven't fooled around at Silver Springs and stuff? No broom closet action?'

My response comes out as a snort. 'What am I supposed to do? Pin him up against the wall and whisper in his ear, "Oh baby, take me right here, right now, right next to the defibrillator?"'

Dreamy eyed, Ray swivels around in his chair and clutches his chest. 'OhmyGod, that would be so romantic!'

In what possible way could that be construed as romantic? I shake my head, laugh, and shut off the camera so future generations won't get skewed impressions about my generation's dating habits.

Eyes spidery with mascara, Cass makes her way over to me in her sky-high heels. She's doing a much better job of keeping up the normal act. Pink chewing gum lolls around in her mouth as she leans over and says, 'I can teach you how to wrangle him.' Those exact words. *Wrangle*, as if he were a steer. 'So you two are going to' – using air quotes – 'watch a movie?'

'What's with the finger bunnies?' I say.

Ray lets out a *psshhh*. 'Everyone knows "watching a movie" is code for having sex.'

Everyone except me, apparently. The Virgin Marilyn. I picture Grace laughing at me: 'Really, have I taught you nothing?' And I would shout back, 'You're not exactly here to teach me!'

Cass says, 'It's just like that time I met that Kevin guy who went to art school and he said he wanted to "show me his motorcycle" one day after class, but then we ended up doing it in his basement.' It's amazing how many of Cass's stories now end with hooking up in some guy's basement/car/backyard. Last year, serious spit swapping began to occur outside our mutual locker, a parade of boys smearing their lips across Cass's like they were trying to repaint her face. At first I thought it looked gross, but now . . .

Just drop it, Linny!

'Pretty, pretty please, come out with us!' Cass squeals. 'I'm sure Lawrence can fit one more, or' – slapping her thighs, like she's calling a dog – 'you can sit on my lap.' Okay, she's totally drunk. Without warning, she crumbles down into the beanbag with me, crushing my side.

'Ow.' I bite back a lecture on personal space.

'We can snuggle up like old times.' She digs her nose into my shoulder. 'Plus we totally have enough vodka to go around. Lawrence won't mind. Will he, Ray?'

I ask, 'How's that going, by the way? You and Lawrence?'

Ray smiles. 'Well. Really well. We're officially boyfriend and boyfriend, which is kind of scary but also incredibly exciting. And he won't mind at all about the vodka. If he does' – scrunching up his face – 'he'll have to answer to me.'

I laugh. Compared to Ray's serious face, his pretend-angry face is about as intimidating as a baby hedgehog. Still, I tell them I can't go to the party.

Cass huffs. 'Can't or won't?'

Mostly won't, for several reasons. People at parties can't look at me without seeing Grace, and getting a good night's sleep is essential. If the resident of 212 Seahorse Drive is another Massive Man, I want to be rested enough to shimmy across the lawn.

Cass and Ray know about the movie but not my morning plans. After everything Sebastian told me at the playground, the trip feels too private.

'Can't go tonight,' I say. 'Strict curfew.'

'Well, boo,' Ray says.

'Yeah, boooo,' Cass says.

They catch melodrama from each other, like germs.

'Oh!' Ray suddenly exclaims. 'I got one! You said that Sebastian wanted to be an astrophysicist, right?'

Where the heck is this going? 'Yes . . .'

'I bet he'd give you a Big Bang!'

Cass and Ray high-five each other. I ask for a ride home, and Ray drops me at my mailbox with a salute. 'Good night, Sister Marilyn,' he says. 'Sweet dreams in the convent.'

I wait for his truck to round the corner before – once again – checking the mail for a letter that isn't there.

THE LEFT-BEHINDS (scene 9)

GRACE'S BEDROOM – EARLY EVENING

LINNY is in the process of tearing apart GRACE's black-and-white room. The floor is strewn with dresses.

We hear GRACE's voice through the cup and string.

GRACE
(angry)
> What do you think you're doing?

LINNY
(yelling)

> What does it look like I'm doing?

LINNY opens the closet, drags out a box of shoes, and begins chucking sandals at the walls. We hear *bang, bang.*

GRACE

> It looks like you're flipping out.

LINNY

> Correct.

GRACE
(softer)

> And you're pissed at me?

LINNY

> Correct.

GRACE

> You won't find any clues in here. I'm sorry.

LINNY
(tired)

> Then just tell me where you went.

GRACE

> How about we make a deal?

LINNY

How about you come home?

LINNY notices something odd; where the shoes collided with the wall, there are holes, and on the other side – pinpricking through – is color.

Sebastian

18.

'Theories regarding the dimensionality of the world are far from set in stone. On the historical side, Minkowski invented $x^0 = ct$, adding to the three dimensions of space.' *A Brief Compendium of Astrophysical Curiosities*, p. 98

'Savannah nixed the prom idea,' Micah says. 'She said it was too early to make plans.'

I stretch out on the couch. 'You actually asked her?'

'I'd rather not talk about it.'

'But you brought it –'

'What about your girl?'

My girl? Can I call someone my girl if she kissed me and then apologized and then said she'd watch a movie with me? I'd rather not bring that up. Confusion doesn't even begin to cover it. Instead, I say, 'We're doing something tomorrow.'

'Have you two . . . you know? BOW CHICA WOW WOW.'

I hope he hears my eyes roll.

'Dude,' he says, 'you're losing your window. It's a precise science.' I start to cut him off, but he only speaks louder. 'Hear me out! Girls decide in the first five minutes of meeting you whether or not they want to hump your brains out. Given that you're stuck in boner-killing Old Peopleville, I'd say you've got some time. Another week, tops. After that and it's over. Trust me, I've done the calculations.'

'Well, *my* calculations say you're full of shit.'

'You can't argue with science.'

'You realize that means you have *zero* chance with my mother, right?'

He pauses. 'Moms are a trickier equation. . . . Are you and your mom still on the outs?'

'Er – sort of. It's complicated. You don't – you don't know the full story.'

'Oh! You're right! You know why that is? You never effing told me.' He sounds half hurt, half like he's enjoying this.

'Fine,' I say. 'I'm going to pose a hypothetical question.'

'You mean you're going to pose a real question that you're trying to pass off as hypothetical.'

'*No.*' Yes. 'What if someone really close to you hid something? Like, something important?'

'Hypothetically?'

'Hypothetically.'

A deep breath rattles through the phone. Then he's silent for a moment. 'Maybe I'd give them the benefit of the doubt. Maybe they just need some time to come clean, because they're afraid of how you're going to react. If you're going to totally lose your shit and start screaming and not want to be friends anymore and fly back from Florida to pummel them and – Okay, okay, okay – I may've touched Savannah's boobs.'

I jerk my head back. 'Is that what you think we're talking about?'

'*Boob*, technically. Just the left one.'

'That's completely your business.'

'You *have* to care a little bit. She's your ex. What if I touched the left one *and* the right one simultaneously? Would you care then?'

'Look,' I say. 'One, I'm serious. Touch both of her boobs, all day every day, and I still will not give a shit. Two, that's really not what I was talking about.'

'I knew it,' he says smugly.

'What?'

'Nothing about this was hypothetical.'

The next morning, Linny's already at the bus stop in a yellow dress, curls pulled into a high ponytail. Shimmering. Like she's not made of human things. Like someone assembled her from glass and flowers and –

Shut up.

Since when did I turn into *that* guy? A guy who uses words like *shimmering*.

Is it warmer suddenly? A few moments ago it was run-of-the-mill Florida hot. Now it's like I've cannonballed into a fire pit.

Quick, picture this:

Cryogenic freezing.

Cold-blooded reptiles.

The Boomerang Nebula (-457.7°F).

None of it works. Still overheating.

Linny shifts her backpack to her left shoulder and spins around. 'Oh hey!' Her eyes effing *shimmer*.

In the understatement of the millennium, I say, 'You look nice,' and she raises and drops her shoulders like she doesn't really believe it. When the bus rolls to a stop a minute later, I have to tear my eyes away from her. *Tear*, like it hurts. We slide to the back, sit two inches apart. This could be horribly awkward, given the kiss, but luckily I'm playing it cool.

'Um,' Linny says, squinting, 'I think you have bird poop in your hair.'

I paw at a spot above my left ear, and, sure enough, white goop coats my fingertips. It's the universe's equivalent of a swift kick in the shins. How did I not feel a bird shit on my head?

Linny laughs. 'Seagulls can be stealthy.'

After the bus stops a street over from 212 Seahorse Drive, Linny and I pace around the block. Pumping each other up.

'Okay, if someone scary opens the door,' she says, 'we just run.'

'Fast as we can,' I say. 'But we've got this.'

'Yeah, totally got this.'

'Absolutely.'

When Agnes, approximately ninety years old and a hundred pounds, materializes at the screen door in a polka-dotted apron, the dramatic buildup (in retrospect) was kind of unnecessary.

I don't beat around the bush. 'Hi, we're looking for the lost possessions of Álvaro Herrera.'

Agnes pauses to consider us, smiles, then swoops her hand. 'Well, come on in!'

Linny says, 'They're *actually* here?'

That's when Agnes notices the bird poop and says, 'Son, I'll get you some paper towels. Don't just stand there letting all the cold air out.' The next thing we know, she's force-feeding us pecan brittle on her back porch. Around us are about a billion citronella candles. All lit. It's just past noon.

Agnes hands me a wet wad of paper that I wipe through my hair.

'About what you came here for,' she begins. Linny and I lean forward. Agnes smiles at us, presses her hands over her heart. 'I have no idea what you're talking about! But you two looked so much like lost puppies that I couldn't say no, and I'd just made all this pecan brittle. Oh – and now look at your faces, you poor things.'

My whole body slumps. Does Álvaro think this is a joke or something?

'Here.' Agnes thrusts the bowl of brittle in my direction. 'Have some more. Sweets make everything better.'

Knocking myself into a sugar coma is a decent option. I grab a fistful and shovel it in. Chipmunk cheeks.

'So what do you need, dears?' Agnes asks.

'Álvaro told us his things were here,' Linny says. 'He gave us this address.'

'Do I know this All-vayro?'

I speak through shards of brittle. 'He wrooote a booook.'

'But he's at Silver Springs now,' Linny adds. 'We thought he maybe used to live here.'

'Ah!' Agnes says. 'Well, I don't know any writers, but I *do* know about Silver Springs. One of the nurses lives around here. Tries to recruit me because apparently I'm old. Hah!' She smacks the armrest of the porch swing, throws her head back, and *he-he-he*'s. 'I tell them time and time again, the day I willingly go into a home is the day Hades turns into a Popsicle stand. My life is here. I've got my kitchen and my books and' – pointing above my right shoulder – 'my cat.'

Just then, the ugliest black cat I've ever seen rams its head into mine. Meows. It's drooling and missing an eye. *Holy shit kickers* is what I think, but I say, 'She's lovely.'

'He,' Agnes corrects. 'As I was saying, I don't want to be

locked away in a place like that. Told when to eat, what to eat, when to sleep, when to relieve myself. No thank you! They'll have to drag me in by my teeth. You get old, and suddenly no one thinks you're *you* anymore. You're just another old bird that flocks to Miami to die, you know?'

No, I don't. But it's the type of idea you can drown in. The type that sucks the life out of you if you think about it too long.

Does Álvaro feel this way, too?

Franken-cat scurries across my shoulder, smashing my moment of contemplation. He launches, sharp claws of doom first, onto my you-know-where.

Estupendo. (It's official: the world's animals are conspiring against me.)

Agnes's eyes twinkle as she shoves more brittle in my face. 'Sweets fix *everything*.'

In my peripheral vision I think I see Linny crack a smile.

'That went stupendously,' I say, clenching and unclenching my jaw.

Agnes waves at us from behind her screen door.

Linny says, 'At least we tried.'

'Sure,' I say, although in actual fact I am not sure. On the bus, I throw my head back against the seat. Keep whacking it until Linny grabs both sides of my face and says, 'Stop. You're losing brain cells.' Her hands are warm. My cheeks turn even warmer. Like she's burning my skin with her fingertips. (In a good way.)

She lets go, mumbles, 'It's frustrating. I get it.'

I say, 'Don't you ever just want to – ?'

'Blow up?'

'*Yes.*'

'Only like all the time.'

'Know what we need?'

'What?'

'I don't know yet,' I admit.

'Well, that's helpful.'

I begin scouring the landscape. 'But I'll let you know when I see it.'

So Linny starts talking about a documentary she saw last weekend, something about SeaWorld. And as I'm listening, I'm watching what's flying by the window:

Option 1) McDonald's

Too greasy.

Option 2) the beach

So it looks like I'm trying to get her in her bathing suit? Pass.

Option 3) funeral parlor

No. Just, no.

We're nearing the stop for a strip mall when – yes! Bally World: Fun for All Ages. Okay, impulse decision. I signal the bus driver and almost immediately regret it, already imagining Micah's reaction: 'You took her to a pit of *balls*? How much more Freudian can you get?'

'Um, what are we doing?' Linny asks.

'Get off and you'll see,' I say, pretending this is a fully formed plan.

She follows me into the half-empty parking lot. Each step I take fills me with dread.

Bells jingle as I open the door to Bally World, which is – as the sign declares – The Best Ball Pit in Southern Miami! For once, advertising doesn't lie. The place is an ocean of Technicolor, the Eighth Wonder of the World.

'You with the McAdams party?' asks the man behind the counter. Approximately a hundred piercings dangle from his face. Magnets must be his mortal enemy.

'Huh?' I say, oh so intelligently.

Slower, like I'm deaf, he repeats, 'Mc-A-dams, twelfth birth-day,' and gestures to one of the two pits, where a contingent of prepubescent boys is beating the shit out of one another with plastic balls. Awesome. He thinks we're here for a *twelfth birthday*?

Puffing out my chest to highlight my man muscles, I say in my deepest voice, 'Nah, it's just us,' and fork over ten fifty for two passes and a locker key. Behind the desk, Linny and I slip off our shoes. There are little blue hearts on her toenails.

Still gripping her backpack, she skittishly eyes the door.

Knew it. She hates Bally World. Probably hates me for dragging her here. Other guys must take her to better places. Restaurants with steak dinners. The planetarium. Establishments that serve alcohol, not cartons of milk.

'We should go somewhere else,' I say, bending down to retie my sneakers. 'This was stupid.'

Dragging her teeth across her bottom lip – 'It's not that.' Her thumb twitches against the backpack. 'It's just, my camera's in here, and these lockers don't look that secure.'

'Oh. Why don't you bring it with you?'

'In the pit?' Her face lights up. 'You don't think that's weird?'

I start to laugh. 'It's a *bit* weird. But I like weird.'

A grin edges up the corners of her mouth. She reaches into the bag. Grabs her camera and a protective lens. Stashes the empty backpack in the locker. At the edge of the pit, I hear the camera powering on. Then the shuffling of feet as we line up next to each other. Words zoom out of my mouth: 'You know there's this ex-NASA scientist who built one of these in his apartment, and it's actually really interesting in terms of physics and what happens when you're at the bottom.'

'Maybe I should try that with my bedroom,' she says. I don't even have to look to know she's goofily smiling. 'My parents would be thrilled.' We hover over the pit for another few seconds before she adds, 'Jump on three?'

Is that going to be our thing? Like at the playground. *One, two, three.*

When I don't respond immediately, she just jumps, sundress ballooning at her sides. (How does she do that? Look like she's suspended in midflight?)

I follow.

Flinging my arms wide like I'm trying to hug the air.

Breaking through the top layer of balls.

Getting swallowed by color.

I lay my body flat and sink deeper, deeper. Roll my wrists and sweep forward in a swimming motion. I feel like a fish breathing underwater. After a fifth-grade presentation about sea life, I became incredibly jealous of fish. Of their gills, especially. How they can swim eyes open, lungs open, without feeling a burn.

After a while, I surface.

Linny's not there.

How long have I been under?

My first thought: *Beneath this ball pit is a loop in the space-time continuum. I have Rip Van Winkled it into the next century.* (I hope I've solved all the mysteries in *A Brief Compendium of Astrophysical Curiosities* by now.)

'Linny?'

Nothing except the sound of young boys murdering one

another in the next pit. (Okay, still this century.)

'Linny?'

Seven, eight, nine seconds pass before the balls rumble and she emerges dolphin-like, camera in hand. 'Oh my God, Sebastian, you have to see this! It's so – Well, come see.' I wade over, waist deep. She rewinds the footage then presses Play.

It's miraculous. She's captured another world. The coolest part is the way the camera snakes through the pit, like it has a tail.

The whole thing seems so natural for her. Like, instead of a hand, a camera grew there. (Maybe I phrased that wrong? Sounds too creepy. She's not a cyborg or anything.)

I reach out my hands. 'May I?'

Hesitantly, she passes me the camera. I sink back and press my eye to the viewfinder, zooming in on her face. 'So, Linny Carson, tell me about yourself.'

'*Ugh*, I hate that question. It's so general.'

'Fine . . . Er . . . If you could have a superpower, what would it be?'

She presses two fingers to her chin. 'Reading people's minds.'

'And why's that?'

She shrugs. Alternates between clinching her lips together and lowering herself deeper into the pit. Only her head floats above the surface, like a flower bulb you could uproot by the ponytail.

'Oh, come on,' I say. 'Tell me.'

'If you must know,' she says slowly, 'if I could read minds, I would've known that Grace was about to leave, and maybe I could've gone with her or stopped her or something. But can we talk about something – literally *anything* – else?'

'Oh, right, er –' I point with my free hand to the camera. 'Is this what you want to do when you grow up? Make movies?'

For some reason, her light fizzles even more. She grabs back the camera and switches it off. 'Yeah. But I can't really talk about that, either.'

I despise the word *can't*. Scientific history is full of hatred for it. *Humans can't fly*, people told Leonardo da Vinci, so he designed a flying machine. *You can't see inside a body without slicing it open* – Wilhelm Conrad Röntgen discovered X-rays. Think you can't clone something? Introducing Dolly the Sheep.

Granted, da Vinci's flying machine didn't work. Didn't even lift off the ground. Much like this conversation.

I'm pretty certain I should backtrack. Or back*stroke*, given the current floating situation. Running through possible discussions:

~~Space ice cream~~

~~The possibility of life on other planets~~

What do people talk about in ball pits? What do people talk about with *girls*? Savannah's tongue was always rammed so far down my throat, word formation wasn't necessary.

Oh, got it!

'Favorite movie. Go.'

She pops up a little. '*Midnight in Miami*.' A little more. 'Ooo, ooo, or *The Godfather*. Or *The Rocky Horror Picture Show*. Or *Dr. Strangelove*. Or –'

I laugh. 'Can't choose just one?'

'Sometimes I think I can, but that's like choosing a favorite child.'

'You have *children*?' I tease.

She whips a ball at me and says, 'No!' And then: 'What about you?'

'I don't have children, either.'

Another ball – *zing*. It connects with my shoulder.

'I meant, what's your favorite movie.' Before *The Empire Strikes Back* forms on my lips, she adds, 'It's probably *Midnight in Miami* now, right?'

Silencio.

Something occurs to her. 'You do like your dad's movie, right?'

Silencio.

'You have *seen* your dad's movie, right?'

Silencio.

'Sebastian! How? You're not even a teensy bit curious?'

I tilt my head, confused. 'Of course I am. I just hadn't seen it before I found out he was my dad and now it's too – it's too –' I stumble. 'Everyone knows him as the famous writer, but I don't want to know him like everyone else does. I want something that's just us.'

An eternity passes.

Then Linny touches my shoulder.

It makes my voice come out jagged. 'That's why I was so mad at you that first day and ran when you opened the door. Because you were one of thousands of people closer to him than I was, and it wasn't supposed to be like that. And I wanted to tell him – right away. But you were always *there*.'

For a second, I think I should've kept my mouth shut, finally used that superglue Mom chased me with years ago. I want to kick myself in the head for saying too much.

But then Linny plunges her hand into the pit. In the seconds before hers finds mine, I swear I've taken a giant leap toward mastering hibernation. My heart practically stops beating.

Fingers: intertwine.

Let me tell you something about hands. They're not one size fits all like hotel slippers. Ours slot together with an audible *chink*. (At least I can hear it.) I trace my thumb along her palm. I am a palm explorer now. Lewis and Clark of the palms.

It's almost better than the kiss.

But is she going to apologize for this, too?

'About yesterday,' Linny says, like she has a transcript of my thoughts, 'I lied.'

I don't ask her to elaborate – because I know what she means. I squeeze her hand and she squeezes back.

A QUESTION REGARDING DIMENSIONALITY:
If the fourth dimension is duration, then can one awesome moment extend infinitely through time?

How is this happening? I didn't think it possible, but it's happening. She likes me. At least, the evidence suggests so.

And I'm *stoked*.

But should I be happy, in the midst of everything else? With nothing I came here to do actually done?

At that exact moment, the twelve-year-olds burst through the wall of introspection and, streaming in like rabid antelope, launch an attack on our pit. Balls grenade through the air as the birthday boy – by the look of his crown – bangs his chest and lets out a war cry.

It is possibly the funniest thing I've ever seen.

Linny

19.

WHO: Captain Matthew Stanley
WHEN: Three and a half nights in December 2013
WHY: He wandered away from his military base and into the Hindu Kush Mountains of northeastern Afghanistan. When he returned to camp three and a half nights later, his superior asked him why he fled. He responded, 'Thought I didn't have any fight left in me, sir. Came back when I realized I did.'
NOTES: When is Grace going to realize it's time to come home? That there's so much left to fight for?

We are severely outnumbered, but we are also *much* more strategic. Climbing onto the side of the pit, gaining the higher ground, is the obvious choice. . . . And that's exactly why we don't do it. Beating the opposing forces requires cunning deception.

'Linny!' Sebastian shouts above the *whiff* of balls zipping through the air. 'Down! Down!'

We're on the same page. I almost shout back, 'Roger that!' but maybe people only say that in action and adventure films.

Dipping below the balls once more, camera still in hand, I follow the curve of the pit's walls, counting: *One, two, three.* Simultaneously, Sebastian and I spring from the pit and launch a counterattack. Fighting one-handed, I'm at a slight disadvantage, but we hold our own until Bally World's manager appears out of nowhere, screaming, 'DID YOU NOT SEE THE SIGN?' He points to the back wall, where a banner clearly dictates: No chewing gum. No shoes. Clothes must be worn at all times. DO NOT THROW THE BALLS.

'Oh,' Sebastian says, looking guilty along with the other boys.

The manager wags his finger at us. 'Last. Warning. Normally I'd just kick you out, but I know this is a birthday party.'

'Yes, sir,' I say as the twelve-year-old army leaves the pit. Sebastian and I wait until everyone's gone to double over and clutch our sides, laughing.

'I feel slightly better,' he says, struggling to catch his breath.

'Yeah, me too.'

We still have half an hour on our rental, so we float in the pit – several inches from each other – and play the Asteroid Game.

'What would you do if an asteroid was crashing to Earth?' Sebastian says. 'Ten seconds to think about it. *And* . . . go.'

'Besides cry? Depends. How long do I have before the asteroid touches down?'

'Let's say twenty-four hours.'

'*Bueno*. I'd say good-bye to everyone I love.' Try to, at least. What if I couldn't reach Grace? 'And then I'd do everything I'm afraid to do. Skydiving, cliff-jumping, skinny-dipping –'

'You *cannot* classify skinny-dipping and skydiving in the same category.'

'Sure I can. Jumping out of a plane, terrifying. Having people stare at me when I'm naked, equally terrifying.'

Without missing a beat, he deadpans, 'Believe me when I say you do *not* have to worry about the last part.' And then all the color rushes to his face. Raising himself a few inches out of the pit, he turns ever so slightly toward me.

Holy bananas.

Is he going to kiss me, like in the movies? I picture *Breakfast at Tiffany's* – George Peppard kissing Audrey Hepburn in the rain. Or *Gone with the Wind* – Clark Gable telling Vivien Leigh, 'You should be kissed, and often.' Heck, I'll even take the upside-down lip-lock in *Spiderman*, logistics of inverted kissing aside.

Because I *do* want him to kiss me – even though he's leaving at the end of the summer, even though I have other things I should be focusing on, even though, even though.

'Linny?'

'Yeah?'

Every ball in the pit is motionless.

'Am I imagining this,' he says, 'or do I still have poop in my hair?'

He bends over and, sure enough, there's a short white streak near the crown of his head. 'Only the *tiniest* bit,' I say, and since the magic is pretty much broken, we step out of the pit and gather the rest of our stuff.

Near the lockers I ask, 'Rain check on the movie? I kind of told my parents I'd be home for dinner.'

'Fine with me,' Sebastian says, and then rather sheepishly, 'That means I get to see you twice.'

It's not as good as a kiss, but it's still like someone has tied a thousand balloons to my body: so light, so happy, at risk of floating away.

Mom and Dad zap away the helium. At dinner, there is a grilling (and I don't just mean the hamburgers that Dad brought back from Shake Shack).

Mom's updo is tighter than usual; it's pulling her eyebrows into near-straight lines. 'I called three times. Where were you all day?' she says, taking a sip of white wine.

You know, just fought off an army, almost got kissed in a ball pit, searched for a lost chapter of a soon-to-be famous manuscript, and ate two tons of pecan brittle.

I swallow a bite of hamburger. 'Hanging out with a friend.'

Dad says, 'Cass or Ray?' He's tucked a white napkin into his shirt collar, which I know drives Mom insane.

'I do have other friends.'

Mom sets down her fork. 'And where did you meet this friend?' 'This friend' rolls off her tongue like it's a disease, as if she's about to add it to the list on her office wall, right under *S is for Syphilis*.

'Silver Springs. He volunteers there, too.'

'Well,' she says, 'is he free four Sundays from now?'

Dropping my burger, I panic. 'Why?' In my mind, I hear Grace laughing, saying, 'Why do you *think*?'

'Please tell me you haven't forgotten about the Future Doctors of America luncheon we're hosting.'

Silence punctures the room.

'You have,' she says. 'Well. Mark it in your day planner, July tenth, like I told you. Why did we even *buy* you that planner if you aren't going to use it? Anyway, the Jeffrey's boy can't make it, and I've ordered enough sandwiches for exactly twenty people.'

Still panicking here. 'So?'

'So invite your friend. I have a right to know with whom my daughter's spending her time.' She points a slender finger at my plate. 'And don't just eat your burger. The vegetables are there for a reason.'

*

As soon as I finish my fresh-from-the-can green beans, I rush back into the safety of my closet, where I rewatch the footage from today. Since I angled the camera upward while filming him, Sebastian appears ten thousand feet tall – because in my mind, he is. Then there's the moment when he takes over the camera, and suddenly I'm full screen. What's strange is, for a moment, I look so blissfully happy, the girl I wish I were all the time. Do I really smile that big around him, like he just told me I get free ice cream for a year?

I rub my fingers over my lips, remembering how it felt to kiss him: soft and reckless at the same time. I rewind and rewind, head growing hotter until I feel thoroughly flambéed. All I know is, when I flick off the lights promptly at 9:00 p.m., the first thing that pops into my brain is Sebastian's hand in mine.

THE LEFT-BEHINDS (scene 10)

<u>LINNY'S BEDROOM</u>

LINNY slips the yellow sundress over her head. It stands in stark contrast to the black-and-white everything else. She runs her hands over the dress to smooth it out, and the yellow transfers like paint onto her hands. It drips onto the carpet.

Drop by drop, color inches into the room.

She spreads her fingers and tries to lift off the ground.

Sebastian

20.

'Gravitational instability is one proposition for the beginning of galaxies. Think of it — our universe could be the result of small perturbations.' *A Brief Compendium of Astrophysical Curiosities*, p. 188

'I talked to your mom last night,' Ana says the next Friday over breakfast. 'She said you texted her.'

Through a mouthful of fried plantains, I say, 'Mhmm.' After the ball pit, I sent her four words: I'm okay. *Te amo.* I wanted her to know that coming to Miami was the right choice. That I don't blame her for the past, but I need to create my own future.

'I think that's great, Sebastian.' Ana beams. 'You look happy. Realmente feliz.'

'Gracias,' I say, getting up and putting my dish in the sink. 'I am.' And maybe it's not just Linny — maybe it's this whole place. Being here with Ana and my dad in Miami. Speaking some Spanish in the house.

She pushes up the sleeves of her magenta robe. Like she's prepping for heavy conversation. 'Is there something else going on with you, *mijo*?' There's that word again! It gives me heart palpitations. 'You seem *extra* happy.'

I inspect the grout between the kitchen tiles. 'Er — nope. Just . . . today could be a very good day.'

'What's today?'

'Nothing in particular.'

'No, it's definitely something. Do you . . .' She slaps one hand into the other. 'You have a date with this girl from Silver Springs, am I right?'

'No.'

'*Sí*. Out with it.'

I roll my eyes. 'We're just watching a movie.'

Ana stands up. Ruffles my hair. 'That's how it starts.'

(See A THEORY ON BEGINNINGS*)*

After five hours of cleaning the Silver Springs kitchen and unsuccessfully questioning Álvaro about his disappearance, Linny and I are padding the pavement to my aunt's condo, her bike rolling between us. My mind's blasting into hypergear, repeating: *Movie. Movie. Movie.*

What if I mess this up? What if I tell her my best joke ('So, a duck walks into an antigravity chamber . . .'), and she doesn't laugh? What if I sit down on the couch and it makes that *pfft* sound, and she thinks it's me?

This is an effing minefield.

When Linny props her bike against the rack, I check for Ana's Toyota in the lot. Nope. She's out.

It's just Linny and me. Alone.

I repeat: ALONE. Truly alone.

I try not to dwell on that. Try not to dwell on the tanned freckles on her shoulders or the stamped feeling of her hand in mine. *But* . . . I have a hot girl, alone, in an empty apartment. For a moment, I feel slightly like (insert ultramanly cool guy here). Then I remember I'm a seventeen-year-old wannabe astrophysicist who's only had one girlfriend.

So, yeah.

Inside, it's blistering. Steam practically rises from the couch. Ana is willing to compromise on everything but the temperature. She says the heat is good for the skin.

'It's good for the skin,' I blurt out, because that's what a normal person would say, right? Sometimes I wonder if I have verbal dysdecorum, which makes sufferers lose the ability to censor their speech.

'Um, what is?' Linny says.

I mumble, 'Nothing, nothing,' and search for a distraction. 'Chicken!' I exclaim, like I've just spotted one sprinting across the yard. 'I can make chicken.'

'That's . . . cool.'

Shaking my head – 'No, I mean, what I meant to say is, are you hungry?'

She's full-on grinning. 'I could eat.'

She follows me into the kitchen as I try to remember where Ana keeps . . . almost everything. Recipes. Baking trays. Spices.

Linny pulls up a chair to the breakfast bar. Studies me intently. 'I didn't know you cooked.'

'Oh yeah' – dusting off the comment – 'all the time.'

I crack open a window, attempt to let out the heat. Unfortunately, it's just as sauna-ish outside.

'Right,' I say, largely to the spoons. 'Let's do this!'

I fumble around for some onions and tomatoes and olives, pull some chicken legs from the fridge, dump everything into a pan (or maybe it's a lid?), find salt and pepper silos on the table, and give the whole thing a really good grind. (That sounds wrong somehow?)

Chicken in the oven, I turn on a timer – fifty-five minutes

should do it! In the meantime, we select a documentary on Netflix about a man who walks a tightrope between the Twin Towers. Then we avoid the couch like it's made of combustible materials. Sitting down means determining how close we're going to be. When it becomes more awkward to hover than take the plunge, I bravely park myself in the middle of the left cushion. Linny plops down on the right. The blob nearly eats her.

'Comfy,' she says, and I laugh. Then she notices the extra pillows. 'So do you, um, sleep here?'

Uh. Have I really just lured her into my bed, after one kiss and a hand hold? 'Yeah,' I say, and bullet forward. 'This-movie-looks-really-good-let's-press-Play-shall-we?'

And it's true, the movie's awesome, and it's even more awesome watching her watch the awesomeness. Eyes: *brilliante*. She really loves this stuff. Mom says that when I'm reading *A Brief Compendium of Astrophysical Curiosities*, I have this enrapt expression on my face. Like a great white could be gnawing at my lower extremities and I wouldn't notice. Now I know the face she means.

'How much of a movie snob are you?' I tease.

She acts offended. 'I'm not a snob!'

'I bet you're one of those people who spell *theater* with an *r-e* at the end and deliberately mispronounce it *thea-TRA*.'

That elicits an eye roll.

I inch a bit closer.

'I'm glad we're hanging out,' I say.

'Technically speaking, we hang out all the time.'

'I mean outside of an old-people's home, without five other people asking for the remote in the game room. And not during a manuscript hunt.'

What I don't say: *It's nice to act our age. Nice to forget about the people without teeth and the smell of sickness. And as much as it kills me to admit it, nice to forget about Álvaro – for just a second. To watch a movie with a cute girl without wondering how I'm going to push 'I'm your son' from my mouth.*

She smiles. 'I know what you mean.' And maybe she actually does.

Pulling lip balm from her pocket, she strokes it over her lips. Does that mean something? Am I supposed to kiss her?

All my systems react.

God dammit, an instructional manual would be useful. *How to Hold a Girl's Hand in Three Simple Steps*. It was so easy in the ball pit.

Yeah, I tell myself. Because *she* took the first quantum leap. Just like at the playground.

Twenty minutes into the movie, as my hand is within 0.002 millimeters of Linny's, the back door swings open and – *clomp, clomp, clomp –* Ana treads into the kitchen. 'Seb, I got a pizza! Not sure what we had in the fridge.' Rounding the corner with the box in her hands, she sees us. '*Hola!*'

Here's the weird thing: Linny and I spring apart. Like we were *doing* something (or thinking about it, at least).

Linny's embarrassed.

I'm *mortified*.

Ana introduces herself by scooping Linny off the couch and into a bear hug. 'I've heard so much about you,' she says, which is not strictly true but humiliating nonetheless.

'Oh,' Linny says, 'good things, I hope.'

'Very good things,' Ana says, at which point I stand up, grab her elbow, shepherd her back into the kitchen.

Whispering to her, 'Not cool.'

'What? I want to make her feel at home. *Mi casa es su casa.*' She holds up her hands. 'But okay, okay, making myself scarce.'

Except she doesn't. Even though Ana's not my mom, she's still mom-ish. Example: She pokes her head out of her bedroom every fifteen minutes. The implication: Linny and I are going to fly on top of each other as soon as she leaves.

I wish we were. I wish we were doing everything there is to do.

But instead of jumping her, I spend the next half hour peering at her from the corner of my eye. Waiting for my cooling mechanism to kick in. Then slowly, slowly, slowly – inching my hand toward hers. Initiate countdown:

Tres,

dos,

(Can you die of anticipation?),

uno.

Mission complete!

Just like in the ball pit, I cradle her fingers in mine. Trace little circles in her palm.

Neither of us looks at the other, like our hands are independent beings. Like we're casually just watching a movie while our hands are making out. I don't want to look down, either. It feels too much like I'm intruding. Like I'm Aunt Ana-ing the situation.

But then, from the corner of my eye, I see Linny turn her neck an inch. *She's* looking at our hands, so I do, too.

Can a hand be hot? Just a hand by itself? (Not like a severed hand or anything. I'm explaining this badly.) It's just that she has a constellation of freckles by her wrist. And cute fingers.

And her skin is unnaturally soft.

Two minutes later, the timer beeps in the kitchen. It's loud. Obvious. But both of us stay still for an inappropriately long time. Hands squeezed together. At some point, the moment has to end. But I'm disappointed that Linny's the one to break away first. Our hands have been smashed together long enough that they make a sticky *thwunk* when separated.

'Shouldn't you take out the chicken?' she says.

From Ana's bedroom: 'Sebastian, turn off the timer!'

So I spring to a stand and trail into the kitchen, Linny at my heels. I slip on some oven mitts and wrench the dish from the oven. It smells . . . interesting.

On the breakfast bar, I set some plates, serve the chicken, and hand Linny a fork. I'm standing across from her, so I witness the first bite. She's smiling. Yes! Smiling! I've done it!

She chews, chews, swallows.

'Sebastian, I have to tell you something.' Smiling turns to laughing. Pointing at the chicken with her fork – 'This is literally the worst thing I've ever eaten.'

'Seriously?'

'Seriously.'

I cut off a small piece and put it in my mouth. Immediately spit it out in an attractive way. 'Oh, gross. What have I done? It's like Frankenstein's monster.'

This makes her laugh even harder. I lose it because she's losing it.

Ana pops into the kitchen. 'Have I missed something?'

I can't catch my breath for long enough to answer her. That is, until she picks up a fork, about to sample the chicken.

'No!' Linny and I yell simultaneously, and she drops

the utensil like it's molten lead.

We decide that pizza is the safer option, so we watch the rest of the documentary while scarfing down double-cheddar slices. As the credits roll, I'm dreading her leaving. We stare at the ticking list of names. Then in rapture at the blank screen until it becomes too weird.

'So,' Linny says.

'So,' I say.

She clears her throat. 'I should probably . . .'

'Yeah, of course.'

We clean up the plates, and I walk her to the front door, where Linny – backpack in hand – clears her throat. 'Um, what are you doing on July tenth?'

Random. But I grin and give an answer I'd heard in a nineties sitcom. 'Hanging out with you.'

Her smile is state-of-Florida big. 'You probably should ask me what we're doing before you commit.'

'Okay, what are we doing?'

'It's kind of awkward, but my parents are having this Future Doctors of America lunch, and they asked me to invite you.' Both of my eyebrows arch toward the ceiling. 'But you totally don't have to come,' she adds, fingers dancing at her sides. 'It's just lots of miniature cheese sandwiches and conversations about medical-school rankings – kind of like gladiatorial combat, except we battle with SAT scores instead of swords, and I spend most of the time looking out the window and wishing I were at the opposite end of the globe, but if you were there it might be tolerable.'

Wow. The heaping-gulp-of-words thing must be contagious.

I take three steps forward. 'Then I'll be there.' Suddenly, I'm hyperaware of her lips. How they're approximately fifteen inches away from mine, definitely within kissing distance. 'We can lock ourselves in your room or something.' I mean it as a joke – to avoid the party – but it sounds like something I'd happily donate my moon rock collection to do.

I lean in as she breathes the words, 'That would be –'

Ana cuts in. 'It was really nice to meet you, Linny!'

Oh no, not now.

I turn around, and Ana's left hand is on the living-room doorframe. Eyes firmly on us.

Kissing moment, killed.

PLEASE, future self. Solve the mysteries of time travel so I can return to this exact moment and *not* have it messed up.

'You too,' Linny says to Ana, and then to me as she's slipping out the door: 'See you tomorrow, okay?'

'Yeah,' I muster, watching her hips swish down the front path. I close the door and glare at Ana.

'What?' she says.

'What?'

'Oh, did I just . . . ?'

'Yep.'

She runs her hands through her waves. 'Oops.' Pause. 'You really like her, don't you?'

'You could say that.'

'Let's talk.' Beckoning me into the kitchen – '*Ven conmigo*. I'm making *frijoles negros*.'

Like black beans will fix the situation.

I march in anyway, as Ana thrusts a wooden spoon into my hand and orders me to stir. Little waves of concern etch her forehead. 'I like her, too,' she says. 'But, now that I've seen you together, I just . . .'

Stirring vigorously, I create a vortex of beans. 'Just what?'

'Don't you think you have enough on your mind? I assumed this was a summer thing, but it seems like more than that.'

The air goes still for a moment. I deliberate between words. 'What if it is?'

'Is what?'

'More.'

Breathing in – 'Then I'm concerned that you're setting yourself up for disappointment with . . . too many things.'

I drop the spoon into the pot and stare at her. 'I'm handling this. And besides, she knows about Álvaro. She's helping.'

Ana unties and reties her apron strings. Picks up a knife and begins to chop (read: attack) an onion. 'Okay,' she says, 'you're right, you're right, it's your business.'

The knife smacks against the wooden cutting board. In the air: the sharp tang of onions. Ana swipes at her cheeks as a few tears run. 'It's just the onions,' she says. 'I'm not crying.'

Extraño. Why the need for clarification?

She repeats it again, forcefully, eyes veiny with red. 'I'm not crying.'

It's an interesting chemical reaction, actually. Enzymes convert the amino acids of the onion into sulfenic acid, which rearranges itself and mists into the air, irritating the eyes. But the onions aren't *that* strong. I'm two feet away, and my eyes are fine.

She says, 'You're a good boy, Sebastian.' Dropping the knife, she presses a hand over my heart. 'Just protect this, okay?'

Linny

21.

WHO: Neurosurgeon Carl Strinberg of a Mount Sinai hospital
WHEN: Three weeks in 2010
WHY: After performing an unsuccessful operation on a nine-year-old car crash victim, Dr. Strinberg hiked the Adirondacks alone, trying to come to terms with the loss. 'At some point I decided to turn around,' he writes in his memoir. 'I always urge my patients to stand up and face their trauma. What kind of person would I have been if I'd kept running?'
NOTES: Stop. Running. Grace.

Ten days later is the Fourth of July, which my sister loves. She never misses an opportunity to strum out 'The Star-Spangled Banner' on her guitar, holding the notes in her best Jimi Hendrix impression. Besides her black boots, that guitar is the only thing I'm positive she took with her. I wonder whom she plays for now, if that's how she's supplementing her life savings on the road.

Instead of being Grace's groupie on Independence Day, I pin Marla's memos to all the notice boards, to which Cass (during her one-day-a-week volunteering) takes the liberty of adding handwritten messages.

NO DRINKING ALCOHOLIC BEVERAGES BY THE POOL.
unless it's tequila. then it's A-OK!
SHOES MUST BE WORN AT ALL TIMES.

extra points if they're leopard print
FIREWORKS ARE NOT PERMITTED.
 . . . until after 5 o'clock, when this place will look like Chinese New Year

'Such a troublemaker,' I half joke, and she winks at me like *It's the only way to live.*

In her infinite coolness, Cass has not one but five invitations to Independence Day bashes. I have five by extension but decide only to attend the Silver Springs 'party,' a liberally used term, considering all the restrictions.

Once there, it's difficult for me to concentrate on anything but Sebastian, flipping burgers on the Rent-A-Grill across the courtyard. He's wearing bright-red swim shorts, and every time he stretches his hands over his head, I can see his back dimples. He has *back dimples*, for goodness sake. I want to press my thumbs into them.

'If you look at him for too long,' Álvaro says, suddenly appearing at my shoulder, 'you will burn a hole in his head.'

Seventeen different shades of pink etch up my neck. Apparently I'm not as covert as I think.

'Oh,' I say, 'I wasn't . . .'

'It will stay between us, *mi amor.*' A low-burning cigarillo is in one hand, and with the other, he strokes his stubbly beard. It's white, as is most of the hair on his head – snowy tendrils springing from the black like untended garden weeds. Even the skin on his hands is changing color. Where it was brown before, now it's elephant gray.

And I really don't want to notice this, but his chest hair's whitening, too.

He's been wearing the same linen shirt for two days now, scraps of paper overflowing from his pocket. Looking at him, it occurs to me that he's probably doing the same thing I do with film: gathering little moments and squirreling them away.

Álvaro rotates his head at an abnormal angle, as if warming up for yoga or a bullfight. 'What do you want to do?' he says. Smoke drifts into my face.

'Well.' I cough. 'I was thinking about getting something to eat, maybe see if –'

He holds up a hand to stop me. It shakes like a windblown leaf. 'No, no. I mean with your life.'

Whoa. That's a little deep for a pool party.

It's not fair that he can do this so effortlessly: shoot me a question that cuts me to the quick. The more times I ask him about Joe, the easier he slips away from the topic. I wish I could be like him. I wish I could have the kind of voice – the kind of presence – that grips people's hearts.

He's just so darn *intense*. Sometimes he'll hypnotize Sebastian and me for hours, relaying stories about his childhood in Cuba. Or I'll arrive in the morning and he'll be rapid-fire punching his typewriter; I almost see smoke rising from the keys.

Other times he's not so okay. Sometimes he looks – I'll just go ahead and say it – dead, like the ghost I thought he was. When I open his desk drawers, I find them stuffed with odd bits of string, more scraps of paper, and leftover napkins from the cafeteria.

I figure that happens when you get old. There are good days. There are weird days.

I parrot his question. 'What do I want to do with my life?'

If he hears me, he gives no indication, just puffs away at his cigarillo. It dangles and bobs as he speaks. 'I'll tell you *un secreto pequeño, niña.* Only two things matter in life. How we love and how much we love. You'll remember that, yes?'

See what I mean? *Intense.* He's looking at me like he's handing me a sliver of his heart. I stutter, 'Yeah – yes, of course.'

Stamping out the remains of his cigarillo in one of the red, white, and blue cupcakes, Álvaro points to a jug of yellowish liquid on the snack table. 'Have you tasted *la limonada*?'

'Um, no,' I say.

Resting his cane against the snack table, he fills two Dixie cups with a lemonade-like substance and offers me one. I take a wary sip. The stinging liquid hits my tongue like an atom bomb. I fight it – but it fights harder, spewing from my lips and Impressionist-painting the concrete.

Tilting back his head, he drains the Dixie cup in one gulp. 'I added vodka.'

Ha! I wonder if *vodka* is the same in every language.

Someone's playing the Eagles' greatest hits over the loudspeaker. Grace's absence slaps me in the face again – she *loves* the Eagles, even though I joke with her that they're an old-people's band. (I guess I have definitive proof now!)

Álvaro snaps his fingers. 'We should dance, *sí*?' Next to the grill is a makeshift dance floor with two or three couples shuffling around it. At first I think he's joking, but he extends a hand, skin crackly like clay baked too long in the kiln. Together we walk (ultraslowly) to the dance floor.

But once there, he is anything but slow. The only thing I can liken him to is a sheet in the Miami breeze, the way it twists fluidly in elegant motion. He's graceful, swift, measured – everything I'm not, apparently.

'Bah!' he exclaims, ten seconds into the dance. 'You are

horrible!' Except he pronounces it in Spanish, *whore-ee-blay*, which sounds harsher somehow. 'I'll teach you,' he says. 'First, stop moving. Enough movement for right now. Your hand, here. Begin on the second beat.'

It should be weird, spinning around the floor with Álvaro Herrera. A month ago, if you'd told me I'd be dancing with a presumed-dead novelist on the Fourth of July, I'd tell you to quit messing with me, but after I learn the basic beat, it feels almost natural. *He* feels almost natural. Sort of grandfatherly. Not that my grandpa had the grace of a professional dancer or even once spiked the *limonada* . . .

'There! *Perfecto!*' Álvaro seems genuinely proud, although I'm still crunching his toes every other step. 'I tell you, I am the best teacher. No one in Miami could move like me. Next week, I'll teach you tango. These dances, very sensual. Done with the right person? Enough to fall in love.' His eyes roam over to where Sebastian continues to flip burgers. 'You are falling, no?'

My voice has something in common with driftwood: it splinters. 'Falling – in love with – Sebastian?'

'Sebas-TI-AN! You look at him like he cups the whole world in his hands. This is a universal look. Believe me when I tell you I know this look.' He spins me in and out, the hem of my shirt flapping with the movement. 'So when do we tell him?'

'*We?*'

His eyes crinkle at the corners as he dissolves into a peal of laughter. 'Oh! *Mi amor! Lo siento*, but it was too easy! No, I will never tell, but you must.' After several more intricate steps, the laughter and the crinkling fade. What replaces them is something much bleaker. The cut – now scarring on his forehead – still reminds me of lightning, and appropriately so, because his face is a thunderstorm. 'You must,' he repeats in a deep baritone. 'You must. You must. If you listen to any one thing, listen to this. Sometimes there are no second chances to say how we feel. I only want to make you understand. You understand this, yes?'

He says it so earnestly, my lungs feel as if they've been pinpricked. 'Yeah,' I gasp out. 'Of course.'

This whole time, I've been thinking of him like Grace. But suddenly I wonder if he *has* a Grace.

'Good. So . . .' He stops dancing and shouts across the courtyard: '*Oye!* Sebas-TI-AN!'

Mildly horrified, I say, 'What are you doing?'

'Giving you a chance, *mi amor.*'

Sebastian appears moments later, wielding a greasy spatula like a baton. My eyes flick between them — Sebastian to Álvaro and back again. Positioned side by side, the resemblance is startling, like they're the same person on opposite ends of the age spectrum. Álvaro releases my grip and makes the swap: me for the spatula. 'I'll take that,' he says, shifting away, 'and you take her. Dance! Dance!'

Slightly confused, Sebastian winds his arms around my waist, his hands on my lower back. Let me repeat that: Hands. Lower. Back.

Muchas gracias, Álvaro.

Sebastian's whole face is lit up. 'Hi.'

'Hi,' I say.

'So, should I be jealous that he got the first dance?'

My instinct is to lower my eyes, embarrassed, but there's nowhere to look except the diminishing gap between us. At my high school's dances, teachers usually dart around with flashlights to ensure we're at least four inches apart, as if three inches of separation automatically leads to babies. Sebastian and I are approaching the danger zone.

'Oh yeah,' I say. 'Superjealous.'

Is it wrong that I want to slam my body into his and roll around on the dance floor in a tangle of limbs like it's the end of the world? Probably.

I am falling, no?

He pulls me infinitesimally closer. 'I like this,' he says.

It's an almost perfect moment – almost, because Cass charges in a minute later, breath reeking of that lemonade. Overhead are blue and white streamers, and she yanks one of them down to wrap it around her neck like a scarf. 'You missed a f-freaking great party,' she slurs. 'But I thought – ya know? Cass, you should be with your friend. Tha's all I thought. So here I am!'

'Are you drunk?' Sebastian asks. He's not a huge Cass fan – I can tell.

'Duh.' She winks, hiccups. 'And I have a sur-prise for you, Lin-a-Lin-Lin.' From her purse she extracts a blue bikini like she's yanking a rabbit from a hat. ''S for you. Go put it on.'

I tell her that underneath my T-shirt I'm already wearing a one-piece. (Florida 101: Always be prepared for the beach.)

'Purrrfect,' she coos as she drops her purse and wrenches up her dress, revealing her sparkly two-piece and scintillating figure. Discarding the dress in a heap on the concrete, she grabs one of my hands from Sebastian's shoulder. Grabs *his* hand, too, and starts dragging us toward the pool. 'Take a walk on the wiiiild side.'

A *swim* on the wild side, she means. Flip-flops gripping the concrete, I say, 'Should you be swimming? Plus, I haven't seen anyone in there all summer.'

'All the more reason to jump. You even know how to have

fun, Lin-a-Lin-Lin? Come on, on, on.' For a moment it's like last year – Cass urging me on to do wild things, except that last year Grace was at her side.

Metal barriers guard the pool to avoid accidental drowning. We hop over them as Cass prods me to strip. Reluctantly, I undress and cover myself with my hands – although I don't have enough hands for everything I want to cover. I mind-film myself a thousand more.

Next to Cass, Sebastian peels off his T-shirt and . . . Whoa. I have to close my lips to keep my heart from lurching out of my mouth. He's like a drawing – all lean lines and perfect hues. In the sunlight, his skin's the color of honey. Back dimples galore.

Teetering at the edge, Cass yells, 'Now!' and I can feel a hundred eyes on us as we pierce the waterline. Streams of water balloon outward. For three seconds it's dreamily quiet, and I remember when Cass, Grace, and I were at swim camp three summers ago, and we shared secrets underwater. Warbles of words we could only speak when no one could understand us.

I told them I'd never kissed a boy.

Cass confessed that, sometimes, she wished she'd been born into another family. Grace said she wanted to be a bird.

My feet touch the warm bottom, and I spring weightlessly upward, breaking the surface again. Sebastian's a blur beside me. I blink, rub the chlorine from my eyes, and watch him shake his head like a dog. Beads of water run down his neck. Down his chest. Probably down his . . .

Holy bananas.

To avoid giving too much away, I finagle a few curls to shade my eyes. Even still, I can tell he's studying me. Because I can't help it; I imagine water sloshing as he walks over, reaches up, and gently parts my hair, tucking wet chunks behind my ears.

But then something abso-freaking-lutely weird happens. He actually does it – walks over, tucks my hair. 'There,' he says, dark-gray eyes catching mine. 'Much better.'

I disintegrate, reassemble myself, and disintegrate again. I want to tell Grace. I *need* to tell Grace.

There are fireworks.

No – I mean *actual* fireworks. The sky pops, becoming a constellation of fizzling color. I wish I had a waterproof camera so I could film it from this angle. Us, down below. Above, all the residents peering up in wonder, like kids seeing the sky lit up for the first time. Álvaro looks happy, too – the happiest I've seen him in weeks.

But then he glances down at the pool, to where we're standing. He stares at us with no recognition in his eyes, like we're not even people but seaweed floating in the ocean. Maybe worse than that. Maybe the water's turning us invisible. He's staring like nothing's there at all.

THE LEFT-BEHINDS (scene 11)

<u>**CARSON FAMILY DINING ROOM**</u>

There are little bits of color in the room: orange flames atop sixteen silver sparklers, lit on a small cake. DAD, MOM, and CASS surround LINNY as they sing her 'Happy Birthday.'

LINNY smiles when the song ends but is obviously unhappy.

CASS
(excitedly)
Go on, blow out the candles!
(chanting)
Blow – them – out, blow – them – out!

LINNY does. A hopeful pause as she waits for her wish.

As DAD cuts the cake, the home phone rings in the kitchen – so loud that it rocks the whole house.

LINNY's eyes widen. She rushes from the table, stumbling to the kitchen against the earthquake-like vibrations. Everyone watches her, unsure.

LINNY
I'll get it! I'll get it!

She answers, breathless.

LINNY (continued)
Hello?

On the other end of the line, we hear a man's voice and banjo music.

CALLER
Hello, there. My name's Buck Johnson, and I know what you've been thinking to yourself. It's that time of year again, and my lawn needs landscaping! I'm here to tell you that at Buck Johnson and Company –

LINNY crashes the receiver on the countertop, taking a chunk out of the granite. Pieces of the ceiling crumble and fall.

She runs a hand over her back, checking for something. When she doesn't find it, she stares at the kitchen wreckage like there's nothing there at all.

Sebastian

22.

'The concept of parallel worlds is passionately contested, but who knows? In another universe, we could be having the same debate.' *A Brief Compendium of Astrophysical Curiosities*, p. 112

The fabric of my swim trunks is way too thin.

This tops the list of the worst possible times and places to get an erection. In the pool. At an old-people's home. With my father fifteen feet away.

But she looks so goddamn gorgeous.

And this is the smoothest I've *ever* been.

And we are so close to each other, teeny-tiny layers between us.

I tell my mind – and let's face it, the stick of dynamite twenty seconds away from forming in my swim trunks – to chill the eff out. I whip out my best boner-killing material (DEAD-PEOPLE-BLOOD-BLOOD-BLOOD-MICAH-HITTING-ON-MY-MOM) until the threat is 85 percent neutralized.

How I'm managing words, I have no clue. Any more clothes off and I'll need one of those Stephen Hawking machines to speak.

I think: I'm going to kiss her.

I'm going to kiss her right here. Right now.

In a parallel world, I already have.

I'm going to tuck her hair behind her ears and kiss her, *finally* – a second kiss.

But then *boom, boom* in the sky.

And then Álvaro's eyes on us.

How am I being cock-blocked by my eighty-two-year-old dad?

After the fireworks fizzle out, Linny, Cass, and I leave the pool, grab some cupcakes, and set up camp on the lounge chairs. A rope of wet hair hangs over Linny's shoulder.

Next to me, she licks off the cupcake frosting.

I nearly lose it.

'May I?' Álvaro says, slow-walking up behind us, pointing his cane at an open pool chair. Cass says, 'Sure,' as he lowers himself down. Adjusts his kneecaps. Even over 'The Star-Spangled Banner' playing in the distance, I can hear his cartilage sliding.

'You look like you're part of the picture,' Linny observes, and I see what she means. To Álvaro's back is a mural. Paint chipping. Ocean, seagulls. It's as if he's bobbing along in the water.

Álvaro twists to view the beach scene and says, 'Ah, so I am.' Turning again to us: 'When I was very young, younger than now, I would swim and swim and swim. I wanted to be in' – snapping his fingers – '*las Olimpiadas.*'

Linny smiles. 'The Olympics? So you were really good?'

'Bah! No, I was *horrible*. But that is *juventud*! To be young is to have dreams.' He crinkles his eyebrows at the three of us. 'You must promise me: do not – do not let anyone tell you that because you are young you cannot do things. That you cannot feel things. It is *because* you are young that you can feel *everything*.'

Just like that, Linny's hand drifts toward mine on the lounge chair. And I *do* feel everything, all at once. When the cleaning crew removes the rest of the streamers, we stay. When the music stops late into the night, we stay. Cock-block aside, I wouldn't trade one second of this everything.

It's Sunday morning. Future Doctors of America lunch day. Already eighty degrees and humid as I bike to the address Linny gave me. On my T-shirt is Einstein sticking out his tongue. Considering that I'm drenched in sweat, it feels like he's actually licking me.

A line of parked cars (all with HONOR STUDENT bumper stickers) snakes around Linny's block. Every house is a weird shade of blue, but I identify hers right away. It's the one with the nuclear-green lawn, she texted me. And she's right. Sprinklers lightly spritz. Neon water pools near the gutter. Their white-porcelain flamingo has a weird expression, like it's choking.

I ring the doorbell once. Twice. Three times for good measure.

A striking man with sandy hair answers the door. Next to him is a striking woman in a beige pantsuit, curly hair pulled into a tight bun. Linny's parents. Must be. They look a lot like her. (If Linny were made of plastic. If Linny had a dial in her back, set to Disapproval.) They throw me a look that simultaneously reads *What's your pedigree?* and *I hope we purchased enough sandwiches.*

'Hi,' I hear myself say. 'I'm Sebastian, Linny's friend?' It comes out as a question.

'Ah,' Linny's dad says robotically. 'Please, please, come in.'

I swipe my sneakers four times on the doormat. It's the type of house that requires clean shoes. Kind of like visiting a nanotech lab.

In the all-white foyer, Linny's mom pinches her chin. 'So, Sebastian, are you at all interested in the medical profession?'

On the nervous scale, I'm a twelve out of ten. It doesn't help that, at that exact moment, classical music switches on somewhere in the house. Long, pounding notes that rattle my rib cage. 'I'm actually going to Cal Tech this fall for physics. I want to study – er – dark matter and stuff and eventually solve all the big mysteries of the universe.'

They nod in apparent approval. Strange how they do it simultaneously. Like bobble heads on the same dashboard.

In my periphery, I spot Linny in a sea of Future Doctors of America, chatting with a vampire-pale guy in a sweater vest. When I catch her eye, she mouths *Excuse me* to him and bolts across the living room. Wedges herself between her parents.

'You're here!' she says as if I wouldn't show up.

Linny's dad: 'We were just talking to Sebastian about his future.'

Linny's mom: 'He's interested in physics. Did you know that, darling?' Turning back to me, 'Marilyn's incredibly interested in emerging scientific research as well, aren't you?'

Linny, devoid of emotion: 'Oh yeah. All about it.'

I remember in the ball pit how she told me her parents would – if they had the opportunity – dress her up in scrubs and a stethoscope. Keep her in a cabinet like a china doll, on display for the neighbors. I think I'm getting a glimpse of what she means.

Linny, to me: 'You must be really hungry. Sandwiches?' Without waiting for an answer, she grabs my elbow and yanks me down the hallway. We pass all her school pictures, arranged chronologically in silver frames. In each picture, her smile fades a little more.

Happy.

Moderately happy.

Glum.

And what's with the nail holes a foot above every photo, like other frames used to hang there?

'Sorry, I just had to get out,' Linny says, bursting into the kitchen. The tile is brilliantly white. The counters, bare (except for the sandwiches). A note on the refrigerator reads: *Grocery Store – Celery, Bleach*. 'My parents can be a bit full-on.'

'Trust me,' I say, 'I'll be the first to acknowledge the difficulty of having parents for parents.'

She nods appreciatively, reaches awkwardly behind her back to grab the end of her ponytail. 'Thanks so, so much for coming.'

'No problem,' I tell her. 'Hey, above your pictures in the hallway . . . ?'

'Grace's photos.'

'Oh.'

'They took them down about two months ago. I can't tell if it was for me or for them. . . . Sandwich?'

Lifting the bread of one of them, examining what may be the only colorful object in the house – 'Is that cheese? Why the hell is it pink?'

'Because it's fancy?' Linny presses two fingers into the sandwich's soft flesh. 'A few times a year – same people, same horrible sandwiches.' Pause. 'Do you maybe want to see my room, before my parents drag me back to the party?'

Wait. What?

Girls' rooms are sacred, mysterious spaces. Mars before *Voyager 1*. To be invited in so casually is mind-boggling.

'You have to take off your shoes, though,' she adds at the bottom of the back stairs. 'White carpeting and all.'

Our socked feet quietly touch the floor all the way to her

room. Once there, my eyes flicker around. 'It looks like a clean room.'

'Well, my parents like it tidy.'

'No,' I say, running my hand against one of the near-bare walls. 'I mean like in a hospital or a lab. Where they strip out all the environmental pollutants – no dust or chemicals or anything.'

Linny smirks. 'My parents would probably consider *you* a pollutant.' Counting on her fingers – 'One, you're a boy. And two, you're a boy who's *not* a Future Doctor of America.'

Both mortal sins, I guess. We stifle laughs in silence as I continue to peer around her room.

'You have a turtle.'

'Hector. He's my sister's. But, you know.'

The door to her closet is cracked open wide enough to see inside. 'Why are there pillows?'

'Hmm?'

'On the floor of your closet. Why are there pillows?'

'Oh – um – I kind of hang out in there sometimes. Don't judge me.'

'Never,' I say, heading across the room. 'But I *am* intrigued.' Opening the door wider, I crawl inside on my hands and knees. Turn around and pop my head between two pairs of pants. 'You coming?'

Hesitating for a long moment, her foot taps the stiff carpeting. Then she makes her decision, slowly walking over and ducking inside. The flashlight app on my cell phone illuminates the space as the door clicks shut. Crossing her legs, she plops down on a pillow in front of me.

It's cave-like in here. Hanging clothes instead of stalactites. And a much, much smaller space. Although I did technically *ask* her to enter, nothing has prepared me for being this close to her. I try backing up, but there's nowhere to go except deeper into the collection of fabrics and throw pillows. Too deep, and I'll look like I'm forming a chrysalis.

Silence.

Opening my mouth seems risky. When was the last time I had a breath mint? (Three months ago. Good enough? No way.) But since Linny's not speaking, I take the plunge. 'Have you ever heard of Schrödinger's cat?'

Not my best opener. Even in the near darkness, I can see her eyes squinting into slits as she studies me. 'No,' she says, half smiling.

'It's a thought experiment. A famous one. So, imagine a cat in a box with a vial of poison.'

Her smile vanishes. 'Why would I want to do that? That's horrible.'

Sinking back into the pillow – 'It might sound kind of twisted, but – er – no real cats are in danger, here.' Grasping at the strings of where I was going, I continue, 'Anyway, until you open the box, you don't know if the cat is dead or alive. It exists in both states simultaneously. It's an unknown.' Linny is still squinting. I'm losing her. Cut to the chase! 'And I just think you should just open the box, with your parents, I mean. Just get the whole not-a-doctor thing out in the open, and then you can see –'

'If any of us are still breathing?' She cracks a smile.

'Exactly.'

She inhales all the air in the tiny space and pushes it out again. For a moment, she seems far away. 'What if I open it and the cat's dead?'

'But what if you open it and it's all cute and cuddly and

jumps up and wants to lick your face?'

'You're one to talk.'

'What do you mean?'

'Álvaro. Telling him.'

'That's different,' I say.

'It's actually exactly the same.'

That's when I see it. A black journal, open at the middle, by her right knee. The name *Álvaro Herrera* written all across the page. I pick it up. 'What's this?

'It's my, um . . . Okay, remember when I said that I was a tad bit obsessed with people who disappeared and came back?'

'Yeah?'

'Voilà.'

'Wow, this is so detailed. Did you –'

Pressing a fingertip to my lips – '*Shhh.*'

Beneath the crack in the door, I hear muffled footsteps. Not from downstairs. From *right outside.*

Oh no.

Both of us hold our breath as my pulse enters stroke range. I prepare for the real possibility of the door swinging open. Of Linny's six-foot-four Viking of a dad wrenching me from the closet. Disemboweling me. Entrails all over the white carpeting.

Step, step, step outside.

Maybe it's not Linny's dad? Maybe they have a morbidly obese cat?

Thirty horrifying seconds pass before she removes her finger from my lips. The footsteps have stopped. Whispering – 'I think it's okay now, but we should really go back downstairs.'

I nod and resist the impulse to mention that I'd like to stay here forever with her.

That's when the door whips open. The lights are solar-flare bright.

If ever I wanted to solve the mysteries of the universe, it would be now. Can matter instantaneously disappear? Oh effing please let that be possible.

Because it's her dad.

'Oh.' He almost jumps. 'I – uh – well.'

This is the end of me. Good-bye, cruel world.

Neither Linny nor I speak. It's a three-person staring contest, and there are no winners.

But then, get this! He closes the door.

ESTOY VIVO. I AM ALIVE.

A PERSONAL OBSERVATION ON PARALLEL WORLDS:
In most of them, I'm probably dead.

Linny plummets her head into her hands. Muffled panic – 'Oh my God, did that just happen?'

Whispering – 'Why didn't he kill me?' Had he been Paul, he would have.

'I actually have no idea.' Cracking the door back open, she peeks outside before instructing me to crawl out. 'Quickly, quickly,' she says, panic still in her voice. She darts into the light, stands up, and begins to race out of her room. I dart out, too. As she's shutting her bedroom door, I hear her dad's voice carrying from the kitchen: 'Didn't find her, unfortunately.'

Linny's mom: 'And this is *her* party. I don't know why she would embarrass us like this.'

Linny's dad: 'I don't think that's her goal, dear.'

'And that boy! You saw that boy.'

'Well – yes, yes, I did.'

'She's just so *young*. She has plenty of time for those things after Princeton, but right now she needs to *focus*.'

Linny and I exchange worried, embarrassed glances. She surges to the back stairs while I barrel down the front with a burst of adrenaline.

Maybe I'm wrong, but I swear that later, as Linny's cutting a cake shaped like a pair of surgical scissors, her mom's putting a curse on me from across the room. I don't believe in curses. But I believe that *other people* believe in curses. Her tight lips smack together and apart. I'm too afraid to look at her dad.

I am the undisputed king of lousy first impressions.

Linny

23.

WHO: Astronaut Jeremy Higgs
WHEN: Early 2000s, seven months after his journey to the International Space Station
WHY: He shocked his wife and two children by taking off at 3:00 a.m. in the family truck. After two days with no communication, Higgs called his best friend and fellow astronaut, Wilson Jones, to come join him in the middle of the Mojave Desert. When Jones arrived, Higgs was sprawled out on the truck bed, gazing at the sky. 'Just look at them,' he said when he heard footsteps. 'See, you're the only other person I know who understands – from here on out, it'll never be as good as those stars.'
NOTES: If I could, I would fill the sky with them for you – just please come home.

Deep in the night, I can't switch off my brain. The pipes are whooshing and the floorboards are settling and a whispered hush is cutting through the backyard. Somewhere, a sprinkler turns on. The streetlamp flickers. My cotton sheets net me like a flounder, no matter how many times I kick them down the bed. Usually I like staying awake after midnight – mostly because MomandDad are asleep, and I can hear myself think without crashing into anyone else's thoughts. But right now, I can't swat away what happened at the Future Doctors of America lunch. My dad just *closed the door*. I think he might've shocked me as much as I shocked him. This is the man who showed Grace and me pictures of STDs when she turned fifteen, almost permanently putting us off the opposite sex. And now he's okay with *a boy in my closet*? Excuse my French, but what the hell?

I'm starting to think that contradictions run in the family. It makes sense that Grace came from this sort of father. After all, she is the Contradiction Queen. She wants to free wild things, yet she has a pet box turtle in captivity. She professes the sanctity of sisterhood yet runs away without her sister. Why couldn't she have taken me with her?

Why am I not strong enough to fly away, too?

What Álvaro said at the July 4th party mulls around with thoughts of Grace. *How we love and how much we love.* Rolling onto my stomach, I dig my chin into the pillows. *How we love and how much we love.* He's a hypocrite, too – spouting these words about love, yet he left Sebastian's mom in the dust.

Why?

Okay, definitely can't sleep.

I slip out of bed, add all this to my *Journal of Lost and Found*, and start cross-referencing all the Seahorse and Seashore Drives in the state of Florida and then expand nationally. There are a couple in Georgia and Louisiana and tons throughout the rest of the country. We could spend our entire lives searching for that chapter of his manuscript and come up with squat.

As I'm rolling this around in my mind, my cell phone buzzes with a text from Sebastian: **Knock knock.**

Um – it's two o'clock in the morning, and he's telling me a knock knock joke? I text obligingly: **Who's there?**

Less than ten seconds later, he responds: **Me, in your backyard.**

Oh God. Is he serious?

A faint *plink, plink* rattles my window. I scramble over and (as quietly as possible) jimmy it open, peering along the roofline. There's Sebastian, standing under the porch light, a pebble balanced in his right hand. His hair's adorably bed headed, but he's dressed in day clothes: jeans and a bright-green T-shirt that claims I EDIT WIKIPEDIA.

He's totally serious. And I'm totally freaking out.

'What are you doing here?' I whisper. Yes, I'm happy to see him. Okay, I'm *thrilled* to see him, but Mom has bionic ears. Given my luck, she'll hear our conversation, peek through the blinds, and ground me for a century. Well, I might already be; after the party, she told me to go to my room and didn't even call me down for dinner.

In Sebastian's left hand is a plastic pack of something yellow and glittery. He whispers, 'I come bearing gifts.'

'At two o'clock in the morning?'

He shrugs and stares up at me with his intensely metallic eyes. Waiting. Waiting for me to let him in. Besides the MomandDad issue, the foremost problem is my reindeer-printed pajamas. Quickly throwing on a hoodie is the only option, because I can't leave him standing in the backyard while I change. I curse Prancer, Dancer, and Vixen under my breath and let my words fall down the roofline. 'Don't move.'

Downstairs is pitch-black except for the blinking refrigerator lights. I brace myself for the creaking sound of the back door opening – *screeeee*. Stop. Listen. No sounds from MomandDad's bedroom, thank goodness.

With two rapid flicks of my wrist, I motion him inside, and he tucks the yellow packet underneath his arm.

'I know it's really late,' he whispers. 'Really, *really* late, and

I don't want to get you in trouble or anything, but I got you something and I've been wondering whether I should give it to you, and I couldn't sleep, so I thought I'd just take a chance and drop by.'

I close the door with a quiet *screeeee*, and then everything is dark.

Except for his armpit. It's glowing.

'What *are* those?' I say.

'I kind of need to be in your room to show you properly,' he says sheepishly. 'Otherwise it's stupid.'

I have no knowledge of Boy in Your House at 2 A.M. etiquette, but saying 'No, get out of here' feels rude. Especially when he comes gift in hand (or gift in armpit). Weighing my options, I swivel around and whisper over my shoulder, 'Okay, but you have to be gone in *literally* two minutes.'

We manage to ascend the stairs and enter my room without bumping into anything. Once there, Sebastian pauses by my desk. 'Now close your eyes.'

'What?'

'Just – please?'

He is the weirdest boy I know.

Squeezing my eyes shut, I take several deep breaths and piano my fingers against my pajama bottoms. Somehow I get the sense that Rudolph's mocking me from near my kneecaps (because really, this must look strange).

Vibrations ripple across the carpet. What's he doing? Did he just pull out my desk chair? I hear the package ripping open, the sound of peeling plastic.

'Keep them closed. One more minute. Almost done.'

My brain's hopscotching all over the place – listening for any noises outside the room, wondering what awaits me when I open my eyes.

'Okay,' he says after an eternity. 'Now.'

Oh my.

Above my head is a glow-in-the-dark constellation – twenty or so plastic stars arranged in a swirl on my ceiling. Sebastian's still standing on my desk chair, reaching up to press the last star into the pattern. Before I can say a word, he jumps in: 'If it's too much, I can take them down, but I just thought that your room needed a bit more – er, I don't know, just *something* – soooo are they okay?'

'They're perfect,' I say, a little louder than I should.

He steps down from the chair and shoves it back under the desk. 'Good . . . so . . . enjoy them, and I'll see you tomorrow?'

'No!' I whisper, snatching his hand as he walks toward the door.

No? Why no? What the hell are you doing, Linny? 'You should stay for a few more minutes, so we can – um – enjoy them together. Just for a little bit. I'm not tired anyway.' Before I lose my nerve, I plop down on my carpet and, releasing my grip on his hand, softly pat the spot next to me.

His grin extends from ear to ear. 'Okay. For a little bit.'

We lie next to each other on our backs, our fingertips touching but nothing else. A little bit turns into three, four, five minutes. A peaceful silence falls over the room. Who else could I do this with? No one. Not even Grace. I know there's no one else who'd tap on my window in the dead of night just to plant stars on my ceiling.

'You called me hot,' I say.

'Huh?'

'At the bookstore. You called me hot.'

I hear him shrugging, shoulders rubbing against the carpet. 'You *are* hot.'

'*Cass* is hot. *My sister* is hot.'

'Linny-I'm-a-boy-just-trust-me-okay?' he says ultraquickly, as if to bypass the subject. 'So what's your wish?'

'Does it count if the stars are plastic?'

'Of course.'

I take a deep breath and hold it. 'You first.'

Instead of answering, he rolls over to face me and, with one finger, traces a slow line up and down my arm. Maybe he *is* answering.

Oh my goodness, is this happening?

I roll over on my side, too, and suddenly he's the only thing in frame. His face snaps into ultradefinition – all the puzzle pieces falling into place. I can see each one of his eyelashes. As he leans in closer, his nose touches mine, and we match each other blink for blink.

He speaks slowly, directly into my mouth. 'You terrify me, Linny.'

I terrify *him*? I'm only 60 percent sure I'm breathing.

'You weren't supposed to be part of the equation,' he says. 'But I'm really, really glad you are.'

Please, please, please let this actually be happening. 'Um, thank you,' I say.

He smiles nervously. 'I guess this is the point where I give you a one-liner to sweep you off your feet.'

I smirk. 'I'm already lying down.'

'Point taken. In that case, I should . . . I should kiss you.'

'Maybe you should.'

'Okay, I will.'

'Good.'

'It's settled then. I'm going to kiss you.'

'Sebastian.'

He draws his mouth the final inch toward me and − Whoa. Just, whoa. Every ounce of sexual tension stored throughout the summer lurches into my lips. His hand finds my face and pulls me even closer, then it's not just the stars but *me* glowing from the inside out.

To be clear: I've made out with guys before, but it always felt like sword fighting and sounded slippery, like fish flopping in a shallow pool. Not this. This is fingers-tangled-in-hair, can't-catch-your-breath, moan-inducing, end-of-the-world-type kissing. Movies don't do this justice. *Words* don't do this justice.

Lips still touching mine, he says, 'You have no idea how long I've wanted to do that for real.'

'Eons,' I say.

'Centuries,' he says, kissing me again and again and again. Then he looks up. 'Although, I do think your turtle is judging us.'

'He's a very judgmental turtle.'

By the time we say good night, the moon has swung off to the side and the (nonplastic) stars are losing their full glow. From the front yard, I watch him bike into the milky blackness. When he's a neon dot at the end of the road, I mouth *Bye* even though he can't see or hear it and then stand with my arms open, palms open, heart open, until I rush back inside, up the stairs, to Grace's bedroom door; and it's only when I'm about to twist her doorknob that I remember. Her absence hurricanes through me, nearly blows me away.

But I still twist her doorknob. I still step into her room, stupidly hoping against all impossibility that she's plunked on the floor, records spread around her, telling me, 'Oh hey, Linny. I've been waiting for you.'

THE LEFT-BEHINDS (scene 12)

GRACE'S BEDROOM – DEAD OF NIGHT

After deliberating for a moment, LINNY seizes the cup and string.

LINNY
(serious)

How'd you do it?

GRACE
(drowsy, like she's just woken up)

Do what?

LINNY

Grow your wings.

GRACE

Oh. I – I don't really know. I just wanted them, I guess.

LINNY

What if I want them, too?

GRACE
(lovingly)

Then you'll get them, my Linzer Torte.

Sebastian

24.

'Just think: in the scope of the human universe, not so long ago, Newton's third law of motion was still a new phenomena. Who's to say that – twenty years from now – we won't say the same thing about all the possibilities mentioned here?' *A Brief Compendium of Astrophysical Curiosities*, p. 399

A THEORY ON KISSING, FEATURING NEWTON'S THIRD LAW:
For every action, there is an equal and opposite reaction. But you will never fully understand this until there is a girl pressing her lips against yours in the same way that you are pressing your lips against hers.

Micah calls five days after the kiss. Although I'm still stoked about it – and even more stoked that there has been *additional* kissing – I gloss over the details of showing up in Linny's backyard with a packet of plastic stars. Micah would probably call me whipped. After a series of BOW CHICA WOW WOWs (him) and SHUT UPs (me), he asks, 'So hey, did you decide on a costume yet?'

Cass has a Halloween party tonight. Yes, Halloween, because (a direct quote from her): 'Getting to buy a costume only once a year is total bullshit.' Apparently she throws a massive blowout every summer. Sends the same invitations:

KEG, JELL-O SHOTS, AND BYOB AT CASA CASS
DRESS UP TO GET MESSED UP

'Nope,' I say to Micah. Unless I want to invent my own superhero, go to the party as Professor Perspiration. (Florida. Summer. Enough said.) For the last seven years, Micah and I have coordinated our Halloween costumes. Stupid, I know – but *two* mad scientists or *two* Super Mario Bros. make a bigger impact than one.

'How about a really ripped Ninja Turtle?' Micah suggests.

'Isn't that just a Ninja Turtle?'

'Point taken. Oh, oh, how about – what's that guy's name? James Dean? Girls eat up that leather jacket shit.'

'That would involve *buying* a leather jacket.'

'What's your budget?'

'Twelve dollars.'

'Ah . . . what's your mom wearing tonight?'

'Good-bye.'

Ana rushes in with her purse, dressed in scrubs and late for work. She hands me a twenty – 'For your costume,' she says – and then plants a kiss on my forehead with, '*Mwa*, be good.' I lock up a few minutes later on my way to Silver Springs.

I get there twenty minutes earlier than usual. On purpose. Don't get me wrong – I love hanging out with Linny. *Especially* after The Night of the Plastic Stars. But it would be nice to have some time with him alone, just Álvaro and me. But when he opens the door, his hair's standing on end. Like the victim of a lightning strike.

'Bad time?' I say, cautious.

He flicks his head from left to right, checking down the hall. 'Did you bring food?'

'Er – should I have?'

'*Sí.*'

'Oh. Okay, I'll – I'll be right back. *Uno momento.*' In a faraway corner of my mind, it probably occurs to me that this is abnormal behavior, but in the moment, I only think burgers. Miami has tons of food trucks scattered around the city and along the beach. Korean bites. Fish tacos. And one right outside Silver Springs: María's Cocina, which specializes in ground beef and chorizo patties on a Cuban roll. The nurses are always raving about them, so I purchase five (I'm not sure how hungry Álvaro is, but maybe five burgers is excessive) and spring back upstairs.

This time when the door swings open, the scent of chorizo hits Álvaro's nose, and I gain immediate entry. Sitting at his desk chair, he spreads out three burgers on his lap. Unwraps the tin foil and lets heat rise up in the air. Handing me two – 'Here, eat.'

'I've actually just had breakf—'

'*Eat.*'

'Okay.' I collapse into the armchair, two burgers in hand, and peel one from the foil. First bite – astoundingly good. Like, if I could marry a burger, it would be this burger.

After another bite, another swallow, I attempt to dive into conversation. 'I'm going to a party tonight.'

Álvaro's mouth is so full, it's like he's storing food for the winter. 'Mmm?'

'With Linny.' That's a loaded phrase if ever there was one. *With Linny.* 'Hey, can I . . . can I ask you something?'

He bobs his head. 'Mmmhmm.'

'Okay, hypothetically speaking, if a girl kissed you at the playground, and then you kissed her on her bedroom floor, and then the two of you kissed each other approximately seventeen times in the last five days – you know, at the beach and stuff – then what does that make you?'

Álvaro swallows. 'A girl did not kiss me at the playground.'

'No, no . . . it's hypothetical.'

'Ah.' Leaning back, burgers at risk of sliding off his knees – 'This person, he likes this girl?'

'*Muchísimo.*'

'Then he must buy her flowers. *He must.*' The way Álvaro says this, so matter-of-factly, makes me feel like an asshat. Like I should've known.

'Flowers,' I repeat.

Just then, a knock at the door, and a few seconds later, Linny pops in her head – 'Ooo, burgers.'

Álvaro smiles at her knowingly. 'Flowers.'

Linny

25.

WHO: Socialite and hotel heiress Poppie Kerr
WHEN: Thirteen days last February
WHY: She told her friends, 'Wait for me by the cab,' and then disappeared from a Paris nightclub. Paparazzi spotted her again at a soirée in Rome. 'I just needed some "me" time, you know?' Poppie said. 'But this party was too good to miss.'
NOTES: Grace has never missed one of Cass's parties. Well, there's a first time for everything.

Half an hour before the Halloween party begins, I'm goofily smiling, sprawled face-up on my carpet in the exact spot where Sebastian kissed me.

Downstairs, Mom is double-checking her tickets for the symphony. 'Third row,' she says to someone on the phone. 'Yes, I specifically requested row *three*.' She sounds higher-pitched than usual – a voice that could bend spoons. A lot of spoon-bending going on lately. It may have something to do with the glow-in-the-dark stars ('Marilyn, what on earth have you done to your ceiling?'). But I make no excuses.

I will never, ever take them down.

I count them now – a habit I'm developing. I'm on *seven* when Dad, dressed in a sleek gray suit, raps his knuckles on my doorframe. 'You going to be okay by yourself tonight?' He gives a small, nervous smile. *Another* one. For some reason, he won't stop small-smiling me since the FDA lunch.

'I'm sleeping over at Cass's, remember? Ray's going to be here in a bit to drive me.'

Mom suddenly appears next to Dad, her beige dress pretty but straitjacket tight. 'Bring an eye mask,' she instructs me. I'm shocked that's all she says. Usually MomandDad insist I skip parties to – I don't know – memorize structures in the human brain or something. At the very least, I expected a soliloquy about the dangers of alcohol consumption and premarital sex. They must be running very, very late to cut corners like this.

As if on cue, Mom taps her watch and says to me, 'Must go. No drinking! No intercourse!'

Ah, there it is – to the point. Mom doesn't mince words. For the first time in my life, I nod but wonder: *What if I did have sex?*

Where did *that* thought come from?

Once MomandDad are gone, I slip into my costume: a blue-and-white dress from the local thrift shop – and tie a black ribbon in my hair *à la* Alice in Wonderland. And when I say *slip*, I mean vacuum-seal myself into it. The top part constricts my boobs like a space-saving bag, which seemed like a good idea when I bought it weeks ago, but now I'm questioning it. After drying the last bit of my hair, I grab my Chuck Taylors from my desk drawer and head downstairs.

Ray has just let himself in – should've never given him that spare key. His boyfriend Lawrence is by his side in a big, honking Stetson and a plaid shirt. 'Hey, Linny,' he says, all smiles and perfect dimples. Sheesh. 'I've seen you around, but it's nice to, you know, meet you. Heard a lot about you.'

'You too,' I say. 'I like your costume. Ranch hand?'

'Bingo,' he says.

'How do I look?' Ray asks, twirling in the foyer. He's wearing a furry yellow jumpsuit bedecked with streamers. 'I'm a *Ray* of sunshine. Get it?'

'So clever!' Ingenuity aside, my lips go pink from clamping them together, trying not to explode into laughter. I have to state the obvious. 'Since when is the sun furry?'

He glares at me.

Lawrence slaps his knee. 'That's what *I* said!'

'And here I was,' Ray says, 'about to tell you how awesome *you* look, Sister Marilyn. But since I'm amazing and forgiving, I'll tell you anyway: Sebastian is *so* going to want to fall down your rabbit hole.'

'Oh my God. I *so* don't want to talk about that.'

He tosses me the keys, uncontrollable grin spreading across his face. 'Then you drive. I'll do the talking.'

THE LEFT-BEHINDS (scene 13)

CARSON FAMILY HOUSE – MIDDAY

LINNY has dragged the cup and string to the roof of her white house, where she is gazing at a slightly blue sky.

Into the cup:

LINNY

How come I always have to start the talking?

After a moment, we hear GRACE through the string.

GRACE

Dunno. You pick up the cup first.

LINNY

What if I didn't?

GRACE

But you do.

LINNY

Humor me.

GRACE

I'm not sure you really want to know.

LINNY

Just – just tell me.

GRACE takes a deep breath.

GRACE

I can't fly when I'm tethered to the ground.

Sebastian

26.

'Although the origination of cosmic rays is a mystery, we do know they are astoundingly strong. Imagine a particle in a man-made collider, then multiple its energy by 100 million.'
A Brief Compendium of Astrophysical Curiosities, p. 205

It's a beehive. Swarms of people buzz in and out beneath black streamers and cardboard ghosts. All clutch red Solo cups. (The people, that is. Not the ghosts.)

THE PARTIES-ARE-LIKE-COSMIC-RAYS PRINCIPLE:
It is exactly like it sounds.

'You want a beer?' Cass yells over the music. Orange lights eerily illuminate her face. Her black-taffeta dress barely squeezes through the doorframe as she yanks me into the kitchen. Extracts two cans from the fridge. Runs her tongue slowly across her pop-in vampire teeth. 'Here,' she says, handing me a can, tilting her head to the side. 'What're you supposed to be?'

I point to the Sharpie mustache I gave myself five minutes ago. The lines curve crazily up my cheeks like my little brother drew them. At least Paul would probably approve. 'Salvador Dalí,' I say.

Cass: confused stare.

Me: 'The Spanish painter?'

Cass: raising an eyebrow.

Me: 'He did all those melting clocks.'

'Mmm,' Cass says, taking a long swig of beer. 'Cool.'

I guess this is what people do at parties. Stand around and chat about things they don't have in common. I'd like to say that, for most of high school, Micah and I avoided parties like the meningeal plague. But usually we just weren't invited, until Savannah and I started dating and the proverbial party doors opened. Even still, we kind of stuck to ourselves.

'Are the flowers for Linny?' she says, pointing to the bundle of sunflowers in my left hand.

'Er – yeah.' Who walks into a party with flowers? Starting to think Álvaro misled me on this one. Changing the topic: 'So your parents are cool with you throwing a massive party?'

Cass shrugs. 'They were hippies in college.'

I wonder if they're upstairs smoking pot or something.

I wonder where *Linny* is – weren't we supposed to meet at ten?

I ask Cass, 'Is Linny here yet?' The music booms suddenly louder.

'What?' Cass yells.

'Linny! Is she here yet?'

'WHAT?'

I give up for now. Popping the can tab, I take a huge, bitter gulp. I've never liked beer that much, but it's a good time passer.

Just then, Cass hisses over my shoulder: 'Would you l-ak me to suck your blud?'

Ray bursts past me, extends his neck – 'But of course, *da-ling*' – and Cass licks his collarbone.

Linny materializes next to me. She pretends to vomit down

her pretty blue dress. 'Guys. Gross.' And then she stands on her tiptoes and plants two kisses on each side of my mustache lines. 'Hi,' she says. 'Sorry we're a little late. Ray got lost.'

What surprises me is how many people are staring at us. Well, at Linny. It occurs to me that Linny must be *popular*. Not just because of Cass – but because she's mind-blowingly beautiful and cool and people notice her, as they should. Can't blame them.

'These are for you,' I say, thrusting the sunflowers at her.

'Oh, oh, wow – thank you.' She presses the petals to her nose. 'They smell like summer.'

'Shots!' Cass says. Ten Dixie cups filled with green Jell-O wobble on a plate in her hands. 'Take one! Take three! And then come dance, *pleeeeeaaaaasssseee*.' Judging by the green hue of her lips, she's already indulged in several.

I pinch one between two fingers and squeeze it into my mouth. Tastes atrocious. Like it's mixed with battery acid instead of water. I spit most of it into my palm.

'Everclear vodka,' Cass says. 'Ninety-five percent alcohol.' To Linny: 'Okay, *dancedancedance*. Grace would've danced with me.'

'Yeah,' Linny says quietly, 'okay.'

Cass herds us into the living room, where a cheap plastic disco ball emits orange, pulsating light. Around us are sweaty people dancing with their sweaty hands above their sweaty heads. Pushing through them reminds me of a salmon swimming upstream.

There are limited dance moves in my arsenal. The robot. The sprinkler. A few salsa steps. None of which I'm about to break out in front of a crowd. Slow dancing is one thing. *This* is not happening.

Linny tiptoes it again, still awkwardly holding the sunflowers.

Her lips brush against my ear. 'I think you're supposed to move at least *one* part of your body when you dance. It's kind of a rule.' Each breath she takes I can feel on my neck.

DO NOT BLOW THIS, SEBASTIAN. I WILL NEVER FORGIVE YOU IF YOU BLOW THIS. JUST DANCE, YOU FOOL!

But I'm frozen.

The whole length of her is pressed against me, and I keep thinking: *Here is a girl who cares about my dad.*

Here is a girl who understands.

Here is an amazing, neurotic, gorgeous girl – and I have so many words for her. Three in particular.

Of any land mammal, the giraffe has the biggest heart, weighing in at twenty-five pounds and two feet long. At least that *was* the case. I may have it beat. (Ha. Pun.)

Because *holy shit*, I'm in love with Linny.

And like an idiot, I begin to say this. I begin to tell her *I love you*. But it comes out as 'I . . . I'm going to . . . I have to go.'

Suddenly, I'm hauling ass across the party.

Bursting through the back door.

Lurching into Cass's garden.

Is this a stress attack? Probably. I may love Linny, but who knows what *she's* thinking? Reading girls is as easy as decrypting messages from alien planets.

The panic has transformed me into a weightless being. Like the time Linny and I jumped off the swings, suspended in air – except hopefully I won't come crashing down this time.

Get a hold of yourself, Sebastian. You're not even drunk. I accidentally say this out loud. A couple interrupts their make-out session to glare at me.

Onward!

The backyard is all grasses and haphazard flower beds. Jungle-like. As I try to remember all the dangerous species in Florida (pythons, panthers, brown recluse spiders), I fumble. Trip. Emit more involuntary noises. Everything is muddled and loud. Across the garden are snippets of conversations:

'She said *what* about your boyfriend?'

'. . . and then I was, like, run bitch run!'

'That's why they call it *inter*course.'

And the cicadas! The goddamn singing cicadas! *Buzzz, buzzzzzz, buzzzzzzz.* Stupid bugs. Why do their aboveground life cycles last a billion years?

To my left, a guy in a soccer jersey staggers from the bushes with beer cans duct-taped to both of his hands. He bends over ninety degrees and projectile vomits onto a tragically placed garden gnome. His girlfriend — or a girl who *wants* to be his girlfriend — rushes over. 'It's okay, sweetie,' she coos, petting his back. 'Let it out.'

And he lets it out. About four times.

Wait.

Five times.

Running away from the vomit smell, I come to an abrupt halt beneath an oak tree. By that, I mean I run directly into one of its low-hanging branches.

Ah! *¡Una idea!* I shall scale this tree like a wildcat! I am Sir Edmund Hillary, and this is my Everest!

After a few attempts, I climb that sucker and feel shielded from the world.

At the same time, so much radioactive energy pulses through me, I'm convinced the branch is going to splinter to bits.

I think maybe I'll live in this tree forever. Create my own

ecosphere. Survive on rainwater and local squirrels. I gaze upward and breathe. Night bleeds through the crisscrossed branches. It's just the sky and me! No one else! No one else can find —

'Sebastian?'

Oh.

'What are you doing?' Linny says, studying me from five feet below, sunflowers in hand.

Valid question. *Panicking about you.*

'All right if I come up?' she asks.

I think I nod.

She's not a gifted climber like me but manages to scoot onto the low branch. Resting the flowers on her lap, she peers from root structure to canopy. 'This is — um — a nice tree.'

Crickets.

Running her hands along the tree branch, swinging her legs — 'You're up here because . . . ?'

Because I love you. 'I don't like . . . I don't like dancing in front of people.'

She giggles, stops swinging. 'So the natural solution is to hide in a tree?'

I crack a small smile despite the panic. 'Obviously.'

'Hey' — turning her shoulders toward me — 'if I kissed you right now, would we really be Sebastian and Linny, sitting in a tree, *k-i-s-s-i-n-g*?'

Another smile. 'I guess so.'

Her lips press against mine. Once. Twice.

'You're so good at that,' I tell her.

She kisses me again. 'I have an idea.'

Linny

27.

WHO: Magician Augustus the Great
WHEN: Seventeen days in 1985
WHY: He evaporated in a poof of smoke onstage during a Las Vegas show. The crowd marveled when he did not reappear; even his assistant worried. He returned in another poof during a rival magician's performance. 'This,' he shouted to the stunned audience, 'now this is magic!'
NOTES: I'm down to magic? Is that how desperate I am?

Thoughts forming, I pull away from his mouth, only an inch. 'I have an idea.'

'What?'

'It's a surprise.'

We jump out of the tree, hand in hand, one of us with a considerable *oomph* (hint: it's not me). I lead him through the tall grasses and around to Cass's garage, sliding my fingers above the doorframe for the spare key. 'Ah, got it.'

'Are we breaking and entering?' Sebastian says.

'Hardly.'

Inside, I lock the door behind us, flick on the lights, and it's still there – the tie-dyed blanket strung in the rafters, throwing colored light all over the room: neon greens and pinks and blues. Cass's family doesn't keep any cars in the garage – only a couch and some Foosball tables – so splotches of color float along the floor.

'Wow,' he says.

'Isn't it?'

By the power tools is Cass's super old-school boom box. I set my flowers next to it, pop open the lid, and say to Sebastian, 'Do you want the good news or the bad news?'

'Good first.'

'Okay – there's an ancient CD!'

'And the bad news?'

'It's a pop band called the Swedish Princesses.'

'Ouch.'

Pressing Play, peppy music *ting*ing through the garage. I do the superdorky thing of pretending to reel Sebastian in, pulling my hands along an imaginary rope. Once he's a foot away, I start bobbing my head, swinging my hips in a circle, my arms wiggly at my sides.

'What's happening?' he says.

'Tie-dye dance! Cass and I did this all the time with . . . with Grace. If you can't dance in front of people, maybe you can dance just with me?'

'That's even scarier,' he deadpans. 'You have no idea how . . .'

The beat continues to pound the walls of the garage. It's starting to match the thumping of my heart. 'How what?'

He switches off the music, shards of blue light breaking and splintering the Sharpie mustache that's snaking its way up his cheeks. His eyes are all over my eyes. Why's he looking at me like this? Doesn't he see how colorless I am?

'How maybe . . . maybe I could be . . .' His voice drops, and he glances down for a moment as if to find it. 'I've never felt anything even close to this.'

Oh. *Oh.*

I swallow. 'You really mean that?'

Smoothing a hand over my shoulder, he says, 'Yeah. Why would you even question it?'

'Because . . . because . . .' Why *am* I questioning it? The reason slaps me in the face – and suddenly I'm holding in tears. 'Because I'm not sure if she even misses me. I keep thinking of her at the end of our street, right after she climbed out her window, and what if she didn't care about me and all the places we were supposed to visit together and –'

Sebastian cups my cheeks, drags his thumbs across them to swipe away a few tears. '*Of course* she misses you.'

I choke out, 'You don't know that.'

'I do. You're a very miss-able person.' He pulls me closer and kisses my nose. 'Remember how I was telling you about *A Brief Compendium of Astrophysical Curiosities*?'

'Yeah?'

'Well, there's this chapter where Dr. Mangum talks about how there might be all these parallel universes, existing alongside our own. Where we're basically the same people, but we make different choices. Lead different lives. I was rereading it the other day, and all I could think about was, in every universe, we'd *have* to be together. I can't imagine any scenario that doesn't lead to you.' His hand is on my arm now, tapping with every word. 'I. Would. Miss. You.'

'Sebastian, that is the corniest thing I've ever heard.'

He rests his other hand on the back of his neck, massaging it. 'Corny in a good way?'

I kiss him with a gust of motion, pushing him a few steps backward, and we sink into the couch behind us, springs creaking. 'In a very good way.'

I used to think that only bad things sneak up on you (monsters in the dark, grief, sisters disappearing out of windows), but as it happens, good things are even sneakier. One second I'm in like with Sebastian, and the next second I'm completely blindsided by love, which is a lot like sunshine: hot, tingly, and all over my skin.

Surely one person can't feel this much without exploding.

And when Sebastian kisses me back, I know he's deep in explosion territory, too. I know this is for real.

'I just want you to know,' he says, voice a whisper, lips still brushing mine, 'although I'm leaving at the end of the summer, I'm not a leaver. I want to stay, just like this, with you.' He crisscrosses a finger over his heart: *I promise*.

And maybe that's what does it.

Or maybe it's because we're kissing in a way that sucks out all the darkness, until the only thing left is color and light.

'I haven't exactly done this before,' he says suddenly.

'And you think *I* have?'

'Well, I thought, you're –'

'No, never.'

'Do people generally put on – er – music or something?'

I shrug. 'Beats me.'

Reaching over the couch, he presses Play on the boom box and bobs his head to the Swedish Princesses like it's his jam. I dissolve into hysterical laughter as he unzips my dress.

Anatomically speaking, everything happens in the proper way. I've seen pictures in MomandDad's office of what's supposed to occur; plastic models, condom displays, and detailed diagrams leave little to the imagination. Grace once told me that real, live penises look like sea monsters, and I can now confirm this assessment. A thousand movie references also shuffle in and out of my brain: *When Harry Met Sally*, *The Notebook*, *Pretty Woman*. But it's still different from what I'd anticipated – gentler and slower, with a lot of pauses and readjustments and bumping foreheads. As it's Florida, and about ninety degrees in the garage, sweat collects in odd places, and we both pretend not to notice, just like I pretend not to notice his out-of-control heartbeat (which is so, *so* sweet). I follow the splotches of neon on his skin with my fingers and then with my mouth.

Afterward, as Sebastian twists one of my curls around his finger, I cradle my chin in his neck and try to piece together how we got here: how he transitioned from the annoying boy in my way to – well, the not-so-annoying boy *very* in my way.

Above the music, there is laughter from the party, and someone is shouting: 'Chug, chug, chug.'

'Should we go back out soon?' I ask.

Kissing my forehead, he says, 'I've never slept with a girl.'

'Um, I know.'

'No – I mean *slept*.' He nestles his head into the sofa arm and pretend-snores. 'You know, *zzzzz*.'

So we slip back into our clothes, switch off the lights, and listen to the Swedish Princesses tumble in the dark. It's the first time in months that I've fallen asleep without seeing her face.

THE LEFT-BEHINDS (scene 14)

<u>BRIGHT-WHITE SCREEN</u>

LINNY (Voice-over)

Is that you, knocking at the door?

GRACE (Voice-over)

No, it's not.

LINNY (Voice-over)

Oh, I thought I heard your footsteps.

GRACE (Voice-over)

You didn't.

LINNY (Voice-over)

What happens when I stop assuming that? One day the
phone's going to ring, and I won't immediately think it's you.

GRACE (Voice-over)

(a smile in her voice)

Then it looks like you're growing some wings of your own.

Sebastian

28.

'After testing the bounds of what was possible – and succeeding – Einstein continued his upward climb.' *A Brief Compendium of Astrophysical Curiosities*, p. 3

I'm learning that things are simpler than I first conceived.

Back up. *Conceived* is the wrong word to use here, considering what happened on Friday night. What I mean is, it made sense. How much simpler could it be – just the two of us, loving each other?

On Monday morning, I walk to Silver Springs with an extra *oomph* in my step, remembering it all. (For the record, the Google image results for 'boobs' do not do the real things justice.) And afterward was good, too. The next morning, her head on the pillow next to me. Twelve millimeters from my face. There was light-blue glitter on her eyelids. Up close was a whole new ball game.

I have sex *once* and I'm already using sports metaphors?

I had sex. Me. With *her*.

(Okay, Micah, touché. Thanks for the condoms.)

The only problem is that it's almost the end of July, and I leave for Cal Tech in four weeks. What does that mean for us?

Still, I feel brave.

THE HOT-GIRL HYPOTHESIS FOR PERSONAL USE:

If I can have sex with a hot girl who I love, then I can say four words.

I. Am. Your. Son.

In the Silver Springs lobby, I tell Linny, 'Today.'

'Today?'

'I'm going to tell Álvaro. Wish me luck.'

Right by the fig tree, she plants a kiss on my lips, reminding me just how brave I am.

My heart is a leapfrog. I can hear each distinct *BA-boom. BA-boom.*

Giving myself an internal pep talk (*Just do it, you coward*), I knock. Wait. Wait a few moments more. The door squeaks open slowly.

Álvaro rocks side to side, holding the doorjamb for support. He's wearing his gray pajamas, mostly unbuttoned, and his fedora. A cigarillo droops between his lips. 'Yes?' he says.

Voice unsteady – 'Can I – can I come in?'

'It's a free country, no?' He opens the door a little farther.

Solid start. Keep up the momentum.

Álvaro shuffles to his desk. Around him are mounds of unsorted fan mail, three weeks of newspapers stuffed between books in the bookshelf.

I take a seat in the armchair. 'I've been wanting to talk to you about something.'

'Would you care for *un poco de tocino*?'

Huh? Bacon?

He passes me a plastic dish with two already-nibbled slices.

'Um, I ate earlier,' I say. 'Thanks, though.'

With a gesture that says *Suit yourself*, he folds one slice into his mouth. Doesn't even bother to remove the cigarillo.

I shoo the frog from my throat. '*Ahemm*. Anyway. About that talk. I was wondering if . . .' Out with it. Out with it already! 'If, hypothetically speaking, you had a son, what would you say?'

There. Those are *almost* the right words. They're out in the world now. Can't take them back.

Álvaro swallows the bacon, stamps out the cigarillo. 'A son?'

'Yes.' I might puke. 'A son.'

Silence ensues – the longest silence in the history of silences. His teeth clack together. Finally, he looks at me. Inhales.

And in those seconds, I swear he knows.

Who I am.

Why I'm here.

What I've been trying to tell him this whole summer.

'A son,' Álvaro says again, more thoughtful this time. Never dropping his gaze from mine. 'I suppose I'd tell him' – pausing, bringing one hand to his chin – 'I'd tell him what it is to be . . . to be a man.'

Not *at all* what I was going for. 'Oh, what I mean is –'

'You see, there is *una diferencia* between what people think and what it *is*. You understand? It is not' – slapping his feeble arms where the muscles should be – 'it is not this. Nothing to do with this. It is . . .' He keeps dragging his teeth over his bottom lip. Looking frustrated. Like his words are in the wind. Eventually: '*Es aprender a quedarse, incluso cuando tu puedes salir.*'

Translation: It is learning to stay, even when you can leave.

His head falls forward. He scrapes at his eyebrows with his fingernails. 'I'm not always good at this. I was not good at this.'

I sit up as straight as I can. 'Álvaro?'

'Yes?'

'I'm . . . The thing is . . . I'm your —'

'There is something familiar about you,' he says slowly.

'Yes! There's a reason for that. I'm your —'

A tap at the open door, then another. Marla pops in. Her voice rattles over to us: 'Mr. Herrera, you don't want to be late for your doctor's appointment.'

'Wait,' I say to Álvaro, 'I —'

But Álvaro is already wobbling to a stand. Gripping his cane. As he leaves, he places a brittle hand on my shoulder. Leans over slightly to whisper in my ear: 'Believe me, *mijo*. No son wants *un padre* like me.'

On TV that night, Morgan Freeman is discussing whether time can run backward, but I can't concentrate.

Believe me, mijo. That word — it's eating me up.

Determined to finish our talk, I borrow Ana's car and drive to Silver Springs around eight p.m. A night nurse signs me in with 'He's in his room but just be quick, okay? Residents need their sleep.'

'It won't take long,' I say, and bound up the stairs. But this time when I knock on his door, there's no response. This time when I twist the doorknob, nothing greets me but stale air.

Was he trying to tell me something this morning?

It is learning to stay, even when you can leave.

I'm not always good at this.

Oh no.

Linny

29.

WHO: *Kenneth G. Locke, author of* A Stranger in the Field, *a novel set in a mental institution*
WHEN: *1964*
WHY: *He faked his death to mislead police after he was arrested for possessing rare, stolen antiquities. He fled to Honduras, and it's pretty unclear why he came back to the US.*
NOTES: *I love his book. That's potentially irrelevant to this investigation.*

Sebastian calls as I'm climbing into bed with my computer. The intensity of his voice makes my stomach clench.

'It's happened again. Linny, it's happened again.'

'Wait, wait,' I whisper, conscious of MomandDad's footsteps trundling down the hallway. Once the sliver of light under my doorway extinguishes, I let out a breath and speak a bit louder. 'What are you talking about?'

'Álvaro. He's gone.'

I shoot up in bed, a searing pain in my shoulders. *'No.'*

'I was trying to tell him I'm his son and figured he wouldn't be so busy at night, so I went back and – and he wasn't there.'

His words are a charcoal pencil, turning everything black. My dad said a similar thing when he picked through Grace's bedroom after she disappeared, as if she were hiding instead of gone: 'I checked her closet and under her bed – and she wasn't there.'

Sebastian continues, 'So the staff checked the rest of the building, and there were all these announcements over the loudspeaker, and they started searching the street and he's *gone*, Linny.'

I know what happens next: Police. Crying. Police. Repeat.

Search parties. Neighbors knocking on your door with groceries. Pitying looks.

Sebastian's voice is heavy and ragged, like he's catching a cold. 'Did you hear what I said?'

'Sorry, sorry. Did you have to talk to the police?'

'Yeah, they're looking for him right now. According to the security footage he broke out through the kitchen again. He couldn't have gone far, right? Where would he go?'

The answer seems obvious. 'Back to where he came from.'

'Which is *where*?' The last word reaches a particularly high octave.

What do I say to that? What did I want my parents to say to me? 'We'll find him, Sebastian. We're going to find him. We'll get to Silver Springs early tomorrow morning and say we left something in Álvaro's room, and we'll —'

'You don't have to do this, you know.'

'What?'

'Tell me it's all going to be okay.'

'It *is* going to be okay.'

He says softly, painfully, 'Can we play a game or something?'

'What kind of game?'

'Categories? One of us picks a category, and we have to rattle off as many words as we can.'

Categories.

Grace and I used to play this when we were kids. She'd

always choose 'names of bands' to ensure a swift victory and then move on to Scrabble. Grace is the reigning Scrabble champion of our family – except that she consistently fabricates words. Once, she tried to convince me that *treehood* was in the dictionary. 'Treehood,' she said. 'The condition of being a tree.' I'm about to tell this to Sebastian, but he interprets my silence as something else.

'I know it's stupid,' he says. 'It's just, there's no way I'm falling asleep.'

Dragging my sheets up to my chin, I whisper, 'Okay, how about . . . "exotic pets"?'

And for the next three minutes we list *capuchin monkeys*, *armadillos*, *coyotes*, and *sugar gliders*, and I tell Sebastian that anyone listening to our conversation would label us clinically insane, straight out of *One Flew Over the Cuckoo's Nest*, but we keep listing and listing and listing.

Eventually, we run out of ideas and end up with animals like 'Um, red chipmunks?'

'Spiky-tailed beavers?' Sebastian says.

'Snakes with fangs?' I say.

'All snakes have fangs.'

'*That* is a good point.'

As I sink deeper into my pillows and plastic-star gaze, we listen to each other breathe on the line.

'This night wouldn't suck so much if you were here,' he says.

'I kind of am here.'

'You know what I mean.'

I do.

'Tell me something good,' he says. 'Something you haven't told me before.'

Since my computer is resting by my elbow, I blurt out: 'I'm writing a screenplay, but – um – that's not entirely a good thing. It's about my sister.'

'Is it sad?'

'Kind of.'

'You never talk about her.'

'Well, she's – complicated.'

'Hmm,' he says. 'Okay. Books.'

'What?'

'New category: "books."'

Fast-forward to the next morning. When I wake up, the phone is still in my hand.

THE LEFT-BEHINDS (scene 15)

LINNY'S BEDROOM

On the floor of her bedroom, LINNY pours over a book entitled *The Art of Growing Wings*. Around her are spots of color, although she is still in black and white.

Closing her eyes really hard as if wishing for something, she feels between her shoulder blades. Nothing is sprouting there.

Sebastian

30.

'Every physicist dreams of that eureka moment.' *A Brief Compendium of Astrophysical Curiosities*, p. 54

The sky is still waking up, but it's going to be a scorcher of a day. Hotter than usual. Linny and I crouch on the curb outside of Silver Springs, clutching our stomachs, waiting for the police to leave.

'Sucks,' I say. Can't even muster the *This*.

Linny touches my knee. 'Let's just stick to what we discussed. I'm going to pretend that I've left something in Álvaro's room, and we'll probably get a little while to look around.'

Tilting my head back to the sky – 'And what if we don't find any clues?'

She crosses her fingers but doesn't say another word.

By 9:30 a.m., the police are gone. As planned, Linny pretends that she's lost a necklace – 'My *favorite* necklace, Marla. From my *favorite*, deceased grandmother.'

So she lets us into Álvaro's room with 'Y'all have five minutes, and then I need my key back. Good lord, it's supposed to be my day off! As soon as you finish, I'm going home.'

His room is messier than yesterday. Toppled piles of typewritten pages are everywhere. *Un desastre.*

'Careful,' Marla says, 'don't disturb anything.'

Disturb anything? How could it be any worse than this?

Walking farther into the mess, Linny gingerly lifts up a few papers on Álvaro's nightstand, scattering cigarillo butts. Her back is to me.

A yellow manila envelope on his desk catches my eye. Fan mail, I think. Except . . .

'Linny.' I clear my throat. 'Linny. Didn't you say you thought your necklace was *over here*?'

She steps across the room and peers at the envelope's address with me.

It's not a package *to* Álvaro. It's a package *from* Álvaro that has yet to be sent.

In shaky blue ink, it reads: *Joe. 112 Seahorse Drive, Miami, Florida.*

Linny and I exchange glances: Joe. Could this be the real address?

The package is unsealed. Inside: about a hundred scraps of paper. The scraps Álvaro's been keeping in his pocket, most likely.

A REVISED RULE FOR SMALL-SCALE OBJECTS IN RELATION TO FATHER-BASED MYSTERIES:
The aforementioned display a high correlation with eureka moments.

Linny's fingers dance on the desktop.

Room, spinning.

Head, clouding.

'Did you find it?' Marla says behind us.

'You know what?' Linny says, turning around. 'I went swimming yesterday at my friend's house. I bet it's at the bottom of her pool.'

Marla eyes us suspiciously, crosses her arms. 'Mmhmmm.'

'I'll check this afternoon,' Linny says. 'Um, cool. That's it, then. You coming, Sebastian?'

We flee down the hall.

Linny

31.

WHO: *Actress Doris Clemens, famous for her portrayal of Perdita in* The Night Robbers
WHEN: *Shortly after the film's release*
WHY: *No one saw her for seven years. Turns out, she had purchased a large, secluded house in Montana's smallest town and had her groceries delivered via courier. The only reason she finally left the house, reports say, was a great flood. Someone recognized her distinctive seagull necklace in the lifeboat.*
NOTES: *How do I summon floods? (Too much? Desperate times, desperate measures.)*

'My *favorite* necklace,' I tell Marla. 'From my *favorite*, deceased grandmother. And obviously she can't get me a new one and I –'

'Y'all have five minutes.'

The stench hits me first; Álvaro's room smells like a damp laundry/old-bacon smoothie. (Yum.) I pick up my feet extra high as I step around the typewritten pages. Somehow the mess is sucking me in, like tornado arms.

Gross. More cigarillo butts on his nightstand. Several land on the top of my right shoe, and as I'm kicking them off, I see it: a sliver of blue tucked into a copy of *The Old Man and the Sea*.

Carefully, silently, I slip the photograph from the book, that splinter of blue sky giving way to a family. Colors burst off the image. There's a woman wearing an orange dress, her black hair pulled into a loose bun. And next to her is Álvaro – the Álvaro I know from his book jacket. He's young, relatively speaking, and is reaching up to push a stray lock from the woman's face. On his head is that trademark fedora, tilted up so you can see his entire face. The woman's looking wobbly eyed at him; Álvaro's looking wobbly eyed at her. Both are smiling these lunatic grins.

And there's a baby in her arms.

No, it's not possible – Sebastian said that Álvaro never knew about him, that his mom didn't tell him. No. This is another baby, another mother. Sebastian must have a sibling.

My index finger runs along the dimpled back of the photograph. And as I flip it over, my heart runs for cover. In blue pen – in handwriting I recognize – Álvaro has written: *Maria, Sebastian, me, South Beach*.

Holy bananas.

Álvaro didn't just leave Sebastian's mom. He left *Sebastian*. He knows about Sebastian!

This all happens in a matter of seconds, but my whole body feels like it's wrapped in gauze. I'm unsettled, can't quite make out the edges of anything – the lamp on the nightstand blurs out of focus.

What on earth do I tell Sebastian? *Do* I tell him? Abandonment is a feeling I know all too well. Why would I put that on someone else?

'Linny,' he says. 'Linny. Didn't you say you thought your necklace was *over here*?'

And in a moment of desperate panic, I stuff the picture into my jean shorts and cover it with my shirt.

THE LEFT-BEHINDS (scene 16)

LINNY'S BEDROOM – THE NEXT DAY

CLOSE-UP –

LINNY again feels for wings that are not there. . . .

Sebastian

32.

'No matter how much we think we understand a question, we may not immediately comprehend the answer.' *A Brief Compendium of Astrophysical Curiosities*, p. 77

Linny insists that bolting this early in the morning – and so soon after a police investigation – looks too suspicious. So we wait, pulling up two chairs in the cafeteria and mulling over our findings.

'Those scraps must be the notes Álvaro's been writing to himself,' I say. 'And he's been sending them to Joe? Why?'

Linny scratches the back of her ear. 'I really have no idea. But . . . I think Joe's really, *really* important to Álvaro, judging by the way he talks about him. Maybe they *did* play dominoes every Saturday – even during the three years that Álvaro first disappeared. That makes sense, right?'

'I guess.'

'Which means that . . . I don't know . . . Joe hid Álvaro? Possibly at the address we just found? I'm willing to bet, if that's right, then Álvaro wandered back to 112 Seahorse Drive.'

'Maybe. But how can we trust that it's the right address?'

She sighs. It could be just me – but I get the feeling something's bothering her. Something more than Álvaro. 'We can't. But it's the best that we've got.'

Just after lunch, we fake food poisoning (highly unoriginal,

I know, but it works every time) and escape the rest of our shift.

'Forget our bikes,' Linny says, bulleting out the door. 'And no buses. Let's take a taxi.'

We hail one down the street from Silver Springs. Inside I blurt out the address and – *vroom* – the driver presses hard on the gas.

Across the seat, Linny grips my hand, but she's not meeting my eyes. Her nose presses against the window. Puffing clouds that fog up the glass.

The beach floats by. Then green and pink buildings. Tourists on bikes. Shops selling neon T-shirts and souvenir mugs with naked women on them. Lots of convertibles with people waving their hands in the air.

Twenty minutes later, we're starting to hit suburbia: manicured lawns, tire swings, little kids screaming through sprinklers in the street.

More puffing from Linny.

When the taxi stops, that's how I see the property: through a haze. Like it's emerging from a jungle mist. We're in the same neighborhood as Agnes's house, only much farther down the road.

'Here you go,' the driver says. He swivels around to face us. A hummingbird tattoo sits above his left eyebrow. 'You want me to wait around for a little while?'

Linny says, 'Um, no, I don't think so, probably not.'

I pull a wad of bills from my pocket, and Linny chips in as well.

As we step onto the sidewalk, the clouds start turning a threatening shade of gray. Like the night sky in *Dark Ops Resolution*.

Peering up, I say, 'That's promising,' and Linny says, 'This definitely seems like the place. Don't you think? The *real* place.'

She's probably right. It's set way, way back from the other houses. Overgrown orange trees abound. You can barely see the house from the sidewalk. The yard's humongous. Wild. Like whoever lives here has surrendered it to nature.

'Wouldn't this be so scary on Halloween?' Linny says, bending down to pick up a decaying orange. 'I bet they don't get a lot of trick-or-treaters.'

It's the perfect place to hide and never be found.

'You ready?' she says.

'No.'

A pause. 'How about now?'

'Not even close, but let's go.'

Fending off orange tree branches, we follow the broken slate pathway to the front door. (One hundred steps. Holding my breath the whole time.) On the exterior, yellow paint peels in wide strips.

'Do you want to knock,' Linny says, 'or should I?'

'You do it.'

Slowly, she raps twice on the door. Maybe no one's home. Or maybe someone *is* home and doesn't want visitors?

Mierda. It's raining. Drip, drip in increasingly large beads. A crack of lightning splits through the sky.

'Did you know,' I ask Linny, 'that forty-nine Americans a year die from lightning strikes?'

Her tank top is already clinging to her skin. (Not that I mind.) 'Well, I do *now*.'

Just then headlights peek through the sheet of rain, through the orange trees. Investigating, we rush back along the slate path in enough time to see a silver Honda slow to a halt in front of the mailbox. Out steps a woman with a bag of groceries in her hands. She trots around the car before she sees us.

And absolutely freezes.

WTF THEORY:
Even if you understand the question, the answer may punch you in the gut.

Linny

33.

WHO: *Richard Walker, animal behaviorist and presenter for* The Magnificent World of Birds
WHEN: *Two days in January 2011*
WHY: *His prized owl, nicknamed Lucy, flew out of sight during a controlled hunt in northwest Scotland. Richard ditched his camera crew and began to look for her; he returned when Lucy did not come back.*
NOTES: *Sometimes I wonder if Álvaro and Grace belong in the animal kingdom.*

In the cab, I almost blurted out everything to Sebastian. It was right on my tongue – a bird about to take flight. *There is a picture in my backpack! Your dad knew about you all along!* Instead, the words built and built until they buried me.

Keeping secrets is wrong, but is telling him worse? How do you protect the boy you love when what you know will break him?

And now doesn't feel like the best time to mention it, as we're standing in the pouring rain, realization knocking us off our feet. You know in movies when, right before a character receives life-altering news, someone says, 'I think you'll wanna sit down for this?' Well, I wish someone had forewarned me and offered a chair.

Even though her paper grocery bag is quickly collapsing,

even though the rain's slicking down her hair, Marla casually clears her throat. 'Miss Marilyn. Sebastian. What are you doing in this part of town?'

Us? What are *you* doing here?

Rain drizzles into my mouth as I stutter, 'There – there was a package in Álvaro's room. It was made out to this address.'

Marla shifts the weight of the grocery bag to her left hip. 'Huh. Sure it was this address? You know Mr. Herrera, he gets –'

'Confused sometimes,' Sebastian says. 'We know.'

Her mouth tightens into a straight line as she sucks on her teeth.

I plunge my hands into my pockets. 'Sebastian and I have been looking for this address all summer, and . . . well, we just want to know what's going on.'

She squints at us. 'What's going on with what?'

Everything I've written about Álvaro in my journal scrolls through my mind, along with everything we've discovered today. *Think, think, think, Linny*. Exchanging a quick glance with Sebastian, who looks equally rocked, I sift through the possibilities and sum up a final theory. 'We just wanted to know where he went, three years ago, and why he came back. Maybe . . . maybe . . . I'm not sure why Joe hid Álvaro, but I think that he did . . . and this is Joe's house?' I must've stumbled onto something, because she goes even more rigid – full-on oak tree. 'Is Joe your . . . um . . . brother or dad or something?'

Out of the corner of my eye, I see a mixture of confusion and anguish invading Sebastian's face. 'Is Álvaro here?' he asks.

Marla examines us for a long moment, threads of hair sopping against her forehead, and then puffs out a gust of air that blows us back. 'Who else knows about this?'

'Just us,' I say.

'In that case, you better come inside before we get swallowed up by this rain.' Following her, we duck underneath the orange trees and hurry toward the front steps, where Marla passes Sebastian the grocery bag and fumbles with her keys, hands trembling. She unclicks the lock, tries to push the door open, fails – and then presses her full weight against it, like she's attempting to break it down. 'Gets stuck sometimes,' she explains.

Stepping inside, I can see why.

Holy bananas to the extreme.

Behind the door is a pile of paperwork that could eclipse the sun, and behind that is its mother. You can tell that at one point the house had an open floor plan, but now it's . . . Okay. Have you seen the TV show *Hoarders*, where people accumulate so much stuff that it threatens to eat them? Like, they're crawling on their hands and knees over piles of empty cereal boxes and tuna fish cans? This isn't far from a TLC special, not far from the creepiest-yet-coolest place I've ever been – think Aladdin's cave; think Álvaro's room at Silver Springs times ten.

But that's not all: I haven't even mentioned the paintings, just visible, hanging on each wall: twelve-foot-tall oils in the brightest colors I've ever seen. They're of a garden. Eden? Wherever it is, I want to go there *now*.

Sidestepping several paper pillars, we follow Marla into the kitchen, where Sebastian *thunk*s the bag on the only empty space on the counter. I drop my backpack on the linoleum – the picture of Sebastian and Álvaro calling out to me from the interior pocket. *Ugh*, what am I going to do about that?

'So if we're going to talk about this,' she says, 'we need some lemonade.'

I almost laugh. 'Yeah, okay.'

And in a voice with no laughter in it, Sebastian says, 'Where's Álvaro?'

'Out back,' Marla says. 'He knocked on my door right after my shift. Almost gave me a heart attack. Lord, I'm telling you, I was glad to see him. Not so glad he wandered off again, but glad he came here. I should've known he would.' She pauses. 'I'll get y'all some towels. Go and sit on the porch. I'll be right there in a minute.' She points us down the hall to a ginormous screened-in porch with double fans, overlooking the garden from the paintings. Now I feel as if I really have been struck by lightning. How many times can you say *whoa* before it becomes redundant? Because: whoa, whoa, whoa.

Once I saw a photo series of an abandoned wedding in the middle of the forest. Trees grew right through the chairs, and every year for twenty years, someone came back to repaint the furniture. The garden's like that: spooky and beautiful at the same time, as if I've stumbled on some nobleman's hideaway from the past. The sky's turned after-storm pink. Light breaks through the lush orange trees as the rain tails off, illuminating the knee-high grasses in scattered light. It must be three, maybe four acres of land – enough to wander without getting lost.

I almost don't notice him at first.

In the center of the garden is a stone table with two seats, grasses fanning around them like crop circles. Álvaro is perched on the left seat, spreading dominoes on the stone. He doesn't look any worse for wear, considering the scare he's given us.

'Álvaro!' Sebastian shouts across the yard. 'Álvaro!'

Álvaro twists his neck in the direction of his name, catches our eyes for an instant, and then resumes his one-person game.

It's unsettling how detached he appears – like that day at the pool when he looked at us like we weren't people at all.

Sebastian's eyebrows inch together until a ridge sprouts on his forehead. He presses his fingers against the screen; I see his Adam's apple bob up and down three times.

Footsteps sound down the hallway. After a moment, Sebastian and I take seats at a wicker table on the porch as Marla plunks down three glasses of pink lemonade and hands us towels. I wring out my curls; Sebastian's hair is spiky and standing on end, and I resist the urge to comb my fingers through it.

Marla collapses into one of the chairs and crosses her hands over her belly. 'Here's the deal. You can't tell anybody. I mean *no one*. Álvaro doesn't want strangers peeking into his life, you understand? All those reporters who were sniffing around? Oh yes, they'd have a field day with this one. Picture it in the *National Enquirer*.' Her hands make a swiping motion like she's buttering the air. '"The Secret Life of a Cult Writer." He won't like it one bit. You wouldn't think it, for how famous he was, but he's a very private person. He likes keeping to himself, just being home.'

We agree to zip our lips, so she begins, 'You were right. My dad's name was Joe.'

'Was?' Sebastian gulps. 'Is he . . . ?'

'He passed away a few months ago. I think . . . I think you should know something.' She studies us for a painfully long moment. 'Álvaro has dementia, most likely Alzheimer's disease.'

I blink. Sebastian blinks. We say, 'What?' in unison. Our hearts are probably matching beat for crazy beat.

All his peculiarities – his faraway stares, the way he hoards used napkins in his desk – I assumed were just par for the course. Aren't all writers eccentric? In the cafeteria that second day, when he was banging on the table, I thought . . . What *did* I think? That he was just old, and that his new surroundings were reason enough for a momentary breakdown? And the pool – should I have known as we were floating there? Should I have known when he kept asking my name? Thinking back, it makes sense – but Álvaro also seems invincible, like having his words captured in film makes him immortal somehow.

Marla's face is a dropped stone, her voice craggy at the edges. 'That's why he disappeared three years ago. Álvaro didn't want people to know about the dementia. He wanted people to remember him as he *was*, not what the disease left. So my dad took him in, and he hid out here. But my dad, he and I didn't speak for a long time, ever since he and my mom split. Did I ever tell you I grew up in Georgia? Went to college there, too – only came to Miami for my job. I didn't even know my dad lived here. Small world, huh? Last year, he found me in the phone book. The goddamn phone book, like I was a plumber or something! "Marla," he says, "I need your help." Just like that. No nonsense. Twenty years go by, and that's the first thing he says. Well, you can imagine I hung up on his ass. Then he called back and told me he had lung cancer. Stage four, he said it was. He gave me this address, and I went over that afternoon. That's when I saw Álvaro. He was sitting in the garden, and my dad, he introduces us and lays it all out. Says this is his best friend and domino partner, Álvaro. Met him decades ago in Maximo Gomez Domino Park. Of course I knew who Álvaro was. All of Miami knew who he was.'

She gazes out to the stone table, where Álvaro is shouting '*Bah!*' at his dominoes. Unlike the rest of the summer, the noise sends chills up my neck. I glance at Sebastian's arms – yep, goose bumps, too. A family of starlings settles in the grass, and another '*Bah*' scatters them.

'Well,' Marla says, 'eventually my dad passed away, and then I took care of Álvaro. Took care of him until I thought I couldn't any more. Until . . .' Trailing off, she lets the last word hang in the humidity.

My stomach inches up my throat. Until what?

She takes a sip of lemonade, swishes the liquid around in her mouth, and swallows hard. 'I tried. Lord help me, I tried, but he just wandered off in the middle of the night, like it was the most natural thing in the world.' Sebastian and I follow her finger as she motions to the back of the property. 'I found him the next morning in a park two miles down thataway. Bleeding all over the place. He fell, I think. Tripped on a tree branch or something, landed on a rock. I don't really know. But I told myself, "Marla, you can't handle hiding someone. You can barely handle *this*,"' she says, gesturing to the out-of-control garden. 'I called a private car company the next day, and – Lord, I had them cart him away, drive him around the block a few times so I could scoot over to Silver Springs and greet him. I thought that if he saw me there, maybe he'd think he was home.'

'So is he going back to Silver Springs?' I say.

'He'll have to, for his own safety. Though the only things he liked there were the food and spending time with the two of y'all. He said you made him feel young again. Only problem now is the police – there's still a silver alert out, but I don't want anything to leak, get to the tabloids. I'm contacting Álvaro's lawyer tonight to figure it all out.'

As I'm processing this, I fall face-first into a heart-stopping thought. The last scene in *Midnight in Miami* is from two perspectives of the same moment in time: Agustina is gaping up at her bedroom ceiling, waiting for Eduardo to come back, and fifty miles away, Eduardo is dying in the sand after being shot by a rival spy. *He pictures what it will be like to be cast away into that sea*, Álvaro writes. *All that is left is for him to close his eyes and shut out the sky.*

I feel dizzy, disorientated, because, am I doing that, too? What if I'm waiting for someone who will never return? Marla *forced* Álvaro to come back into the world, and he disappeared again anyway. Realization drops on me like a thick, itchy blanket. There's a possibility that Grace will never come back, and for the first time I'm forced to wonder if I would survive it. How could I live the rest of my life without my sister? How could *she*?

Sebastian makes a hitching noise. 'Sorry, but – this, this doesn't make any sense.'

Marla frowns at him. 'What do you mean?'

'Álvaro's fine. Alzheimer's? No. He's fine. He's . . . he's writing a new novel!'

Rubbing my eyes, stopping a few tears in their tracks, it suddenly strikes me that Sebastian's channeling Agustina, too. How far into the fog is Álvaro? Forgetting some numbers in an address is one thing. Forgetting your best friend is dead is another. Does he even remember that he has a son?

And what about the picture in my backpack? Wouldn't that break Sebastian even more?

'I'm sorry, honey,' Marla says, 'but he's not fine.'

Sebastian pushes back his chair and stands. 'No. You've got it wrong.'

Marla stands, too, as if prepping for a brawl, but instead of lifting a fist she raises a finger. 'There are a few things y'all need to see.'

THE LEFT-BEHINDS (scene 16, continued)

. . . and on recognition of her winglessness, LINNY droops her head
to the ground.

Sebastian

34.

'Oftentimes, the outcomes astound us. Always prepare for the possibility that nothing is as it seems.' *A Brief Compendium of Astrophysical Curiosities*, p. 302

Álvaro is my father. Let's call that x.

Álvaro has Alzheimer's. Let's call that y.

$x + y = z$

That means z is what happens when you add *Dad* and *Disease*. It's one equation I'd rather not solve.

Álvaro's okay. *Has* to be okay. Because if he loses his yesterdays, I lose my chance at tomorrows with him.

Marla disappears inside, emerges a minute later with shoe boxes in her hands. 'This should explain a few things,' she says, dropping the boxes on the table. 'All that stuff in the house? Most of it's Álvaro's – he keeps *everything*. I can barely see my dad's paintings. That isn't even all of it, if you can believe that. Some of it I've been bringing to Álvaro at night.'

Linny clears her throat. Motions to the shoe boxes. 'So what are – what are these?'

Marla points to the left one. 'Well, that's all five hundred and sixty of Álvaro's notes.' Sitting down again, leaning back in her chair – 'He sends one package a week. You know how I collect all the residents' mail? Well, he had the address wrong almost every time, but I knew they were supposed to come here.'

I ask the obvious question. 'What are they for?'

'More like *who* are they for. Half the packages were made out "To Joe." I've been trying to work it out, and I think Álvaro writes down what he remembers – random bits, you know – and sends them here for safekeeping. Only thing is, he's forgot the crucial part.' She closes her eyes. 'Lord, he's been writing to a ghost.'

The porch spins.

If Álvaro can't remember that his best friend died . . .

¡No es posible!

Don't think like that. He's fine.

Because the alternative is too painful to think about. How Álvaro's brain may not be fixable like the cut over his eye. How the stem cells can't regenerate back from goop. How, if he was going to know me, I may've already lost my chance.

'But –' I stammer, 'what about his new novel?'

Linny wriggles a sheet from the second shoe box. Scans it. Typewritten words run together and are haphazardly capitalized.

'This is . . . ?' she says. 'Is this . . . ?'

Marla hangs her head. '*Midnight in Miami.*'

What?

No.

Realization beats loud. Obnoxious drums in my ears.

No!

Words flop out. 'He's . . . he's writing it all over again?'

Linny's jaw drops toward the table as she grabs my hand. Fingertips digging into my skin as the weight of all the evidence drops.

THE NOTHING-IS-AS-IT-SEEMS PRINCIPLE:
(This is self-explanatory.)

'Holy shit,' I say. '*Shit*.' Blood rushes to my face, so many things hitting me at once. Dialing back the summer, I try to remember Álvaro mentioning *Midnight in Miami* explicitly. He didn't. Not once. It was always 'his next novel.' He doesn't have any idea that he's already written it.

'Does he remember he's famous?' Linny asks.

I stumble over more words. 'This is like . . . this is like . . .'

This is like, he'll never know me. This is like, I could tell him why I'm in Miami, and he could forget the next day.

After all my theories, it's so disastrously simple.

He didn't disappear into another dimension.

He wasn't stuck in a parallel universe.

He's not a time traveler.

He's just an old man with a common, horrible disease. Nothing astrophysical about it.

Marla says, 'Oh honey, I know y'all have grown attached over the summer. But you must've thought something was wrong, right?'

'I noticed,' Linny says, 'but I didn't think that . . . Well, what happens now?'

'I know he wants to be here. Kind of like a homing mechanism. Is that what it's called? With the birds? But even if he's wandering back here, I can't let him stay. I can't watch him all the time – and it's too dangerous for him to be on his own.' Pause. 'You okay, honey?'

Who, me? Oh, fine. *Muy bien*.

I'm just an atom that's splitting.

A little-known fact is that Einstein originally thought the big bang theory was crap. He couldn't imagine a world without any yesterdays. I can't imagine a world where *Álvaro* doesn't have any yesterdays. I'm 100 percent unprepared for any of this. Like I've been jettisoned into the thermosphere without a space suit, and micrometeorites are pelting me in the face.

Because words refuse to exit my mouth, Linny fumbles through an explanation. 'Sebastian is . . . well, he's . . .'

It explodes out of me. 'I'm Álvaro's son!'

Marla clutches her heart with both hands. All three of us whip our heads toward Álvaro, who *must've* heard.

But no. He's engrossed in his dominoes.

And then Marla's grabbing my head and dragging it to her chest, where she rocks me. 'Honey, I had no idea. Oh honey.'

'He doesn't know,' I say softly into her shirt.

She hugs me tighter, because he never will.

In another taxi, Linny's front teeth pinch her bottom lip. 'I don't know what to say,' she whispers eventually. 'I didn't — if I'd thought about it for even a *second*, I never would have been so gung ho about his new novel, never would've —'

'It's okay.'

The air's warm. Sticky. So are her hands when she grabs mine. 'No, it's not.'

She has the driver take us to Zoo Miami, because it's near Marla's house. And neither of us wants to go home. Although it's an hour and a half before the zoo closes, Linny insists, 'This is the best time to visit. Tourists usually leave by lunch.'

At the gates, we purchase two passes. Hold hands as we meander toward the elephants. (And try to avoid the elephant in the room.) 'Did you come here a lot as a kid?' I say.

She tilts her head from side to side. 'Not *a lot*, but sometimes. Grace didn't like it. All the cages.'

We stop in front of a large enclosure where two African elephants are spraying their backs with water. 'But there aren't any cages,' I say, wiping sweat from the back of my neck.

'All this space is deceptive. Look at them, though. They're not exactly free.' She does the same – swiping away a bead of sweat balancing on her forehead. Then she fixes her glance on me. 'Your neck hasn't stopped twitching since we left Marla's.'

'Oh.' I grip a hand to my throat as if that'll stop it. 'Didn't notice.'

An elephant trumpets. Linny's right – a lot of the tourists are gone, the paths nearly empty. It feels like it's just the animals and us.

'Do you want to talk about it?' Linny asks.

I shake my head no, but when I do, words come out. 'I keep replaying everything Marla said, and it makes sense but it *doesn't*.' I puff out a long stream of air. 'At least all the secrets are out now.'

Linny coughs. 'Yeah. Thank goodness for that.' But her words sound flat. Distant. Like the tide is dragging her voice out to sea. 'Let's look at the big cats next, okay?'

'Sure. Okay.'

At the lion enclosure, she pulls her camera equipment from her backpack. 'Do you mind?'

'No, go ahead.' Pointing to a bench nearby – 'I'm just going to sit down for a minute.' I take her backpack off her hands. 'Here, it'll be easier for you to shoot without holding on to this.'

For a split second, her feet are cemented to the ground. She tugs at an earlobe. But then, rolling her shoulders back – 'It'll only take a sec.'

I ease in the bench, drop the backpack by my feet, and cradle my head in my knees. I can't stop thinking about Álvaro, how he will never know me like I want. How, under a microscope, his nerve endings must look like exploding stars. Maybe they'll develop a cure soon? Like, in the next couple of weeks.

No. Probably not. But there's nothing like a sick parent to make you wish for miracles.

I'm still in this position – head tucked between knees – when I notice that the backpack has yawned open. In it, I see: three years' worth of change. Hair ties.

And something flat, tucked into the interior pocket.

Almost like one of those microfiches (micro-fishes?) that Linny and I gathered clues from at the beginning of the summer. Did she take one or something?

Curious, I grab the edge and pull.

Blink.

My heart lurches into my mouth, because it's a photo. It's a photo of my mom and dad – *my parents* – together. Mom's in bright orange; Dad's touching her hair. They're smiling at each other.

And I'm smiling at them.

I *know* it's me. At one week old, I already had a full head of chestnut hair.

It's Murphy's Law. When things can get screwed up, they will. (I would like to propose a revised version: When things can get worse, they will do so exponentially and with all the force of a kick to the balls.)

So . . . my heart splutters. *So . . .*

He knew about me.

I picture a parallel universe. The three of us in the backyard we could've had. Álvaro and Mom are holding hands, desperately in love, beneath a maple tree that the three of us planted together.

Then I see the shit world as it is: Mom, crouching by my knees last month, telling me a story. 'I never told him about you, Sebastian. He left before I could.' That's all it was – a story, something she invented to shut out the stupid truth. No truer than the stories I'd invented. Álvaro's no more a good dad than he was a tuna fisherman.

He left us. Not just my mom. *Me*.

This whole summer, I've been plotting how to tell him. How to say it *just right*. I never thought that seventeen years ago, he'd already decided he wanted nothing to do with me.

More images come: the first time I saw Álvaro, in the cafeteria. The first time I told him my name. 'Saint Sebastian,' he'd said. 'Patron saint of archers and dying people, no?' At the time I didn't think much of it. But did he know then, by my name, by my eyes that look so much like his? Did it ever cross his mind, even once, that the little bundle of joy in the photo grew up to be me?

Mijo. Mijo. Mijo.

The corners of the photo are dog-eared. Fingerprints are on the gloss. Álvaro's? Linny's?

Linny.

Linny knew. Linny *knew*? How long? Did she know when we were . . . ?

I raise my head from my knees and look at her. Viewfinder pressed firmly to one eye. Filming a lion stretching its paw.

Should I sprint up to her so she can tell me it's all an elaborate misunderstanding? Martians framed her. I will gently shake her shoulder, and she'll smile at me and say, 'Yes, Sebastian. Of course aliens planted that photo in my backpack.'

But what if that doesn't happen? How can I love someone who lets me be the last to know?

I try to re-wedge my brain back into place. Fail.

Knuckles, quickly turning white.

Breath, steady as an earthquake.

In *A Brief Compendium of Astrophysical Curiosities*, Dr. Mangum discusses a space roar: 'This radio signal from outer space is six times louder than NASA predicted. Why is this so?' The first time I heard the term *space roar*, I imagined Atlas the giant bellowing. His voice echoing. Forceful. Loud. Filling the farthest corners of the universe. This is the kind of roar I have in me now.

I want to shout until another galaxy hears it.

But I can't. . . . I can't do this.

AN INVERSE MODEL FOR THE SUCCESS OF SPACE ROARS:
The greater the desire to emit such a sound, the greater the possibility that it comes out as silence.

Facing Linny is not an option. If I don't hear her say she kept this from me, then maybe she didn't.

I slip the photo into my pocket, and then I'm rushing out of the lion exhibit. Past the elephants. Into the parking lot. Down the street. A trapped scream burning up my lungs.

Don't know where I'm going. Just — away.

Linny

35.

WHO: *Sebastian*
WHEN: *This afternoon*
WHY: *Because of me. Return date unknown.*
NOTES: *Things fall apart.*

You shouldn't have given him the backpack.

Concentrating on the lions is about as easy as dismantling the Berlin Wall with a toothpick. How can I focus on anything but Sebastian, crouched on a bench, my backpack (with the photograph!) wedged between his feet?

But if I'd said 'I absolutely NEED to hold on to the backpack,' that would've looked too suspicious, right? How has everything suddenly kaleidoscoped into chaos?

Turning my attention to the lioness in front of me, her long tongue ruffling the fur of her cub, I convince myself it'll be fine and do my best to get one usable shot. The after-rain sun is still throwing mottled light all over the long grasses, and the male lions are lazily devouring a shapeless, red carcass that might've been a deer. I zoom in on the cub instead, follow the outlines of her newborn form, and notice how the mother is cradling her like nothing bad will ever, ever happen.

At first I don't even hear the footsteps. At first I'm so sucked into the shot – for *literally* a split second – that the pounding of sneakers on asphalt doesn't break my concentration. But then a wave of realization crashes into the back of my neck. I spin around, almost dropping my camera.

My backpack's there. Sebastian's not.

Calm down. Maybe he . . . needed an urgent bathroom break?

Rushing to the bench, I drop to my knees and fumble desperately through my backpack. I feel in the pocket, around the edges, in every corner. *No, no, no.*

The whole zoo seems to tilt on its axis as I grab my stuff and dash toward the exit, calling Sebastian's name. But when I reach the parking lot, I only see the back of his head, bobbing off into the distance.

THE LEFT-BEHINDS (scene 16, continued)

LINNY's eyes snap to focus. We see that she is crying.

Sebastian

36.

'We are fairly certain that the universe began with a big bang . . . but how will it end?' *A Brief Compendium of Astrophysical Curiosities*, p. 43

I've had approximately twenty-five minutes of a wild sprint through the street to string together my thoughts. In which time I've narrowed them down to one: *What the actual fuck?*

When something dramatic happens, it's natural to act dramatically. That's why I'm hunched on the curb outside a 7-Eleven. Not quite believing what's happening but trying to slurp myself to death anyway.

This Slurpee tastes *red*. Like high fructose corn syrup and a number 40 dye and other things that will surely give me debilitating stomach cramps. I've had two Slurpees in under twelve minutes. Wobbled back inside for another refill. The guy behind the register probably thinks I'm casing the place.

In my chemical haze, three things occur to me. 1) The human bladder can comfortably hold two cups of liquid. I'm well past the danger zone. 2) Floridians buy way too many powdered doughnuts. And 3) I WAS WRONG ABOUT ABSOLUTELY EVERYTHING.

I set Slurpee number three between my feet and examine my knees, which are moderately bleeding. After bolting, I sped around in a blind flurry, tripping a few times on the pavement.

Ended up three and a half miles away, dry-heaving beneath an overpass. Because I did not see this coming. Not at all.

My energy level is so high I'm vibrating (although maybe that's from the Slurpee). Even sitting on the pavement I'm twitchy, can't sit still.

I pick up the Slurpee, take another hit, and dial Mom's number.

Two rings, and then she picks up, excitement in her voice – 'Sebastian! Oh, Sebastian, I'm so happy to hear from you.'

'I, you –' I splutter, staring at the photo in my left hand.

'Sweetheart, what's wrong?'

I'm so quiet, I can barely hear myself. 'Álvaro left me, too, didn't he?'

A pause on the line. Whispering: 'Who told you?'

'No one,' I say. My lungs have forgotten how to accept oxygen. I'm dizzy.

'No one. No one ever tells me anything.'

'I love you,' she says. 'I love you *so* much, Sebastian. I couldn't let you . . . I couldn't let you go through what I went through.'

Too late. Everything aches.

There must be another pause, because Mom says, 'Talk to me, Sebastian.'

But I *can't*. Doesn't she understand that? How can I talk when I can't even breathe?

It starts to rain again.

'How old was I?' I finally manage. 'When he left?'

Mom is quiet, silence prickling the phone – I can tell she's deciding something. 'Eight days old.'

I dump out the rest of the Slurpee onto the concrete, watch it swish with the rain and trail into the gutter like foamy blood.

'I have to go,' I say.

'Sebastian, I —'

But I can't hear another word without fucking exploding. I end the call, slap the photo — image side up — onto the concrete, and leave it as I bike away, rain splattering all over our grinning faces.

Linny sends me eight texts and calls three times before I switch off my phone.

I keep picturing her *knowing*, while we were . . .

I guess it doesn't matter now.

By the time I take a taxi back to Ana's, my chest burns. Literal heartache. The condo door is unlocked, like Ana's expecting me. I wobble in, panting and unsteady from the Slurpee/sprinting/grief combo. She's at the dining-room table. Drilling her fingers against the wood.

'I was worried sick about you,' she says when she sees me. And she *looks* sick. Red rings her eyes. Sweat rings her armpits. In sum: she looks completely unhinged. 'You were supposed to be home *four hours ago*, and then your mom called and I —'

'Did you know, too?'

She scratches at her skin. Her voice is the low end of a bell curve. So quiet it's concaving. 'Yes. But Sebastian, *cariño*, your mom and I agreed that it was best for you to keep believing what you believed.'

When will this family learn that secrets always explode?

Sweeping her hair into both hands, she sighs, then lets her waves down again. The room is a box of tension. 'Sit down and we'll talk about this.'

'*No gracias.*'

'Sebastian.'

I shake my head, hair flopping in my face. Full rocket-charged, I lunge into the bathroom and lock the door. Spend the next forty minutes lying in the empty bathtub, fully clothed, because that's the only place I can be alone. Ana keeps knocking. Sure, she probably has a key – but she's too afraid to open the door and catch a glimpse of my man bits, forever scarring our relationship.

Scarring it *further*, I guess. It already needs stiches.

After the 107th knock, I bust out of the bathroom, out of the condo, into the street – needing to get some air. And then I'm on Ana's bike, unsure of where I'm going until I'm at Linny's house. It's dark.

I turn on my phone and dial her number on the edge of her lawn. She answers 'Hello,' and immediately I want her to tell me it isn't true. But deep down I know it is.

When I say 'We need to talk,' I already know it's over between us.

A THEORY FOR THE END:
(See RELATIONSHIP WITH A GIRL*)*

Linny

37.

NOTES: Why am I still doing this? What's the point?

Sebastian's waiting at the end of my street, far enough away from my house that MomandDad can't peek out the blinds and see. It's just after nine at night, the sky heartsick blue and quickly bruising to black. As I walk up to him, I almost comment that I feel like a shadow in this dark. But he won't look me in the eyes, doesn't even respond when I greet him with a weak 'Hello.' Something terribly dark is trying to escape from his mouth.

'Hey,' I try again, but I fear it's too late for *hey* and *hello* and *how's it going*. In my stomach is a pile of stones weighing me into the blacktop. One more rock and I'll be practically underground, scampering around with the mole people.

At Marla's house, I should've said something. I should've told him every little detail of everything I knew. I should've placed the photo in his palms, because now explanations are slipping through my fingers like water.

I didn't want you to know what it felt like.

I was protecting you.

How flimsy do those words sound, now that he's swaying from side to side in front of me, intermittently blocking the moon?

After a long moment, he speaks in a shredded voice. 'I am *always* the last to know, and I thought you – I thought . . . Why didn't you tell me?'

I chew on my lips. 'Because I didn't want to hurt you, and I . . . I probably would have told you eventually, but –'

'Eventually? Wow, thanks. Glad I'm so important that you'd get around to it *eventually*.'

'That's not what I –'

'Did you know when we were having sex?'

My heart treadmills. 'What? No! Only since this morning, when we found Joe's address. It was . . . Álvaro kept it on his nightstand, tucked in a book.'

'So you knew the entire time we were with Marla.'

'Yes, but –'

'Jesus, Linny. Doesn't this' – he motions between him and me – 'doesn't this mean anything to you? I thought we were . . .' He trails off as the air twists and burns around us. 'All I can think about is how you *lied* to me, like everyone in my family.' The way he says it does something weird to my skin.

'Sebastian, I didn't *lie* to –'

'I think it's best if we don't speak for a while.'

I almost tumble forward. Might as well have said, 'I think it's best if you don't breathe for a while.' Same effect. 'Oh' is all I can muster. What did I expect, for him to immediately understand my reason for not telling him? For us to have a nice little chat at the edge of my neighborhood in the dark? I get this shredded thing more than ever. 'Do you just need some time?' I ask, hopeful.

His jaw clenches. He's chewing the angriest piece of gum. 'Time won't fix it, Linny. I'm going to college at the end of the summer anyway, so . . . I think maybe, I don't know. . . .'

No. Please. Please. Please. Don't say it.

You know how people claim that when you die your whole life flashes before your eyes? I can attest that the same thing happens during breakups: every moment of your relationship, frame by frame, whips through your brain.

Cinderella shoe. Ball pit. Kisses under glow-in-the-dark stars.

His skin to my skin, coated in color.

'I think maybe it's wrecked,' he says in a volcanic voice, his hands like birds scattering, 'this thing between us.'

The words scorch my skin. *Wrecked*. And he thinks I'm the one who wrecked it.

I feel myself nodding. Why on Earth am I nodding? Maybe my neck's the only working part of my body. Everything else is immobile, smothered. I mind-film the street – all the Dolphin Egg Blue houses collapsing.

At this point, would *sorry* make a difference? No. The answer is definitely no.

Tears burn my cheeks, and at first I assume it's raining. But no, it's me. I'm breaking, sinking, leaking from the inside out.

'You know how this feels?' Sebastian continues, tearing up a bit himself. He doesn't finish the thought, even though I already know how it must feel: worse than betrayal, an ax-mark through his trust.

Say something, my every brain cell screams. *Anything!* But all I do is watch dumbly as he runs a hand through his mussed-up hair, clasps his handlebars, and says one last thing: 'I loved you, you know?'

No, I didn't, not really. The past tense of the word socks me right in the cheek. Judging by the creases in his face, love has transformed into something very different.

The worst thing? I love him – present tense.

In the movies, girls always fall for guys who are a little broken; but usually, they're not the ones to break them.

Maybe Álvaro broke him first. Maybe we used the same ax.

Sebastian's feet are a whir in the pedals, speeding away like I'm a bomb about to explode this whole neighborhood to smithereens. (Maybe I am. Sure feels like it.)

Four days ago, he was saying, 'I'm not a leaver,' and what does he do the first major chance he gets? Why does everyone leave me when I need them to stay?

When he doesn't look back – not once – an overwhelming need to run floods through me, so I do; I spin around and sprint, praying I'll go so fast I'll sprint myself back through time. I run until my hands bleed into the air. I run until my breath is faster than I can catch. I run until the stars on my shoes can't hold on any longer, until they lose their grip and slip off like they were never there.

It rains.

In classic films, rain symbolizes renewal, but on the first day of Sebastian not speaking to me, as rain seeps under cracks in doors and windowpanes, I realize that's a bunch of boloney. I feel just as wrecked as I did before.

Early in the morning, I call in sick to Silver Springs. It's the truth, isn't it? All my symptoms mimic the flu. In the shower, I double over from all the guilt and hurt flooding my abdomen in electric waves and afterward plunk down on my bedroom carpet, my hair still wet. Staring up at the plastic constellation on my ceiling, I pray that it has retained some magical wish-upon-a-star quality. So far, no luck. By ten a.m., Sebastian hasn't texted, called, or sent a carrier pigeon.

I press my lips together to keep from screaming bloody murder.

The rest of the morning, I gorge on M&M'S, watch *An Officer and a Gentleman*, absorb none of its plot, contemplate if happy endings are only realistic in unreal worlds. But most of all, I think of Sebastian.

I think of us in Cass's garage. I think of us putting each other back together, only to tear ourselves apart.

Checking my phone once more – seeing there's nothing from him – is enough to tip me off the edge. My heart guides my fingers, knowing just what to do.

Cass answers groggily on the third ring. 'Linzer Torte?'

'Hey' – forcing out words – 'can I come over?'

I can hear her sitting up, concerned. 'What's wrong?'

'Just, can I come over?'

'Yeah, yeah, we'll make breakfast or something.'

'It's noon.'

'We'll make noon breakfast.'

In her kitchen twenty minutes later, I run my fingers over one of the orange streamers still hanging from the party. 'Haven't cleaned up yet?' I say.

Cass grips her temples, obviously hungover. She's wearing a royal-blue dress with a crisscrossed back, like she passed out after the club. For a second, I feel even worse. Did she go out with Ray last night? And why wasn't I invited? 'My parents thought the streamers added a certain je ne sais quoi. But that's besides the point.' She throws a hand over mine on the countertop. 'What's going on?'

I steady myself. 'It's about Sebastian.'

'Oh my God,' she says. 'Are you okay? Did you two . . . Linny, did you have sex?'

Seriously? Can she read it on my face?

'No, of course not.' It's a knee-jerk reaction, what I've been blurting out for years. I don't even know why I say it — because this time I'm no longer the Virgin Marilyn. I quickly realize that Cass would make me feel like I've joined a club; all the specialness would leach out of it, and I want it to be ours — just mine and Sebastian's — a little bit longer. Isn't that all I have left?

Cass says, 'Half the school saw you guys making out in that tree, you know. It wasn't too far of a stretch. . . . So what's happened then?'

There's a fumbling down the stairs as Ray emerges in jeans and a pajama top, scratching his head. 'Waffles or pancakes?' he says before he sees me, and then: 'Oh, Linny's here! Hi! Definitely waffles.'

I'm pondering what about me inherently signals *waffles* when Cass explains Ray's presence. 'We had a late night last night and his parents are in New York.' To Ray: 'Linny was about to tell me something,' and instantly all eyes are on me. It's too much. Are the lights getting brighter?

'Not before waffles,' I say, attempting to sound cheery.

Cass surveys the fridge, which has a few lonely cans of beer in the vegetable containers.

'Can you put alcohol in waffles?' Ray asks.

'Why would you *want* to?' I say.

'Doesn't matter.' Cass slams the fridge. 'My mom forgot to buy eggs. And flour. And sugar. Soooo . . . Pie in the Sky?'

'Pie in the Sky,' Ray repeats.

The three of us hop into Cass's mom's Subaru, Cass (still in clubbing clothes) at the wheel. Light pours into the car. Obviously hungover, Ray groans, 'So. Bright.'

'Kind of ironic,' I point out gloomily, 'coming from a former Ray of sunshine.'

Ten minutes later, we rock up to the bakery. It's kind of our place since Grace left. Sometimes we'll skip third-period gym and drive here to stuff our faces with double-chocolate mocha chip cookies. Cass always claims, 'It'll just go to our chests,' and who can argue with that logic? (Well, Ray. He has no desire for boobs.)

Inside, Pie in the Sky is air-conditioned bliss. We order coffee and enough pastries to feed a small African village.

'We'll take seven croissants,' Cass says, 'and three chocolate doughnuts.'

'And coffee,' I grunt. 'Just — all the coffee.'

Cass and Ray are already at our usual table — the one at the back, by the windows — and Ray is still complaining: 'So. Freaking. Sunny.'

As I sit down, Cass waggles a piece of doughnut under Ray's nostrils. 'Take a bite. Yummy, yummy, soak up the alcohol in your tummy.'

'Are you trying to make me barf?' Ray says, but eventually submits. Mouth reluctantly full, he asks me, 'You okay, Linny?'

I can't tell him. I can't. It's too complicated, too embarrassingly personal, but maybe I can abstract the situation?

'Cass, remember when we were kids,' I slowly begin, 'and our moms told us not to swallow watermelon seeds, because they'd grow inside our stomachs?'

'No,' Cass says.

'Well, *my* mom said that.'

'Your mom is terrifying.'

'Point taken. Anyway, I feel like that. I swallowed this *thing*, and I thought it wouldn't grow into something, but –'

'Oh, honey,' Ray says, cutting me off, a smile inching up his face. 'Your parents are *gynecologists*. You should know you can't get pregnant from giving a blow job.'

To our right, an elderly woman stops midbite and puts down her croissant to glare at us.

'Oh my God,' I say. 'That's not at all what I'm talking about.'

A stab of sadness flashes across Cass's face as concern shoots to Ray's eyes. 'Okay,' he says. 'Then what *are* you talking about?'

The shop suddenly feels very hot. Is the air-conditioning still on? 'Okay, something's happened with . . . Well, I found out a secret and I kept it from Sebastian, and he knows now.'

To Cass and Ray, secrets are like catnip. 'What is it?' they say simultaneously.

'I probably shouldn't tell you, but . . . it kind of affects his entire life.' *And we broke up because of it*. Somehow, those last words turn to thorns – won't unstick from my throat.

'Then why didn't you tell him?' Cass says immediately.

Because I thought it would destroy him, and it did anyway.

'It's complicated,' I say.

Cass's eyes widen. 'You *did* sleep with him, didn't you? Oh my gosh, you totally slept with him.'

Ray reminds me of a deer that's just been spotted by a hunter; if he stays perfectly still, maybe it will all go away. 'Not that we're judging you,' he quietly adds.

'No,' Cass says. 'We totally are judging you, and not because you lost your virginity. Because this is *exactly* what friends are for, Linny – you're supposed to tell us things! We're supposed to *talk* about things.' I'm not entirely sure we're discussing sex anymore. Her voice is climbing a roller coaster; it hitches at the top. 'Do you know what it's been like for me? Do you have any idea? You think I want to talk just for *you*? What about me, Linny? Have you ever asked how *I'm* doing? It's like you've completely forgotten that Grace was mine, too!'

My stomach mirrors her voice as I go down, down, down – and then down some more – because I didn't mean to forget. I was shoved so quickly into the hole that Grace left, I never stopped to *truly* consider that someone else was in the pit with me.

I don't know why it's hitting me so hard now. All those parties she invited me to? Maybe she wasn't just trying to get *me* out of the house. Maybe she was trying to preserve *herself*, our group, what's left of us. She has a Grace-shaped hole in her heart, too, and she's just trying to plug it up. When I couldn't make room to care about her, she was still working hard to care about me.

Even though I'm running over solutions to fix this, all I can come up with is, 'Cass, I'm . . .'

She explodes. 'And what about Ray? You know, he and Lawrence broke up last night, but I doubt you would've asked about it. Stop being so selfish, Linny.'

I chance a look at Ray, but he won't return my glance. Is it possible to feel any worse?

'Whatever!' Cass yells. She says to Ray, 'I think we should go.'

So we do. Most of the pastries are uneaten. The baker boxes them up and says, 'See ya soon' as Cass and Ray trail out the door in a different direction from me. It's hard to imagine we'll ever go there again.

It's so much easier in film. You don't like a scene? Delete and rewind. In real life, you get dizzy on the spot and grit your teeth in aching silence. There are no do overs, no second takes. You perform the scene and then live with the consequences.

These are the consequences.

I can't stop hurting the people I love.

THE LEFT-BEHINDS (scene 16, continued)

CUT TO –

Blackness.

Sebastian

38.

'I am moved to believe that scientists who attempt to solve these mysteries will stumble upon additional conundrums. It is a perpetual spiral.' *A Brief Compendium of Astrophysical Curiosities*, p. 399

Instead of returning to Silver Springs, I read Dr. Mangum's book from cover to cover and flip through the TV channels. End up watching the weirdest stuff. At noon, I kid you not, there's *Sock Puppet Theater* on channel 7, followed by some cheaply funded documentary. A bearded ornithologist is drawling on about geese migration.

It's so effing boring.

I watch the entire thing because Linny would.

Turns out, scientists don't know a whole lot about why birds skedaddle every year. It's a genetic impulse. They might navigate based on the stars or magnetic fields. The guy massages his beard and explains, 'The most important environmental cue is the scarcity of food.'

I get that.

But why do they fly back?

If there's enough food in their winter home, then why do these stupid birds travel another thousand miles to get back to where they came from? Why do they keep picking up and leaving, over and over again?

More importantly, why am I getting so worked up about it?

THE BIRDS CONUNDRUM:
If birds fly back, then why couldn't Álvaro return to my mother, to me? Why does one mystery end at the same time another begins?

On-screen the geese are in a V formation, and the ornithologist is saying how they can only flock together. How they wouldn't survive alone.

This is the type of thing I'd discuss with Linny, if she were here.

But she isn't.

She isn't here when Ana and I make coconut chicken. She isn't pressing her nose into my book to ask what I'm reading. She isn't resting her head on my shoulder, telling me she's sleepy. She isn't here to talk about how everything got so effed up. And it's killing me. She stays away, like I told her to.

Until she doesn't.

The day after we break up, the doorbell rings late in the afternoon.

Ana answers in her scrubs and repeats what I told her to say in this situation. 'Sorry, he's not here.'

Linny's voice: 'Oh.'

I wonder what she's thinking. Because of course I'm here. Where else would I be?

'It's not done yet, but could you give this to him?' Linny says. 'I want him to know why I did what I did.'

'Okay, sweetie,' Ana says. 'I'll give it to him.'

I cave in to temptation. Rush over to the blinds. I want to see if she looks as sad as I feel. She does. *Worse* than I feel, if possible. She stays on the doorstep a few moments, even after Ana shuts the door.

Linny's head whips to the side, to where I am.

Damn it. She must've seen the blinds rustle.

I shrink back into the living room, where Ana gently sets a small stack of papers on the coffee table. 'For you,' she says.

I peer down at it. On the front page in large script, it reads:

The Left-Behinds
by Linny Carson

Linny

39.

WHO: *Javier Rojas, a firefighter*

WHEN: *Seventeen hours in 2015*

WHY: *The Chilean government reported the tragic death of Javier, who rushed into a burning courthouse in Viña del Mar, attempting to save two judges. But really, he was alive; during the building's collapse, a wooden board struck him in the temple, and he escaped through the back exit in a serious daze. According to the news stories, Javier wandered the streets for seventeen hours, concussed, until he finally remembered where he was — and who he was — and walked back home.*

NOTES: *Huh. Remembering who we are. Who ARE we without her?*

Eerie doesn't begin to describe the feeling of coming back from Sebastian's house and seeing Mom perched on the couch. Not scrubbing the tile. Not flipping through medical reports. Just . . . sitting, rigid and upright. She says nothing as I slip upstairs, says nothing as I shut my door to the world, says nothing as I notice that where the plastic stars once were there are now blank spaces on the ceiling, white paint flecks chipping, one or two falling like first snow.

(Note to self: Install padlocks on door.)

Maybe I suck in a breath or clench my teeth or jam my fingers into fists. I don't know. I can't feel anything except the movement of my feet trouncing down the stairs.

MomandDad are both in the living room now – Dad flipping through *Scientific American*, Mom still sitting, picking bits of lint off the pashmina pillows.

'Why did you do that?' I exclaim. 'Do you have any idea how much those meant? How much . . .' I falter, raise my hands to the back of my head because I genuinely fear it's about to roll off.

'Darling,' Mom says, slowly crossing her legs. 'You're obviously going through –' She glances at Dad for the right word, but when his lips remain motionless, she pushes on. 'Let's call it a phase. Even so, you can't just decide to desecrate your ceiling without asking our permission.'

'But it's *my* room.'

'And *our* house.'

I flinch.

Tenting *Scientific American* in his lap, Dad asks, 'What are we talking about?'

Huh. Mom acted alone. Have things *actually* changed since he found Sebastian and me in my closet? 'Marilyn glued some cheap plastic stars to her ceiling,' she says. 'Completely destroyed the paint job when I took them down.'

'Why?' Dad says.

'That's a good question, Marilyn. Please tell us what you were thinking.'

'No,' Dad says, inching forward on his chair, 'I mean, why'd you take them down?'

She waves her hand dismissively and digs into me again. 'I'm sorry if you find our rules too restricting, but throwing fits doesn't change anything. Like it or not, you are going to follow the rules, because they're there for a reason. They are there for *structure*. You need that now more than ever. . . . You know, when you're thirty-five and a successful doctor, you're going to think: "Thank God my parents had rules. Thank God my parents wanted more for me than I wanted for myself."' She drags in a breath. 'It's probably best if you go to your room.'

Me too. I think it's best if I never come out again.

But for some strange reason, my legs don't move. My lips do. 'Why can't you see that I'm not happy? That you're *squishing* me, just like our clay people. Just like Grace. And now she's probably never coming back!'

What did I just say?

I slap both hands over my mouth, trying to prevent any other words from seeping out. But it's too late – I let out a crazy, sad groan, and my words form fists that smack me silly, straight into a wall of pulverizing sadness. For the first time this summer, I wonder if I've been living in black and white on purpose, if living in a colorful world means fully accepting that she's gone.

You know that rule I have about not making waves? Well, pretty sure I've just initiated a tsunami.

I said *Grace* – out loud, to *them*.

I brace myself for the impact, but the strangest thing occurs: gruff words blast from MomandDad – and they're not directed at me.

Dad exclaims, 'This is exactly what I've been talking about, June,' and Mom pushes back, 'Eric, not now.' Almost forgot, MomandDad have names. Almost forgot they were capable of fighting. Usually if they do, it's about little things: Dad forgetting to empty the recycling bin, Mom leaving the downstairs bathroom light on until it fizzles. On the subject of me, they've been unanimous for as long as I can remember, and *especially* since

Grace left. To hold this family together. Now their voices rise to screams.

In my mind, I can see the rope fraying between them, getting more and more slack until it drops to the floor in a resounding *thud*. MomandDad sever into Mom and Dad, two separate and distinct people, who continue to explode several feet from each other, enough sparks flying that the carpet might go up in flames.

Dad's aging a year a minute as cryptic phrases fly from his mouth: 'You should have gone, June. You should have been there. We should have both been there. . . .'

Mom's removing the bobby pins from her bun, all the while shouting, 'That was not what was best for them, Eric, and you know as well as I do that structure is best. What kind of mother would I be if . . .'

Whoa. Hold up. Gone where? I try to get in a word, but Mom and Dad edge me out, the creases in their foreheads so deep, you could row canoes through them. A million thoughts dart through my mind, but foremost is what Sebastian said when he and I were in my closet, about opening the box.

I'm unhappy to report that the cat is dead. None of us are breathing.

Mom starts tearing up suddenly, and then the real tsunami hits – she *sobs*, her whole body convulsing and making noises like something is dying inside of her, which I guess it is. I quickly scan the room for glass objects, because it looks like she wants to break something. Dad crosses his hands over his chest, as if he's trying to fold himself up and disappear.

I've never seen them like this. Never.

Not even right after Grace left. They were breaking down then, too – they were just breaking down *together*.

This lasts for an eternity (the crying, the wish to be anywhere but here), but then Mom declares through a sob that she's very busy — she has journals to peer review — and without another word retreats upstairs to her bedroom, her hair unraveled at her back. Dad's hair looks different too: thinner, patches of white cresting his temples. How long has he had a bald spot, and why have I never noticed?

I collapse onto the bottom stair and inhale gulp after gulp of air. (Well, at least one of us is breathing.)

'I have to —' Dad begins, and stops. His hands travel to his pockets. 'Have to . . . see about . . . yeah.' Then he leaves me on the stairs, and moments later I hear the roar of his Volvo driving away.

And again, it's my fault. Everything breaks in my hands.

Dad doesn't come home for three hours. When he returns, he spends another fifteen minutes puttering around the garage, the car doors opening and closing. Through my bedroom window I see him finally cut across the yard, swiping yellow dust off his hands. I don't question it. I don't want to know where he's been, what he's doing. I've had enough complexity to fill several lifetimes. Instead, I lie on my bed, look up at the blank ceiling, and write a film in my head: *The Girl Who Built a Time Machine to Erase Her Mistakes*. (It's a short movie. I don't succeed.)

So I lift Hector from his terrarium and let him crawl around my floor, leaving a trail of turtle poop on the white carpet. I think about Hector's family, wonder if they're missing him — if they're falling apart, too.

Five minutes later, there's a knock at my door. So light, it's like rain falling. I pretend I'm asleep.

THE LEFT-BEHINDS (scene 17)

MIAMI BEACH DAY

We see from LINNY's perspective as she opens her eyes. The mostly blue sky blinks in and out of view.

She is lying in the sand near the boardwalk and sits up to see ...

... she is completely – and rather frighteningly – alone. The sand is black, the sea white.

Then:

LINNY
(to no one)
How did ... how did I ...?

We hear the flutter of wings from above.

And see a break in the clouds.

Sebastian

40.

'Although we can only infer its existence, we know that dark matter neither emits nor absorbs light.' *A Brief Compendium of Astrophysical Curiosities*, p. 211

In my dream, Álvaro is dark haired again. Leading me through a swamp of paper. Gone are his orthopedic shoes. I wear knee-high boots to wade through the swamp.

The angrier I get, the higher the paper tide rises. Eventually we're floating on our backs like starfish. Above, no sky. *Solo blanco*.

I sit up and tread paper, furious. 'Did you know all along?'

He's four feet away and drifting farther. I wonder if he hears me.

'When you first saw me,' I say, louder this time. 'Did you know I was your son?'

Álvaro shrugs. Paper ripples above his shoulders. 'I don't know.' Still on his back, he removes a cigarillo from his pocket. Lights up. I notice the skin around his neck is beginning to pucker. 'How can I know? Everything slips. I hold on to nothing.'

I shake my head, fuming. 'How can I believe you?'

I tell myself it's okay to yell at him because 1) He's young now, and 2) He looks healthy. Yelling at an Alzheimer's patient is unacceptable, but this floating man's not even sick.

'Do you know what you've done, Álvaro? Do you have any effing idea?' I pound the floating papers, but they sink.

Álvaro's voice chokes through smoke. 'Any idea of what?'

I feel a faint suction from below.

Oh no.

I try to grasp something. Anything. But the papers sink. Fifteen feet away, Álvaro's skin turns transparent.

His hair goes white.

His body crumples.

In one fluid motion, the papers absorb him. I swim over. Try to part the swamp. I hold my breath and dive under. But suddenly whatever's tugging him tugs me.

It has my feet.

It pulls me into the deep.

I wake up.

I'm lying on my back like in the dream. My cell phone's buzzing beneath the couch pillows. Groggily, I answer.

I've watched enough movies with Linny to know this is what they say: 'There's been an accident.' It sounds so removed. To someone, somewhere in the world, an accident has occurred.

At first all Ana says is 'Sebastian,' and I know from the way she breathes it. Just know. 'Álvaro,' she says. 'There's been an accident.'

Even if I watched a thousand movies in a row, those words – said about Álvaro – would still hit me like an asteroid to the chest. I recall how giraffes clamp their nostrils closed during sandstorms. But as far as I know, no animal can shut down its eardrums and block out sound. Wish I could have been the first. Didn't hear 'There's been an accident.'

Ana says, 'I'm coming to get you.'

The line goes dead.

A THEORY ON DARK MATTER IN THE REAL WORLD:
It exists.

*

The waiting room wall is becoming my best friend. It's the only thing holding me up. Leaned against it, I survey the chaos. Emergency room doors bang open and closed. Someone is screaming. The intercom crackles and pops.

In Ana's car, I made a list of everything I wish I'd said to Álvaro. I mentally crossed most of it out.

~~Why didn't you tell me?~~

~~I think I might hate you.~~

~~I will never forgive you.~~

I *want* to hate him, after everything he did. I want to think he's an asshat. I thought maybe he'd changed, that I should give him the benefit of the doubt. But who does that to a mother? Who does that to a baby?

But what kind of son hates a father with Alzheimer's?

The list ended up being only one item long: *No matter what, I'll be there.*

Down the hall, Ana – still in blue scrubs – is speaking with a doctor who crosses his arms a lot. Definite arm crosser. Definite floor gazer. There's nodding and more nodding. Every few minutes a different nurse's aide pops up like a Whack-A-Mole. Offers me hot coffee or a copy of *Us Weekly* (magical cure-alls, apparently).

But no one will tell me anything.

Is he still in the ER?

The ICU?

¿Está despierto?

Can I see him?

Hence, my friendship with the wall. I lock out my knees to keep from tumbling.

Before too long, another nurse – one of Ana's friends, I think –

trots over from his station to rub my shoulder. 'Might as well sit down, son. It's probably going to be a while.'

Son? Is he effing kidding me?

Worst possible word to use.

I shrug him off and decide to pull out *The Left-Behinds* from Ana's purse. I grabbed it on the way out of the condo. Haven't read more than the first page since Linny dropped it off, but I guess I've got nothing but time.

So I start reading, right there against the wall.

The script begins with two sisters together. It changes to two girls apart. The wings are cool, the writing's good, but I don't completely understand why Linny wanted me to read this.

That is, until I flip to the last page.

THE LEFT-BEHINDS (scene 17, continued)

GRACE descends onto the sand, yellow wings outstretched.

LINNY
(shocked)

> Am I . . . I must be dreaming, right?

A shrug of GRACE's wings.

GRACE

> I'm not sure it makes a difference.

LINNY stands up.

LINNY

    You can't be serious.

GRACE frowns. Clearly, she isn't following.

GRACE

    Um –

LINNY

(fully shouting)

    You show up NOW after ALL THIS TIME, and it DOESN'T
    MAKE A DIFFERENCE?

GRACE

    That's not what I –

LINNY

(partly shouting)

    They're not growing, Grace, okay? You got your stupid wings,
    and I'm stuck here. You left me, do you understand?

GRACE is on the brink of tears.

GRACE

    I'm not sure you're the one who understands.

LINNY

    Really? Oh, really?

(inhaling sharply)

    You were supposed to love me most in the world, Grace, and

you left me behind. You did it on purpose. That's the thing.

You knew you were abandoning me, and you did it anyway.

The last three sentences are circled in blue ink, with stars around the words.

Oh. Oh, Linny. I get it.

Being left behind is one thing. Being left behind *on purpose* is infinitely shittier. All the things he's missed. My first science fair. My prom. That time I built a rocket in the backyard. He's missed all of it intentionally.

This – this shit right now – is exactly what Linny was trying to avoid, and I've been a grade A asshat in return.

Good work, Sebastian. Good fucking job.

I debate whether I should call her. (Con: I deserve a kick in the nut-sack. Maybe twelve kicks. Pro: Seeing her. Hearing her voice.)

Decision made. No matter how much I effed it up, I hope she'll understand why I'm about to tumble.

I press Call, and when she answers 'Sebastian,' all the words congeal in my throat.

'There's been an accident,' I say eventually.

'Are you okay?' Her breath is heavy. 'What kind of accident?'

I tell her that a nurse at Silver Springs heard a thud in the night. That she saw Álvaro face-up in a pile of papers in his room, body contorted like a bird that just flew into a windshield. 'They think he slipped – hard – and hit the back of his head on his desk,' I say. 'He lost a lot of blood, but . . . Well, they don't know much yet.'

'Is he . . . ?' She stops. 'Do you think he'll be all right?'

'Maybe.' I don't really say the word. More like vomit it. 'Maybe. I hope so.'

'I'll be there in twenty minutes, tops.'

'It's . . . it's too far to bike.'

'I'm taking my parents' car.'

'They'll never let you out of the house at two in the morning.'

'Who said I was going to ask them?'

'Linny . . .'

'What my parents think is *seriously* the last thing on my mind right now, okay? See you soon.'

I hang up the phone and grate my fingers through my hair just as Ana finishes nodding at the doctor. Walking over at a remarkably slow speed, she presses her back against the friendship wall. Drapes a heavy arm around my shoulders.

'He's in the ICU. Jay says we should have the next update in under an hour.'

'Why so long?'

She's back to her nurse voice. 'The doctors need time. Álvaro has experienced a pretty serious head trauma. He was dead for two minutes. It's now wait and see.'

Dead. He was already dead.

My heart constricts. Think I mean that figuratively? No. I mean a giant literally rips open my chest. Grips my heart in his meaty hand. Squeezes.

Squeezes until no blood flows.

Squeezes until Ana has to shake the breath back into me.

She clutches both of my shoulders and says, 'Look at me.' Clinical nurse no longer. 'Whatever happens, everything will be okay. You are so strong, Sebastian. So strong.'

Not true.

I am a Lego set that someone has hammered apart.

I am a tiny speck of space dust.

'So strong,' she repeats. 'And I'm so sorry things didn't turn out like you'd hoped.'

I'm still chewing on that thought fifteen minutes later when two things happen simultaneously.

The first: an Indian doctor with an unreadable expression emerges from behind the double doors.

The second: Linny bursts into the waiting room. She's breathless and wearing her reindeer pajamas, like on the Night of the Plastic Stars. As soon as she spots me, she runs. Literally *runs* across the room to my side. Out of her mouth flies: 'Any news?'

The doctor clears his throat. 'Are any of you the family of Álvaro Herrera?'

I clear my throat in return. 'Me. He's my dad.'

'How old are you, son?'

'Seventeen.'

A pause. 'Are there any adult family members present?'

Ana steps in before I lose it. 'Tom,' she says, because of course she knows this asshat. 'I'm his guardian. Is there news?'

Dr. Tom's eyes flicker from Ana to me and back again.

Why isn't he saying anything?

Speak, damn it! Speak!

And he does.

And the words infiltrate the air.

And I take one step backward.

And Álvaro's gone.

A SECOND THEORY ON DARK MATTER, BASED ON CURRENT OBSERVATIONS:
It can consume the entire world.

Linny

41.

WHO: *Álvaro Herrera*
WHEN: *Three years, then a day, then forever*
WHY: *Alzheimer's. Confusion. Loneliness. All the sad things.*
NOTES: *I don't think he's coming back this time.*

Even after Ana and Sebastian return home, I stay one, two, three hours. Leaving makes it real. Leaving makes it over.

Slumped on a waiting room couch, I contemplate forever, because that's what's getting to me – not that Álvaro died, but that he died *forever*. A resurrection happening twice in one summer is highly unlikely.

Hadn't I been bracing myself for this? Yes and no. He was old, yes; he had an incurable disease, yes, but part of me still viewed him as invincible. All of me *wanted* him to be invincible.

How long can I stay here? How long before reporters touch down like vultures on a fresh kill?

Too many firsts tonight. I've never sneaked out in the middle of the night, never commandeered the family Volvo, never seen a boy cry right in front of me. It's not the first time I've been in this hospital, though. I had a bone-breaking spree in the seventh grade: wrist, arm, and big toe in quick succession. (Blame it on soccer, which Mom insisted I play to showcase my well-roundedness.) Grace would try to sidetrack me from the pain, holding my face in her hands and demanding, 'Hey, hey, look at me. Do *not* think about elephants,' and inevitably – for a few seconds, at least – I thought about elephants instead of my splintered bones.

I would give anything for her to be here, for Álvaro to be here, for all of us to be thinking about elephants.

The sun's poking through palm trees by the time I peel myself off the couch. As I sag out of the hospital, my eyes wander across the emergency room parking lot, and then in a jolt-to-the-heart kind of way, I realize I'm looking at Marla's silver Honda – and Marla's in it. Her hands are glued to the steering wheel, even though the car's motionless. The way she's crying and shaking, I'm surprised the car doesn't move, surprised the continental United States doesn't move.

She sees me. For one shuddering moment, we lock eyes, and we are two people who've lost the same person – because it *is* a person who we've lost, not just a story in a journal.

Mom and Dad jump all over me before I even turn my key in the lock. Mom's in her monogrammed bathrobe, hair wet and tucked behind her ears. Dad looks uncharacteristically disheveled. He hasn't even ironed his jeans. 'Oh, thank God,' he says, pulling me inside. 'You're safe. Now we can ask where the hell you've been for the last four hours.' I've never heard his voice so strained. He's angry, yes. But there's another layer to it: fear. His face is beyond pale. 'We thought you . . .' he begins, but doesn't finish.

Thought I what? Disappeared like your first daughter? Guilt flutters through me like bats. I tell them to go find another cave.

Mom sounds even worse – gravelly – like she's been out-smoking Álvaro for the past eighty years. 'I called everywhere,' she says, choking back a sob. 'To think I'd wake up at two in the morning to see my child driving off! You know you're not allowed to drive without our permission. And *certainly* not at two in the morning.' She leans in and attempts to catch a whiff of my breath, and I smell her sadness in return. Her nose twitches like a bomb-sniffing dog at the airport. 'Have you been drinking?'

'No,' I growl. Though, wobbly as I am, alcohol is the obvious assumption. 'I'm going to bed,' I try to say, but the words emerge in a slow jumble: 'I'm bed . . . going . . . to.'

'Are you on *drugs*?' Mom exclaims, not fighting the tears any longer. 'Or were you with that boy? That's it, isn't it? You were with that boy! If you end up pregnant –'

I push through them and head toward the stairs.

'Marilyn,' Dad says sternly to my back, 'tell us what's going on.'

In the last four hours, I've changed. This girl standing in front of my parents is wilder, stormier, seems like she could light the room on fire. She's sad and angry and tired of all this crap.

It's been two directors against one Camera Girl for too long.

I begin with his name, Álvaro Herrera, but then I stop abruptly. Saying it feels too much like conjuring a ghost.

'What?' Dad says.

I try again. 'Álvaro – he – it's so weird, because I played dominoes with him two weeks ago – but the hospital – I was at the hospital – we were friends – and then he was gone.'

After a moment, Mom says, 'Oh.'

Dad takes a step toward me. His voice is noticeably softer than before. 'I'm so sorry to hear that, Marilyn.'

Mom wipes away a few tears from her eyes. 'Me too. But that still doesn't excuse sneaking out of the house at all hours of the night. You could've woken us up, told us what was going on.'

I scoff. Actually *scoff* at my parents. 'Could I? Could I *really* have done that?'

'Don't take that tone –' Mom begins.

I bat back at her. 'You just don't get it, do you? I can't say anything, in any tone, because I have no voice in this house. I can't even – I can't even *breathe* without asking your permission.'

'That's not true,' Mom says quietly.

'Oh yes, it is! God. I don't even want to be a doctor!'

The room, the house, the world shakes. This is what I've been avoiding all summer. *For your entire life, Linny.*

Mom laughs the saddest laugh. 'Of course you do.'

'That's what *you* want, not me.' I say it forcefully, clearly articulating each word. 'And Grace didn't want it, either.'

Jeez, this girl *is* a forest fire. Where has she been for the last sixteen years?

I'm tired of being stuck in black and white, of hiding in my closet instead of being out in the world, of downplaying how much I want to be me – the *true* me, not some cardboard cutout of the girl my parents want. Maybe it's time to flip around the camera, take a good look at myself. Maybe it's time to stop being one leg of a tripod and start standing on my own.

Is this how Grace felt?

Clearly, Mom and Dad are stunned. Mom's hand flies to her mouth then migrates to the rest of her face, patting it, perhaps checking to see if she's dreaming, while Dad hangs his head – in worry, disappointment, disgrace?

Dis-grace. I *have* become like her.

'Now if you'll excuse me,' I say, already halfway up the stairs, 'I'd like to be alone.'

THE LEFT-BEHINDS (scene 17, continued)

GRACE swipes a tear from her cheek.

The beach feels very quiet and still.

GRACE
(barely audible)
> I don't think you need them.

LINNY
> What?

GRACE
> Wings. You never needed them.

LINNY
(exasperated)
> Then how am I supposed to fly after you?

GRACE
(gently)
> What if you aren't supposed to?

LINNY

But everything feels so – so – I don't know. Colorless. It's like you've taken all of it with you.

GRACE blinks once. Laughs.

GRACE

Then I guess you aren't looking very hard.

Sebastian

42.

'It is thought by some that, 13 billion years ago, the universe underwent a dramatic change. The fog cleared, allowing in ultraviolet light. What may have caused this alteration is unknown – but its impact is abundantly evident.' *A Brief Compendium of Astrophysical Curiosities*, p. 189

When my *abuelo* died, neighbors swamped us with lasagna. Meat lasagna, vegetable lasagna, tofu lasagna. This is different. A quarter of Miami knows Álvaro died – all the major Latino news stations are flashing his face across the TV – but no one knows to bring us lasagna.

For two days, Ana keeps asking me if I'm okay.

Translation: How does it feel?

On my eleventh birthday, Mom gave me an iguana. I named him Dr. Spock and spent two months' allowance buying him a plastic igloo and miniature palm trees for his cage. Three days after my birthday, I woke up to find him belly-up. Little iguana legs stiff. Eyes forever opened.

It feels like that.

Only a billion times worse.

And rationalizing the biological aspects behind it doesn't help. Yeah, yeah, I understand the cycle of life. From ashes to ashes. All that shit. But how can someone die when everything between you is even more unsettled than it was before? How can someone die when you just realized you love them? If you don't know if they love you back?

At the beginning of the summer, I had a three-step plan: 1) Fly to Miami, 2) Talk to Álvaro Herrera, and 3) Glue all my broken pieces back together.

Besides step one, mission not accomplished.

Words, still inside me.

Pieces, still broken.

I think the only person more obliterated by Álvaro's death is Mom. I'd called her the morning after it happened, my throat Sahara dry.

'What's wrong?' she'd said, and I told her. For the next sixty seconds she hadn't said a word, just sobbed quietly into the receiver. Then, in a spluttering voice: 'I'm so-so-so sorry, Sebastian. For everything. For not telling you.'

'I could've handled it,' I'd said, 100 percent positive it wasn't the truth.

'But *I* couldn't handle it,' she'd said. 'I didn't want to see you even the littlest bit unhappy, and I tried so hard not to think about him.'

'Am I . . . ?'

'Are you what, *cariño*?'

'His only kid.'

A long breath. 'I – I think so, but I don't know. He said I was his biggest love, but . . . your father was a very complex man, Sebastian, and our relationship was complicated. Even now, I hate him. Absolutely *hate* him. But I also love him very, very much. I'm . . . I'm going to be honest with you, Sebastian. *Dios, dame fuerza.*' The Spanish pummeled me. God, give me strength. I'd thought, *Why does she need additional strength?*

What could there possibly be left to say?

She'd spoken clearly, enunciating each word. 'Your father and I – we kept in contact a bit.'

My lips moved, but nothing came out but a weak 'Whaaaat?'

'A few times a year,' she continued. 'He checked in when he was – well, when he was up to it – but then he disappeared three years ago. The phone calls stopped. And I thought . . . I thought what everyone else thought. I should have told you, but . . . I couldn't stand the thought of him breaking you.'

I'd wanted to tell her I understood. Wanted to forgive her.

But I just needed time.

A THEORY FOR UNIVERSE-ALTERING PHENOMENA:
To minimize the impact of aforementioned occurrences, retreat to earlier times.

In the living room, I hang sheets between the TV and the couch. Prop up the middle with breakfast bar chairs, erecting the kind of fortress I used to make when I was younger. It's stupid. I know it's stupid. But feeling like a kid again – like this can be fixed with a Band-Aid or a chocolate milk shake or a sheet fort – is the only thing keeping me sane.

On the second day, the front door of the condo creaks open.

Linny: 'Do I need a password?'

'Nah,' I say, unable to summon any lightness in my voice.

She finds an opening between the sheets, crawls in on her hands and knees, and sits nearby, stretching out her tan legs to full length. Bouncing her knees against the ground. 'Soooo?' she says, and in the same breath: 'I almost asked how you're doing. Stupid question, huh?'

'Kind of,' I admit. To be honest, part of me doesn't want to speak to her – this girl who broke my heart – but more words come. 'I keep telling myself that out of the 13.7 billion years that the universe has been around, this doesn't even register. It's not a big change. It's not even a blip. Should that make me feel better or worse?'

Linny shrugs and says, 'Both, probably.' Her hair hangs across her shoulder in a long braid. She undoes it and immediately begins braiding it again. Nervous fingers. 'I've been dreaming about him,' she says. 'Last night I swore he was sitting across from me in my desk chair, and I kept telling him he should leave, that he didn't have much time left – that he should run, just run.' She looks up from her braiding. 'Does that sound crazy?'

'No.' I blink at her, remembering my own dream. 'Did he . . . I don't know. Did he look happy?'

Her smile is full of sadness and something else. 'Yeah, he did.' A pause where she blows air into her cheeks, then pops them. Tilting her head back against the couch and sighing – 'God, how'd everything get so screwed up?'

I wish I could trust her completely again. I wish I could love her again – but I don't know how. So instead I say, 'I read *The Left-Behinds*.'

'And?'

'And I understand it. One hundred percent . . . How does it end?'

'I'm not sure. . . . I'm not sure I *want* it to, you know? If it ends, there's . . . What if there's nothing left?'

A pause.

'Just because it's the end of one thing,' I say, 'doesn't mean it can't be the beginning of another.'

We sit in thoughtful silence for a minute before she nods. 'Okay,' she says. 'So what do we do now? Turn off the lights and make shadow puppets?'

I grin a little. 'What are we, twelve?'

'Oh, come on.' She spreads her fingers into antlers. 'I do a pretty mean moose.'

'Not as mean as my soaring eagle.' I lock my thumbs together, flap my hand-wings, let out a *ca-caw*. It's stupid. It feels nice.

Linny switches off the lights and illuminates the flashlight on her phone, a narrow band of light targeting the sheets. For three minutes, we transform the fort into a menagerie: silhouettes of alligators and bunnies and bears. For a few minutes, I forget.

And when I remember again, we kill the lights, and Linny brings my head to her chest. I repeat: to her chest.

As in boobs.

As in wow.

In any other situation, great. But since I'm still experiencing the giant-squeezes-heart-in-chest feeling, it's significantly less awesome.

She rocks me back and forth, fingers running through my hair. 'Sometimes things don't make sense,' she says.

I want to tell her that they *should*.

That there are rules and laws and theories.

That everything is explainable.

But I don't really believe that anymore. I just squeeze my eyes shut and try to feel okay.

Linny

43.

WHO: Norwegian painter Oskar Thorsen
WHEN: Three weeks in late 2009
WHY: His neighbors filed a missing person's report, and the police scoured Oskar's small town of Otta, Norway, finding no trace of him. Oskar later reappeared with a colorful, new painting in his hands; he'd been holed up in one of his property's three cellars. 'Sometimes bright things only spark in dark places,' he declared to the local newspaper.
NOTES: Really?

The night before Álvaro's funeral, I count sheep with no success. It's kind of hard to sleep when you feel as fragile as a hollowed-out egg, when you're mourning and you love someone who may never love you back.

Around four a.m., I give up and go downstairs for a glass of milk. The milk carton, I notice just in time, is six days past its expiration date. I'm pouring chunks of Dairyland's Best down the drain when I notice the flicker at the end of the hallway – a stitch of light pulsing beneath the door that leads to the garage.

Huh? Carton in hand, I tiptoe down the hallway and open the door.

Oh!

'God, you scared me,' Dad exclaims, raising his hands in the air like a caught robber. He's arched – very bizarrely – over a large sheet of plastic wrap, his hair burning silver in the lamplight. 'Didn't think anyone else was up.'

I want to tell him I haven't slept for two days, but all I do is shake the empty milk carton. 'It's gone bad.'

'Ah.' One hand rubs the back of his neck like he's working out a kink. 'Your mother's been a little lax on the groceries lately.' He means: Your mother hasn't been herself lately. Your mother has been so disappointed in you lately, she can't remember to protect her family from potentially deadly milk microbes.

That's when I notice the paint cans by Dad's feet, next to the mound of plastic wrap.

'None of us is ourself lately, though, are we?' he says, standing straight up and tucking his hands into the pockets of his jeans – the same pair as yesterday? Did he ever go to bed?

'I guess not.'

'Here' – beckoning me closer – 'I want to show you something.' I set down the milk carton on Grandpa's woodworking shelf as Dad kneels and pries the lid off one of the paint cans. Wow. It's so bright, like bottled sun, like a shirt Sebastian would wear. Totally not what I was expecting.

'According to the man at Ace Hardware, it's called Laughing Yellow.' He pulls a three-tiered color swatch from his back pocket. 'No, my mistake. *Giggling* Yellow. I tried to' – awkwardly clearing his throat – 'match the color you had in your room. Before.'

Before.

My room was yellow before it was white. And he remembers that – and he *cares*? Who is this man, and what has he done with my father? I surreptitiously bend over and check that my real dad isn't masked and gagged beneath the Volvo. 'And it's . . . it's for my room now?' I ask.

'Yes.'

'Mom's okay with yellow?'

Without missing a beat, he responds, 'Your mother doesn't have to preapprove everything.'

She doesn't? Could've fooled me.

'But it helps to get a head start on her finding out,' he says, face splintering into a lopsided grin. 'I wasn't going to wake you for another half hour, but now that you're up' – closing the lid, handing me the paint can – 'help me carry this stuff upstairs. Quietly.'

So together, we creep through the house – as silently as you can creep with paint cans, brushes, tape, and twelve feet of crinkly plastic. Together, we lift my bed on *one, two, three* and move everything to the center of the room, shrouding it in white cloth.

After taping off the baseboards and coating the carpeting with plastic, Dad opens the lid again, swirls the paint with a stick, and holds up a clean brush. 'Go ahead, kiddo.'

I almost start crying because I can't remember the last time I wasn't 'Marilyn.'

He waggles the brush at me until I take it, dip it into the yellow, and run a streak across the nearest wall. Dad picks up a roller, and we work silently side by side until the first wall, then all the walls, are giggling out loud.

He suddenly says, 'I had this crazy idea that maybe we'd even paint the ceiling. Too much?'

'Maybe a *little* much.'

'Well, I bought plenty of extra cans, in case we change our minds.'

Outside, morning is rolling in. Chirping robins replace a symphony of crickets and frogs.

Dad says, 'Today is going to be –'

'Hard,' I finish for him.

'Yes. Hard.' He blinks a few times, swipes his eyes with the back of his hands, and makes a weird noise in the back of his throat, like he decided to clear it again but then changed his mind. 'This whole week has been hard.'

He means because of me.

He means I toppled the tripod.

'And I just want to let you know,' he says, 'how unbelievably proud of you I am. For holding up during such a hard time . . . and also for reminding your mother and me . . .' He trails off. 'I'm very sorry, Linny. So very sorry.'

'It's okay, Dad.'

'No, it's not, because you and your sister are truly talented, and I apologize for not telling you sooner. We should be telling you every day. We should've told *her* every day.'

I must be looking at him like paint's pouring from his ears, because he adds, 'I saw your documentary, the one about Grace.'

'You *did*?'

He nods. 'I was a little late coming from the practice, so I had to get a back-row seat. But I watched it from start to finish. And the entire time I couldn't get over it. My daughters.'

'But –' I stutter. 'Why didn't you say anything?'

He peers down at his hands, which are giggling, too, but decides to curve an arm around my shoulders anyway. When was the last time he hugged me? When was the last time I *let* him? Has he been trying all along?

'Because I'm human,' he says. 'And because I've wanted things for you and Grace for so long, I never stopped to consider if you wanted them, too. But I will. From now on, I promise I will.'

I lean into his side, close my eyes, and nod.

'Can *you* just promise *me* something?' he says.

'Anything.'

'I let it slide once because you were having a hard time already' – clearing his throat again – 'but no more boys in your closet.'

Mortified as I am, I laugh. 'Yeah, okay.'

Together, we quietly stare at the walls.

'You know what I just thought of?' Dad says. 'Yellow. The color for missing people.'

Two hours later, Dad dons a suit and tie, and I iron my only black dress. Paint flecks are in our hair.

THE LEFT-BEHINDS (scene 17, continued)

LINNY watches GRACE for several moments. The wind picks up.

Over LINNY's right shoulder, a crack in the sky comes into focus. It's almost indistinguishable – like two bits of fabric joined together. Around it are flecks of color.

Sebastian

44.

'No one knows how gamma ray bursts originate. These energetic explosions are brighter than anything else in the universe and are often preceded by an afterglow, which is longer than the original event.' *A Brief Compendium of Astrophysical Curiosities*, p. 67

'You've grown,' Mom says. 'You know that?'

Ana picked her up from the airport last night, and we ate a painfully silent dinner. (I made Cuban sandwiches. Hard to eff up.) Mom's making an attempt at conversation now. Scooping her waves into a loose bun directly on top of her head. She's wearing a standard black dress.

I, on the other hand, didn't pack for a funeral. Mom offers to take Ana's car and drive me to the mall, 'pick out something nice' for the service.

Don't care if it's nice, I tell her. My only stipulation is that I'll never have to wear it again.

In the end we buy a fairly average gray suit. (Not black. It may be a funeral, but it's still early August in Florida. Things are shit enough without absorbing a billion photons of light, roasting me like a pig on a spit.) A wide silk tie rounds off the look. It's Álvaro's. Marla dropped it off – so I'd have something of his. Although it's approximately twelve shades too purple, it still smells of cigarillos. So I obviously have to wear it.

'That's festive,' Mom says.

'Yep,' I respond as I adjust the knot. Keep adjusting it. Spend the fifteen-minute drive to City Cemetery alternating between too tight and too loose. The only sound in the car is the *pssssshh* of the air-conditioning and Mom clearing her throat, preparing for the conversation we won't have. Every few seconds, Ana side-eyes me from the driver's seat. Probably checking to see if I've hurled myself from the vehicle. (Thought about it. Couldn't bring myself to do it.)

Ana switches off the engine and softly ruffles my hair. For once this summer, I don't hate it.

Outside, a mass of black is assembling – hundreds of people who heard about Álvaro's death on the news, online, in a newspaper – all coming to pay their respects. I even spot a few residents from Silver Springs. No reporters so far. At least I can be thankful for that.

We exit the car and follow them down a low hill, toward the graveside. Palm trees flank the rectangular hole in the ground. Seeing the casket (monstrous, shiny, blue) tugs at all the strings I have left.

My legs become spaghetti. Knees: knocking together. *Es un milagro* I'm still standing.

All of a sudden Linny appears by my side. Yellow speckles her forehead, her cheeks, her eyelids. 'You look like solar activity,' I tell her, noticing a long, golden streak on her arm. 'What happened?'

She shrugs away a smile. 'Long night . . . I think someone's waving at you.'

Opposite us, peeking out from the crowd, is Micah.

Micah?

Wearing a suit jacket over a black Metallica T-shirt (hey, at least it's black), he waves once more and makes his way through the throngs of mourners to bear hug me.

'How'd you find out?' I say after I regain oxygen.

'Your mom called mine. Plus, I saw it on the news. I just didn't know he was your –'

'Yeah, I know.'

He runs a hand through the front of his hair, which has grown a solid three inches over the summer. 'You could've told me, man.'

'I know. Sorry, I – hey. Aren't you missing orientation at Berkeley?'

'Don't worry about it, dude. Besides, how else was I going to meet this *chica* right here?' He faces Linny and extends his hand. 'Micah. I'm sure you've heard a lot about me. You're even prettier than on Facebook.'

'Ha,' Linny says, shaking his hand as my face turns red. 'Thanks.'

A minute later, the priest begins to speak about how 'it was Álvaro's time.' Two things about those words crawl under my skin: 1) how he makes it sound like there's a giant stopwatch in the sky, waiting to beep when it's time to die, and 2) how it's past tense.

Was his time. (Was it?)

Was a good person. (Was he?)

Was ready for the next life. (What about finishing this one?)

THE AFTERGLOW PARADOX:
A person's brightness increases after they are gone.

Then mourners are laying white flowers on the coffin. Except me. From my pocket I toss a packet of cigarillos on the pile.

They lower him down. Mom scatters a fistful of dirt into the hole. Then Ana and Marla do. Then I do. *Plink, plink, plink.*

Almost everyone is leaving, hauling grief back into cars.

We wait until the cemetery workers begin shoveling in the dirt. *Plink*s turn to *plop*s.

In fifth grade, Micah told me to hold my breath in graveyards. 'It's not polite to breathe when others can't,' he said. I guess the same applies to speaking.

No one speaks. No one has to.

The day after the funeral, Micah and Linny team up to keep me distracted. Micah – who's leaving for the airport tonight – unpacks his Xbox 360 from his suitcase because, as he says, 'Wouldn't dream of going anywhere without it.'

Turns out, Linny is a *Dark Ops Resolution* master. Even better than Micah.

'Bastards!' I shout at the TV screen, although part of me is stoked that Linny's the one kicking my ass. Judging by the river of blood cascading from my player's every artery, he should be deader than dead. 'Remind me! How the hell is this supposed to help me cheer up?'

'Get up!' Micah screeches, by way of answering. 'Up! Or she'll shoot you again!'

'I AM DYING MICAH HOW CAN I GET UP?'

'You are seriously off your game, man.'

'I've been a bit distracted lately!'

'Nah. That's not it. You've always sucked, and I think this

summer has only increased your suckage.'

Classic Micah.

Wanting to rise to the challenge, my player resurrects himself for three final seconds and places a shot exactly right – dead center in Micah's player's right butt cheek.

Linny's entire face goes bright pink. She's trying so hard not to laugh, because laughing's still not acceptable, right?

Micah takes advantage of the I'm-staring-at-Linny distraction and shoots my dead player in the left foot. I throw him a look that bursts Linny's efforts. It sounds so strange – laughter echoing through the condo.

'Sorry,' she says, zipping it immediately.

I say, 'Don't be.'

'Linny!' Micah shouts, breaking into a grin. 'Shoot him! Shoot him!'

She shoots, all right – into Micah's player's *left* butt cheek. She laughs once more and sticks out her tongue at him.

And that's when there's a knock on the door. Since my player's bleeding out on some nondescript rooftop, and Ana and Mom have gone somewhere (beach, coffee shop, who knows?), I throw up my hands and say, 'Fine! I guess *I'll* get it.'

When I wrench open the door, my gut reaction is that someone else has died. What are you supposed to think when a statue-like dude in a black suit shows up at your doorstep? Given his forehead crease and downturned smile, he looks like a man who gets paid to deliver bad news.

I chicken out. Slam the door shut before he has the chance to tell me: 'There's been an accident. Your whole family has perished in unfortunate circumstances. In fact, a freak nuclear disaster has wiped out everyone else in the world.'

'Who was that?' Linny says, peeking her head around the corner.

'Er – Girl Scout.'

'Oh, oh!' Linny squeals. 'Let's get some Thin Mints.'

'No, don't –'

But she's already swung the door back open. The man is peering up at the sky, like he's bird-watching or something. He snaps to look at us. 'I apologize for the interruption. I'm looking for the family of Álvaro Herrera.'

Adrenaline shoots right to my heart. 'Why do you want to know?'

Linny elbows me gently in the ribs.

'I'm Walter Gomez, Señor Herrera's lawyer.'

My stomach yo-yos and so do my vocal chords. Every time I try to push out words, they zoom back down my throat. Thankfully, Linny takes the lead. 'Sebastian is . . . well . . . you have the right house. Come in.'

'Thank you,' he says.

Micah drops the video game controller as Mr. Gomez enters the living room.

'Um,' Micah whispers to me. 'Am I missing something?'

'What's this about?' I ask.

Mr. Gomez's eyes take stock of Linny and Micah before finally settling on me. 'I am sorry for your loss, Sebastian. Is there somewhere that we can talk privately?'

A balled-up sock bobs in my throat. I gulp, nod, signal to Micah and Linny that it's okay.

Mr. Gomez follows me into the kitchen, where he opens his briefcase on the countertop and leafs through neatly filed paperwork. He fishes out an envelope from the bottom of the case and hands it to me.

'Álvaro instructed me to give you this letter. I can certify that he authored it.'

I grip the paper. *Really* grip it. White knuckles. It's like ten thousand eyes are watching me. What if I don't like what the letter says? The skin on the back of my neck prickles. My stomach demands that I prep my throat for the likelihood of vomit.

'How –' I stammer. 'I mean – when did he write this?'

Mr. Gomez rubs a hand over his bald, shiny head. 'I can't be one hundred percent certain when he wrote it, but Señor Herrera entrusted me with the letter a little less than a year ago and instructed me to deliver it to you only after his passing.' He roots around in his briefcase again. 'I would also like to discuss with you the matter of Señor Herrera's will.'

I swallow the sock in my throat. 'What about it?'

'He left everything to you, Sebastian.'

He *what*?

My brain has no idea how to respond.

With joy?

Anger?

Sadness?

Everything's oozing out of me at once. 'There has to be some mistake.'

'No mistake,' Mr. Gomez says, pulling out another set of papers. 'Is there a guardian around so I can go over the particulars with you?'

I shake my head until I shake right out of my skin. 'Sorry. Can I just let this sink in first?'

Mr. Gomez studies me for a moment then extracts a business card from the pocket of his suit. 'Of course. When you're ready, give me a call. I'll be in the area for the next two days.' With that, he takes his leave.

The letter from Álvaro is still in my hands. I should rip it open. Hungrily devour it. But . . . these are the last words from my dad. I want to save the letter until I'm stronger. Until I can read what it says without falling apart.

Linny pokes her head into the kitchen. 'Everything okay in here?'

I surreptitiously slip the envelope into my back pocket. 'Yeah. You up for another round of *Dark Ops*?'

Linny suspects something. She tilts her head. Surveys me up and down like, *I thought we weren't keeping secrets anymore*. '*Dark Ops* is fun, but –'

'Cool, then let's go.'

But instead of following me back into the living room, she grabs my elbow, opens the back door, and yanks me outside. We stand barefoot, grass between our toes. 'I know you well enough to recognize when you're not okay,' she says. 'What did the lawyer tell you?'

Telepathically, I implore an alien spacecraft to beam me up so I don't have to discuss this. I'm not ready to think about what it all means.

I stare at the grass.

'Oh,' she says as if realizing something. 'If you don't want to talk about it with me, I understand.'

'It's not that I don't want to talk about it *with you*.'

'Then what is it?'

Sighing, I reach into my pocket. Show her the letter. 'Álvaro wrote something for me a year ago. Haven't opened it. What if he tells me he hated my mom? That he was having an affair? That he –'

'Whoa, whoa. I don't think he'd write that.'

'That's just it. We don't know him, do we?' I flail the letter, feeling like a gutted fish. 'Why the hell did he leave me everything in his will?'

'What?'

I pretend I didn't hear what she said. Letter flailing again: 'This could literally say anything!'

Her eyes pierce mine. She stretches her hand in the direction of the envelope. 'It'll be okay. There's only one way to find out.'

I release the letter into her grip.

All of a sudden, she drops into the grass, crossing her legs by my ankles. 'Sit,' she says. 'These things are always better if you sit.'

So I plop down next to her, and she gingerly slits open the envelope. I clamp my eyes shut. Focus on the words as she reads them slowly.

Dear Sebastian,

You have every right to be angry. When you finish reading this, I hope you are less so. I do not want to think, do not want to believe, that I have lost you forever.

Know, I love your mother. My heart is bursting, still. When you were born, you looked so like her. All that hair! Your smile – I remember thinking it was mine, too. I already knew what a great man you would become.

Understand, many years ago, I was not in a good place. I drank and I drank and I drank. Your mother, she tried to help me, but you came along – and I was joyous! You were beautiful! My son! Beautiful! I could not do this to you. I beg you to understand.

Forgive me. If God grants me one selfish wish, it is for you to forgive me.

After rehab, I came looking for you and your mother. I found a phone number first, and your mother and I spoke of you, but then you had a new family, a good father and a brother and your beautiful mother. I wanted to see you happy, and her happy, so I kept watch from a distance. I have been out of your life for so long, it is better for you this way. But I tell you, it does not mean I love you any less, my son.

There are so many things I want to write, too much to write here. I wish things had turned out differently. I wish I had turned out better, for you.

I love you, my Sebastian,
Álvaro

My eyes spring open. In my periphery, I see Linny folding the letter. Holding it tight to her chest. 'Wow,' she says.

Every muscle and bone in my body springs awake.

He came looking for me.

Yeah, he wasn't a candidate for World's Best Dad, *but he came looking for me*. I made him fly back.

'I guess that solves a few mysteries,' Linny says.

More than she knows. Ever since I'd found out that Álvaro knew he had a son, I assumed he never loved me. Now I know differently. Maybe I'll never figure out if he knew me when he saw me at Silver Springs, if *mijo* was a coincidental phrase or a clue. I have this letter, and that's enough.

Linny crinkles her forehead. 'They're really similar.'

'Who?'

'Álvaro and Grace. I thought there was this magical answer

for why people leave and why they come back, but maybe it's really simple. They want space to figure out why all their bird bones broke, and they fly home when everything heals.'

'*Toda la cura*,' I say.

Theoretically, everything should be explainable. But what if the explanation is that things are a gazillion times simpler than we think? That we don't need formulas and theorems to figure out our own lives?

What if it's as simple as a boy loving a father? A girl loving a sister?

A boy loving a girl?

Linny's blue eyes squint. She looks so unbelievably beautiful that it happens immediately: I love her again. Now that I think about it, I never really stopped. Just went into hibernation for a while. I decide to trust this feeling.

Because sometimes you don't get second chances to say things – sometimes you don't even get a *first* chance – I blurt it out. 'I love you, Linny Carson.'

I grip the sides of her face and pull her until our noses touch.

She says, 'I love you, too.'

THE AFTERGLOW PARADOX 2.0:
Brightness can dim and revive in unpredictable ways.

Linny

45.

WHO: *Linny Carson (aka, Camera Girl)*
WHEN: *Half her junior year and most of the summer*
WHY: *Her sister, Grace, left, so she hid, too.*
NOTES: *Took you long enough.*

Biking back from Ana's, I veer left before I get to my house, stop, walk up another set of porch stairs, and rap on Cass's door. She answers, an unraveled look consuming her face. In a pair of rhinestone sandals, she shifts from one foot to another. 'Yeah?'

'I want you to have something,' I say, dropping my backpack and rooting through the front pocket. 'Here.'

I hand her my *Journal of Lost and Found*, and she flips to the front, where Grace's loopy handwriting informs me about Hector's feeding schedule. Her fingers fumble through the pages, pausing over the Álvaro Herrera section. I hear the confusion in her voice. 'What is this?'

'What I've been doing since Grace left. I thought – well, I thought it might help bring her back, but that seems kind of silly now. I just wanted to explain why I've been acting so . . . crazy. That's probably the best word for it.'

She fans the pages again, stopping to skim a few entries, shaking her head slightly as if a stray hair is tickling her nose. 'I'll be right back,' she tells me suddenly.

I wish her thoughts were as open as my book. 'Oh,' I mutter. 'Okay.'

She dashes upstairs, and I count the bricks on the side of her house, a knot twisting in my throat. Her foam-soled sandals clomp the carpet all the way back down. She's carrying something – a blue spiral-bound notebook – and she passes it to me with both hands, arms outstretched, like she's presenting a birthday cake. 'I did sort of the same thing.'

I take the notebook and open the first page – flip to the second, third, fourth, keep going until I hit the back. On every page is a list with lines crossed out.

'Are these –' I begin.

'Places where I thought she could be. Places she talked about when we were growing up. Would you believe I called every campground in Florida *and* Alaska? She always talked about Alaska with me. My dad had a heart attack when he saw the phone bill.' I look back up at her, astounded. She makes a sound almost like a laugh. 'I *told* you. I miss her, too.'

I knew this, but I didn't *know* this, so intimately, so wholly. I break first, hugging Cass and closing my eyes for a moment; and as she squeezes me in return, I feel time blowing away like sand, think for the first time that maybe it *is* possible to turn back the clock – just keep turning and turning until we reach a place where everything isn't so broken.

'I am so over this fight,' she says into my curls.

'And I'm so, so sorry.'

She pulls away and rubs at her eyes, little swipes of mascara now fading off into her hairline. 'You should text Ray. He misses you.'

'I miss him, too . . . How's he doing?'

'Better,' she says with the hint of a smile, 'now that he and Lawrence made up. You know, even though it's only high school, I kind of feel like they're made for each other.' We talk for a few minutes longer – about Ray, about the improbability of love lasting years and years and years, how sometimes it does – and then I'm on my bike again.

'Hey, Linny?' she calls to me from her porch. There's a pause. 'You think she's ever coming back?'

I tell her the truth. 'I don't know.'

Sebastian's flight leaves tomorrow morning, so this afternoon I'm arranging flowers to pin in my hair. The last time he sees me (rephrase: the last time he sees me *this summer*), I want to look as colorful – and as unforgettable – as possible. Lining up five yellow daisies from Joe's garden, I rake my fingers through my curls to prep it for braiding. On my desk is a mirror, and that's how I see Mom approaching, her footsteps barely audible against the carpet. Her bun is looser than usual, a few stray curls swaying around her ears.

I like her like this – smudged, without all the clean edges.

In Dad's study there's a picture of her at fourteen, visiting Nigeria, her hair swept into an emerald-green ichafu – a head scarf flowering toward the sky. We look almost identical: bronze skin, tons of freckles. For most of my life, she's suffocated her freckles beneath layers of sticky foundation. '*God*,' Grace once said, 'don't you just want to take a wet cloth to her face or something?'

I imagine doing this now, wiping my thumbs across her cheeks.

She stops several feet behind me and says, 'It's tonight, isn't it?'

Yep. The idea dawned on me two weeks ago, and since then it's been a whirlwind of video editing, equipment checklists, and handing out flyers (as well as spending a quarter of my life savings). Cass and Ray have been helping out.

Still, I don't understand how *Mom* knows what tonight is. Dad must've told her. He and I've been talking more lately – at breakfast, when he gets home from work. Last night as I was passing through the living room, he patted his hand on the sofa and said, '*Anna Karenina*'s on TV. Want to watch it with me?' We even made popcorn, like old times, and call me crazy, but I got the sensation that Grace was there, watching it with us.

'Yeah, it's tonight,' I say to Mom, only half turning around in my seat.

'You doing your hair?' Her fingers dance awkwardly by her sides, and there's a moment when I think she's going to offer to braid it for me. Instead, she says, 'Well, I'll let you finish getting ready,' although none of her muscles moves. Years pass. I fiddle with the flowers, and when I look back at her, she's leaning against my bed, the white blanket crinkling against her gray dress.

'Should we talk?' she says. Based purely on the steadiness of her voice, she could be asking if it's supposed to rain on Tuesday, or if I picked up a half gallon of milk on my way home; but I see how her fingers curl, how she forces out a breath afterward, like she's blowing out a candle.

I say softly, 'Are you going to yell at me again?'

A little less steadily now, she says, 'I'm going to try my best to listen, but I do want you to understand that what happened to us this year was . . . unthinkable to me. Unthinkable. And I held on to you too tightly, just like I held on to Grace.'

It's the most she's said to me since the morning I came back from the hospital, *and* she's speaking about Grace. Even saying her name. I'm not entirely sure how to respond.

'I just couldn't let her go,' she says. 'I just couldn't let her go, and she went anyway. She – it's probably my fault.'

I swallow.

Mom picks a speck of lint off her knee. 'She came to me, asking to go to a music conservatory in Ohio. Oberlin. And . . . I told her no.'

'She . . . she . . .' I'm processing, but it's difficult – like straining boulders through mesh. 'She didn't tell me about that.'

Mom's voice splinters, tears forming in the corners of her eyes. 'She *did* leave me a note, Linny. Under my pillow. She left me her acceptance letter to Oberlin, and I keep checking to see if she's enrolled, and –'

'What?' I stand up. 'Why didn't you say anything to me?'

'Because you would've *followed her*, Linny. You would've camped out in Ohio for the whole summer, and we never would've seen you again. It's just like with the stars – you look at them all night, and you'll' – waving a hand as if cleansing the air – 'start wishing you're anywhere but here.'

'*That's* why you took them down?'

'Yes, and I'm – Oh, I'm saying this so badly.' She gestures for me to sit. 'I still want you to go to Princeton. I still want all the best things for you – the things women like us didn't always get to have. But if I don't accept that it's your life, truly *your* life, then you'll run. I know you'll run. And I don't want to have to sit up every night worrying about you, worrying if you're hungry or scared or cold or if something bad has happened, something *very* bad.' Her voice hitches.

I stumble through words. 'I'm – I'm not Grace.'

'We know, Linny. Grace is . . . she's a lot sadder. You may not remember all the times she – Well, it always seemed like she was somewhere else. And I'm so sorry for that, because you two are so close.'

'*Were*.'

'*Are*. She never left you, Linny. She left *this*.' She interlaces her fingers in her lap. 'Do you . . . I was looking at some old pictures the other day, and do you remember our trip to Minnesota?'

'Yeah,' I begin cautiously. 'I was about nine. Didn't we go to that restaurant where they served moose burgers? And Grace pretended she was Tiger Lily and swiped your red lipstick across both of her cheeks. . . . I remember thinking that she looked so cool.'

There's a faint upward movement in the corners of her mouth. 'Funny.'

'Why's that?'

'Because in every photo, she was looking at you.'

A thought sears into me: For my entire life, I've been waiting for Mom's blessing to reach inside myself and ratchet up the color, but what if it's been up to me all along? What if I'm my own Color in Chief? This whole time, have I been just as bright as Grace?

Mom's neck is going splotchy like a giraffe's, and in those moments, I picture her alone in our attic, where she keeps the family photos. I picture her holding the Tiger Lily picture in her rubber-gloved hands. Two daughters, down to one – like tearing the photo in half.

So I lean forward and wrap my arms around her, remembering what Álvaro said about the camera and dimensionality. *Life on a small screen has no texture. Smooth as paper.* Mom and I've gone through so many bumps – mountains, even – but I suspect that no matter how I decide to write my script, *our* story is far from finished.

Her touch is soft now, like the sun on my skin.

Hector's watching the whole thing unravel – or *re*-ravel – and that's when I get an un-freaking-believable idea. I release Mom, check my watch, and blurt out, 'If we leave right now, we can just about make it.'

'What? What do you – ?'

'Dad!' I yell. 'Meet us at the car!'

And that's how I end up driving two miles over the speed limit in the family Volvo, with Hector (and his terrarium) in the passenger seat and Cass, Mom, and Dad in the back. The near-evening sun is still hot and flooding through the open windows, coating everything in pale-orange glow.

'This is it!' I say, pulling over five minutes later at a side-of-the-road pond. 'She said it was three miles away, and had some benches and – Yes, this is definitely it.' Checking first for alligators (nope, coast is clear), we all step out of the car and onto the freshly mowed grass, dew seeping into my sandals; from the passenger's side, I lift out Hector and walk to the edge of the water, where the four of us (well, five) gather in a circle.

'Who wants to do the honors?' I say.

Dad scratches the back of his neck. 'I'm not exactly sure what we're doing here, to be perfectly honest.'

'We're letting her go,' Cass says, matter-of-factly.

'I thought Hector was a *him*,' Dad says.

'Think about it, Eric,' Mom says, and Dad *ah-ha*s after a dawning moment.

Hector is wiggling in my hands, little turtle legs propelling him slowly through the air. I try to pass him to Cass, who says, 'No, you do it, Linny.'

'Yes,' Mom says, then Dad: 'You do it, sweetheart.'

So I kneel down by the shore and guide Hector into the pond. At first he's unsure of what to do – legs, motionless – but then he takes one or two tentative steps, dipping beneath the warm blue.

He doesn't look back.

When I stand up, Cass threads her arm through mine, rests her head on my shoulder as we watch the water rippling, and I am so happy that she's here with me – that the glue is sticky between us again. 'Do you think his turtle family has written a *Journal of Lost and Found*?' she says.

I laugh. 'Of course. What would the "why" be?'

'Kidnapped. Released.'

'And the notes?'

She smiles. 'People are good after all.'

THE LEFT-BEHINDS (scene 17, continued)

LINNY turns, sees the split sky, and wanders toward it.

LINNY (Voice-over)

> What I'm wondering now is whether it's always been my choice. If all I had to do was take three steps forward and release myself.

Then LINNY reaches out and finds the edge of the crack, peeling back the sky. On the other side is color, a sharp contrast to the black-and-white world.

Sebastian

46.

'The research into extra solar planetary systems attempts to tackle a controversial hope – a wish not to be alone in this vast, vast universe.' *A Brief Compendium of Astrophysical Curiosities*, p. 303

When I step off the bus, a hundred people are clumped at the beach, just a few blocks from Silver Springs. The sky is dark, but I swear it's like walking directly into the sun. Bright lights. The flicker of a huge movie projector.

Linny pops into view, daisies like satellites around her head. 'Surprise!' she shouts, grabbing my hand. 'Come on, everyone's already here.'

We weave through pockets of people until we see them. On a cluster of multicolored beach towels: Ray and Cass. Linny pulls me down to their level. Their grins stretch so far, they could pass for Cheshire cats. (Except not in a creepy way. Maybe I'm describing it wrong.)

'What is this?' I ask.

They all jump in at once.

'Well, I –'

'Linny planned it –'

'OMG, it's so romantic –'

Linny holds up her hands and smiles. 'I just thought we should do something for Álvaro. And for you.'

I'm still trying to figure out what the heck's going on when the screen lights up in neon. And I hear Álvaro's voice.

He's on the beach.

This beach.

And he's just spun around to face the camera, his eyes several feet wide. 'Where have you been?' he says. 'I didn't expect to see you again.'

A few screws in me twist loose. Okay, more than a few.

It's his cameo in *Midnight in Miami*. A trickle of applause runs through the crowd.

Then, more Álvaro: still on this beach, except he's an old man. Wisps of grayish-black hair in his eyes. The camera zooms in on his wrinkly face. 'All these little bumps,' he says, 'that is life. Given enough time, *todo se cura*.'

Everything heals.

He was saying that to *me*, wasn't he?

I whisper to Linny, 'This is from the day he broke out of Silver Springs, right?'

'Yep. Keep watching.'

The camera pans to the left – and there I am. Drinking in Álvaro's every word. And then there's Álvaro and me playing dominoes. Álvaro and me sharing a Cuban sandwich over lunch. Álvaro and me watching *Roman Holiday*.

Álvaro and me, Álvaro and me, Álvaro and me.

This is the part where something should combust. My heart. My brain. My gut. But it's the opposite.

THE THEORY TO END ALL THEORIES:
In this vast universe, the only positive constant is love.
(I don't feel even remotely alone.)

The screen goes dark for a second before the opening credits of *Midnight in Miami* roll.

Of course. *Of course* I'm seeing this now.

Although I'll never know for sure, I think Álvaro would've wanted me to see this movie. Why else would he write the book over again if it wasn't immensely important to him? If he wasn't trying to hold on to it? Why wouldn't I want to be a part of that, a part of him?

Leaning into my shoulder, Linny says, 'I thought if you were going to watch his movie for the first time, it should be here and in this way. On the big screen.' She bites her bottom lip. Dips her eyes down to the sand. 'And I went back and forth about whether I should show the new footage of Álvaro, because I didn't want to show anything he didn't want seen, but he's so happy here and . . . Please say something.'

Hadn't realized I wasn't. Thought I was yelling 'I love you, Linny Carson' at the top of my lungs. I'm so happy my dad got to meet my girl.

'You are really something else,' I tell her, kissing her cheek, watching her face light up as bright as the screen.

I sink into the storyline. Into the neon-lit streets of Miami after dark. I quickly realize that the people who criticize the movie don't *get* it. Yeah, it's about sex. Yeah, it's about spies and guns and too much alcohol. But mostly it's about love and all its complications. How stories tangle and intertwine. How things get effed up and then effed up some more. But in the end, Agustina still loves Eduardo, and he's still head over heels for her.

Here's the kicker: in the closing scene, you don't actually see Eduardo die. It's implied, but *he never closes his eyes*. You see him lying in the sand and then only the imprint of his body.

Something about this is absolutely hysterical to me. I start laughing – then *really* laughing, gripping underneath my ribs because it almost hurts.

To the casual observer, I've lost more than one of my marbles.

Linny says, 'Um, are you okay?'

People several towels over shush me. Throw me nasty looks for laughing during the death scene.

'BUT IT'S NOT A DEATH SCENE,' I want to tell them. 'It's a *disappearance* scene.'

I don't believe in signs, but this sure feels like one. Otherwise, why would I be the only one laughing, the only one who gets it? Score one for a *padre-hijo* connection.

As I'm thinking this, I'm also remembering how I barreled out of the hospital without viewing Álvaro's body. How he wanted a closed-casket funeral. It's a dangerous thought. But I think it anyway, for just a second. That instead of dying, Álvaro shifted off to a margarita bar to cha-cha-cha until closing time. Maybe – as we're all mourning him – he's dangling off a dock somewhere, his wrinkly feet dipping into the water.

Linny repeats, 'You okay?'

I tell her honestly, 'I think I will be.'

After the rental company packs up the projector and film, after everyone folds up their beach towels, the four of us stay. In what I now know to be typical fashion, Cass rips off her shirt. Windmills it in the air like a lasso. She's wearing a hot-pink bikini top. 'Anyone up for a late-night dip?'

Ray pipes up, 'Cass! Near midnight. Sharks.'

'Don't be such a spoilsport,' she says. 'We'll just dip our toes in.'

So we all make our way down to the surf. The waves crashing into our ankles immediately bring me back to Álvaro's breakout day. We stood here, side by side. The three of us – free.

I can tell Linny's thinking the same thing.

'I miss him,' she says. 'This is going to sound kind of corny, but I think I needed him this summer, in a completely different way than I thought I did. He broke me out of something.' The others are splashing off to the side, so for a moment it feels like it's just Linny, Álvaro, and me. 'Before you guys,' she continues, voice thick, 'I thought I was going to explode.'

'Have you ever seen an exploding star?' I say. 'Because it's possibly the most beautiful thing you'll ever see. *Kaboom*. So many colors.'

She smiles. Moonlight rolls along the waves.

'I can't believe you're leaving tomorrow,' she says, gently kicking the water.

Me neither. 'Does that make me a complete asshole? I'm supposed to be a stayer, not a leaver.'

She interlaces her fingers in mine. 'You can be both, just as long as you come back.'

'About that. I was thinking about spring break in Miami? And maybe you could visit Cal Tech over fall break or next summer or anytime, really, because you will never pick a date when I won't still be in love with you.'

'Is that so?' she says.

I kiss her nose. 'It is.'

'Well, maybe I'll see you even sooner than that. I didn't want to tell you before it was officially done, but' – she takes a massive breath – 'I know how I'm going to end my screenplay, so I'll be touring some film schools in California, and –'

'That's *awesome*,' I burst, because it is. Because no matter how good things are elsewhere, I know we'll keep flying back to each other.

That's one mystery, solved: how to fix broken pieces. I go over the revised plan once more.

Step 1: Fly from LA to Miami. ✓

Step 2: Get to know my father. ✓

Step 3: Fall in love with a girl. ✓

Linny

47.

My dearest Linzer Torte,

How's it going?

That's not a good enough opening, is it? I'll start over.

If you're reading this letter, it means I've gathered up enough courage to mail it, and I've found a place that sells stamps. As I write this, there's a man outside my window screaming about a flat tire. Gosh, he looks ticked. . . .

But, I'm procrastinating. Okay.

You're probably expecting to hear that I'm sorry. I so wish I could tell you that I was. But the truth is a lot more complicated. I'm happy I ran. No matter how hard it's been out here, at least I wasn't <u>there</u>.

Everything got to be too much. (Again, not good enough, right?) But there's no other way I can explain it. I told Mom I wanted to go to music school instead of Princeton — maybe she's told you this by now. Anyway, she flipped. I flipped.

And I couldn't handle it. That's on me, Linny. Not on you. You did nothing wrong — and I wish I'd told you that.

I've been thinking a lot about what I want to say to you. What I've come up with is this: You are still my sister. You will always be my sister. You are stronger, braver, wiser than you think. You are not the sum of other people's expectations. Their dreams do not have to be your dreams. You are lovable, and you are loved. I hope that's enough.

If you're not too furious, give me a call sometime, okay?

All my love to Hector. Tell Mom and Dad I say hi. Parents weekend is in September.

A million warm wishes,

Grace xoxo

Her letter arrives the last day of summer, in a plain cream envelope postmarked Oberlin, Ohio. On one corner of the page, she's drawn clef notes, and in the other corner is her phone number. That's the best part, besides knowing she's okay. Finally, *finally* I'll hear her voice again.

What I'll say after hello, I have no idea. Maybe I'll tell her that I understand why she left without me, that she couldn't fly if I latched on to her heels. Maybe I'll tell her that I was wrong – instead of trying to draw her back, I should've allowed myself the freedom she chose.

I smooth the letter's edges on my desk, setting it next to two other things.

The first is Sebastian's copy of *A Brief Compendium of Astrophysical Curiosities*, the one he's been clutching all summer, the one he placed in my hands before leaving three days ago. He's underlined, highlighted, and circled a sentence for me.

Remember to keep your head up in the sky; otherwise, you'll miss the stars.

The second thing is Álvaro's typewriter, which Sebastian insisted that I have. 'To finish *The Left-Behinds*,' he said.

I think again about what my first words should be, how the end of one story – and the beginning of another – should read. I hadn't realized this, but on a typewriter you have to press the keys extra-hard. You have to mean it.

My fingers jam each key, until the first direction appears on the once-blank page.

Enter LINNY into a colorful world.

Acknowledgments

A billion to the third power thanks to:

The amazingly talented Claire Wilson, agent extraordinaire, who I'm convinced is actually Wonder Woman. From our earliest meeting I knew that she understood this story's heartbeat, and it is infinitely louder and stronger because of her. Thanks also to Rosie Price and the lovely RCW team.

I'm pretty much the luckiest author alive to have not one but two extraordinary editors. Thanks to Jocelyn Davies at HarperTeen, whose enthusiasm for this book was only matched by her warmth and insight into its characters; Linny and Sebastian are extremely lucky to have met her. Thanks to Rachel Petty at Macmillan UK, who said during our first meeting that she 'just wanted more' of my story; those were perfect words. I have given so much more because of her guidance and passion. Quite simply, this book would not be this book without Jocelyn and Rachel, and I am eternally grateful.

Everyone at HarperTeen, Epic Reads and Macmillan UK deserves a loud round of applause. Bea Cross, Kat McKenna, and George Lester – you are excellent humans. To designers Rachel Vale and Aurora Parlagreco, I want to shower you with praise for creating such magical covers! To all my foreign publishers as well, for continuing to make my dreams come true.

I wrote a good chunk of *Birds* in the Creative Writing and Publishing MA at City, University of London. Special thanks to my exceptional mentors, Clare Allen, Keren David and Julie Wheelwright, and my writing group. A big shout-out to Lin Soekoe and Helen Pain for their unwavering support and general loveliness – you brilliant, brilliant women!

A huge thank-you to Alice Swan and Leah Thaxton at Faber & Faber, for cheering on my successes and providing unparalleled guidance. To Grace Gleave for her kindness and encouragement.

The UKYA community is spectacular. Truly, truly spectacular. Thank you especially to Claire's Coven for welcoming me with open arms, and to my fellow 2017 debuts for sharing this journey with me. Rebecca Barrow, Ali Standish, Kristina Perez, Rebecca Denton, Alice Broadway, Vic James, Cecilia Vinesse, Lisa Lueddecke, Natalie C. Anderson, Ruth Lauren, and Katie Webber – you have no idea how much our ongoing emails mean to me. On the other side of the pond (and in Australia!), all the emoji hearts to Kayla Olson, Anna Priemaza, Tanaz Bhathena, Jilly Gagnon, Cale Dietrich and Kate Watson.

I've also had the extreme good fortune of meeting a group of veteran writers who are basically kick-ass in every way. Thanks to my mentor Emery Lord for her down-to-earth grace, to Alwyn Hamilton for talks over wine, to Jeff Zentner for inspiring not only me but also a generation of readers, and to Sara Barnard and Harriet Reuter Hapgood for Mexican food and just being awesome. I'm lucky to know all of you.

For Keebe, Pete, Katherine and Sarah at McIntyre's – thank you for championing excellent books and for being the best bookstore in the South. And Mouse, who read an incredibly early chapter of *Birds* and told me it was good, even when it was still very drafty.

Book bloggers! I love you! Thanks for your gorgeous pictures and wonderful tweets. And Brian Cox! You don't know me, but hello! Your books are pretty awesome and greatly informed my understanding of the universe. (Any errors here are firmly mine.)

I'm lucky to have an incredible support network in America and in the UK. Ellen, thank you for being a splendiferous maid of honor, for keeping me calm-ish during edits, because my wedding was in capable hands. Grandma Pat, I love talking with you about books – always have. Miss Wilson, you saved me in high school. Chris, best father-in-law award goes to you. To my professors at UNC, especially Dr. T, so many thanks for believing in me. For most excellent Spanish language guidance, thank you to Nicole Pradel, Mandy Morine and Eric Ramirez. I wish I could name everyone – and it's becoming a bit Oscar-ish, *get off the stage, Carlie* – so just know that I appreciate each and every one of my neighbors, classmates, and friends. There was a time in my life when I didn't have so many people to thank, and the biggest blessing – far greater than publishing this book – is having you all by my side.

To all the girls out there who dare to dream: please believe in yourself, because I believe in you. I promise that life is so much more than middle school and high school.

Jago, thank you for *Pretty Little Liars* and *Vampire Diaries*, Indian food breaks, and – you know – marrying me. Everything in my life is brighter because you're in it. Maybe someday I'll write that book about the penguin guards.

To my dad, Jim – I am shocked that you read *The Lady of the Tree* without cringing. Thank you. I have never doubted even for a second that you believed in me. From Waffle House chats to now, you've always encouraged me to be who I am.

And most importantly, my mom, Jen – the smartest, kindest woman I know. How do I even begin to thank you? You are the reason I'm a writer. You read me *Harry Potter*, channeled Agnes, and literally supported me in every way possible in every thing possible. This book is for you. I am blessed that you chose me.

About the Author

Carlie Sorosiak grew up in North Carolina and holds two master's degrees: one in English from Oxford University and another in Creative Writing and Publishing from City, University of London. Her life goals include travelling to all seven continents and fostering many polydactyl cats. She currently splits her time between the US and the UK, hoping to gain an accent like Madonna's.